PRAISE FOR
The weight of winter

"*THE WEIGHT OF WINTER* SHOULD SECURE PELLETIER'S PLACE ON THE LIST OF MAJOR AMERICAN WRITERS. . . . *THE WEIGHT OF WINTER* IS THAT GOOD. IT IS AS REAL AS LIFE."
—*Nashville Tennessean*

"HEARTRENDING. . . . PELLETIER IS AN AMBITIOUS, FEARLESS NOVELIST."
—*Washington Post*

"WHAT AN INCREDIBLE RIDE . . . as full as life is of hilarious lows and heartbreaking highs. . . . *THE WEIGHT OF WINTER* LEAVES US LAUGHING AND CRYING, SPELLBOUND BY THE WONDER OF LIFE."
—*Memphis Commercial Appeal*

"THERE IS NO SHORTAGE OF ACTION, BOTH TRAGIC AND COMIC. . . . The story begins with the first snowfall in early November and ends around Thanksgiving, by which time the prospect of months of low temperatures and high drifts has set off a fine series of explosions. . . ."
—*The Atlantic*

"POWERFUL STUFF. . . . Routines get elemental at 45 below, and nobody can make the page exude cold better than Cathie Pelletier. . . . HER SENTENCES ARE AS SHARP AND UNIQUE AS SNOWFLAKES. . . ."
—*The New York Times Book Review*

Other Books by Cathie Pelletier

Widow's Walk *(poems)*
The Funeral Makers
Once Upon a Time on the Banks

The weight
of winter

The weight of winter

a novel by
Cathie Pelletier

WASHINGTON SQUARE PRESS
PUBLISHED BY POCKET BOOKS
New York   London   Toronto   Sydney   Tokyo   Singapore

Grateful acknowledgment is made for permission to reprint excerpts from the following copyrighted works:

"Ships That Don't Come In" by Paul Nelson and Dave Gibson. Copyright 1989 by Maypop Music, a division of Wild Country Publishing and Warner/Tamerlane Publishing.

"All My Ex's Live in Texas" by Sanger D. Shafer and Lyndia Shafer. © 1986 by Acuff-Rose Music, Inc. Used by permission. All rights reserved. International copyright secured.

"Snowbird" by Gene MacLellan. © 1970 Beechwood Music of Canada. All rights for the U.S. controlled and administered by Beechwood Music Corp. All rights reserved. International copyright secured. Used by permission.

"anyone lived in a pretty how town" from *Complete Poems, 1913–1962* by E. E. Cummings. Reprinted by permission of Liveright Publishing Corporation. Copyright © 1923, 1925, 1931, 1935, 1938, 1939, 1940, 1944, 1945, 1946, 1947, 1948, 1949, 1950, 1951, 1952, 1953, 1954, 1955, 1956, 1957, 1958, 1959, 1960, 1961, 1962 by the Trustees for the E. E. Cummings Trust. Copyright © 1961, 1963, 1968 by Marion Morehouse Cummings.

A Washington Square Press Publication of
POCKET BOOKS, a division of Simon & Schuster Inc.
1230 Avenue of the Americas, New York, NY 10020

Copyright © 1991 by Cathie Pelletier
Cover design by John Gall
Front cover illustration: Grandma Moses: *The Old Oaken Bucket, the Last.* Copyright © 1989, Grandma Moses Property Co., New York

Published by arrangement with Viking Penguin,
a division of Penguin Books USA Inc.

ISBN: 0-671-79387-X

Library of Congress Catalog Card Number: 92-39708

First Washington Square Press trade paperback printing August 1993

10 9 8 7 6 5 4 3

WASHINGTON SQUARE PRESS and colophon are resigtered trademarks of Simon & Schuster Inc.

Printed in the U.S.A.

*This novel is for
my great-niece, Shawna Cathie O'Neal;
my godchild Ashley Norris Gauvin;
and my nephew Martin Louis Pelletier,
with the hope that they will grow up
in a world that respects all living creatures,
the air, the earth, and the future,
although I have great fears.*

And also for my nephew, Kirk St. Amant.

The history of America is the history of its small towns. For better or worse, small town values, convictions, and attitudes have shaped the psyche of this nation.

—Jacket notes for *Small Town America*
by Richard Lingeman.

Acknowledgments

My thanks to:

Jim Glaser, for fifteen years on the roller coaster, and never a dull ride.

THE NEW YORKERS: Rhoda Weyr, my agent, also known as Fortuna; Amanda Vaill, my editor with the third eye; Scott Edward Anderson, for the hubcap; Beena Kamlani, in honor of Beena Gifford, her namesake; Paul Slovak and Faye Darnall, who agree that T.S. Eliot could be done in rap; Hal Fessenden, for his view of the Statue of Liberty; and Jane Rosenman and Mary Ann Sacco, in memory of phone booths and cappuccinos.

THE MAINERS: Louis Allen Pelletier, Sr., and Ethel Tressa O'Leary Pelletier (Dad and Mom) as always; Joan St. Amant and Elaine Desjardins, my sisters; Mary Bossie McBreairty, who is greatly missed, but who lives on in a letter she wrote to me in 1969; Jonah Hafford, who read my stories to our captive fourth-grade class; Jackie Saunders, my seventh- and eighth-grade teacher, who told me that I should become a writer; Fred Malmborg, for pushing me onward; Brian Springer, wherever you are, for insisting on excellence.

The University of Maine at Fort Kent crew: Lisa Ornstein, for the friendship and the music; Julia Bayly, for lots of stuff, including use of her name; Dr. Roland Burns (as usual), Dr. Richard Dumont, Naomi Nicholas, Beth Pinette, and John Labrie for the great support; Professor Roger Paradis, for twenty-two years of encouragement; Sylvia, in the bookstore; all my Creative Writing students, especially Don Dufour for reading the rough draft.

THE NASHVILLIANS: My niece Dee Dee Pelletier (soon to be Dr. Diana Pelletier) in hopes that she will give me veterinary discounts in return for this ad; the following good friends, for their companionship, or for allowing me to wantonly use their family names: Paul and Sue Gauvin, now in Mankins, Texas, and greatly missed in Nashville; Randy and Suzi Vanwarmer, you were always there "Just When I Needed You Most"; Cathy Gurley, also known as "I'll Call You From L.A." Gurley, and Meagan Gurley, the adopted godchild; Carl E. Hileman, the wild man from Illinois; Bob Zimmerman, who is not related to Dylan; Steve Womack and Cathy Yarborough, for those evenings at The Third Coast; Bob McDill, for all those incredible songs; Patsi Cox, in memory of the day we were expelled from a graveyard for being too noisy; Ruth Sloan Brown, a toast to the old days; and in memory of Clubby, the Wonder Cat.

Larry Owens, who told me the line about land being too poor to raise hell on with a fifth of whiskey; Paul Gauvin, who gave me the idea of (1) the sandwich with writing on it for *The Funeral Makers*; (2) the "a man only gets married a few times in his life" line for *Once Upon A Time On the Banks*; and (3) the notion that someone might be "lucky just to have electricity," in *The Weight of Winter*. And songwriter Jennifer Kimball, for whom Miss Kimball, the schoolteacher, was named.

THE NEBRASKANS: Eleanor Marie Glaser Ryan, my idol, my soul-sister, my friend, for her part in raising Jim; Robert Louis Glaser, the quintessential big brother; Pat Ryan, for so many years of "pats" on the back; Kenny and Diane Ryan, also known as "Ozzie and Harriet," and Heather, Steve, Jennifer, Melanie, Derek, Shawn, and Callan; Gerry, Lisa, and Tony Ryan, for the white pelicans; my dear friend and former Spaldingite, the brilliant musician Dr. Joan Poland Wildman, for introducing me to Jim Glaser; lastly, Chi-Chi the dog, the Spalding farm, and the old Cedar River.

The weight of winter

The First Storm: Not Just the Ground Is Barren

As Amy Joy Lawler waited by her mailbox, several fat flakes of snow winged softly out of the gray sky. She wiped them from her face but did not notice the ones that landed soundlessly on the strands of her hair and disappeared there. She stared down at the *A. J. Lawler* on the mailbox. The snow had already clung busily about the letters that spelled *Sicily Lawler,* the second name painted on the box. As Larry Monihan swept by with the town plow, Amy Joy Lawler stared at the lettering with interest. It was as if some cosmic penmanship had erased her mother from the world, had wiped her out. Amy Joy stared at it as though there were meaning to the act, before she slid a mitten across the letters and brought the name back to life. *Sicily Lawler.* The mailman was late again today. Maybe it was snowing even harder in St. Leonard. "It will be all snowflakes soon," Amy Joy thought. "Tons of it for months." What

1

had she always promised herself, each year when autumn's dead foliage bent in the wind and then broke beneath the weight of winter that would cover the Mattagash Valley for six full months? What had she dreamed of? Warmth, somewhere, and long strings of brown sand between her toes, and green—yes, *green*. How Amy Joy missed that color all during the time when things were white: rooftops, black spruce, automobiles, fences, the frozen river. It wasn't that the color white bothered her really, except the town seemed drained of color, all the green seeped away.

Amy Joy shivered inside her plaid woolen coat and waited for old Simon Craft to finally nose his way around the turn in his mail car.

"A bill from J. C. Penney's," Simon said. "A card from your kin down in Portland, a wedding invitation from Tom Henley's girl—I must've delivered fifty of them already today—and a flier from the Women's Legion Auxiliary for the Thanksgiving Day Co-op Dinner." With one wrinkly hand holding a used handkerchief, he wiped his bulbous nose. With the other hand, he passed Amy Joy Lawler her mail.

"Thanks, Simon," Amy Joy said. "What's a Thanksgiving Day Co-op Dinner?" she asked as she studied the home computer flier. It used to be that the Women's Legion Auxiliary printed their fliers by hand. Technology was apparently rampant.

"The Women's Auxiliary decided to cook up a bunch of turkeys and trimmings and just have the whole town come to the gym for their Thanksgiving dinner. All for four ninety-five and no cleaning up the dishes afterwards. That's what my better half likes most about the idea. She said she can just get up and walk away like she never even ate there. They're gonna have all kinds of contests and prizes and even a play afterwards. My two grandchildren been dressed up like little Pilgrims all week. And what money they bring in above their expenses will go to Ernie Felby's wife." Simon sniffed a runny nose as he spoke. "She's got all them kids, you'll remember."

"What's wrong with Ernie?" Amy Joy flipped through the mail in her hand. It would be nice, one day, to get mail and be surprised by the origins of it, by the senders. But Simon Craft had believed for almost forty years that the mail belonged to *him,* that he was kind enough to let other folks handle it, open it, read it.

"I'd say a lot is wrong with him," Simon declared. "He died three months ago. Cancer."

"No kidding," said Amy Joy. She had opened the card from Portland. It *was* from her relatives there. How could she have, even for a second, doubted Simon's telepathic abilities?

"The Felbys might be hippies, but they still got feelings," Simon said. "And it looks like they had a bushel of friends. I bet that man got almost fifty get-well cards. One even come from England. I gave up counting." Simon waved his hand to pshaw the foolishness of his even having tried.

"A book of stamps," said Amy Joy. "Please." She laid a five-dollar bill on the stack of *Bangor Daily* newspapers inside the car.

"You need to get out more, Amy Joy," Simon said. He selected the stamps, all Jack Londons, and gave them to her. "Seems like I been harping to you almost twenty years about the bird being on the wing, as they say. Even that bird is getting real old."

"Thanks, Simon," said Amy Joy. "I do remember hearing about Ernie. I guess I just forgot."

"Oh, yes," he said, and pointed a bony finger. "If you look beneath that flier on the bottom of the stack, your electricity bill came. Probably your last low month before winter."

Amy Joy looked. It was there, of course, one of Simon Craft's children, one of his little white homing pigeons.

"I got it," she said. "Thanks." She pulled her mitten back on and glared up at the sky. It was dull gray with snow, the mountains dark whales beached on the horizon.

"I better get the mail put out before this storm comes down on us full blast," Simon declared. "I don't believe in that hail-or-sleet-or-snow slogan, you know. That was written in warmer climes. I believe in sitting out a storm."

"I don't blame you," said Amy Joy. Once, during a blizzard, he had sat out for four days. But so had everyone else. Sometimes the world needed a little cuff on the ass from Mother Nature, a warning to slow down.

"I wanna see you at that Thanksgiving dinner," Simon warned

The First Storm: Not Just the Ground Is Barren

sweetly. "There'll be lots and lots of eligible bachelors, mark my words, and four ninety-five is quite a deal."

Eligible bachelors in Mattagash. Amy Joy considered this. He must mean Nolan Gifford, Oliver Hart, and Moss Fennelson.

"Be still, my heart," thought Amy Joy.

"The women even put up a poster at The Crossroads," Simon added. "And you know how they feel about *that* place. I hear they're trying to call an emergency town meeting to get the dry vote back. Just between you and me, I think some of them women watch *Sixty Minutes* too much. They're always sneaking up on an issue. But this co-op dinner ain't a bad idea, and I think you oughta shake a leg and come down there."

"I'll see," Amy Joy offered.

"And remember, it's for a good cause," Simon reminded her. "That poor woman ain't so much as gotten a sympathy card from her folks down in Boston. But she gets her share of bills, I can tell you that much."

"I'll try, then," said Amy Joy.

"She's still paying Cushman Funeral Home for the burial," Simon whispered, a delicious secret he saw fit to share with Amy Joy Lawler.

"In that case, I'll really try," Amy Joy lied.

"Oh, by the way . . ." Simon raised his voice again, away from the soft tones of gossip to the feisty notes of proclamation. "Did you hear that Paulie Hart won a thousand dollars in the state lottery? The lucky numbers was eighteen, twenty-two, five, seventeen, and seven. Ain't that the luck of the Irish?"

"He's been spending over a hundred dollars a week for the past three years on tickets," said Amy Joy. "It sounds more like the luck of the stupid."

By the time Simon Craft's tires caught the remaining tar and spun back onto the road, snow was buzzing about Amy Joy's head in threateningly fat flakes. She watched as his taillights became bleary red eyes in the storm, then winked out. When she pivoted on her heel for the short walk back to the house, both names on the mailbox had been leveled over with snow.

"I must call Conrad Gifford to come and shovel the porches," Amy Joy thought. The yard had become a sea of snow. For that she would need to call someone with a plow. Several high school boys made extra money that way, on Saturdays, with their fathers' four-wheel drives. Using as many of the same footprints as she could, Amy Joy followed the crooked path back to her front porch. It had been only a few hours since the first darkening of the horizon, and now nearly four inches of snow lay on Mattagash.

Amy Joy stood in the doorway to her mother's bedroom and cleared her throat softly a few times until Sicily came awake from a snoring little nap and said, "What? Tell me what you *asked* me then, and I'll answer you."

"I didn't ask you anything," Amy Joy said. "We'd been talking and you fell asleep, so I went out for the mail."

"What come?" asked Sicily. She pulled herself up a bit on shaky elbows as Amy Joy reached to help her.

"Don't," Sicily said stiffly. "I ain't helpless, you know, like some old piece of driftwood."

Amy Joy sighed softly, so that Sicily would not hear. "The electric bill," she said. "J. C. Penney bill. A flier Simon says is for a Thanksgiving Day Co-op Dinner."

"I wish Simon Craft would pay our bills instead of read them," snapped Sicily. "That man is a better gossip than any woman *I* ever knew."

"And you've known the best," Amy Joy thought. "All gold medalists."

"That all?" asked Sicily.

"An invitation to Junior Ivy's retirement party," Amy Joy said, reading.

"You mean that big lug is old enough to retire?" Sicily asked. "My God, where does the time go?"

"He must be just over sixty," said Amy Joy. "But with his money, I suppose he can retire whenever he wants to." She tossed the card onto the kitchen table.

"We only hear from them people when they want a gift," said Sicily. "The last hint we got along them lines was that graduation card this spring from one of his granddaughters. I tell you, in my day we considered ourselves lucky just to *go* to school. They didn't have to give us a money order to do it." She swung her feet out of bed and her legs dangled there, too short and thin to touch the floor. "Amazing how we hear from near strangers every time there's a graduation or a wedding or a baby born."

"And not necessarily in that order," said Amy Joy. "Besides, Junior's got enough money to buy what he wants. I think he's just being friendly. I'm gonna send him a congratulations card. He *is* my first cousin, after all."

"You notice we don't hear from someone who's just hit the lottery."

"Get back in bed!" Amy Joy ordered, suddenly noticing Sicily's posture.

"I ain't an invalid," Sicily insisted. "A little cold is all that's wrong with me."

"Nobody said anything different," Amy Joy soothed, pushing her mother gently back onto the bed. "No one said you were helpless, or an invalid."

"I ain't too old, either."

"Who said you were? But you *are* contrary. Now get back into bed until that cold passes, or you'll be asking for pneumonia. It's snowing so hard outside that you won't be able to stare out the window anyway. I'll bring you the new crossword puzzle."

"You don't like for me to do the crossword puzzle," Sicily snipped. "You say I just mess it up so you can't do it."

Amy Joy took a deep breath and stared steadily at Sicily. "I believe I said that once, in 1972 or 1973. It's now 1989. Can you let it go?" Amy Joy could see, before her eyes, the countless, useless fill-ins she'd had to erase over the years, when her mother was finished with the puzzle, so that she could jot in the proper answer herself. What had one of the many been yesterday? A five-letter word for "City of Light." Sicily had scrawled *Tampa* instead of *Paris*. When Amy Joy asked her why, she had replied, "Ain't that where Disney World is? There must be plenty of lights."

"Well, it seems like just last week you said it," Sicily whined. She slid her legs under the covers and lay back on the pillow.

"Maybe to you, Mother, 1972 seems like last week. But believe me, it was a long time ago."

"See!" Sicily spat, shaking a brittle finger. "*That's* what I mean! You're trying to make me believe I'm senile! Oh, what did I ever do to deserve an end like this?"

"Do you want a list?" thought Amy Joy. She threw the crossword puzzle onto the foot of Sicily's bed, but Sicily kicked it off quickly with her foot.

"Suit yourself," said Amy Joy as she gathered up the mail.

"You just read the Bible and see what it says about daughters trying to pack their poor old mothers off to nursing homes," Sicily threatened. "You'll do an about-face, I tell you."

"What *does* it say?" Amy Joy stopped at the doorway to ask.

"You know very well," warned Sicily.

"No," said Amy Joy. "Tell me. What does the Bible say about nursing homes?"

"Lots," said Sicily. "That I can assure you."

"Well, assure me by telling me a little, never mind lots. What does it say?"

"For your sake," said Sicily, "I hate to even think of it. It makes Sodom and Gomorrah look like a picnic." *Sodom and Gomorrah.* Sicily's favorite twin cities.

"And just what is it you're referring to?"

"The punishment God wields down to unloyal children," Sicily said. "That's what."

"Mother, I mentioned once, one time, *uno,* that you might like the social atmosphere at the St. Leonard nursing home, what with your good friend Winnie Craft down there entertaining legions daily with her gossip."

"Now listen to you," said Sicily. "What's poor Winnie ever done to you? If the Lord was to come to St. Leonard tonight to take Winnie Craft to heaven, how would you feel?"

"If the Lord comes to St. Leonard tonight, he'd better have snow tires," Amy Joy said, her eyes staring out beyond the pane of Sicily's bedroom window, to the snow falling over Mattagash. "Besides, Winnie Craft has never been a focal point in my life, so I probably wouldn't notice if the Lord bundled her up and took her."

"No," Sicily shot back. "And that's just the problem. You *ain't got* any focal points. Not even one or two."

Amy Joy sighed. "We're back to me not having any children and therefore you no grandchildren, aren't we?"

"You did it out of spite," said Sicily.

"Shit," thought Amy Joy. "She'll be banging this drum even after I go through menopause."

"You did it out of spite just to keep me from them." Sicily tugged at the lace border of her pillow. Amy Joy looked away from her mother's spotted hands. She remembered when they had been smooth and white as snow.

"Maybe I did it out of love," said Amy Joy. "Maybe I kept *them* from *you*."

"It ain't like you're barren or anything." Sicily ignored the slight. "Besides, God can cure barrenness. 'He maketh the barren woman to keep house, and to be a joyful mother of children.' You'll find that in Psalms."

"One of these days I'm gonna look all that stuff up," said Amy Joy. "I swear you write most of it yourself."

"I'll bet you five dollars," Sicily offered, her hand extended. Amy Joy ignored it. "And I'll bet you something else," Sicily went on. "When I'm laying out flat next to my sister Pearl and my sister Marge, right here in the Mattagash Protestant graveyard, I hope you'll realize then how you've treated me."

It had been nearly two years since they'd buried Aunt Pearl. Amy Joy remembered the snowy day when she went to the graveyard, months after Pearl died, and stood before the best tombstone Junior Ivy could find for his mother, the Ivy Funeral Home super deluxe. And she had watched as the snowflakes ate away at the letters, *Pearl McKinnon Ivy, 1909–1987,* until the engraving disappeared in a swirl of snow. Like Sicily's name on the mailbox earlier, like her own name. Amy Joy knew that nature eventually takes back everything it has loaned to the temporary world. *1909–1987.* It took it back quickly too. "We're *all* disappearing," Amy Joy had thought, that snowy day in November, the first snowfall of 1987, when she had finally, quietly, gone to the graveyard to say good-bye to Pearl. She had found a solace in her aunt Pearl, which was unusual for two people who had begun their acquaintance on such terrible terms. But Amy Joy had grown up, and Pearl had discovered in her the daughter she never had. She had given Amy Joy the knowledge of the old settlers, the McKinnon ancestors, who had come up the Mattagash River from Canada and founded the town. She had passed the torch on to Amy Joy and now—Sicily was right—Amy Joy had no children waiting behind her to take it up for themselves.

"The Bible says to honor thy parents no matter what." Amy Joy realized Sicily was still quoting. "It doesn't say *unless they're old.*"

"I asked you *once,*" Amy Joy said, "after we first visited Winnie at the home, if maybe you'd like to live there."

"That's like a posse of men coming up to you with a rope and asking you what you think of hangings, and then never mentioning it again," said Sicily. "That rope gets to preying on your mind."

Amy Joy again stared out the big picture window that overlooked the Mattagash River. She wondered how many more days before it froze over and then immersed itself in the endless white of the fields, the ridges, the footpaths. She could almost feel the house being covered in snow, each feathery flake causing little goose pimples to spring up on her arms. This was the McKinnon homestead, the house that Marge, oldest of the sisters, had left to Sicily and Pearl. Pearl had stayed on in it after her husband, Marvin Ivy, died, and had allowed Amy Joy to move in. That was in 1969.

"I need to get away from Mother," Amy Joy had told Pearl. "I love her, but she's driving me crazy."

It was only a matter of a year before Sicily moved in.

"I'll just stay until after Christmas," Sicily assured her stunned relatives as she bounced past them to claim Marge's old bedroom.

"Who would've known she meant Christmas 1999?" Pearl remarked two years later, when it was more than obvious, even to the dog, that Sicily intended to stay. But now Pearl was gone, and soon the earth would be coming for Sicily, and Sicily was all that stood between her daughter and the fate even McKinnons must bow to.

"And I have no intentions of getting onto that senior citizen bus neither," Sicily threatened. "Wipe *that* out of your mind. If *you* can't take me to Watertown to shop, I guess my shopping days are over."

"Why won't you ride in the bus?" Amy Joy asked.

"Because them old people look like a busload of them muppets you see on TV," Sicily said, "what with their heads all bobbing and their hair flying."

"You're not serious, Mother, are you?" Amy Joy had promised herself not to engage in another disagreement with Sicily, but sometimes the pull was too strong. "You could go shopping, have a snack, see a movie in Watertown. The senior citizen bus takes them all over."

"I know what you're going to say next," Sicily prophesied. "You're going to say that even Winnie Craft rides on the bus."

"I'm surprised she's not driving it," said Amy Joy, remembering with chilling certainty Winnie Craft's domineering personality.

"There you go again with your knifelike tongue," Sicily said.

"Forget about the St. Leonard nursing home," Amy Joy told her mother curtly. "It was only a suggestion to begin with."

"That's good news," said Sicily. "I feel like I just got a last-minute pardon from Governor McKernan."

"I thought you'd enjoy being around folks your own age instead of me," Amy Joy offered.

"You keep me young." Sicily smiled.

"I'm almost forty-five, Mum," Amy Joy said. "We're both going to run out of luck one of these days."

"You'll manage," said Sicily. Her cold was suddenly better, she herself rejuvenated. Amy Joy was not surprised. She watched as Sicily buried a pretend sniffle in her handkerchief.

"Albert Pinkham is there too, you know," Amy Joy plodded on. "And so is Blanche."

"If Blanche's Grocery hadn't burned to the ground, she'd still be going strong," Sicily predicted. "She would've kept busy."

"Claire Fennelson is there."

"Lordy," said Sicily. "*There's* a strike against going. I hope they keep their piano locked up. Claire thinks she's Liberace. I remember one Tupperware party when she played 'Nearer, My God, to Thee' so many times that we was all wishing she *was* a little nearer."

"Well, maybe one of these days you'll change your mind," said Amy Joy. In the year that Winnie Craft had been at Pine Valley, the St. Leonard nursing home, she and Sicily had made a dutiful monthly visit. "You might even be lucky enough to get a room near Winnie. Wouldn't that be nice?"

"What's a three-letter word for 'chemical suffix'?" Sicily asked, ignoring her daughter's question.

The Giffords Glissade into Winter: Big Bucks in the Lottery

Do you hear the children weeping, O my brothers,
Ere the sorrow comes with years?
They are leaning their young heads against their
    mothers,
And *that* cannot stop their tears.

—Elizabeth Barrett Browning,
"The Cry of the Children"

*B*y late afternoon, Mattagash was safely buried beneath a solid foot of thick snow. The town sent out its plow, driven by Larry Monihan, who had placed a bid for the job and won it. The yellowish paint of the machine pushed like sunshine across the blankety white, leaving behind a passable road for the townsfolk. Dead goldenrod stood along the highway and in the fields, up to their tops in snow. Amy Joy Lawler's bird feeder had attracted black-capped chickadees, gray jays, and an assortment of evening grosbeaks. Winters in Maine weren't kind to the birds. Or to deer. Or coyotes. Winters in Maine weren't kind to people. Only the wise black bear was smart enough to crawl into some murky dark den and wait until the entire fluffy shebang was over.

A cold wind, snow-filled and rolling up from the icy water, slapped Pike Gifford, Jr., age thirty-one, in the face as he stood on the back porch of his house and gazed down on the Mattagash River. His stepcousin Billy Plunkett stood beside him, shivering in the wind, wearing only a faded sweatshirt. It said *My Friends Went to Florida and All I Got Was This Damn Shirt.* The men had stepped outside briefly to check on the storm.

"Son of a bitch," said Pike. "We're up to our asses from now until April."

"It's here to stay, all right," said Billy. He snapped a cigarette off the ends of his fingers and watched it sink, sizzling, into the snow. Three of Pike's children were sliding down the hill, their necks wrapped warmly in thick scarves, their hands in bulky mittens. Two of them, the boys, were in a fight over the biggest, fastest sled. It was a Woolworth special, bright orange, with two rope handles attached to the plastic body.

"Kids don't lay on their stomachs anymore to slide," Billy observed. "It can't be much fun sitting up like that."

"You boys take turns!" Pike hollered at them. "And give your sister one now and then."

"Shit," said Billy. "We used to slide on a chunk of linoleum and were darn glad to get it. We used to dream of getting a nice wood sled with metal runners. Nowadays kids don't even know what them sleds look like. They got Flying Saucers and Magic Carpets and all sorts of gizmos." He adjusted his hat, pulled it down a bit to cover his ears. It said *Damn Sea Gulls!*

"Remember the time you cut a swath of carpet out of your mother's kitchen floor and we slid on that?" asked Pike. He slapped his leg festively in memory of the event.

"Yeah, well," said Billy. "I was in a bind at the time." More snowflakes bombarded the back porch of Pike's house. At the bottom of the hill, one of the boys overturned on the Woolworth sled, allowing the other to steal the apparatus from him. A volley of cries and protests rolled up the hill.

"Eat some snow!" the larger boy shouted as he shoveled a mittenful into the smaller boy's mouth. "It's full of germs!"

"Daddy, make him stop!" the smaller boy yelled, but Pike ignored the plea.

"I don't know what's worse." Billy sighed. "All this goddamn snow, or all them summertime blackflies."

"Well," said Pike, "at least the snow don't bite."

"The hell it don't," Billy shot back. "What about frostbite?"

The wind came up the steps in heavy gusts of snowflakes. The rocks along the Mattagash River lay like large white polar bears. The pines, the spruces, the tamaracks, the heavenly birches, all fluffed white. In the wind they scattered themselves in tufts of soft down. The sky was dark, swollen with more snow to come.

"I'm freezing my balls off," said Billy. He lifted his glass to his lips. It was a juice glass belonging to Pike's wife and was covered with fragile daisies. It was full of straight, cheap vodka.

"Tell them kids to stay away from the river," a voice said sharply from behind them. It was Lynn, Pike's wife, her face barely visible in the crack of the kitchen door. "They fall in, they'll freeze to death in a second. We won't even find them until spring." The door slammed with a wide spray of snow.

"Wasn't that music to your ears?" Pike asked Billy. "Wasn't that what you call one of them *symphonies?*" He raised his own cold glass of daisies and looked at it. It would be six months before a daisy even considered sprouting in Mattagash. Snow swept down from the porch roof in a flurry of wind and pelted the fleshy necks of the two men. They scooped it off.

"Reed, you fucking bastard," Pike heard his younger son shout into the wind. Reed dropped his sled and ran back to the slanderer, buried him face down in the snow, and administered several well-weighted punches.

"Your mother says that if you fall in that river," Pike yelled to his children, "she ain't even gonna look for you until next spring!"

"Dirty prick," Pike's daughter screamed at Reed as she kicked one of her little boots into his back. "Daddy said to give me a turn!"

"Listen to her," Pike chuckled. "She can fight back just like a boy."

"I hear that Paulie Hart won a thousand bucks in the lottery this week," Billy said.

"As if Paulie Hart needs to win money," Pike noted sadly. He spit a warm little hole into the snow by the back step. "What is he anyway? Early twenties? No wife. No kids. No bills."

"He started working for the P. G. Irvine Lumber Company the minute he got out of high school," Billy said. "And his paycheck has gone to buy lottery tickets ever since. So you might say he had bills."

"Well, I seen all the first storm I care to see," said Pike, and he followed Billy Plunkett back into the house.

On Pike's living room floor Conrad, his firstborn, twelve years old, lay sprawled on his stomach in front of the television/VCR. He was watching a movie his mother had rented for him at the Watertown Movie Factory.

"See you later?" Billy asked his cousin. "Ronny's been home a whole month from the navy, but he's still buying the drinks." Ronny Plunkett was Billy's big brother.

"I don't think so," Pike said, and then winked knowingly. "I'll probably stay home and watch a movie with the kids." He winked again as Lynn banged a pot in the kitchen sink. The music of it rang out loudly.

"Okay then," said Billy. "See you tomorrow." He went out into the first permanent snowstorm of 1989. Pike watched Billy's taillights, cloudy with snow, swing around and around like crazy flashlights. Billy was busy executing half a dozen cop turns in the slippery yard. Then, as Pike watched, Billy drove a straight path across the yard and up onto the main road. Then he put the pickup in reverse, backed up to within a few feet of the house, shifted into first, and retraced the same track. Billy knew that if Pike had his heart set on tipping up a couple at the local bar, he'd need a path to the road. The old Chevy clunker couldn't tackle snow like the invincible Dodge Ram with its four-wheel drive. With a neat trail packed down all the way to the main road, Billy straightened the truck and made a zigzaggedy dash for The Crossroads. Pike smiled.

"What a character," he said to his son, who was deep within the drama of the movie. "A real cowboy, that cousin of mine." He heard Lynn grunt from the kitchen. More utensils banged, forks and knives being roughly stacked in the dishwasher, which Lynn had picked potatoes to buy.

"Did you tell him to make that track to the road?" Lynn asked.

"No." Pike answered the question from the living room. He preferred being where Lynn—or Judge Wapner, as he called her—couldn't see him. He had heard Lynn tell her sister, Maisy, when they thought Pike was asleep on the couch, that she could read Pike Gifford like a book. "It'd have to be a comic book, then," Maisy had answered. Pike and Maisy weren't the most loving of in-laws.

"Why'd he do it, then?" Lynn asked. He could hear the icy anger in her voice. Pike could do a bit of book reading himself.

"He's just got a big heart, is all," Pike answered. "Nothing wrong with things being *big,* is there?" He grabbed his genitals dramatically and shook them. Conrad ignored him.

"His heart is about the same size as his brain," Pike heard Lynn say. "And next to Billy Plunkett's brain, a pea would look like a boulder." He listened with a wry smile on his face. Let her rant on. It was only a matter of time before he would be telling Billy about it at The Crossroads, two frosty shots of vodka in front of them, the snow above their heads covering the roof, the town, hiding them from their women, their children, and sometimes the law. It was no secret that Giffords and Plunketts had seen their share of misdemeanors. But Pike Gifford and Billy Plunkett regarded this truth as a kind of family curse.

"Look how much trouble the Kennedys has been in," Pike liked to point out.

"And for *felonies,*" Billy always added.

"What movie she rent?" Pike asked his son. He settled down on the sofa and put his feet up on Lynn's Naugahyde hassock.

"*Rambo,*" Conrad said.

"Shit!" Pike lamented. "That big Wop? He'd *better* get behind a machine gun. A real man could whip his ass in a second." He sloshed his vodka about in the glass. The fifth he'd come home with earlier in the day was almost empty, had disappeared as if beneath a cold snow in Pike's gut, a place that was now warm. In just an hour Billy had helped put a mighty dent in the bottle. But Pike had another one stashed away upstairs, beneath the socks in his sock drawer. Pike Gifford was never afraid to look at the bottom of a bottle.

"Just watch the movie," said Conrad.

"Big Italian Wop," Pike muttered.

"Shut up," threatened Conrad, "or I'm turning it off."

"Don't you even consider talking to me like that." Pike shook a finger at his son.

"Go to hell," Conrad said softly.

"Nice talk for a kid," Pike observed.

"I got it from *you*," the boy answered.

"The fuck you did!" said Pike. Conrad continued to watch the movie, an orange ring of Cheese Twist crumbs about his mouth. Pike listened for sounds in the kitchen, determining Lynn's mood. He was growing restless. Billy must be just driving into the yard at The Crossroads.

"Hey, Lynn!" Pike shouted. "You gonna make us some popcorn or ain't you?" More noises, brittle and angry, volleyed back from the kitchen as a blender was washed and dried. Seeing that Conrad had gone back to the drama of the movie, Pike threw a sofa pillow at him. It bounced off the top of the boy's head and he jumped in honest surprise. Rambo had been ready to attack.

"Ma, make him quit!" Conrad wailed. "I can't watch my movie!" He got up and rewound the suspenseful scene. "Leave me alone," he said to his father, and then lay back down on his stomach, hands beneath his chin. He wished he had arms like Rambo. He would crush his father, Pike Gifford, Jr., the way you crush a snowflake. The way Rambo crushes a Commie. He wished he had an AK-47 like Rambo's. He would blast away at his father, splattering red blood and Gifford guts all across the white dooryard.

"You think you're it, don't you, punk?" Pike asked his son. He said this carefully, each word measured out slowly, icily. He saw Conrad stiffen, his facial muscles tighten. "You think you're the bull's dick, don't you?" Conrad stared hard at the TV and said nothing. The little game of kidding each other was over. Pike saw a soft tremor, like a tiny spurt of electricity, course through Conrad's right arm. It was trembling. As his father watched, Conrad took the arm out from beneath his chin and plunked it on the floor. He seemed embarrassed by it. Pike threw another pillow, this time roughly. It mashed against Conrad's nose, then fell to the floor. Tears filled the boy's eyes but he kept them on Rambo. Rambo was blasting the Commies, giving them what they deserved and then more.

"You think you're Rambo, don't you? You pale little trickle of horse piss."

"Leave him alone," said Lynn. She was standing in the doorway to the living room, a hand on one hip, a dish towel in the other. "He ain't done nothing to you."

"Oh, look who's here!" Pike squealed. "It's *Miss* Rambo. You must be here to rescue this little faggot!"

Conrad jumped to his feet and stopped the movie. He pushed *eject* and waited until the tape popped out and into his hand. He grabbed the box it came in, a picture of Rambo with his gun on the cover, and bounded away up the stairs. In seconds a door slammed heartily. Lynn went back into the kitchen and opened the refrigerator. She stared vaguely inside, not wanting anything from there but simply waiting.

"You let them kids rule the roost," she heard her husband say. He had come into the kitchen to empty the last of the vodka into his summery glass. *Roost.* Lynn stared at the seven eggs sitting happily in their little nests, *roosting.*

"I'm the one who has to put food on this goddamn table," Pike said, thumping the kitchen table as he spoke, "and I can't even sit in my own living room and watch a goddamn Wop in peace." He was thinking how Billy would be polishing off his first drink at The Crossroads, probably ordering a second while he pumped quarters into the jukebox.

Lynn stared at the food in the refrigerator. Carrots. Milk. A huge bucket of margarine. A liter of generic cola. Pork chops. A few scraggly strips of bacon. The cheapest cuts of chicken and meat that money could buy. She'd had fifty-some dollars in food stamps that week. Leftover cream-style corn, also generic, sat beneath a transparent wrap that was too cheap to stick to the dish. A slab of cut-it-yourself bologna, what the kids called Canadian steak, lounged in a corner. A bushel of bright red hot dogs, full of God knows what, looked almost pink and flowery in the fridge's light. This mess of chicken parts and other unthinkable remnants of the animal world would have to feed the six of them for more than a week.

"You want to stare at something cold, go out on your back porch and stare at the goddamn sky," Pike said. "It'd be a hell of a lot cheaper on our electric bill." *The electric bill.* Last month's had been $128.40, and she had gone to her mother, had bitten her lip, swallowed her pride, jumped down from her high horse —all the things her father had predicted she'd do—to borrow money to pay the bill. A very angry woman from the electric company had phoned and warned her for the last time. Cold weather or no cold weather, kids or no kids, the juice would be turned off.

"Please don't tell Daddy," Lynn had asked her mother. "You know how he loves to say he told me so."

"Well," her mother said as she handed over the money, "he *did* tell you so."

Pike had been on workmen's compensation for two years, another family characteristic. A baffling back injury sustained in a trucking accident had put him there, and had linked the destiny of the Giffords again with that of the Kennedys.

"Just say you got the same back problem that President Kennedy had," Billy had advised Pike. "Except he got his in a boating accident." Billy had been using *Kennedy back* as the excuse for his own disability, and it had worked so well that he saw no reason why two Mattagashers couldn't suffer from the same malady. So he had given the mysterious ailment to his cousin Pike, as though it were some kind of gift. No one felt sorry for Pike. He'd been hoping to acquire a good injury, nurse it for life, as his father, Pike Senior, had advised him to do.

"Get in the habit of wincing every third step," the elder Pike had explained, in an effort to teach the younger Pike how to evade the false-claim detectives sent out by workmen's compensation. But even with this steady income the checks were not so high that a family of six could relax, and Lynn always felt lucky to see half of Pike's check. The Crossroads saw the other half.

The children came in from outside and stomped snow from their boots. Julie and Stevie, the seven-year-old twins, made a dash for the refrigerator.

"Stay on that rug," Lynn said as Julie reached past her and grabbed a string of hot dogs, four of them, tied together with small red umbilical cords.

"Give me one," Stevie begged. He grabbed at a hot dog so greedily that it broke from the string and came away in his hands.

"No, Stevie. Get your own!" Julie cried. "These are mine."

"Put them back!" Lynn shouted. "I'm gonna make a hot dog casserole for supper tomorrow night." But she didn't have the energy to go after the hot dogs. Pike's next move was more important than hot dogs anyway. She stared at the chicken breasts and wings and thighs still oozing juice in a poorly wrapped package and remembered a segment on *60 Minutes* that exposed chicken production for what it was. Still, Pike and the kids kept on eating it. Who'd even be able to tell if Pike ever got salmonella?

"You got *three*," said Reed, age ten, who was next in line to Conrad. "Hot dog face," he said, and slapped a wet mitten, beaded with snow, across Julie's nose. She began to cry loudly.

"Shut up!" shouted Pike. "A man stays home for a quiet evening with his family and he has to listen to all this wailing about hot dogs. Besides, according to that Ralph Nader, all hot dogs is is rat shit, and there you are fighting over them." Julie quit crying and bit into the bright red hot dog.

"They're red like that 'cause they're made of pure blood," Stevie whispered to her. "*Rat's* blood." But she ignored him by biting off a second large chunk.

"Did you buy us some Megabuck tickets, Mama?" Reed asked. "It's up to four million dollars. No one won again last week."

"I bought five," said Lynn. She stared at the small light bulb inside the refrigerator and realized that she, too, was forced to come on at the most surprising moments, to the commands of other people.

"Stevie's putting on my turkey outfit!" Julie cried. "Make him take it off, Mama. Miss Kimball said we ain't supposed to wear them until the night of the play." Stevie paced about the kitchen, the turkey's bill opened to show his face, the red plastic wattle shining brightly.

"Gobble," Stevie said, now feeding the turkey's mouth a red hot dog. "Gobble, gobble." Julie began to cry.

"Stevie, put them damn hot dogs back," Lynn snapped. "And take off that foolish suit."

"Let him wear it," said Pike. "He's just being hisself."

Julie stopped crying and clapped her hands. "Stevie's a turkey," she chanted. "Stevie's a turkey."

"Are we gonna watch *Rambo* now?" Reed asked his mother. Lynn closed the refrigerator door and retreated to the cupboard. She took down some IGA popcorn and tore a hole in the plastic bag.

"Look, kids," Pike wheezed. "Miss Rambo is gonna pop popcorn with her bare hands." The kids all tittered, still chilled as little icicles. Tonight it was Conrad's turn, as usual. Things hadn't changed. That was all that mattered.

"Just don't say anything," Lynn thought. "Swallow your pride. Bite your lip. Do all that shit you've been doing a lot of lately." She dug the old popcorn popper out from its spot on the bottom shelf where she kept her pots and pans.

"Did you rent *Rambo*, Mama?" Reed asked, and dropped his soggy mittens on the rug.

"Put them on the register to dry," Lynn said. She wondered how she was ever going to last through six months of winter. She wasn't ready for it this year, there was no doubt about that. Not another winter with Pike anyway. "Once the kids have their Christmas, that's it," she'd already told her sister Maisy, just that morning, when the first snow had begun to fall. "I'll do a little spring cleaning come April and Pike Gifford's gonna be among the trash I throw out." But this time she couldn't catch hold of the thought, as she had on other occasions. This time, this day of the first big snow, was different. "You've been promising to do your spring cleaning for years," Lynn told herself as she poured a couple capfuls of vegetable oil into the popper. "Every year's the same. All you throw out is old clothes, and broken dishes, and good intentions. And every year Pike Gifford's roots go a little deeper." It would be a long white wait until spring, and now, with no hope looming up ahead even if it was *false* hope, with no ear of corn in front of the donkey, how could she endure?

"Ow!" Stevie screamed. He had plunked a finger down in the oil of the popper, which was hot enough to be sizzling.

"What would make you do that?" Lynn asked in exasperation. "Reed, break me off a piece of my aloe plant." She blew coolly on Stevie's finger. "That'll take care of it," she said. "Aloe's the best thing for burns."

"You ought to put it on your biscuits, then," Pike said, and the kids laughed again. "It's not me," each thought unconsciously, and felt a smooth rush of relief. "I ain't seen a biscuit come out of your oven yet that wasn't black. You been making nigger biscuits ever since we was married."

Lynn tossed the rusty beads of corn into the oil and watched them spin in the heat.

"You rent *Rambo* for us, Mama?" Reed asked again as he rubbed the sticky, clear medicine of the aloe plant onto Stevie's finger.

"Yes," Lynn said. "I did." She placed the lid over the cooking kernels. "Conrad has it upstairs. He'll come back down when the popcorn's ready."

Pike had finished the last swallow of the vodka. He slammed the empty glass down in the sink so hard that a crack streaked up the side of it, quick as a flash of lightning. Billy was probably trying to get up a game of cribbage, right at that minute, down at The Crossroads, the jukebox sweetly urging him on.

"By God, he won't watch a television set of mine," Pike threatened. "Not with the kind of mouth he has. When he learns a little respect, maybe then."

Lynn sighed, a soft sigh, more like the sweet rush of wind when it's filled with snow, tired, heavy, sleepy. She turned and looked at her husband as he leaned clumsily against the kitchen sink. He was well named. He looked enough like the older Pike Gifford to be his clone. Or maybe his ghost, come up the snowy hill from the old river, booze-heavy, vengeful. He had that dark, curly Gifford hair, a bushel of it. Huge dark Gifford eyes. A Gifford swagger when he walked, wagging that lean, long Gifford body like it was a tail, or something special. And he was more than a near clone of the elder Pike. He was a repetition of all the older man's mistakes on the planet.

"Like father, like son," Pike Gifford, Jr., had made mention of, many times. It was his favorite toast. Lynn had seen him hold his glass up to Billy's and boldly sing it out. *Like father, like son.* Now the senior Pike was dead. No one knew where the excessive booze left off and the heart attack began. But the heart, with more than enough help from the spotted liver, had taken away Pike Gifford, Sr., and left a younger version in his son. Lynn looked at her husband. She had—*hadn't she?*—loved him dearly once. Once, she had defied her own family to marry him.

"Why don't you go on out, then," Lynn said sharply, each word spaced carefully, fiery words, all the letters sizzling like popcorn kernels. "Why don't you go on out and find Billy. You know he's waiting for you at The Crossroads."

Pike's eyes gleamed. What was it that was so damn exciting about a game played well? The *power* of it, that was what. Those Donald Trump types, they know only a part of the secret, sitting around their oval tables and chewing the big business fat. They know how to mold deals, shape concrete and steel into tall buildings. But Pike Gifford knew well that real power comes from bending and shaping human beings.

Julie climbed into his lap and put her arms around his neck. "Ain't you gonna watch *Rambo*, Daddy?" she asked. "Ain't you gonna watch that big Wop?"

"So," Pike snarled at Lynn. "If it's a choice between me and that little bastard upstairs, you'll take him?" He plunked Julie down flat on the little balls of her feet, and grabbed his jacket from one of the nails Lynn had driven into the wall by the front door, to accommodate a family of jackets. "I try to make these kids mind," he said, "and you jump in and stop me. Well, by Jesus, *you* put up with them."

"Gladly," Lynn whispered, but Pike heard her. He spun around and caught her by the throat with one hand, pushed her against the kitchen sink.

"What?" His face was red with fury. Lynn closed her eyes. She felt his fingers prodding deep into her throat, cutting off her air supply. "Don't let him see it," she told herself. "Don't let him see the fear." Then she was strangely surprised to realize that there was no fear. Not even a morsel. The corn was popping now, roughly, against the plastic of the lid, angry little faces popping loudly in hopes of escape. Lynn closed her eyes. *Pop. Pop.* She remembered, once, when he had touched her neck at the Watertown drive-in, a sweet touch, his fingers running like petals along her skin, his lips following wetly. *Pop. Pop. Pop.* Then the fingers left, left red prints on her throat, little forget-me-nots in the snow, but *left*. Lynn opened her eyes and saw the front door closing. She stood in the kitchen and stared out past the frills of the curtains. Pike was at the car, wiping snow away from the windshield with his arm. Then he disappeared behind the wheel. The headlights blazed on, catching the snow in the very act of falling, catching the *power* of the snow. It would control their lives for another six months.

"I could've stayed upstairs," Conrad said, peering over her shoulder. "I could've watched *Rambo* tomorrow."

"Never you mind," Lynn said. "The popcorn's almost done. It's a night to be in, watching the TV. Not out there." She looked back again to see her husband's taillights drive off into the storm. She wondered how many days, how many weeks, how many months now she had been hoping something would happen out there, some tragedy—a bar fight with a broken bottle, a twisted, metallic car wreck, a bleary liver just suddenly exploding. Something that would assure her that the man she married would never come back home again. She wondered what day it was that the fear had turned to hate.

"I hope they don't close The Crossroads," she heard Conrad say, his throat tight with emotion. And she knew what he meant. *At least he ain't home here all the time.* Lynn was thinking the same thing.

"I'm going headfirst into winter with a real bad attitude," she thought.

Lumbering Pitfalls:
Elvis Comes Forth at
Radio Shack

> Jesus said, Take ye away the stone. Martha, the
> sister of him that was dead, saith unto him, Lord, by
> this time he stinketh. . . . And when he thus had
> spoken, he cried with a loud voice, Lazarus, come
> forth.
>
> —John 11:39, 43

*D*avey Craft shoveled his front porch and then scraped a narrow path out to the mailbox. He would call his father later and ask to borrow the pickup with the plow on it. Davey turned his face upward to the gale and surveyed the sky. The bulk of the storm had fallen the day before, and when the kids had managed to go off to school that morning, there had been hope that the storm was over. But now the flakes were beginning to swirl again, and snow hung dark as a swarm of bees above the treetops.

Davey watched as the cloudy puffs of his breath mushroomed into the cold and then dissolved.

"Damn," he said, and the word burst out of his warm mouth, took shape in the air before him like a little ghost. It would be a long six months. Already his skidder was broken. The piston had snapped and then pierced the block of the motor. It would cost him forty-five hundred dollars to repair it. Forty-five hundred he didn't have. He didn't have a savings account with forty-five cents—where would he get that kind of money to put into his checking account?

"Daddy?" A child's voice came to him above the scraping of the shovel, and Davey saw a blurred face behind the living room glass. A small white hand waved. It was Tanya, his only girl, home sick from school again. It was getting to be a habit with her. Davey waved back. If the snow came more thickly than this, his other children would appear out of the drifts on the long yellow bus, a streak of sunshine in the storm. But in Mattagash, Maine, buckets of snow had to come down before school closed. Otherwise, the kids would be going to school all summer to make up the snow days.

Davey Craft clomped the snow off the shovel and then his boots. He leaned the shovel against the door where he would find it again in a few hours, after the dusty snow had begun to fill in his work. Inside, his wife was peeling potatoes at the sink. The sick child lay on the sofa watching a Disney movie on the VCR.

"Still coming down?" Charlene asked.

"Is the Pope still Catholic?" Davey tossed his wet mittens at the rack Charlene kept near the back door for wet winter things, or the limp summer things the kids wore to swim in the river. The mittens bounced off the top of the rack and dropped heavily to the floor.

"Don't be throwing things, Dave," said Charlene, who didn't bother to look up from the potatoes. "The kids are bad enough."

"What did the doctor say about Tanya?" Davey asked as he unlaced his boots.

"He took another blood test, this time for mono." Charlene cut the potatoes in half and then plopped them all into a pan of water. "He thinks that might be why she's tired all the time." She snapped the burner of the stove on high and waited as it turned orange with heat.

"Goddamn doctors," Davey muttered. "According to them, if

you live you must've been okay, if you die you wasn't okay. And either way it costs you an arm and a leg."

"This far north, we'd do just as well to ask a witch doctor what he thinks," said Charlene. She turned the heat beneath the sputtering pan down to medium.

"They're all alike no matter where you go," said Davey.

"You gonna get that piston fixed in the skidder?" Charlene asked. She had opened a can of corn beef and was now slicing it.

"You gonna win the lottery?" Davey answered her, and went into the living room to kiss the warm forehead of his sick child.

Charlene stopped her busy hands to stare idly out her kitchen window. The snow had picked up momentum, maybe somewhere up north in Canada, and now Charlene could see the yellow lights of cars inching along the one ragged road that cut through the heart of Mattagash. The roads were looking dangerous. She suspected the kids would be home soon, now that the first real big permanent storm of 1989 seemed intent on making itself known to all those folks who still held green summer images in their foolish heads. How had she ended up in Mattagash, next door to the North Pole? No wonder her own parents had left it for industrial Connecticut in 1959 to find good, lucrative factory jobs. Charlene Hart had been born in New Milford, Connecticut, in December of that same year, to former Mattagashers. She had trekked north with her parents during an occasional summer vacation, but that was her only experience of the town.

"The end of the world," Charlene muttered as the town snowplow poked its nose around the bend. Charlene watched it coming slowly toward her, inching past the ruins of Albert Pinkham's motel. It was there, at the Albert Pinkham Motel, that Charlene's family had stayed during those Maine vacations. She hadn't minded the visits back then, and rather enjoyed jumping out of the big shiny Buick her father had proudly driven back home for all the unfortunates to view. Charlene remembered how easily her country cousins had been impressed as they gathered around her like Munchkins, inspected her city clothes, the braces on her teeth, the transistor radio in the shape of a Coca-Cola bottle. It was that same transistor that Albert Pinkham, proprietor, had smashed with a hammer when Charlene left it playing on the cement walkway outside her room. "Lord have mercy," Albert Pinkham said, when Charlene showed him the wires inside the smashed plastic, the two tiny batteries. "The Bible says strange things will happen just before the end of the world," Albert had explained. "I just figured singing pop bottles might be one of them." But even someone as cautious as Albert Pinkham couldn't keep an eye on things forever. Mattagash's only motel had fallen into disrepair as Albert grew toward his own physical downfall. With no family to tend to him, he had gone, reluctantly, to live at Pine Valley. Sometime after that, ruffians had thrown rocks to break out all the windows. Then Charlene noticed that the front door had fallen off one hinge and was dangling. Now the motel's shutters hung diagonally from their windows. Aging red bricks had cascaded down from the chimney earlier in the fall, and lay hidden beneath the snow. Rumors were that the pot smokers among Mattagash's newest generation held wild parties at the old motel. What would Albert Pinkham think of that? Charlene smiled, remembering the day of the smashed transistor. Instead of reimbursing her for the radio, Albert had merely gone on to charge her fifty cents for the rental of a nail clipper. Charlene smiled until she remembered where she was, back in Mattagash permanently, soon to turn thirty, and about to be buried alive beneath tons of white, indifferent snow.

She had met David Craft at a wedding reception. Mattagashers stuck together in Connecticut, even if they hadn't liked each other back in northern Maine. In Connecticut, Mattagashers all looked alike, and sounded alike, and suddenly there didn't seem to be so much reason to dislike each other anymore. So those who had been enemies back on the historic soil of the first settlers suddenly discovered the logic of safety in numbers. It became the *city slickers* against the *country bumpkins*. And when one had a wedding to shout about, the rest came from their respective cities and shouted. Their city-born children might not know or understand the old northern Maine roots, yet they learned to recognize the faces and the Mattagash twang. But facial smiles and the tinge of an old Irish brogue were not enough to warn this new generation of how interrelated they were. Parents silently hoped their daughters would marry city boys, their sons new-blooded Connecticut girls, who would spread some good genes about the twisted family tree. When Charlene could not resist marrying the handsome, self-assured David Craft, she did not think they were even remotely related.

"Your grandmothers was sisters for starters," Charlene remembered hearing, when she first announced their engagement. It had taken her mother a full hour, with a sheet of paper before her, to explain the genetic complexities. "Your dad is a first cousin to Davey's mom back up in Mattagash. Davey's dad is, I think, my second cousin on one side and third cousin on another. Your dad and I are related a few times too."

Now that Charlene had looked in all the old church records, had studied birth and death certificates for the nighttime genealogy class that helped her pass her first Mattagash winter, she knew the truth. She and David Craft were related all over the place on a family tree that had a writhing mass of earthworms for branches. It was an extreme case of love that had prompted Charlene to move back north when Davey lost his job, then his confidence, all in one hot-pavement Connecticut summer. But he had money in the bank, and he had a burning urge to move back to Mattagash and put that money to work in the woods.

"Go to Maine," her own father, now proudly one of only a dozen plant managers at the Ronder Plastics Company in New Milford, had advised. "After all, you was spawned there," he reminded her. Charlene smiled.

"When we passed the *Leaving Mattagash* sign, I waved for you, too," her mother loved to tell her. "Even though you was only three months along inside me." Now Charlene wished she could wave good-bye for herself. In person. The remnants of Davey's confidence were being scattered about the white pines like broken and discarded shards of a lumberjack's machinery. If she didn't get him to hell away from the woods, which was eating his spirit alive, stealing his money, sneering at him, slapping him with blackflies in the summers and whipping him with snow in the winters, he would be a hollow man when he came to the twilight of his years. He would be a dead stump left behind in the forest until the first strong wind came to level him. The woods was a real whore.

"If we don't get out of here," Charlene thought, "we'll all be lost souls." And she wondered if maybe Bennett Craft, Davey's younger brother, would be alive and well if he hadn't moved back to Mattagash. But Benny had committed suicide the autumn before, had shot himself out on the hardwood ridge that followed the Mattagash River. "Depression runs in the family," Lola had informed Charlene. But whether it did or not, Davey still hadn't accepted Bennett's death. Several times that autumn, just before the wind took the colored leaves away, Charlene had caught Davey staring out at the ridge, his eyes hard and unblinking, unable to cry. When Charlene Craft looked at that same ridge, covered with poplars and rock maples, it reminded her that this was her third winter.

"The third time tells the story," she'd told Davey that morning at breakfast. "I'll know by spring if I can handle it anymore. If I can't, Davey, I'm taking the kids. So help me, if you won't come with us, we're going alone." Now she was sorry, standing there and watching the hordes of flakes pelting the window, that she had chosen such a time to threaten him. He had enough on his mind as it was. Coming back to Mattagash with a fancy big New Yorker and ten thousand dollars in his savings account had been a fine thing. Even his brother Peter Craft, who had himself worked long enough at Pratt & Whitney to come back to Mattagash twenty years earlier and open Craft's Filling Station, could not imagine himself such a lucky man. Yet Davey and Charlene Craft had watched that money siphon itself off like a slow, steady leak, and when it was gone, not even a stain was left, not even a memory. Now Davey was just another lumberman being chewed up alive by the woods. As the first big snow of 1989 filtered down upon the dried stalks of autumn, Davey Craft had already been forced to have his father cosign for him at the Greater Northern Bank.

That loan had been to put four new tires on the skidder and buy it its costly chains. Tires were five hundred dollars each. Chains were a thousand dollars a set. But without the skidder Davey would have no way to drag the logs he'd cut out of the woods to the trucks waiting to haul them away.

"I could buy diamond necklaces for some prostitute," Davey had told his father, on the awkward drive home, "and it would be cheaper than putting chains on that goddamn skidder."

"No prostitutes in Mattagash," his father had said glumly, his eyes on the meandering road ahead of them. Now, forget the chains. Davey had left the skidder—with its broken piston and motor block—sitting where it was, its red-orange ass up in the air, had come home to measure his frustrations out in shovelfuls of fat snow.

Charlene glanced in to see that Davey had fallen asleep sitting on the sofa, Tanya's little brunette head nestled in the crook of his arm. A small twitch pulled occasionally at the corner of his mouth, a nervous tremor. Tanya was softly singing "Santa Claus Is Coming to Town."

"He's only thirty-five years old," Charlene thought, "and he's already a hundred percent beat."

"Santa Claus is coming, Mom," Tanya said, her pale round face like a little moon lodged in Davey's arm.

"He might be coming empty-handed," Charlene thought. "He might be coming for nothing." She took the potatoes off the burner and quickly deposited the hot pan into the sink, where she would mash them. She heard the screech of the school bus as it swung into the snowy yard and braked. Its door popped open and Charlene's two boys, Christopher and James, ages ten and eight, jumped out into the gusty white yard, their arms flailing snow at each other. Charlene glanced at the clock. Ten-thirty. She would now have the boys for lunch at eleven. She could only hope that the snow would quit sometime soon, or at least by nightfall, so that the chunky old plow could make things orderly by morning and allow the school bus passage.

"They'll drive me crazy if they're home again tomorrow," Charlene thought. She went quickly out the front door and stood shivering in her jeans and blouse until the boys heard her and ceased their snow wrestling.

"Daddy's asleep on the sofa," Charlene told them.

"What's Daddy doing home so early?" Christopher asked.

"The skidder broke," said Charlene.

"Again?" Christopher was genuinely concerned for a second, until he brought a mittenful of snow up quickly and rubbed it into James's face.

"Stop it, Miles!" James shouted.

"Ma, James says I'm too short to be Miles Standish," Christopher said. His cheeks were rosy with cold.

"You're even too short to be Christopher Craft," James said, and began shaping a snowball.

"Stay outside and play until I call you in," Charlene told them. "Daddy didn't sleep a wink last night."

Inside, the phone rang just once before Charlene caught it up. She walked with it, its long cord coiling behind her, out into the laundry room, where she could shut the door and talk without waking Davey. It was Eileen Fennelson, whom Bobby Fennelson had wed in the service. Eileen had no Mattagash roots whatsoever and refused even now to put any down.

"What do you think of this storm?" Charlene asked her. "Not exactly your idea of getting back to the land, is it?"

"Bobby just informed me I won't even *see* land again until April or May," Eileen whined. "I feel like I'm out to sea. This isn't Arizona, Char. What in hell will I do?"

"Get a satellite dish," Charlene advised. "That's what I did. Believe you me, it helps. I don't know what the old-timers did, and I don't care. Get a satellite dish."

"Bobby and I are fighting all the time now as it is," Eileen said. Charlene could tell by her breathy words that she was in the process of lighting one of her sixty daily cigarettes.

"Are you smoking again?" she asked Eileen. "I thought you said last week that you had it licked this time."

"Yeah, well, I thought so too until Jesus decided to dump the down out of his pillows all over us." Eileen laughed, and Charlene could hear her intake of smoky breath. "Beth's teacher told the class that's how snow is made. Beth is in the fourth grade, Char. Is that too young to be told the truth about frozen water vapor? I tell you, I'm not made for this country. I'll be a suicide case by Christmas. Mark my words. You'll find me hanging from the old birch one of these days."

"Just dig your heels in," Charlene told her. "Go out and get some exercise."

"At least you're from Connecticut," Eileen said with dismay. "You've been *introduced* to snow. I feel like I'm being attacked right now. There should be some kind of halfway house for first-timers like me. You know. *Little* snowstorms. Someone serving hot coffee. Talking me down."

"What are you and Bobby fighting about now?" Charlene put a load of whites into the machine and turned it on. If she was stuck in the laundry room for a time with the phone, she might as well do a bit of work. And she expected to be on the phone for a lengthy chat. Bobby's Arizona wife was known all over town—and this was one time Charlene had to agree with the gossips—as finicky.

"It's Bobby's family again," Eileen said. "You remember the Munsters." Charlene smiled. Eileen had been a breath of fresh air when she moved to Mattagash six months ago, straight from Germany, when Bobby's twenty-year enlistment with the army finished. "And it's his friends, too," Eileen went on. "It's this whole damn town." Charlene sighed. Maybe the whole town was saying *she* was finicky too, because when it came to the shortcomings of Mattagash, Charlene Craft had a long, long list. "They drop in at any time of day." Eileen was still complaining. "It's impossible to sit around in my P.J.'s for a cup of coffee because any ragamuffin can come through the door. They don't even knock." Charlene sighed again. Why did this all sound so familiar? Because she and Davey had argued about just the same thing.

"Gee, it's really coming down, isn't it?" Charlene asked. If she joined in with Eileen by listing her own grievances, they'd be on the phone all day. She glanced at the clock. Five minutes to eleven. She would need to finish preparing lunch—or dinner, as they called it in Mattagash—and then wake Davey from his few minutes of earthly relief. He had to solve the problem of the skidder as soon as possible. *How,* Charlene was pressed to know. "Listen, dear, it's gonna be a long winter," she reminded Eileen. "And, as Dorothy once said, this ain't Kansas."

"It ain't even New Jersey."

"You're gonna have to grin and bear it."

"But, *Char.*" Eileen had begun a perfect protest, when Charlene heard the beep that meant another incoming call. All progress was inching its way to Mattagash, even call waiting.

"I gotta go, sweetie," Charlene said. "Another call. Keep the chin up."

"Why? It'll just get covered with snow."

Charlene pressed her finger down on the button and Eileen was lost in the white swirling storm, cut loose somewhere on the telephone wires lining the main road. It was Davey's cousin Lola on the phone. Charlene winced when she heard the voice. If she had only known, she would have let Eileen drone on and on. Lola Craft Monihan. Cousin-in-law. Another reason to pack everything she owned into a U-Haul and haul ass back to Connecticut.

"Say hello to Mr. Winter." Lola was poetic for such a blustery day. "It sure is coming down, ain't it?"

"Yes, it is," said Charlene. "At least the kids are loving it. They canceled school."

"Well, if we *wanted* Arizona, we would *move* to Arizona," said Lola. "At least that's what I was just telling Dorrie." *Arizona.* They must have been gossiping about Eileen again, their favorite pastime—a pastime against which not even a satellite dish could compete.

"I was telling Dorrie," Lola went on, "about that time me and Raymond drove out to California to see his cousin and take the kids to Disneyland. We almost died in that earthquake, the one that weighed seven on that earthquake scale."

Charlene closed her eyes and listened to her cousin-in-law's

Mattagash twang bounce along the snowy wires. She put the load of whites into the dryer and packed the washer with Davey's work clothes. She added some extra detergent. The gummy stains of spruce and fir were something TV housewives never mentioned in all those Tide commercials. She swept a remnant of cobweb down with a dirty towel, then wondered if she should wait until spring to paint the laundry room. She was surprised to hear Lola still on the line, had forgotten her there, in some kind of snowy, electrical limbo.

"Who would *want* to get up and look out their window every morning just to see one of them big cactuses staring back at you, hardly a leaf on it. No sirree. I was just telling Dorrie. We had us a trip to California once and it's enough to satisfy me. The only time I want to see six lanes of traffic again is in my nightmares. And we almost *died* driving across dusty old deserty Arizona. I'll stay right here the rest of my life, thank you, in good ole northern Maine and love every blessed minute of it. There ain't nothing them states out there got that we don't."

"I'd better call the kids for lunch," Charlene said, and had planned to add something about their surely being starved, but Lola cut her off.

"Me and Dorrie just had our dinner at The Crossroads," said Lola. "We'd never go in there at night or anything, it being a bar, but we do stop for dinner once in a while, or for a take-out pizza. Did you hear that Maurice got himself a microwave put in and now he serves hot sandwiches and pizzas?"

"I hadn't heard," said Charlene, and was glad that she hadn't.

"What are you baking for the Thanksgiving Day Co-op Dinner?" Lola asked. "I'm gonna bake six loaves of bread. I'd just like for someone to tell me how many loaves I already baked this year."

"I think we'll have our dinner here," said Charlene, wondering, "What must it be like to have dinner with an entire town, most of whom you don't know, the others you don't like?"

"The newspapers is still claiming Elvis is alive," Lola announced. "They even showed what he's supposed to look like. Someone photographed him outside one of them Las Vegas gambling places. He's got long hair, but he's bald on top. And he's still real plump." Charlene smiled. The *newspapers,* her ass. When Lola said newspapers she meant *Star, Enquirer,* and *Globe.* When Lola said news show she meant *Geraldo.*

"I was telling Dorrie about it a few minutes ago and she almost fell out of her chair into a dead faint," Lola plowed on. Charlene could hear children in a bitter argument, their voices welling up to a frenzy, somewhere in Lola's house. She must be keeping Dorrie's bratty grandchildren again.

"Dorrie said that last week she was at Woolworth's in Madawaska looking for percale sheets 'cause the perma-press get them little lint bumps after a few washings, and who should she see buying handkerchiefs but a man who was the spitting image of Elvis except, and listen to this, he was *bald.*" Charlene heard Davey mumbling on the sofa and then a long sick sigh from the chest of her daughter. "Dorrie and me don't know what to make of it, now that experts claim Elvis would be bald by now," Lola was saying. "It seems like too much to be a coincidence. And northern Maine'd be the perfect place for him to hide. Who'd ever look for him in Madawaska? We're taking a trip down to Woolworth this week and just keep our eyes open."

"Davey's here for lunch," Charlene said slowly. She wondered if Lola knew about the broken skidder, but had no intentions of telling her. Lola loved for hard times to strike, even upon her relatives. And Charlene wouldn't be too surprised if Lola already knew that Davey's father had cosigned for him at the bank the previous week. Davey had met Booster Mullins on the narrow road to Watertown, and Booster had, as is usual with travelers on a tiny road, waved and tooted recognition. "He's probably wondering what we were doing on our way to Watertown," Davey had said, and Charlene knew what he meant. She had learned, in her three Mattagash years, that you could meet an entire busload of male Giffords and no one would think twice, but for hardworking men to be seen on their way to Watertown in the middle of a good workday meant that machinery was broken, or they needed to talk to the folks at the bank.

"I hear Davey's skidder is broke again," Lola said. "I bet he hates the thought of another loan. If it ain't one thing in this woodsworking business, it's another." Charlene leaned back against the washer and let out a long breath. How did they do it? By God, she *was* surprised. She was always surprised. So Lola had a week to figure out the loan, but the skidder had broken just that morning. How could one tiny little town stay so on top of things without being computerized? "Well," Lola kept on, "maybe he'll get as lucky as Paulie Hart and hit a nice lottery jackpot."

"My potatoes are boiling over," Charlene said, a rush of emergency in her voice.

"Oh, listen!" Lola stopped her. "I forgot the real reason I called you." *Let the potatoes burn* is what she was really saying. Charlene bit her tongue. If they didn't get away from Mattagash by spring, they would find *her* hanging, next to Eileen Fennelson, from the old birch tree.

"Amy Joy Lawler's pregnant," Lola whispered, as if the screaming children behind her could possibly hear. "The girl who works for Dr. Brassard at the health clinic in Watertown is married to Angelique's son, of Angelique's Hair Factory. Angelique's daughter goes to school with Prissy Monihan's daughter at the University of Maine. When Prissy's daughter come home for Labor Day weekend, she told Dorrie's daughter, and *she* called Dorrie right up the minute she heard. Amy Joy went in and had a pregnancy test done. They claim the test was positive." The *they* of a small town. Who were *they?* A collective mind? A large queen bee, fermenting with gossip?

"It's all over town," Lola added with smug satisfaction. Charlene had no doubt of that, what with Lola and Dorrie at the helm of the good ship *Gossip.* And the town of Mattagash, Maine, was like a sheet of pure ice. Bad news seemed to slide over it. "Can you just imagine?" Lola was now saying. "They don't know yet who the father is, but they think it might be Oliver Hart. He's the one who come home from Vietnam with a duffel bag full of medals and just shut himself up in his Daddy's old house." Charlene imagined, suddenly, a large modern office building, with wide windows and plenty of parking space, a sign on the door: *They,*

Inc., a place where bad news and good news were sorted over like mail, and decisions were made as to which news would be made public. *They* never talked about their own.

"Let's look at the facts," Lola said. "Unless she's seeing a married man—and I wouldn't put that an inch past her—the only bachelors in town even close to Amy Joy's age is Nolan Gifford, Oliver Hart, and Moss Fennelson. I personally think that Oliver Hart got too much of his vitals shot away in Vietnam to be chasing after Amy Joy. And I doubt that Moss is even interested in a woman," Lola added. "He took dancing lessons for almost a year at the college in Watertown."

"It's like *Big Sister Is Watching You,*" Charlene thought. It was true that most men in Mattagash were too worried over bills, or politics, or maybe even booze to join in with gossip of a feminine nature. They waited for car wrecks, the occasional suicide, an in-state murder, theft—the *important* slices of a town's life. Let the women sort out the gynecological gossip.

"She's forty-four years old," Lola said with disgust. "She should have grown kids, like the rest of us her age, not babies. Anyway, Dorrie's calling that hippie woman who sells cucumbers to Amy Joy to see if *she* knows anything."

"Another call coming in," Charlene warned, her voice full, again, of emergency. She could say, "Someone just shot a bullet into my head, Lola," and Lola would say, "Okay, but just one more thing." Emergency meant nothing to Lola Monihan. To Lola, all life had become one long, dragged-out emergency. Charlene put the phone down on its cradle. Poor Amy Joy. She'd met her only a few times but had pity for her, to be lingering along unmarried in Mattagash, Maine. Now Charlene felt the utmost compassion. It was a terrible thing to be on Dorrie and Lola's hit list.

"Davey, wake up, honey," she whispered. Tanya had fallen asleep too, her forehead warm and sweaty in Davey's arm. Davey opened his eyes and looked blankly at his wife's face, until he remembered who she was, who *he* was, and then he closed them again.

"Jesus," he said. "I just dreamed I won the lottery."

When the Old Become Young: The Downhill Slide into Pine Valley

> "Virginia Mullins should be shot for doing that to her own mother. I'll tell you one thing. The day will never come when I let a parent of mine spend their last days at an old people's home."
>
> —Lola Craft Monihan.
> Tupperware party, 1978

Amy Joy Lawler opened the passenger door of her brown 1982 Cavalier and allowed Sicily to swing her legs out of the car and plant her feet firmly upon the snow-packed driveway. They were at Pine Valley, the St. Leonard nursing home, to visit Winnie Craft. The day was brilliantly blue, river and sky competing against the white hills and fields. The first storm of 1989 had settled in, with one or two lesser storms packed on top of it, by the time Amy Joy and Sicily made their monthly visit to Pine Valley, known as Death Valley to all those reckless celebrants of youth who passed by, sometimes tooting their horns drunkenly in the heart of a boozy night.

"This better not be a trick," Sicily whined. "This better be our regular visit. I've heard of children tricking their parents in ways like this. This better not be another case of *cheese in the trap*."

"It isn't," Amy Joy assured her. "I wouldn't do that to you." She took Sicily's arm and guided her to the entrance door. "The yard is slippery. Watch your step."

"You watch *your* step," Sicily threatened. "If there's someone waiting in there with a big butterfly net that's got my name on it, be prepared for trouble. I intend to bolt."

"Oh, Mother," said Amy Joy. "What do you take me for?"

"And just what did Winnie Craft think of *her* precious daughter, Lola, for years, until she was forced to move in with her?" Sicily reminded her own daughter. "Wasn't it Lola this and Lola that? You bring up Lola's name to her now and listen to what Winnie has to say. Lola told her she was taking her to Watertown to get her hair trimmed at Angelique's Hair Factory, and before Winnie could shout "Fudge!" she was a permanent resident here. She had no choice. Lola refused to take her back home. Where could poor Winnie go? She can't live alone no more."

"That's a shame," said Amy Joy.

"She ended up getting her wings clipped instead of her hair trimmed," Sicily said. She was taking her time as she put one rickety foot in front of the other.

"I'd never do such a thing," Amy Joy soothed. "You can stay with me as long as you want." She herself knew Lola to be the kind of creature who would trick her own mother into a home. Lola had once, twenty years ago, been Amy Joy's friend. She had been Amy Joy's maid of honor, had been there to see Amy Joy jilted by a Frenchman from Watertown, a *Catholic,* something akin to a devil worshiper in Mattagash. Amy Joy had known all about Lola's gossiping disloyalty.

"You might say our friendship ticket has expired," Amy Joy told Lola when she called, a year after that fateful day in 1969, to say that she herself was getting married and could they finally bury the hatchet? The only place Amy Joy cared to bury it was between Lola's thin shoulder blades.

"Besides," Lola had added, "I'd love to borrow them brides-maid gowns of yours that never got used."

"Oh, Lord," Sicily said suddenly, and stopped on the bottom

step leading up to the front door. Out in the bright, telltale sunshine, Amy Joy noticed how pale her mother had become, how shrunken in her big woolen coat.

"What if Winnie begs us again to take her home?" Sicily's wrinkly little mouth pursed itself with the question. "You know she called again yesterday to ask me."

"You just pretend you're hard of hearing," Amy Joy advised, and realized this was an impossibility to ask of one of Mattagash's finest gossips. Sicily had been a real contender in her day.

"But there's that extra bedroom of Pearl's . . ." Sicily began. A soft white spittle formed on her bottom lip like a little snowfall.

"Mama, let's go in," Amy Joy insisted, and tugged at Sicily's arm. Sicily calculated the remaining steps before she lifted a foot to try one. With the slow-footedness of old age, she climbed all six and waited at the top as Amy Joy knocked loudly on the door.

Amy Joy felt sheer despair settle over her again. She was entitled, wasn't she, to one last stab at life before she laid down the sword? The truth was that Sicily would have better company at Pine Valley than she found back at the old McKinnon homestead. She stayed on the phone to Winnie all day anyway. Why not be there in person? Besides, Amy Joy was accustomed to spending the long daylight hours of summer along the Mattagash River and in the deep woods, collecting her wildflowers to be dried and pressed between the pages of a book. In the summer Amy Joy abandoned Sicily for the meadowsweet, field mint, yarrow, caraway, the rare St. John's tansy, the wild cucumbers that grew on vines along the edges of the wood. In the winter, even on those blustery, snow-swept days, Amy Joy went on snowshoes to quiet places, too narrow for the noisy snowmobiles. She went about the winter hills, leaving Sicily behind to complain on the phone to Winnie about abandonment, as she switched from channel to channel with her remote control and waited for Amy Joy's return. Now it was becoming a danger to leave Sicily alone for very long at a time. What if she fell? Should Amy Joy, then, forfeit the rest of her own life to look after what was left of Sicily's?

"I'll come visit you every day," Amy Joy had promised, when

Sicily complained of loneliness. This was the very first time the subject of Pine Valley had floated up between them. "And you wouldn't be lonely at Pine Valley. You'd have all the company you could stand over there." But Sicily preferred her own room at the old McKinnon homestead, her birthplace, and continued her lifelong quest to instill enough guilt in Amy Joy to control her. Amy Joy knocked again on the heavy door.

"We could make Winnie's Christmas this year," Sicily said sweetly. "All we have to do is take her home with us, and today could be the day we tell her."

"Three minutes ago, you were about to collapse with fear that I might be putting you here against your will," Amy Joy said. Her patience was waning, as it always did. She hated it when Sicily managed that. Yet, three or four times a day, Amy Joy lost her grip on her emotions and lambasted Sicily with a few good facts of life. "Now that I tell you I won't do that, you want to bring Winnie the Poop home."

"Don't call her that," Sicily scolded. "You're as bad as Lola." Amy Joy looked at her mother. *That* was an insult of utter magnitude to Amy Joy, and Sicily knew it.

"I'll tell you what," Amy Joy said. "Why don't you and Winnie move in at the house, and *I'll* come live here."

"We'll visit every day," Sicily said. Amy Joy was about to waltz her ornery little mother down the Pine Valley steps and into the car, give her a breakneck ride back home, when the door flew open.

"Come on in," a girl from Watertown whom Amy Joy knew only as M. J., told the pair on the porch. She was one of the regular workers at Pine Valley. "You'll freeze to death out here."

Winnie Craft was already stiffly settled in the lounge where the social hour was held. She wore a pair of nubby wool slacks under her dress, and what looked like two sweaters. Her hair was gossamer as snow. She was staring at Amy Joy with an inordinate interest.

"They keep the temperature in here at sixty-eight," Winnie griped immediately, before the visitors had removed their wraps.

"One of these mornings we'll get up and find frost on everything."

Amy Joy undid her scarf and placed it, along with her gloves, inside the pockets of her coat. Then she helped Sicily off with hers. She wondered how Winnie even knew it was the social hour, considering that she had gossiped every second of every waking minute of her life—a life full of social hours.

Sicily gave Winnie a big hug. They appeared almost conspiratorial. Amy Joy smiled cautiously. Surely her mother hadn't promised to break Winnie out of Pine Valley.

"They claim they're gonna bus us all over to that co-op dinner on Thanksgiving Day," Winnie said. "Those of us who can still sit up."

"Ain't you lucky," said Sicily, patting Winnie's bony arm. "Amy Joy won't take me. She says we're gonna eat our dinner home alone, like a couple of nuns. Amy Joy says it's Thanksgiving dinner, not a jamboree."

"*You* said the part about the nuns," Amy Joy reminded her.

"Albert Pinkham's giving them a hard time again," Winnie whispered suddenly, and nodded at a figure slumped in a wheelchair. He was pointed toward the sunny window, as though enjoying the day. But his eyes were shut, his tongue lolling about in his open mouth.

"This is only the second time he's come out of his room since he's been here," Winnie reported. Amy Joy gasped. It had been only three years since she'd seen Albert Pinkham, yet she wouldn't have recognized this old man who was caving into his own bones, like an avalanche.

"Albert calls the staff goddamn Frogs," Winnie offered further. She was, Amy Joy noticed, still happily able to finger all the hairs in her nose, albeit her hand now shook during this consummate work. "He says he didn't live his whole life speaking the King's English in Mattagash only to die among Frogs in St. Leonard." Winnie fingered as she spoke. "He says one night, after they turn out the lights, he's heading back to his motel."

Amy Joy thought about that. The old-timers, and even many young-timers, were still hanging on to the prejudices as though they were heirlooms. It was a lucky thing Mattagash had no blacks. She could imagine one hanging from each and every lynchworthy pine.

"How's your mother?" Sicily asked. This was one of life's little ironies. Winnie's mother was still alive, well beyond a hundred years old, and in another room at Pine Valley.

"I was in to see her this morning," Winnie said. "She seems to be resting well enough. The Women's Auxiliary wants to present a plaque or something to her at the Thanksgiving Day dinner. That peaked-faced girl of Rose Monihan's come and asked me if it was okay for them to wheel Mama into the gym, even though she ain't aware of things. They thought it would be good for the little kids to sort of see her, her being the oldest Mattagasher and all."

"That's real nice," said Sicily. "I wish *I* was going to that dinner."

"I dreamed of Morton last night," Winnie said wistfully.

"Poor Morton," said Sicily. Morton was Winnie's brother, who had died in his sleep when he was only thirty years old. At the time, the doctor couldn't figure out why the incident had occurred, but the whole town knew that Morton was so stupid he had probably just forgotten to breathe.

"That old woman from Watertown died last night," Winnie added. "I heard them take her out."

"Which old woman is that?" Sicily asked. Amy Joy watched the two old women referring to someone else as such.

"Remember the one who was doing the needlepoint of that moose scene?" asked Winnie. "It said *Maine, Vacationland* over the antlers."

"Yes," said Sicily. "Now I remember her. She had an awful steady hand."

"Well," Winnie said flatly. "It's even steadier now."

"Too bad she couldn't have finished it," said Sicily. "She'd put an awful lot of work into it."

"The family would've just thrown it out anyway," Winnie said. "Nothing means anything to folks anymore." A small piece of silence fell upon them. Amy Joy wished the mood were more festive. Her greatest prayer was that one day Sicily would throw up her hands in jubilation and shout, "I love it here, Amy Joy! Please, God, let me stay!" Then maybe Amy Joy could go off somewhere and live a life of her own. Maybe she'd even leave Mattagash.

"Mrs. Faber, from right here in St. Leonard, pees the bed like a baby," Winnie whispered suddenly, and Sicily gasped.

"No!" Sicily said. "Don't tell me."

"Every single night," Winnie assured her. "I heard the girls say so," she added for validation.

"Imagine that," said Sicily. "She was such a snob in her prime. Remember the fur coat she ordered through the mail? You'd have sworn all them little minks committed suicide just to be in *her* coat, to hear her talk."

"Them minks was from Germany or someplace, wasn't they?" Winnie asked, as though the creatures were tourists.

"Oh, to be sure they were," Sicily said. "Our own minks weren't good enough for her. And then, that was in the fifties. We was fresh from a war with Hitler, but there was Mrs. Faber wearing his minks." Amy Joy imagined an army of tiny Nazi minks.

"From snob to bed wetter," Winnie said.

"Are you sure they said Mrs. Faber?" Sicily rarely asked for documentation, generally taking Winnie at her word.

"Every single night," Winnie assured her again.

"Back to being a baby," said Sicily softly. "I guess that's what the Bible means when it says the old will become young." Amy Joy felt the social awkwardness that had inched in around the conversation and settled itself down. Old age pressing down on them like an anvil. *Will this happen to me?*, Winnie and Sicily were asking themselves. Amy Joy could almost hear the unspoken questions running around and around in the coiled mechanisms of their minds. *If this can happen to Mrs. Faber, how can it not happen to me?* Even Amy Joy had begun to count, by tens, the number of years before *she* would be the same age as Sicily, as Winnie, as Albert, as Mrs. Faber.

"They keep a diaper on her night and day." Winnie's voice

was a child's now, small and uncertain. "They feed her food mashed up tiny enough for babies."

"That arrangement of flowers is beautiful," Amy Joy said firmly. Her voice was the voice of an adult, loud with pretense, a mother's voice placating the children. Sicily stared at the flowers with relief. It was good to have Amy Joy around. Someone had to stop the train of memory once it got rolling, to slap a foot down hard on the brakes. Otherwise, one would slam into questions, doing a hundred miles an hour and unable to stop.

"It's like summer to have such pretty flowers," Amy Joy went on, and certainty filled the air again. "There's almost two feet of snow out there, after all."

"The staff ordered them," said Winnie, her voice bouncing back from the horrible edge of that great, familiar void. "Someone had a birthday." She was back to her old mocking self. She seemed to be staring at Amy Joy again, at her waist—no, her *stomach.*

"Those mums are so colorful," Amy Joy noted. She saw Sicily's face finally relax, the troubling questions about the future flown.

"They ought to spend any extra money in the budget on food," Winnie snapped. "Not flowers. I doubt they paid for them out of their own pockets." Amy Joy noticed that Winnie's lips had grown thinner than she remembered them, as if they were disappearing.

"She probably wore them out," Amy Joy thought.

"And you say the food is usually cold?" Sicily inquired, and then gave Amy Joy a plaintive look as Winnie described the culinary horrors at Pine Valley.

"Absolute slop," she finally summarized.

"Well, Mama," Amy Joy said. "Maybe we should go now." She had seen Albert Pinkham twitching like an old leaf in his chair, quaking.

"He cries all the time now," Winnie whispered.

"Poor soul," said Sicily. "Don't his daughter, Belle, ever come up from New Hampshire to visit?"

"Not anymore," said Winnie. "Not since her mother died. Nobody to drive her now. I hear she's blind as a mole."

"Well, there's a line in her family tree that goes back to old Caroline McGilvery. She brought an eye disease over on the boat with her from Ireland," Sicily said, as though retinitis pigmentosa were something Caroline had packed. "The Giffords come down from them too," Sicily reminded her friend, "and look at how many of them was always driving off the road or bumping into walls, unless they was stealing something. Sarah and Albert would've died rather than own up to them family skeletons, but Belle's living proof."

"Sarah Pinkham did think she was a peg or two up the ladder, didn't she?" asked Winnie.

"I always thought Sarah would come back to Albert one day," said Sicily.

"Lord, woman!" Winnie was surprised. "You must be talking about a different Sarah Pinkham than I am. Sarah wouldn't have took Jesus back, under them circumstances."

Amy Joy had stood up and was waiting anxiously for Sicily to finish her chat. But this caught her. She could barely remember Sarah Pinkham, a pinched, thin-faced woman, or her daughter, Belle, who had eyes like a large looming fish, eyes swimming behind thick lenses. And no matter that this incident had happened thirty years ago, this incident between Albert Pinkham and his wife. When it came to Mattagash gossip, time had no dimension, no limitations. Gossip curved somewhere out in space and flickered back. Gossip was an unbroken, unwavering line that touched generation after generation after generation. It was a continuum. Mr. Albert Einstein would have had a field day in Mattagash, Maine.

"She accused him of bedding down with that strip artist," Winnie said. "Remember?" As if Sicily didn't. As if any townswoman worth her tongue would, *could* forget one of the high dramas that, like supernovas, occur sparsely in small towns, if ever. "She'd never forgive him a thing like that," Winnie added with finality. "Not Sarah."

"Poor Sarah," said Sicily. "I hope she has peace, wherever she is."

"I hope that strip artist ain't there too," said Winnie. "If so, there won't be any peace for anybody."

"I hope it's warmer, wherever they all are," Amy Joy interjected. "Could we please go now? It's time for Winnie to have her supper."

"Don't remind me," said Winnie, and waved a hand to pooh-pooh the food.

"You poor, poor thing," said Sicily magnanimously. She looked sweetly at Amy Joy. "Just think of all the wonderful food we get to eat at home."

"I heard the food here was pretty good," Amy Joy countered.

"There ain't nothing, though, like a home-cooked meal," Sicily argued.

"You eat TV dinners and pour hot water over packages of instant soup, Mama. I wouldn't call that home-cooked."

"Sounds pretty good to me," Winnie said, and licked her disappearing lips.

"It's where you eat it that counts," Sicily said scientifically.

"How's Lola these days?" Amy Joy asked Winnie, and watched as a tremor rushed over her. She knew what Amy Joy was up to. She was saying, *Why doesn't your own daughter, your own flesh and blood, come and take you home to a fine dinner?*

"She comes in plenty to see me," Winnie lied. "Them kids of hers are so big I hardly know them from time to time."

"How nice," said Sicily soothingly.

"They make me stuff, day in and day out," Winnie lied again. But she *imagined* the sweet picture in her mind and smiled warmly. "Mittens," she said. "Crayon pictures. Cakes and cookies." Her eyes misted. Amy Joy looked away, but Sicily rushed to her friend's defense.

"There now," Sicily rattled. "Look what you've made yourself go and do. You've made yourself get lonesome for all them sweet grandchildren of yours."

"The dirty little devils!" Winnie cried out. "If they ever do make me a crayon picture, they can just keep the damn thing!" She was weeping openly now, loudly. A member of the staff came to investigate.

"Mrs. Craft," the young woman said gently. Her name tag read

Nadine Auclair. She was very sympathetic. "What's wrong? Are you sad again tonight?"

"No!" Winnie shouted. "I just won the damn lottery. Of course I'm sad, you nincompoop. I'm crying, ain't I?" She turned to Sicily and grabbed her hand. "See? What did I tell you? They treat me like I'm a baby."

"Now you have Mr. Pinkham going," Nadine said somewhat sternly. Albert had suddenly burst into tears.

"It would take a cattle prod to get Albert going," Winnie cried. "So don't you blame me." She clutched at Sicily's arms, and Sicily wrapped them around her.

"Shh," said Sicily.

"They blame me for everything," Winnie sobbed. "You know damn well that Albert Pinkham wouldn't do a single thing unless he *wanted* to." Nadine wheeled Albert Pinkham past the social hour crowd and disappeared down the corridor with him. His sobs followed them, echoing along the tiles until the door to his room was softly closed.

"There, there," said Sicily, and patted Winnie's plump hand. Amy Joy reached into the pocket of her coat and found the woolen gloves she had crammed there. Nadine returned and beckoned her aside.

"I don't know what we're going to do with her," Nadine whispered. "All the others manage very well. They seem to enjoy themselves until Mrs. Craft stirs them up. I hope she doesn't discourage your mother's notion of Pine Valley."

"Discourage her?" said Amy Joy. "She lives for moments like this. Look at her." Sicily had inched her way around to Winnie's back and was massaging her neck as deftly as an expert.

"Breathe in deep now," Sicily was saying, and Winnie was doing her best to comply.

"I can't offer her this kind of melodrama at home," Amy Joy said. "She's pretty bored over there."

At the front door, Amy Joy and Sicily came face-to-face with Dorrie Fennelson Mullins, Lola's comrade in good gossip and bad news. Dorrie had been most pleased over Amy Joy's shattered wedding plans.

"Why is it," Amy Joy wondered, "that if you have only two enemies in your life, you'll bump into them all over the world?" Lola and Dorrie were hers.

"Well, Amy Joy," Dorrie purred. "It's been absolutely ages." She was wearing her padded stadium coat, which went all the way down past her knees.

"Has it?" asked Amy Joy. She had run into Dorrie at the post office less than a month ago. Sicily hobbled past and began her descent down the front steps just as a small dark-haired woman appeared behind Dorrie.

"Don't fall, Mama," Amy Joy warned. "I'm right behind you." She was sure that this would be a signal to Dorrie that she was in a small rush. But Dorrie loomed heavily before her, her body vaporous and vague and bulging with the work of having borne seven children. It had also kept David's House of Doughnuts in Watertown operating quite nicely in the black.

Nadine stood quietly, one hand on the door opened to the cold, and waited. Chilly air rushed in and met the warm, hoisted up Dorrie's big burgundy coat, exposed part of her meaty calves. She slapped the coat down and held it with her hand. The thin little dark-haired woman smiled weakly.

"You *look* well," said Dorrie.

"Shouldn't I?" Amy Joy asked.

"Oh, I guess so." Dorrie sighed fully. "I keep forgetting that you got neither chick nor child to look after. If you had a house of kids driving you crazy, well, that's a whole other story."

Amy Joy stared at her flatly. Dorrie, who had babies as though they were gold medals, prizes, tickets to heaven. Her house had always reminded Amy Joy of a picture she'd seen once of the old woman in the shoe: kids in the windows, kids on the front porch, kids on the roof.

"I tell you what," Dorrie said. "It's a good thing all my kids is growed up, some with kids of their own. I needed the rest. I told Booster that if we had had one more baby, I would've become a Catholic. They probably would've made me a saint."

"On the other hand," said Amy Joy, "they might've just burned you at the stake." She imagined Dorrie's ovaries popping, all her tubes sizzling like bacon. Dorrie let the slight drift by. She had a point she wanted to make, and stopping to be insulted would prevent it. Also, it was very cold in Mattagash. One had to be quick with one's barbs in the wintertime.

"And what about you?" she asked, her voice feigning a long and tender relationship with Amy Joy. "Good heavens, but your biological clock must be ready to blow all its springs. That clock'll put you into orbit if you ain't careful. You'll end up on Mars."

"I'm not worried about it, Dorrie," Amy Joy said. "So don't you be." She slid past the heavy woman, her purse held close to her chest, her scarf fluttering.

"Well, you should," Dorrie called after her. "*I* wouldn't want to end up on Mars."

"No, of course you wouldn't," Amy Joy said. "There are no doughnuts there."

"Come back soon," said Nadine, all ashiver, and she closed the door to Pine Valley.

Dorrie was aghast. Her face fluffed up with anxiety, the anger narrowing her eyes. She carried her hundred extra pounds over to the lounge and plopped down.

"We're here to see Claire Fennelson," Dorrie huffed. "I'm her daughter and this here's her daughter-in-law."

"She just went back to her room," Nadine said. "It might be easier on her if you visited her there. The social hour's over anyway."

"That's just fine and dandy," Dorrie said to her sister-in-law as they followed Nadine through the shiny halls, past aging legs dangling off bedsides, past wrinkly little men inching their way along the walls, tiny women standing in doorways. But Dorrie was oblivious to them all. "Amy Joy can be as sarcastic as she wants to. The whole town knows. Having an illegitimate baby at forty-four. Have you ever heard the likes?" Wrinkly men clung to their walls as Dorrie swooshed past, like a big angry breeze. Tiny women shrank back from doorways. Legs stopped dangling and slid under covers.

"How far along is she?" the sister-in-law asked. She was quite uninterested in Dorrie's saga, but she knew she'd better ask anyway.

"We ain't really sure." Dorrie's breath was rattling in her chest like a little train, her heart pulling all those cars behind it.

"Mrs. Fennelson," Nadine said, rapping on a door. "Your daughter's here."

Claire Fennelson looked as though she'd been wakened from a shadowy, bad dream. Or perhaps she'd been pulled out of the safety of someplace warm and sweet, afforded her by her subconscious, only to be faced with the horribly vague, sad truth of life.

"What day's today?" she asked Nadine.

"Sunday," Nadine answered.

"Mama, we come to visit you, sweetheart," Dorrie shouted. Wrinkly men in other rooms canted their heads and listened. Tiny women scrunched up their faces.

"This is Larry's wife, Edie, that he met and married in the army. She come to visit you all the way from Worcester, Massachusetts. You remember Larry? Your oldest boy?"

Claire Fennelson smiled widely. "Larry," she said, slowly and surely, as if it were the correct answer to a tough question she'd been working on for years. She waited expectantly, her eyes on Dorrie's face.

"Poor woman," Dorrie whispered to Edie. "You'd swear she was on the *Wheel of Fortune*. That's what them contestants look like just before they buy a vowel."

"Where's Larry?" Claire Fennelson asked, and looked above the heads of her visitors. She grew quiet as different images fluttered about in her mind: Larry at five, Larry at sixteen, Larry in his uniform—because memory, like the gossip in Mattagash, never ages. It simply grows larger and brighter. *Larry!*

"Every time we come here," Dorrie whispered, "we have to goddamn bury Larry all over again."

"Don't tell her, though," Edie said. "It'll only upset her."

"Larry's keeping house!" Dorrie boomed, and Larry's mother smiled to hear this.

"I wish the hell he *was*," Edie thought. "Considering what I've spent on baby-sitters in my day."

"You mark my words," Dorrie said, and opened the card she had brought with her. *Happy Birthday to a Wonderful Mom* it said. She put it in the old woman's hands and it wobbled there. "Amy Joy's gonna wake up one morning and instead of being on a pedestal she'll be eyeing ground level."

"Do you know who the father is?" Larry's widow asked, and opened her own card. *A Birthday Wish for a Special Mother-in-Law.* "Did you say it was someone from town?" She needed to keep Dorrie talking. The visit would pass more quickly.

"I'd give up a winning lottery ticket just to know." Dorrie sighed and unwrapped some birthday underwear. "Lola thinks it's Oliver Hart, our local war hero. But I got a feeling Oliver is more interested in Moss Fennelson than he is in Amy Joy. Moss took a bunch of dancing lessons at the college. Need I say more? Hey, come here a minute," she said suddenly to Edie, who was unwrapping a cotton nightdress. "I got something to show you." Edie followed her out of the room and down the hallway. Tiny women pulled back from doorways. Wrinkly men quaked in their pajamas. Feeble hands reached for the walls.

"What room is old Mrs. Mathilda Fennelson in?" Dorrie asked the first staff member she saw. "I used to know, but I forgot."

"Are you family?" the nurse asked suspiciously.

"I'm her granddaughter-in-law." Dorrie was annoyed by the question. What did they think she was going to do? Steal an old person?

"Room thirty-two," the attendant said. "Down the hall, turn right, the first room on the left."

"She's a hundred and seven," Dorrie whispered as she and Edie stared down at the spindly shape. "She ain't talked in years. Who knows what she's thinking of, or even if she *can* think. But everybody in Mattagash is related to her a dozen times over. That's why they're gonna give her a plaque on Thanksgiving Day."

"I'll be damned," said Edie.

"She's been here at the home since day one," Dorrie said, pleased with herself for showing Edie, a bona fide city woman, a treasure her streetwise eyes had yet to behold. Dorrie left off with her whispering and returned to her usual boom. "She's been here at Pine Valley forever."

"Imagine that." Edie fidgeted with a curl that had come loose inside her scarf. She had made several visits to Mattagash with the kids since Larry's death. She felt she owed him that much. Now the children were all grown. If they wanted to visit the twisted horde of their paternal relatives, they could do so on their own. This was Edie's last trip. She had, after all, remarried years ago. Enough was enough. "I guess my kids are her great-grandchildren, then."

"Naw, she's Booster's grandmother, not mine," Dorrie said. "But she *is* my cousin in a lot of different ways. She was a Craft before she got married, and my grandmother was a Craft."

"Who did this woman marry?" Edie asked. She noticed the blood running like old blue rivers beneath skin stretched on the hands, the temples.

"She married Foster Fennelson," Dorrie said, and quickly read the signature on a Hallmark card that was decorating the bedstand. "Larry and me is in one Fennelson line, and she married into another one. Them Fennelson lines is so twisted they look like that sign on a doctor's door. The one with the snake in it."

"Did she have many children?" Edie asked.

"She raised a whole bushel of kids," Dorrie said, and then shooed a fly away from the old woman's face. "You wouldn't believe the tragedy in that family. You think the Kennedys are cursed? Remind me someday to tell you all about the line of Fennelsons this poor woman married into. She married right smack dab into a curse."

"A curse?" Edie asked.

Dorrie nodded with a chilling certainty. "One of the old McKinnons cursed one of the old Fennelsons for stealing some pastureland, and it's been passed on ever since. Thank God it didn't come down to Booster."

"What do you mean?" Edie asked.

"One of this old woman's daughters was Justine. Booster is Justine's son," Dorrie explained. "They say that only the men in that family, the sons, passed that bad-luck gene on. So Justine couldn't give it to Booster. She did have it, though. She went out to the mailbox one day to see if her mail had come, and the dry cleaner's truck from Watertown struck her and killed her dead." Edie's eyes widened at the dramatic lilt in Dorrie's voice. "The roads was icy and the driver said he didn't see her," Dorrie added. "However, if you ask *me,* and I say this even though she was my mother-in-law and I loved her, she was probably trying to look across the road into Edna Hart's windows and didn't see that truck coming. When Simon Craft, the mailman, finally pulled up to the box to deliver her mail, he found her. She was stiff as a poker by then. The temperature was below zero that day. Poor soul. She'd been waiting for two months for her Sears, Roebuck order to come and, sure enough, wouldn't you know that was the day Simon brought it." Edie felt her breath catch. As much as she wanted to shake off the notion of a curse as silly, she had to admit Dorrie was certainly a storyteller, her voice rising and falling like Hitchcock music.

"I tell you what," Dorrie whispered. "Old Rose Kennedy can't hold a candle to this poor soul here." She pointed dramatically at the old woman on the bed.

"Just her sons had the bad gene, huh?" Edie asked. Mattagash was more interesting than Worcester, it was true. If only they had a mall, Edie wouldn't mind her visits quite so much.

"Well, no, all of her daughters got it except Winnie, who's here at Pine Valley," Dorrie explained patiently. Edie had always been, and Dorrie was the first to mention this, a little bit slow-witted. "Of course, Winnie did lose the tip of her finger in an electric knife accident, but if you ask me, just being Winnie is curse enough. The other daughters got that gene from their father. They just couldn't pass it on. All but two of this woman's children died young and most from violent deaths. One of them, Elizabeth, is an old maid. Her bad luck was to be infertile and then move to New York City. She's been mugged a million times. But just between you and me, I think the reason she's infertile is by choice.

I strongly believe Elizabeth is of the opposite persuasion. Her hair ain't more than an inch long anywhere on her head."

"The others all died violent deaths?" Edie asked.

"All except Morton, Booster's uncle. He died in his sleep a long time ago. But they say he was so stupid it was hard to tell if that was good luck or bad."

"I'll be damned," said Edie. She reached a finger out to touch the gnarled skin, to see if the old woman was real. The skin was warm, blood pumping somewhere, life inside the shell.

"It's *her* old house that's now The Crossroads," Dorrie said. "Maurice Fennelson, who runs it, is her grandson."

"Wonder how she'd feel to know that," said Edie.

"Well, from what I hear on the wind, Priscilla Monihan from right here in town is trying to get The Crossroads closed down," said Dorrie. "The Bible can say what it wants, but there ain't no one can clear a temple faster than Prissy."

"Do you suppose she can hear us?" Edie asked. She had noticed an ear peeping out from the tufts of gray hair, like some old vegetable growing unnoticed.

"She's the oldest living person in Mattagash, Maine—maybe even the whole country," Dorrie bragged. "President Reagan sent her a special letter when she turned a hundred."

"Hell, someone'll be sending *him* one pretty soon," Edie said, and she and Dorrie muffled laughs, each with a hand to her mouth.

"It would be her great-grandson who just won that thousand dollars in the lottery," Dorrie said, adding even more family history and mystery. "Paulie Hart. He picked eighteen, twelve, six, seventeen, and nine. Do you realize I picked three of them same numbers myself? That's how close I come."

"Well, that's pretty lucky, ain't it?" Edie asked. "I guess he couldn't have got the bad gene either."

"He's Morton's grandson," Dorrie explained. "All that got passed down to Paulie was the *stupid* gene."

"Look there," said Edie. "Her lids just fluttered."

"Ain't she the oldest living thing you ever laid your two eyes on?" Dorrie asked.

"Not really," said Edie. She was, after all, a well-traveled woman, having been married for a short time to an enlisted man. "When Larry was stationed out in California," Edie said, pride in every word, "before he went over there to Pork Chop Hill, we piled into the Buick one Sunday and drove out to see a whole bunch of them redwoods."

FROM
Mathilda Fennelson's Bible

McKINNONS

WILLIAM
BRANSFORD   *Came to Mattagash in 1833*
JASPER

BRANSFORD	*marries*	AUGUSTA
MCKINNON	*1831*	HART
b. 1808		*b. 1811*

LEWIS	*marries*	RACHEL
MCKINNON	*1855*	HART
b. 1832	*(1st cousins)*	*b. 1838*

ELIZABETH	*marries*	NATHANIEL
MCKINNON	*3/1882*	CRAFT
b. 1865		*b. 1864*

MATHILDA ANNA CRAFT
b. December 16, 1882
(marries Foster Fennelson 1896)

Mathilda Fennelson
Is Beginning: Postscript from Pine Valley

> Be beginning; since, no, nothing can be done
> To keep at bay
> Age and age's evils, hoar hair,
> Ruck and wrinkle, drooping, dying, death's worst,
>   winding sheets, tombs and worms and tumbling to
>   decay;
> So be beginning, be beginning to despair.
>
> —Gerard Manley Hopkins, "The Leaden Echo"

I woke up on my hundredth birthday and thought I was young again. So I tried to get up out of my bed, and couldn't. Imagine that. I just wanted to get up out of that bed and *I could not do it.* It was as if my body was a turtle shell with 1882 carved on it by a penknife, and I was just a living muscle struggling around inside. The king of England is to blame for all this.

Me and this town was born at the same time, in the same year, and you might say for the same reasons: folks doing what they had no business doing. The king of England wanted white pine to build the masts of his ships, and that selfish notion alone brought my maternal great-grandfather to this town. I used to think a lot about that, you know, how one feller way over there across the ocean changed the lives of so many folks. He even changed their countries. My great-grandfather Bransford McKinnon was a Canadian until he and his two brothers come looking for them white pines. That was in 1833. They was given grants to the land they might settle on, so Bransford and his brothers brung their wives, and what tiny children they had among them, and they come way up here in the wilderness. It weren't just the pines that lost their roots before this whole shipbuilding scrape was over. And you know the funny thing? There weren't one of them old-timers ever *saw* a ship, let alone a king. They come up here in pirogues, dug-out canoes. They thought they'd staked a claim in Canada, but it was a big mistake, you might say. They were really in the United States of America. That's how all us loyalist descendants here ended up Americans. But just the same, them McKinnon boys come without ever looking back, and because of that, my great-grandmother ached to go home right up until the night she died.

It was almost fifty years later that Mattagash made up its mind to form a township. A lot of folks had come here by then, including my father's people, to join up with the log drives, and raise their families. And I suppose, since it looked like it was going to last, they decided to make it official. That was in 1882. In that same year a couple of foolish young people who had no business at all getting together did just that. They never would've met if their ancestors hadn't come looking for pine trees. They probably wouldn't even have been born. Them was my parents. They got married in March, and I come along in December. Looking back on it now, I wish the king had found some other way to sail his ships, without them white pine masts. I wish the king had had other things to do.

The day me and this town turned a hundred years old, you'd have thought *we* was royalty, instead of born out of royalty's whims. That was some years back. I don't remember now just how many, but they had a big party for me. Folks I didn't even know come and stared down at me like I was already dead. They read me like you might read a tombstone, an obituary. So I did what any self-respecting woman would do. I packed up and moved further back inside my head, where I wouldn't have to look at them. That's no different than buying a ticket on a train or a bus. A ticket is something that takes you where you want to go. So I moved back up into the woods by Mattagash Brook, up where I was born. I went for free. I just looked at them all and realized that I was tired of hearing them talk. After living for a hundred years, you deserve some things. So I turned the sound off, you might say, and suddenly everything I saw out there was like a big television screen. Just a picture with no noise at all. I could see their faces, could even recognize a couple of them as my own children, children old enough to be dead themselves. I could see their mouths opening and closing, and I knew words must have been pouring out. But I couldn't hear a single one. I heard the water, instead, at Mattagash Brook, the way it cascades over the rocks, catches up crayfish and inch-long trout. People are foolish, you know, when you quit listening to them. Their mouths kept coming at me like they was goldfish in a tank, grandchildren, great-grandchildren, great-great-grandchildren, God only knows how many generations of them has been born out of me. I give up counting years ago. But now it's all pure silence. Sometimes, when I ain't prepared, they get a word or two to come through. Every now and then, folks I ain't ever seen before come into this room. "Grammie! Grammie!" they shout. "Can you hear us?" The lines are down, my eyes say back to them. There's been a storm and the lines are all down. A real bad connection. So go away and leave me alone.

Sometimes Winnie, the most despisable of all my children, comes and puts her ear next to mine and listens for the longest time, like she might be able to hear what's going on in there. Maybe she thinks there's people living inside my head. Chairs being pushed around. Dishes washed. Babies crying. Maybe she thinks I'm raising my family again, without her. She was always the jealous type. Get your ear away from mine, you old fool, that's what I don't tell her. Get your old ear out of here. I ain't no seashell, and there ain't no babies in here. I didn't get off the train in the middle of being big all the time with children, which I always was back then—me, and the pigs, and the cows, and anything else that was female. I had thirteen babies. Or was it fourteen? One of them died inside me and I used to wake up at night and think I heard it crying. But it was me, crying in my sleep, crying because I was glad that baby was dead. And I knew that God knew. It was an awful burden to carry that child until it was born. It was winter and the ground was frozen so hard you couldn't take an ice pick to it. We put it in a little wooden box, and then buried it in the snow behind the barn, so no animals would find it some hungry night. When spring come, just before the wild apple trees fell into their bloom, and the river was free of ice and flowing good, we loaded it into the canoe and brought it down to the graveyard at Mattagash Point. That's where we buried it, without a marker or anything. Back then only a few folks could afford to mark their dead. It was a boy baby and, in my heart, I named it. I named it Last Baby Fennelson, but I never told anybody, 'cause I didn't want anybody to know, especially Foster. He'd have done all he could have, out of spite, to give me another one. He tried anyway, but my womb was all wore out by then. You've seen an old towel so threadbare there's nothing left to wring out of it? That was me. But God has punished me for being glad that baby was dead. He's making me live forever, like Methuselah, and that's an awful thing to do to one of your children. I wanted mine dead, but God wants his to live and live and live. You might say I'm condemned to life. I already seen most of my children buried. I don't know anymore how many of them's left. I think some of them got too old to visit. Maybe only Winnie's alive now. She's contrary enough to outlive us all. By the time I turned a hundred, I had grandchildren with full heads of gray hair. I've been around so long now that I wonder if anyone even remembers who I am. Maybe I'll be in this world after my descendants are all dead and gone, and strangers will be poking me with a stick and asking, "Who is she anyway?"

No, I didn't stop the train for any more babies. I took it further back to where I could see the wild cherry blossoms, white as snow on the branches. They grew all around the upper pastures and down to the river, then along its bank. *Wild* cherry trees. Imagine that. And beechnuts. And pines so thick and full it was dark as night beneath them. Sometimes we'd peel gum from a spruce tree and pop it into our mouths and chew it until it didn't taste so bad, and then, after a time, it even tasted good. That was nature's gum, not some of the store-bought foolishness that folks started buying. There's fly wings and mice droppings in store-bought stuff. That's what Winnie told me once. She said that nowadays everything you buy has got its share of something awful like that, and it's okay with the government. Can you imagine that?

I made a mess in my bed today. Think about that. I was always such a neat and clean person, and I kept my kids that way, no matter how much work it took. I had to make my own soap, remember. And I washed everything in a wooden tub, was as pleased as Punch when Foster got me a galvanized, store-bought one. My firstborn, Walter, was the hardest child to train that I ever saw. He'd just squat wherever he was and go in his pants. He's dead now. World War I. But that child could've been in church, it didn't matter. He'd just squat.

They sent the nurse to clean me up. She kept a sour face, but it weren't her fault. She should be around young folks all day, and not us spoon-fed corpses that look up from our beds and ask if we're dead yet. I even tried to tell her that there was nothing spiteful in what I did. I guess it happened with me the same way it did to Walter. There was just a burst of warm bubbles inside me, and then it was over. I wanted to tell her that, so I pushed my thoughts forward, felt them all rise up in me, even tasted the words rolling around on my tongue. But I couldn't spit one of them out. My mouth felt like it was full of chokecherries instead of words. It was all drawn up and thick. That nurse stripped me, changed my bed, dressed me back up like I was some old doll, and yet I couldn't say a single word to her. You're really home, you old fool, I told myself. You wanted to go there, like a sick dog, just in case God changes his mind and lets you die. Well, now you are. Put your suitcase down. Take off your hat. You might as well dust everything off and enjoy the view, 'cause ain't it good to be back? For almost forty years now I've twisted and turned my hands on my lap like I was knitting something. But nothing ever come of it, just the twisting and the turning, and staring at the television, or at plants in my window. If I'd had yarn and needles, there'd be sweaters everywhere. If I'd had yeast and flour, I could've fed the multitude. But it goes nowhere, that useless work. There's just imaginary socks, just loaves of bread I'll never eat.

I wish, though, that I could've talked to Elizabeth again. She's my daughter who couldn't have her own babies. The one I named after my mother. My youngest child. The last time I saw her— oh, I just can't remember the year—she'd come from whatever state it is she lives in now. She sat there with her big eyes full of tears, and held my old hand, and touched my old face with her lips. They were like bird feathers brushing up against me. She's the only one who's kissed me in years. All the others, all them children and grandchildren, think I'm too old. They don't want to take any chances, I guess. Maybe they think my face might crumble and fall to the floor. Maybe they think they'll catch something from me. You've caught it already, you silly geese, that's what I'd say if I were still talking to them. You came into this world afflicted with what I got.

When I opened my eyes this morning, I thought I saw Foster sitting next to me. It was like he was in a room full of smoke. He was almost here, almost wasn't here. "Tildy, oh, Tildy," I heard him whisper. Or did I imagine that? Foster, can you smell the thick smell of pine? Listen! The whippoorwill has come back to his tree. Remember how, when the kids was little, we'd stand on the porch and listen? It must be night again, 'cause that's the only time he'll come. He sleeps all day, Foster, all day in the forest. And he looks so much like the leaves that you could step on him if you ain't careful. Sometimes I still stand on the night porch and hold the lantern up to catch his eyes, and Foster, they light up like real rubies. Them eyes are so fiery and red they belong on a woman's necklace. But he goes off with his treasure before anyone comes too close. Another place, another time, I might have been that whippoorwill.

Pike Dilver Gifford: Lynn Stays Out of the Mattagash River

> Little Dickey Dilver
> Had a wife of silver;
> He took a stick and broke her back
> And sold her to the miller;
> The miller wouldn't have her
> So he threw her in the river.
>
> —Mother Goose rhyme

Conrad Gifford, age twelve, stood at the top of the stairs and listened to the disagreement downstairs between his parents. Either it would die away and they would fall asleep angry, or it would build toward some terrible crescendo. Like a snowstorm or a hurricane, fights at the Gifford house had to simply be ridden out, endured, lasted. Conrad stood in the moonlight filtering in through the upstairs window, and in the swath of faint light issuing from the plastic Cinderella plugged into an outlet in the bathroom. Light from the television set down in the living room came up to him, a blue light that flickered mindlessly on the stair steps. A television set running all by itself, everyone too angry to watch it.

"Just wasting electricity again," Conrad thought. He leaned a shoulder against the window frame and waited.

The fight must have originated in the kitchen—at least that's where it was coming from when Conrad roused in his sleep and finally came wide awake to the familiar sounds of it beating on the floor beneath his bed. There were some things you could count on in life. One was the sound of the old Mattagash River, the grating of it against the rocks, so harsh in the summertime that it sounded like a fine downpour of rain. Another was the snow, coming to find the little town each October or November, and staying until you were crazy from it. Another thing you could depend on was the fighting. And Conrad was the lightest of sleepers, maybe because he was the oldest child. They seemed to wake to the fights in order: Conrad first, ten-year-old Reed next, and then the twins. Pecking order had descended into their dreams.

Conrad looked out onto the Mattagash River, which had not yet frozen but lay bluish and cold in the moonlight. The moon was spectacular. All around the house, the fields of snow shimmered, sparkled, cold with excitement. Conrad saw the twins' sled parked against a birch tree in the backyard, left behind from their afternoon sliding bout. He was always lecturing them to put the sled in the cellar after sliding, so that Maine's harsh winter would be kinder to it. In the moonlight, the sled's red paint looked purplish as a bruise.

"I'm sick and tired of borrowing money to pay our bills," he heard his mother say from the kitchen below. Her voice sounded like it was coming from another house, another family, or maybe even from out of the old television set. Its blue light flicked and danced to each of her words. But this wasn't Lucy and Ricky.

"You drink more money than you bring home to this family," Lynn said. Her words were followed by a harsh slap. Something broke.

"I don't need no female telling me what I should or shouldn't do," Conrad heard his father say.

"Don't hit me, you bastard!" Lynn Gifford screamed. "You wake them kids and you're a dead man."

"And what are you gonna do to stop me?" Pike's voice taunted. There was another loud slap. Spook, the family dog, whined from the sofa downstairs. *Stop*, the whine said. *Please stop.*

"I'll go upstairs right now and drag them little bastards out into the yard if I want to," Pike threatened. "And there ain't nothing you can do about it." Conrad heard ice cubes rattling. His father was throwing three into a glass and then filling it with vodka. Conrad didn't have to be there to know this. He'd seen it too many times.

"Leave them alone," Lynn cried. "They gotta get up for school in the morning." Conrad caught his breath. He looked back out at the magnificent, crusty, moonlighty snow, so cold to eyes gazing out from a warm house. His mother should never call attention to the children. His mother should know better, after all these years, as Conrad knew better. She should say to Pike, "Please go beat the kids. Please keep them up all night so that they'll be dead on their feet at school." Then the fun would be gone, stolen from him by someone smarter. But the problem tonight was that Lynn had been drinking too. She and Pike had gone to a wedding reception at the Knights of Columbus in St. Leonard. Lynn's cousin had married a Frenchman, intermarriage being a common thing now among the Scotch-Irish and French-Canadian descendants of the Mattagash River Valley.

Conrad felt Reed's presence behind him. Reed, the second to awake.

"He hitting her?" Reed asked, and Conrad nodded. The twins came out of their warm bunks to stand, rubbing their eyes, in the doorway.

"Go back to bed," Conrad whispered to them. "I mean it, and I ain't telling you again. You'll miss the school bus in the morning. Go on now." They disappeared back into the black cave of their bedroom. "Shut their door," Conrad said to Reed. His eye caught the night-light in the bathroom, the plastic Cinderella. She was smiling serenely, lighting the way for little children in the dark. She'd had some pretty tough family problems herself.

"You think it'll get out of hand?" Reed asked him, and Conrad nodded again.

"She's been drinking too much," he said flatly.

"Shit," said Reed. "We'll never get up in the morning, and I got a test in math." He leaned his palms against the frosty window, and stared out at the wintry night that had unfolded itself all around the house, diamonds in every packed flake of snow. "Pretty out, ain't it?" he asked, and Conrad said, "Yeah." A loud crash rose up from the kitchen.

"Don't!" They heard Lynn shout.

"I wish the river'd hurry up and freeze over," Reed said, "so we could skate." Conrad made no reply. His ears were listening to the semantics of the fight, determining the tactics, calculating the damage. Reed abandoned the moon, and the river, and the birch tree with its red sled, and came back to stand next to his brother.

"How is it?" he asked.

"I can't tell yet," Conrad said tersely. He tilted his head and aimed his right ear at the kitchen, a stethoscope picking up the very heartbeat of the fight. "It all depends on what she's had to drink." He was afraid his mother may have had two many rum and Cokes. Rum made her want to fight back, brought out her anger.

"I hope she ain't had rum," Reed said. He'd heard Lynn say so dozens of times, so he had it on good authority: "Rum makes me crazy," Lynn was known to admit.

"You get out of here!" Lynn sobbed, "or I'm calling the sheriff." More glass broke in the kitchen, a wintry music, as though a hundred icicles had fallen. Lynn was crying loudly now.

"You put me out!" Pike Gifford shouted. "You miserable bitch. You go ahead and try to put me out."

Conrad felt his fingers roll themselves up into his palms. His whole body trembled. He stood in the blue moonlight, in the flickering light of the television, and waited.

"Think we should sneak down and call the sheriff?" Reed asked his standard question at this stage of the fight. Conrad shrugged.

"Let's give it another minute," he said. "He might be too tired or drunk to keep it going." They had called the sheriff on their father twice before at the height of the stormy fight, and he had made them pay for it, when the aftermath had passed. The slaps were a little heavier, and so was the humiliation, the more stinging of the two punishments.

"Get out, I said!" Lynn screamed again. The twins opened their door and peered out like little mice. Their faces were ghostly blue.

"Now!" Conrad whispered, and pointed a finger at them. Their faces disappeared as the door closed quietly.

"I think we better call," Reed whispered. "It sounds like he's dragging her or something." Indeed, chairs were scraping along the kitchen floor, and Lynn's sobs were becoming fiercer.

"You're the one who's getting out," Pike Gifford was saying to his wife. As Conrad and Reed listened in the moonlight, the back door into the kitchen opened with such force that it banged loudly against the wall. Spook was beside himself now, his barks volleying up to the boys from the kitchen.

"Get away from me, you mangy mutt!" Pike shouted, and Spook howled in pain. "You git out on the porch too. The both of you can sleep out there tonight."

"No, please, Pike." Lynn was begging now, the rum fight gone out of her. "Leave me alone. I won't say nothing else."

"You can say all you want to," Pike snarled. "Just say it out on the porch, to the dog. You're lucky I don't drag you down to the river and stick your head under."

The door to the twins' bedroom opened again and they stood there, a halo of moonlight around them. Julie had her thumb in her mouth again and was sucking it frantically.

"He kick Spook?" asked Stevie. But this time Conrad didn't tell them to slink back inside their room and wait for the fighting to subside. It was as if he didn't hear Stevie's question, or Julie's wild sucking, behind him, in the blue winter moonlight of the house. He was listening to something else, to a medley of his father's boozy lullabies, a tune that stretched out from the time he could walk to the time he could finally *act*. And that was now. He was twelve. He was a man now. Enough was enough.

Conrad went into his own room, the one he shared with Reed, and rummaged around in the dark until his hands felt the cool aluminum of his baseball bat.

"What you gonna do?" Reed's whispery voice asked him. "You crazy? He'll kill you."

"Stay here with the twins," Conrad said. He was no longer whispering.

"You crazy?" Reed asked again. "You know for sure he'll kill you."

"Stay here," Conrad said, but Reed followed him down the stairs. The back door was still open, a cold gust of river wind sweeping about the room. Spook's barks were coming from the porch now, cold, crisp, the echo of them bouncing off into the night.

"Pike . . . for God's . . . sake." Lynn's sobs came from outside, and broke her sentence with large pauses. "I'll freeze to death," she cried.

"You should've thought of that before you took to running your mouth off," Pike said. He was trying to step away from Lynn and pull back into the kitchen, but she held tightly to his legs.

"Let go!" Pike yelled. Spook grabbed his pant leg and tugged, along with Lynn. He still wasn't sure if it was war or if it was play. Humans were very complex creatures.

Conrad stepped into the kitchen directly behind his father, who had his back to him. Pike was busily trying to kick Lynn away from his legs. Conrad raised the bat and held it straight up, with both hands, high above his head.

"Pike, *please,*" Lynn begged. Her head jerked backward onto the crisp snow of the porch. In an instant she saw her oldest son silhouetted in the warm yellow of the kitchen door, something shiny as silver in his hands, something like a chance, an opportunity, glowing there in the doorway. Her eyes met Conrad's. *Don't hit him,* her eyes said. Conrad read this quickly. He had grown up with subtle implications, with thousands of messages behind one single glance. He knew the books that lay behind one small word. This was the shorthand of a family abused. *Hit him and you'll never live in peace here again,* Lynn's eyes warned her son. Then she closed them, released her grip on Pike's leg. She would rather freeze to death in the car than have Conrad take his father down to the mat. But Conrad's eyes were talking too. Conrad's eyes were saying some important things. Lynn had read them like little obituaries, brimming with the sad facts of his life. *I have no peace here anyway,* his eyes said.

Pike sensed him there, sensed something behind him, a memory maybe, of when he himself had wanted badly to rise up against Pike Gifford, Sr., on his mother Goldie's behalf, to strike at his own father with tiny, useless fists. But he never had. Now, for a quick, vaporous instant, part of him was almost proud to see Conrad do so. By Christ, he had passed on something good, after all. Then the feeling was gone, forgotten. With Lynn no longer clinging like a burdock to his legs, Pike turned. Time slowed down for the family, the way it does for the occupants of a car wreck. Time became watery slow motion. *Take note,* time warned. *Something very important is happening here.*

"You'd better not," Pike Gifford said, just as Conrad brought the silver bat, as if it were a pure flash of lightning, down on his head. It caught his left temple, and Pike crumpled beneath the blow of it. He went down on both knees and then stretched out across Lynn's body, his mouth opened to the snowy night as blood trickled from an inch-long cut on his head.

"You didn't kill him, did you?" Reed asked as Conrad handed him the bat.

"Naw," said Conrad, and his throat was so thick with victory, his Adam's apple drumming so fiercely, a little war drum, that the tiny word nearly stuck there on his tongue. "Naw," he said again, just to be sure it hadn't, indeed, stayed in his mouth.

"He kill him?" the twins asked, from behind Reed's position in the doorway. Julie was wearing the head to her turkey costume.

"Naw," Reed said, passing on Conrad's triumphant message. "He just knocked him out."

Lynn had stopped crying. The mascara she'd applied earlier with such finesse had washed with her tears down from her lashes. But beneath the black ring of her right eye, a real black eye was growing, a purply flower blossoming amid the November snows. And on her right arm, her left leg, more bruises were sprouting silently under the skin. Flowers from her husband, Pike.

"Get him off me," Lynn said. Conrad and Reed rolled their father over onto his back as she pulled her legs out from under the weighty body. With Conrad's help she managed to stand. A fight was a sobering thing, but still, she was rickety with rum and adrenaline. She would feel the bruises in the morning.

"Jesus, Conny," she said. "I wish you hadn't done that." Conrad said nothing. Instead, he looked down at his father, at the fresh trickle of deep red blood oozing slowly out of Pike's temple and onto the white snow. He tingled all over, little jets of electricity darting beneath his skin, as though his entire body were asleep.

"Reed," said Lynn. "Go call the sheriff. Tell him the cut's gonna need some stitches." Reed disappeared into the living room.

Julie and Stevie stepped, in their stocking feet, out onto the back porch and carefully inspected their father. Julie was sucking her thumb through the plastic beak of the turkey mask.

"Get in here," Lynn told them. "You look like them Munchkins gathering around the dead witch."

"He ain't breathing," Stevie said, ignoring his mother.

"Yes he is, he is too, you stupid you," said Julie, her words coming from behind the immovable beak. She plunked herself down on Pike's stomach, as though it were a bench. Or perhaps a nice flat stump on which a turkey might roost.

"He's got lint in his nose," Stevie observed, leaning in closely, inspecting his father's face.

"For Christ's sake, get in this house," Lynn moaned. "This ain't the fair. You'll freeze your feet off."

"That ain't lint, it's a booger," Julie announced.

"Jesus," said Lynn. "Sometimes I don't know what in hell to do with you kids." She began to sob again.

"And sometimes we don't know what to do with *you*," Conrad thought. But he couldn't say it. Nor could he move, not within the confines of his electrified body. His eyes were fixed on the red blood he had caused to ooze from his own father. Already it was turning icy in the cold, a bloody little river freezing over.

Reed came back to the porch. "The sheriff's coming," he said.

"What'd he say?" asked Lynn. She had always liked Pierre Latour. He seemed human about his job, and that made a huge difference. Lynn knew that if you put most men and women into a uniform, they go crazy.

"He said someone should've laid the son of a bitch out before this," said Reed. "He said this better not be another wild-goose chase."

"Are they gonna take him to the emergency?" asked Lynn. "He needs to go to the emergency."

"Shit, you really nailed him good," said Reed, gazing for the first time down upon his father's countenance.

"I want the quarter!" screamed Julie. She and Stevie were wrangling over the contents of Pike's pockets. "*You* take the jackknife."

"I already got a knife," Stevie whined. He grabbed slyly for the quarter. It fell from Julie's hand and rolled across the porch, leaving a tiny road behind it, a snowy little wake.

"Bastard!" Julie shouted. Her turkey face stared blankly at her brother.

"Take them kids inside before they freeze to death in front of our very eyes," Lynn told Reed. "They're out there like two little Judas Iscariots, fighting for them quarters."

"Get in that house," Reed said. "You'll never get up in the morning." He grabbed Julie's arm and dragged her off Pike's body. He scooted her into the kitchen and then came back for Stevie, who had his hand deep into Pike's shirt pocket.

"How much money is this?" Stevie asked Reed, holding up a fistful of crumpled ones with a fiver sprouting greenly from the midst. "Will it buy me a comic book and a Pepsi?"

"I want a Pepsi too!" Julie shouted from the kitchen.

"He needs to go to the emergency, Reed," his mother urged again. Reed pushed Stevie into the kitchen, then gave each of the twins such a hardy shove that they found themselves reeling into the living room.

"The sheriff said he'd take him," said Reed.

"He needs to go, all right," Lynn sobbed. Conrad said nothing.

"Sheriff says this is the last straw," Reed said as Pike groaned heavily in his vodka dreams. "Either you sign a warrant, the sheriff says, or he ain't coming the next time we call."

"I'll sign his damn old warrant." Lynn sniffled. "It ain't no warrant I'm afraid of." She looked up at Conrad, who stood frozen, that shiver still encasing his entire body. He had never felt such an extraordinary thing before.

"I'll tell Billy it was me hit him," Lynn offered. Her black tears were sparkling. "He'll be sure to end up at Billy's when he gets out. I'll tell Billy first thing tomorrow it was me."

But Conrad remembered the look in his father's eye before the bat came down like a judgment. *You'd better think about this,* the look had said. Pike Gifford would wake up in the morning, Conrad was very certain, knowing two things: the first, that he was in jail with a tremendous hangover; the second, that his oldest son, that yellow trickle of horse piss, that bull's dick, that little fairy faggot, had caused the throbbing in his temple by wielding a bat against him.

"Oh, Conny," Lynn muttered again, now with a cold finger pressed to her husband's bleeding temple. "I wish to hell you hadn't. I wish you'd stayed upstairs until it was over. You know they can't last forever anyway. If he'd locked me out, I'd have walked down to Maisy's. I just wish you hadn't."

But Conrad wasn't listening to his mother's rattling words. He could still feel the frosty aluminum of the bat in his hands, could remember that flash on his father's face when he realized that the *trickle of horse piss, the little fairy faggot,* was indeed going to swing. There was a vestige of fear there. Conrad hadn't realized that fear grew anywhere inside his father. This was new knowledge, given him as a reward for his bravery, his initiation, his journey into the ritual of his manhood. But another feeling pressed heavily upon his mind as he watched his father's labored breathing, his mother's black tears. It was the sensation of the bat in his hand, the weighty impact of it as it connected to flesh and bone, then bounced away. Something grew in Conrad, too, that he had not known was there, and its appearance had caused the ecstatic tingling, like no other sensation he could ever remember. Now Conrad knew something that his father had known all along: the sweet, magical, addictive pull of power.

Immaculate Footsteps
in the Snow:
Elvis as Everyman

> The hero has died as a modern man, but as eternal
> man—perfected, unspecific, universal man—he has
> been reborn.
>
> —Joseph Campbell,
> as quoted in *Mythology*

*I*n Dr. Brassard's waiting room at the clinic in St. Leonard, Charlene Craft wrapped her feverish daughter in a blanket and then lifted her up, light as a snowflake.

"Okay, Tanya," Charlene said brightly. "Upsa-daisy. Let's go so you can watch your *Fraggle Rock* tape before the boys get home from school." Tanya's thin little arms shot out of the woolly blanket and wrapped themselves around Charlene's neck.

"I want Daddy," a voice in the blanket whispered.

"Daddy'll be home for supper," Charlene promised. "You can have all of Daddy you want after he eats."

Charlene hoisted Tanya easily into the front seat and snapped the bundle securely with a seat belt. The past few days of riotous sun were slowly disappearing into what the weathermen in Bangor were predicting would be eight inches of pristine snow. Already

Charlene could see a dark heaviness in the sky above the horizon, a sky full of imminent snow.

"Now don't you unwrap yourself," Charlene warned her child. "Even though the car is warm, you might still catch a cold."

On the ride home, a drive which took them toward the grip of the storm-to-be, Charlene thought of Dr. Brassard's soft words, the little beads of perspiration on his forehead, the pastel paintings on the warm walls of his office. Now, in the car beside Tanya, the warmth of the room had faded, the words had turned icy.

"I've ruled out both mono and rheumatoid arthritis," Dr. Brassard had said. "But why her ankles and knees are swollen I just can't imagine."

"She says her arms and her feet feel like there's pins and needles in them," Charlene had told him. That's why he had suspected the arthritis. "And it's getting so that she hardly wants to get off the sofa. She used to have so much energy."

"We can run some basic neurological tests in Watertown," Dr. Brassard had added. "But if those tests don't show us anything, we may have to send her to Boston." *Neurological.*

As she drove the aging New Yorker over the snaky road back to Mattagash, Charlene wondered where they'd ever get the money for something like that. At least she'd kept up the insurance policies for illness on the kids. She and Davey had been forced to let their own policies run quietly out. Davey had an entire folder in the filing cabinet marked *Canceled.* Where *would* they get the money? She heard Tanya sigh, a small child's sigh, a child tired of being sick, of tests, of lying idly on the sofa while her brothers played roughly in the lovely snows of youth. Guilt washed quickly over Charlene. How could she even remember that such a thing as money existed when her baby needed those doctors, those prescriptions, those fancy city tests, and the expensive airplane rides that would take her there? Charlene felt the strong pinching pain between her eyes, a pain that had seemed to be waiting for her at the *Welcome to Mattagash* sign the day she moved to town —at least, it seemed to start about that time.

"Darn it," she thought, and pressed a finger to the flat surface of her temple, applied pressure. "My migraine is back."

Tanya was asleep by the time Charlene rolled into the dooryard. The blanket had fallen away from her face, heart-shaped and porcelain, so Charlene stared at her daughter for a few seconds, at the brownish-red ringlets, the dark eyebrows, the eyelashes so thick there might have been mascara on them. Then she opened the door to the cold. Already snow was busy in the yard, establishing itself on windowpanes, fluttering like white moths about Davey's yard light. But the snow would not sparkle beneath that light when evening fell. The light was something else filed under *Canceled,* fourteen dollars a month too much to pay for such a luxury item. The family had learned to rely again on the moon for that convenience, and on flashlights.

Tanya stirred in Charlene's arms and opened her eyes. "It's snowing," she said softly.

"Yes, it is," said Charlene, and then covered Tanya's face again with the blanket, hoping to protect her from the cold, from the storm, from the horrible tests that might lie ahead.

"Is Daddy here?" the voice came out of the blanket to ask.

"He will be soon," said Charlene, and stepped with careful feet upon the powdery surface of the front porch. She would send the boys out after supper to shovel off the first accumulation, then again in the morning before school. Surely, by then, the snow would be finished, but who knew for certain, up here at the North Pole, Maine.

After supper Davey played a game of Candyland with Tanya while the boys shoveled snow and Charlene did the dishes.

"You didn't *let* me win, did you, Daddy?" Tanya asked.

"No sirree," said Davey. "It was a battle every inch of the way."

"Someone just drove in," Christopher, shovel in hand, opened the front door to announce. The red of his cap had nearly disappeared beneath a soft ridge of fresh snow. He beat the cap gently against the door, restoring its bright color and the sunny yellow lettering: *Husquevana Chain Saws.* Christopher had been given the hat as a gift by the chain saw dealer in Watertown, when his father had purchased a 266 model in late summer.

"It's Lola and Dorrie," James poked his head past Christopher and stated formally, as though he were a small butler ushering in royalty. Dorrie and Lola stomped snow from their boots and paraded past the boys without even a feigned acknowledgment. Between them they had eleven noisy, sweaty children; someone else's offspring reminded them of their own maternal burdens.

Charlene's first response was to throw herself between the clothes rack and the refrigerator, so that she could slump to the floor behind the wet socks and mittens and hide forever from the stormy intruders. What on earth could lure them out on such an evening? Rain, sleet, and other forms of precipitation might keep Davey's uncle, the pluckless Simon Craft, at home with his feet up, but Dorrie and Lola were undeterred by weather conditions.

"We can only stay a second or two," Dorrie announced, a statement Charlene knew to be a lie of the highest order. The last time Dorrie had promised such mercy was at breakfast, two weeks earlier, and Charlene had ended up fixing lunch for them both.

"What in the world are you two doing out on a night like tonight?" Davey asked them as they unbundled, Lola a small-boned blond creature, Dorrie as bulbous and meaty as well-wintered beef on the hoof.

"I got Booster's pickup with the plow on it," Dorrie announced, and Charlene imagined them blazing fresh trails of gossip all over the woodsy northlands. Here was the type of pioneering woman who gladly went West with tattered, ill-planned wagon trains: *You'll never guess what happened the day we overturned crossing the Missouri River.* Charlene imagined the Lolas and Dorries spread across history: *That was the night Sacajawea slapped Meriwether.* And she could even imagine them beyond American limits, changing the courses of events elsewhere: *Yes, she most certainly did say, "Let them eat cake." I should know. I was there.* She imagined them existing for all time.

"Has Prissy called you yet to sign her petition?" Lola asked.

"What petition is that?" asked Davey. Charlene felt like weeping when she saw Davey taking two cups out of the cupboard. He poured the guests some tea.

"She wants an emergency town meeting," said Dorrie. "She wants another vote on the wet/dry ticket. She says we need to close down The Crossroads." She blew on the hot tea and it rippled.

"I ain't signed it," said Lola. "Raymond has yet to admit to me that he goes there. You should hear some of the crazy stories he comes up with."

"Well, *I* ain't signing it," Dorrie snorted. "The last thing I want is for Booster to be home every night."

"Oh, by the way," said Lola. "Did anyone find out where the ambulance went this evening? It went up through town and then back in a flash, but we've yet to find out why. At first we thought they must have accidentally driven past Pine Valley. Mama's there, you know, and I worry about her."

"We also thought it might be old Mrs. Fennelson," Dorrie added. "Booster's grandma. She's gonna be a hundred and eight next month and the Women's Auxiliary is planning a big Thanksgiving bash for her. They think she might be the oldest person in Maine."

"She's *my* great-grandmother, too," Lola said competitively.

"Yeah, but Booster's related to her in a hundred different ways," Dorrie allowed. Lola thought deeply about this.

"So am I," she snapped. "And so is everybody in Mattagash, for that matter." She and Dorrie glared at each other. Charlene knew that if poor Mrs. Fennelson were in the room at that very moment, Lola and Dorrie would pull her old arms off in a tug of war. *Red Rover, Red Rover, I dare Grammie Fennelson right over.*

"So where did the ambulance go?" Davey asked.

"No one knows where it went," Lola said, ignoring Dorrie's puffed red face. "And I never caught a word about it on my police scanner. It had to be a false alarm or we'd have heard by now." Ambulances screaming through the black nights and sunny days of small towns meant something bad had happened to someone you knew. Not necessarily someone you liked. Just someone you knew.

"No, we can only stay a minute or two," Dorrie announced again when Davey offered them a snack, and Charlene caught the rewrite immediately. From *seconds* to *minutes*. Next it would be hours. So that's how Dorrie craftily enlarged her visits. She stole time, willfully, right from under their noses.

But on this night of snowy nights, the women did stay only twenty minutes, arriving closer to the truth, perhaps, than was customary for either of them. They had other places of business to be on this wintry, tempestuous night, as Charlene was soon to learn.

"The minute it stops snowing tomorrow, we're off to Madawaska," Lola announced. She and Dorrie sucked loudly at their tea and stared at the plate of freshly baked brownies Davey had placed before them. The brownies stood only a remote chance with Lola, and none at all with the bulging Dorrie. She ate two within a minute—Charlene glanced at the clock and timed her—as well as two more with her second cup of strong Mattagash tea. Brownies going into the large burner her body had become, fuel to keep the heavy train moving along.

"We're going back to Madawaska to check on the latest development on Elvis," Lola continued, and Charlene vaguely remembered having heard this nonsense somewhere before, on the telephone, perhaps, during one of Lola's many calls—conversations Charlene rarely listened to, much less remembered.

"Brenda Monihan saw him this time," Dorrie said, brownie bits peeking from between her teeth.

"Who?" asked Davey.

"Brenda swears she saw a man who was the spitting image of Elvis, down at Radio Shack in Madawaska, buying guitar strings and picks," said Lola.

"So she followed him to the drugstore"—Dorrie picked up the mythic saga—"where he bought a box of Dexatrim."

"Does that, or does that not, sound to you like he's planning a comeback?" asked Lola, excitement wet as snow in her eyes. Dorrie's own eyes were on the last brownie, which clung helplessly to the plate beneath her knifey stare. Charlene pushed it toward her, and it met its fate quickly, painlessly. *It ain't over 'til the fat lady eats the last brownie.*

"Thanks," Dorrie said, still swallowing. "I hated to eat the last one, but if no one else was going to, it'd be a shame to let it go to waste." Charlene wondered how Booster Mullins had survived all these years, married to this huge woman. She imagined Dorrie as a ravenous spider, with poor Booster clinging to the outer fringes of their webby bed, holding on for dear life, loath to cause any vibrations that indicated *prey caught.*

"You're kidding, of course," Davey laughed. He looked at them carefully. "My God, you're not kidding. They're *serious,*" he said plaintively to Charlene, and she nodded, thinking, "Yes, of course they're serious. You're looking at the products of nearly two hundred years of inbreeding, kiddo."

"Be one of them doubting Thomases if you want to," Lola said. "But Elvis ain't why we're out tonight. We got another mission." She said this in a little singsong, a teasing riddle, as she and Dorrie piled into their new coats. Mattagash women selected their winter coats carefully; they would become a familiar print to the whole town by the following spring, a license plate of sorts, dog tags.

"Why *are* you out tonight?" Davey asked. Charlene cringed. Why did men do those kinds of things, give in so easily to the wiles of silly women? Charlene would have replied curtly, "Oh, really?" and then perhaps offered some weatherly tidbit. But she would never ask the mission of these women, these Jehovah's Witnesses of gossip.

"We're conducting a detective-like investigation," Lola said. She and Dorrie guffawed coarsely enough to be qualified members of the construction crews who used to whistle at Charlene on those Hartford streets, men stories up and still building. But that was in Charlene's other life. Now the tallest building she could hope to see was Harmon Monihan's three-story house, with the pointy-roof attic, the architecture of which had beset the entire town with uproarious laughter.

"We're gonna find out who's impregnated Amy Joy Lawler," Dorrie said, the "impregnated" a breezy little whisper intended to save Charlene's children from the truth about the origins of life. She pulled on her man-sized gloves with surprising deftness.

"Word's all over town she's expecting," Lola explained. "They think now that maybe it's Nolan Gifford. He's one of the good Giffords and he ain't married."

"He just bought a second skidder," Dorrie said, "and now he's contracting on his own for P. G. Irvine Lumber Company. His car ain't never in his yard at night and we never see it at The Crossroads."

"So we been driving back and forth now and then in the evenings," Lola added, "to see if we can catch someone coming and going."

"You've been driving by her house?" Charlene asked. She hoped Davey was listening to this.

"Just until she goes to sleep," Dorrie explained good-naturedly.

"Hell, our kids is all growed," Lola said. "Raymond and Booster spend so much money at The Crossroads we figure they probably pay the electric bill over there. So why not have our own little excitement? It's free."

"You drive by her house and *spy* on her?" Charlene asked again.

"But we ain't seen a thing yet," Lola said. "Not a single track, not even one made by her cat."

They ambled to the door. Two of the kids' school pictures on the bottom shelf of the bookcase fell noisily as Dorrie rumbled past. Otis the cat flew for safety. Where was Chicken Little? Dorrie stopped and gazed down at the pictures, one James, the other Tanya with her valentine face. Charlene stood the frames back up.

"You must have a loose board in this floor," Dorrie said. "Booster could fix that for you." Then she plowed on.

"Don't people know how fat they are?" Charlene wondered. "Don't they realize how they frighten the rest of us?"

"So far we can't find a single trace of anyone coming around over there," Lola said. "I'm beginning to think it's like one of them immaculate conceptions, the kind the Catholics have." Charlene had forgotten how annoying Lola's trumpeting laugh could be, especially when accompanied by Dorrie's trombone.

"Don't let them Catholics fool you," Dorrie warned. "If somebody'd had the foresight way back then to look around Mary's house, they'd have seen plenty of tracks in the snow." She ambled out the door and onto the front porch. Snow squeaked painfully beneath her boots. Lola followed, like a pitifully thin, misplaced shadow.

"Well, good-bye," Lola shouted in to Davey, who waved to his cousin from the kitchen table.

"Don't get stuck in Amy Joy's yard," Davey yelled back.

"You ever want to take a little trip to Madawaska with us," Dorrie turned and offered Charlene, "you just call."

Charlene said a fast, chilly good-night—thank God for some things about winter—and closed the door on these creatures of the night. What could be more torturous than an eighty-mile round-trip ride with Lola Monihan and Dorrie Mullins, bouncing from the bony Lola over to the mattress that was Dorrie's body, and then back again? Charlene shuddered. Tanya stuck her small sick face up from behind the armchair where she'd been crouching.

"Are they gone?" she whispered.

With the children in bed sleeping soundly, Charlene knew the time had come when she could no longer avoid the medical events of the day. She hadn't wanted to go back over Dr. Brassard's conversation so quickly because there had been no answers in it. She hated being without answers. Some things she knew for sure: It was snowing heavily outside, her children were sleeping warmly in their beds, and her husband was stretched restfully upon the sofa. Why, then, cut through the tranquillity of this scene with a swath of uncertainty?

"Well?" Davey sat up on the sofa to ask her. "What did the doctor say?"

"Not much new," Charlene said, and realized immediately that something—she wasn't sure what—was changing the course of their family life together. It wasn't just money. It was something more precious than that.

"He must've said something," Davey said. "For Christ's sake, what are we paying him for?"

"Money isn't the issue at a time like this," said Charlene, remembering her own guilt, earlier in the day, about such things.

"That's not what I meant," Davey answered.

"I know," said Charlene, and was at once sorry she had called him on it in an attempt to assuage her own guilt. "He doesn't think it's mono after all. She's never once had a sore throat, remember, and it's been eight weeks. He said there should be signs of it letting up if it's mono."

"Did you tell him how the rash on her neck cleared up after a couple of days?" Davey asked.

"He said now he thinks it was only coincidental, and not a symptom of the larger illness."

"The *larger* illness," Davey said, and shook his head.

"He said six years old is real young to have mono in the first place," said Charlene. "Or rheumatoid arthritis, for that matter. But with her being tired all the time, and with her joints being swollen, and what with that little rash, well, he just doesn't know. They can only run superficial tests at the clinic."

"*Superficial* tests?" Davey sighed. His wife was starting to talk like a doctor running for political office, and he was paying for her campaign in costly office fees.

"He said to give it a few more days," Charlene added. "Just in hopes that it is a virus of some kind and she'll pull out of it. If not, he wants to run some neurological tests in Watertown to see if there's trouble in the brain, and if that don't work—" Charlene stopped in midsentence. Davey had enough worries, didn't he? Would it be right for her, as his wife through richer or poorer, to censor a few unpleasant facts?

"Well, what?" asked Davey.

"We'll have to send her to Boston." Charlene imagined an airplane, full of people drinking and laughing and reading magazines beneath their little ceiling lights, an airplane making its way through a gray sky of snow toward Boston, a frightened little girl alone in one unlighted seat, being tested in, oh, so many ways.

"I could never let her go alone," Charlene thought. "Neither would Davey. We'd sell the house first, rather than let that child go alone. We'll get the money if we have to sell our car." Then she remembered that the bank owned those items anyway, when you got right down to it. Well, they didn't own her relatives, and Charlene would beg airplane tickets if she had to. She and Davey could sleep at the Y's. Tanya wasn't going *anywhere* alone, not if Charlene could help it. But maybe in a few days it would all be past them. Tanya would be back to her bouncy self, and airplanes would fly to Boston well enough without her.

"You know," Davey said finally, and Charlene remembered him there, on the sofa beside her. "Mama still thinks it's chilblains. She said that's what the rash looked like."

"Please, don't bring that up." Charlene sighed deeply. Mother-in-law. "She's been calling me twice a day and telling me *chilblains, chilblains.* All she really wants to say is that I don't dress Tanya warm enough."

"Well," Davey said. "Maybe she's right. Folks around here sometimes know a lot more about illnesses than city doctors."

"Davey," Charlene said. She worked with the short little curl, the one she had loved from the first moment she laid eyes on David Craft, way down in Connecticut, long before Tanya Craft was even imagined—the ancestral curl that had given Tanya her own thick ringlets. "Your mother sees frostbite in everything. She's not a doctor, you know."

"And what does the doctor say?" Davey asked. "Did you even ask him about chilblains?" Charlene sighed again. She had, honest to God, asked the doctor about chilblains because Selma Craft had her daughter-in-law secretly hoping it was nothing more than exposure to the elements. Charlene wouldn't be surprised anyway. Her child wasn't created for these horrible temperatures. But Tanya had started complaining of fatigue in September, and as much as Charlene hated northern Maine, she had to admit that September up there was so pretty it hurt your eyes.

"Well? What did the doctor *say?*"

"He laughed," said Charlene, and suddenly Davey was on his feet, surprising her with his quick movements. She had thought *he* was getting slower every day too, like his sick daughter. But now Davey was spry with anger. He threw the sofa pillow against the wall. It careened off and landed noisily on a bottom bookshelf, where the school pictures of the children fell again with soft little thumps. The cat jumped from its curled sleep and skittered, yowling, into the kitchen. Davey slammed his right fist into his open palm.

"Then why doesn't he tell us?" Davey cried. "Why does the son of a bitch laugh when all we want is an answer?" He leaned against the doorjamb, the kitchen light coming in and framing him there in a soft sheen. Charlene could see tears sparkling in his eyes.

"We just gotta wait," she said.

"Christ Almighty," Davey said quietly. "Is he telling us that there might be something *seriously* wrong with her? That this ain't something that'll just go away?"

"He's saying to give it a few more days until these new tests come back," said Charlene.

"I'm going for a drive," Davey said.

"It's snowing," Charlene reminded him, although a drive might be a good idea. If it weren't for the snowy roads, she would take a long, peaceful ride herself. Davey wasn't the type to hang out at The Crossroads and guzzle beer with his cronies. He preferred, instead, to buy one or two Buds at Marshall's Grocery, then sip them in front of the TV. Once in a great while, when the tension in the house grew heavy, Davey would hop into his pickup and cruise along the river road, or just sit in his truck on the flat by the river and watch the black water rush by in the night. After all, Charlene reminded herself, these woods, the fields, the river, were the very roots of his childhood, his closest, oldest friends.

"Be careful," Charlene said. "But if you run into a ditch, just call Dorrie on the CB. She'll come plow you out." Davey smiled, a weak smile. A sense of humor, Charlene knew, would save her damn marriage. Money certainly wasn't going to do it.

"What's her handle?" Davey asked.

"Big Mama," Charlene said. "Big *Nosy* Mama." Then she gave him a quick little kiss.

Charlene watched his truck disappear into the storm before she switched the TV station to *Thirtysomething* and sat down before its fictional drama. That was her, all right. *Thirtysomething.* They should set one of those episodes in Mattagash, or better yet, let the regulars winter there. It wouldn't be long before they'd all be in a fight, the cast, the crew, the writers.

"It's possible, it's just possible," Charlene mumbled, "that all she really has *is* chilblains." And as the television flickered softly, Charlene returned again to the land where hope was alive and well, where it never snowed, and little girls never went anywhere alone.

Crossroads in a Snowy Wood: The Pilgrims Gather at the Tabard

> It's only life's illusions
> That bring us to this bar,
> To pick up these old crutches
> And compare each other's scars.
>
> —Paul Nelson and Dave Gibson,
> "Ships That Don't Come In"

*T*he warping bar at The Crossroads had been built in the shape of a large horseshoe, for good luck, so that its customers could rally around it as though it were a big conference table. By 1989, religions and heritages collided quite peacefully at The Crossroads. Marriages were so common between the French-speaking Catholics and the English-speaking Protestants that duels fought nowadays were fought from other primal sources. They were still territorial, although the real estate market was near the bottom. They still dealt with the courtship/mating game, although the pall of AIDS hung so heavily, even over the northerly Crossroads, that a rejuvenated notion of courtly love seemed to exist, at least until closing time. And feuds were still mainly old family grudges, passed down from ancestors to the descendants. Someone's grandfather might never have gotten the chance to air his grievances toward one of his contemporaries, so they lay dormant until his grandson got drunk enough to settle the fifty-year-old squabble.

Other changes had come to the remote area as well. Oral history was no longer a form of entertainment, not when it had to compete with the new gods—the snowmobile, the television set, VCR movies, and a burgeoning state lottery. If it wasn't tribe against tribe, Catholic against Protestant, then it was Maine resident against those six magical digits that could turn a lumberjack into a millionaire overnight, and could make heavy-thighed Cinderellas out of any number of housewives. It was *deus ex machina* among the piney hills and valleys, but God was arriving upon a new kind of gadgetry. He was now in the whiny buzz of the red-orange skidders, in the chain saw's toothy spiel, and in the lottery machine that spit its dream-filled tickets out into the hopeful hands of this new breed of Mattagasher. Machines had taken the place of all the old country customs. God was now the *start* button on the microwave, the *play* button on the VCR, the *channel* button on the remote control—and the best place to worship in this newly hewn religion was at The Crossroads.

The evolution of The Crossroads had the same kind of history as the good old U.S. of A. itself. It was a hardworking man's destiny to push to the ends of his emotional limits, to expand beyond the familiar territory of his wife's kitchen, to seek solace from a long day's work which, by Puritan ethics, should bring one a just reward. Manifest Destiny, Mattagash style, had demanded the opening of The Crossroads, where just rewards were a dime a dozen, and even cheaper at happy hour. It took a new breed of philosopher to overthrow the rusted political minds of the past which had always voted to keep Mattagash a dry town. And a new voice arrived in Billy Plunkett, tired of driving all the way to Watertown for a quick beer or two. Like some woodsy existentialist, Billy reminded everyone that their ancestors had always liked a brew stronger than tea, even if the Holy Rollers kept it hidden in barns, or in fake Bibles. "If God hadn't wanted us folks up here in northern Maine to drink," Billy said, during his campaign for wet votes, "he wouldn't have created the Budweiser truck." Machines had, indeed, made themselves known everywhere, and it was this Sartrian *Existence Precedes the Essence of Booze* notion that the new generation of Mattagasher, one that already had seen its share of Boston-bought pot and other illegal sundries, took to instantly. At the town meeting of 1989, every self-respecting imbiber within miles turned up to vote. In the school's gymnasium, debates raged on well into the afternoon while outside, oblivious to the needs of the townsfolk, a new crop of pussy willows, those ancient catkins, were being blown about in the late-March winds. By the time the votes were begrudgingly counted by Prissy Monihan, a teetotaler if ever there was one, things were looking pretty moist for Mattagash. And with society demanding change or threatening revolution, Maurice Fennelson, who had read Dale Carnegie's *How to Win Friends and Influence People,* decided to do just that, provided those friends never asked for credit. With a few coats of paint, a few tables, chairs, and a jukebox, Maurice remodeled the old Fennelson homestead into The Crossroads.

In its day the building had lolled up on the grassy knoll overlooking the mouth of Mattagash Brook, which ran into the Mattagash River ten miles from the thrust of town. It had been built in 1894 by a man named Luther Monihan, no doubt a distant relative of Prissy's—another of life's ironies. Foster Fennelson, Maurice's grandfather, husband to Mathilda—who was now lolling herself in St. Leonard's nursing home and God only knows how old—bought it from Luther in 1897. Maurice had seen pictures of the house in its prime, Brownie snaps of the enormous front yard which had once accommodated large Sunday picnics, dozens of hens with chicks trailing happily behind, and sweaty lumberjacks just stopped in for a tin dipper of water and a quick smoke before launching out on a spring log drive. Maurice had seen pictures of folks he never even dreamed of, great-great-aunts in high stiff collars, with their slender young hands grasping the white rails of the magnificent veranda. He had seen great-great-uncles with cocky smiles perched atop a slew of haying wagons, the smoke from their pipes spiraling into some old, forgotten autumn air, the wooden spokes of the wagons locked in time. Several of the first settler families had seen fit to build their homes there, but new folks coming into the area were reluctant to live so far back in the wilderness. The tiny gathering at Mattagash Brook had died away as quickly as the settlement at Mattagash had flourished. With the passing years nature had begun to reclaim the area, had sent vines and ferns and mosses up out of the heart of the land to cover again what man had interfered with. None of Foster and Mathilda's children wanted the old house, so it had gone to Casey, their youngest son. Casey was Maurice Fennelson's father.

In 1960, two years after Foster Fennelson died, Casey decided to move the main part of the old building into Mattagash, where it could be renovated to become the new town hall. There was still enough road left on which to drive a truck to Mattagash Brook, so one summer afternoon, while the sky was alive with heat lightning, Casey and several of the townsmen rolled the house up onto a flatbed and drove it slowly into town. Left behind to rot in the upcoming wilderness were the summer kitchen and the red-roofed barn. No one told Mathilda about the change. She was seventy-eight years old by then, living with her daughter Winnie, and still believing she would be allowed to go back home one day, to the old house, to set up housekeeping once again. What she didn't know wouldn't hurt her, and the town was in desperate need of a big building. But folks had bickered so much about what the old homestead was worth, and where it should ultimately stand, that Casey had said to hell with them, and left it languishing on his property, catty-corner to the old Mattagash River. When Casey's skidder turned wheels up in the woods one muggy, black-flied, summer day in 1968—another casualty of the Fennelson curse, it would seem—no one told Mathilda that, either. By then she was already eighty-six and permanently ensconced at Pine Valley, serving the rest of her life sentence. The news that her youngest son had preceded her into death would only be painful. Maurice, her grandson, inherited the house after Casey's death, and if he had any say in the matter, there would be different pictures taken of the old Fennelson homestead. Maurice expected that nowadays Kodaks and video cameras would be making memories out of any number of pickup trucks, and snowmobiles, and rattly Chevrolets, instead of the rickety hay wagons of yore. But the faces, Maurice knew when he looked at the old photographs belonging to Mathilda, the faces hanging out at The Crossroads in 1989 would be almost the same as the faces in those photos. Time might change knickers into jeans, or boots laced to the knees into tennis shoes, but some things time couldn't tamper with, and those were the thin, narrow noses of the old settlers, the Irish-blue eyes, the wisps of hair yellow and brown as all those old autumns past.

It was out of this architectural folklore that The Crossroads was eventually born. Maurice carved a lovely wooden sign, in the English fashion of The White Stag or The Boar's Head. Beneath the words *The Crossroads,* two graceful roads curved up to a single point and met happily. After a consultation with his sister / business partner, Maurice painted these roads a watery blue, making them rivers instead.

"After all," Sally reminded him, "this town's name means 'where the two rivers meet.'" So, at the bottom of the sign, this historical reminder appeared. It made a terrific slogan. *The Crossroads. Where Good Friends, Like the Rivers, Meet.* Maurice hung the sign outside, suspended by heavy chains, so that it could rock sweetly, even in the strongest of river winds. He then reminded everyone that the site on which the tavern stood, the one lying catty-corner to the river, was reputed to be an old Malecite Indian burial ground, and would surely bring the Great White Drinker any amount of good luck. Not realizing that he had his omens mixed saved Maurice and his clientele from most of the psychological hazards that threaten trespassers on sacred soil. When Maurice was granted a liquor license from the state, he hung it with such pride on the wall behind his bar that it might have been a high school equivalency diploma. With the wheels of democracy spinning in his favor, he chose a beautiful Saturday in May for his grand opening, one that brought with it the aroma of wild apple and cherry, a sky bluer than the old Mattagash River, and the biting freshness of retreating snow. It would seem the old Malecite chieftains were, indeed, smiling their toothless smiles. A full house at the grand opening appeared to be the perfect send-off. Oh, it was true that among the Crafts and Monihans—those Jesus-loves-me-more-than-he-loves-you types, those snowbound, mosquito-bitten Carry Nations—a great wave of protest rose up in a judg-mental cloud, one that was ignored. And it seemed to the patrons of The Crossroads that despite the dreary prophecies of these temperance agitators, God had better things to do—in the Middle East, for instance—than lift a single finger to level The Crossroads. God could even find his work cut out for him back in Ireland, back in the old country, for Chrissakes, where people threw bombs out of their cars instead of beer bottles. So, despite the quibbling storm that always surrounds a controversial institution, Mattagash's first bar was born; and, as with that inevitable westward expansion, the rest is history.

Sally Fennelson-Henderson, who worked four nights a week behind the horseshoe bar, said the occasional fight that did occur was connected, one way or another, to the moon.

"I've seen people get along all month like they was blood brothers," Sally once remarked. "Then as soon as that damned moon turns full, they'll be at each other's throats like werewolves." And it was the same moon—at least Maurice and Sally hoped so—that spurred the Mattagash Temperance Squad on toward a petition to close the place down.

"I wish them women would have an Avon party," Maurice said, when he heard about the uprising. "Get their minds on per-fume or something."

"It's the moon," Sally predicted, and wiped clean an ashtray. "It'll pass."

Moon or no moon, The Crossroads sat looking out over the banks of the Mattagash River, a river that had been witness to some of the biggest, daringest log drives of the last century. But the drives had ended. Tractors had been born, and they went into the woods and built roads so that trucks could travel deep into the forest until they reached the logs. Once, man had needed the old river to bring the logs to him; now he went in his fancy machines and got the logs himself, and he threw the river away, as if it were an old shoelace. But two or three old-timers still sat on rickety stools at The Crossroads to teach the younger generation about the days when nearly fifty million feet of lumber rattled past their doors each spring, at the peak of the drive, when the river was *running* with logs.

"It was a wooden river then," the old-timers told the young-timers, and their weary eyes would meet momentarily, remembering the curved feel of log beneath their caulked boots, remembering whose father had gone under and drowned when a jam broke, remembering their youth as if it were something they could go and look for one day, along the river, if only they had the eyes to find it.

The log drives had ended, and the descendants of those old lumberjacks now owned expensive skidders, machines that cost as much as a Mattagash house. And they owned the best chain saws from Norway and Sweden. Swedish words like *Jonsered* and *Husquevana,* Japanese words like *Tanaka* and *Shindaiwa* had now entered the language of the woodsmen, and could be heard in among the white pines and the black spruce instead of the jaunty old lumberjack ballads. The men worked now for the P. G. Irvine Lumber Company, a large conglomerate from Canada which had eaten up the state of Maine as if it were a mincemeat pie. The P. G. Irvine Company owned almost as much of Maine as Mainers did. It owned the men, too. Their choice was a simple one: go to Connecticut and lose yourself in those faceless factories, and in backbreaking construction jobs, or work for P. G. Irvine, the old Canuck son of a bitch, and take just what he wanted to pay you, and shape your life to his set of rules, while you cut down the wooded heritage of your ancestors. Considering all that, The Crossroads was a damn good idea.

Several complacent deer heads adorned the walls of the bar, the antlers used as natural hatracks, an action that might even please the Malecite skeletons beneath the floor. Most men who frequented The Crossroads kept their hats on. Maybe they were in a hurry to get home to supper after one quick drink. Maybe their heads were cold. It didn't matter anyway, because no etiquette demanded removal of the garment. The hat was a part of the job, of the lifestyle. One wouldn't ask a man to remove his *scalp* because he happened to step inside one's door. But the more serious-minded regulars, the ones who came after supper and stayed until Sally bellowed last call at 12:45, usually hung their hats, as if they were well-won coats of armor, on the obliging antlers.

Several hats were regular danglers, and could be seen nightly on the racks. They sang out advertisements for a variety of products and companies: *Jonsered Chain Saws, John Deere Tractors, P. G. Irvine, Inc., Louis A. Pelletier Lumber Company, Aroostook County: The Crown of Maine, Blanchard Logging.* You could tell a lot about the man by the hat. Billy Plunkett's had a shitty-brown plaster spill on the visor, and *Damn Sea Gulls!* above it in red letters. It was a statement of what he viewed as his perpetual good humor and his lackadaisical approach to life. Pike Gifford's hat, a floppy green felt, had a small replica of a Budweiser beer can pinned to the brim. The message read *Open in Case of Emergency.* The rest of the hat was littered heavily with feathered fly hooks of all sizes and bright colors. Seeing Pike Gifford in this hat, at a distance of ten or twelve feet, one might think that a large swarm of varied tropical insects had, for some instinctual reason known only to them, settled down to colonize on Pike Gifford's head. The appearance of the felt fly hat was even more confusing in the midst of heavy winter, when most of the fake flies ended up coated with little snowy hats themselves. But it bespoke Pike's lifestyle; he had never worked so hard at anything as he had at fishing.

By the time the big wooden sign, describing rivers and friendships, was creaking painfully in the snow-filled blast of November wind coming down from McKinnon Hill, the sea gull hat and the floppy green menagerie had been dangling from one of the deer racks since suppertime.

"The crowd's gonna be slow tonight," Sally said, looking up from her *People* magazine to eye the snow filtering down beneath the pole lights. "Unless we get the Mattagash Milers Snowmobile

Club." Snow didn't bother Sally. She had only two hundred yards to walk and she'd be home. She needed the business too, so if even a gaggle of folks were willing to take their own snowy chances with fate, and occasionally pump the jukebox full of quarters, Sally was willing to let them.

There were three young women from St. Leonard huddled at a table that had been pushed snugly against the wall. Above it, a ruffed grouse—what the locals called a "pat-ridge," spread its lifeless wings in an artificial pose. To the right of the table, atop a Ms. Pac-Man machine Maurice had purchased *très* cheap in Quebec City, a full Canadian lynx appeared ready to leap from its post and rush headlong into the stormy night. He peered intently down at the women. Beneath the softly tufted ears, his marble eyes caught the neon flash of the Miller High Life sign. Along with the stuffed birds and assorted deer heads, *Felis canadensis* was intended, at least in the dense wilderness of Maurice's thinking, to call to the patron's mind the quick flush of grouse on a cool summer evening, the velvety lips of the deer on a mountain freshet, the tawny, cream-colored grace of the lynx as it descended with deadly accuracy upon a snowshoe hare. But the lynx was now so old—it had been trapped by Maurice's father—and the grouse had lost so many feathers in its bumpy move to The Crossroads, that the animal corpses added little more than a graveyard pallor to the atmosphere. One regular customer, Ronny Plunkett, who was back in Mattagash after twenty years in the navy, had gone so far as to insist that the lynx *smelled*. "I think whoever stuffed it left the guts in it," he told Maurice.

And another critic, a canoeist and animal lover from out of state, who was camped on the flat by the river, had even suggested cruelty.

"I love animals too," Maurice had explained patiently to her. "*Your* way, you only get a glimpse of them. *My* way, you get to look right up their assholes."

The women from St. Leonard, who had noticed the lynx at Maurice's grand opening, now no longer saw him there, crouched, dead, forgotten—just as they failed to hear the rattle of precious bones beneath the floorboards of the pub. They went on talking gaily, instead, in their Franglais, their French mixed with English. Maurice scarcely paused when one of his St. Leonard clients told him they'd just bought a new car "*avec* air condition." Nowadays, among the youngest of the St. Leonardians, French was no longer spoken at all, and only a trace of the old Québecois accent could be heard in their English. Supply and demand had propelled many young St. Leonard girls to smile their best smiles at the Mattagash males. And the males had been smiling back for a long time now. The Crossroads simply gave them larger berth in which to mix. And pretty Mattagash girls—the prettiest goddamn girls in Aroostook County—had been twirling on their stools and whispering about young men with last names like Robichaud, Grandmaison, and Bellefontaine. Difficult names for them to spell, much less pronounce. But they had learned to spell *Mattagash* as first-graders, and now they were ready for the tough polysyllables of the outer world. It was true that the purists of town, those who preferred genocide to integration—the Crafts, the Monihans, and their ilk, the hierarchy now that the McKinnons had faded away —would go barren to their coffins rather than let French Catholic blood leak into their veins. But all that interbreeding was beginning to take its toll. "It's getting to the point now," Willy Fennelson once noted, "that you need to know algebra just to do your family tree." The Crafts and the Monihans might think they could control the very network of their DNA, but there were silent, invisible things called chromosomes, so strongheaded themselves that they had never even heard of the Crafts and the Monihans. And the time comes when families, like worn ropes with dangerously thin spots, must untangle themselves and own up. Unbeknownst to all but the amateur genealogists in town, The Crossroads was a blessing in disguise.

"When's Maurice gonna put a couple quarters of his own into this big metal hog?" Billy Plunkett asked as he kicked the jukebox. Merle Haggard stammered a bit in the midst of a song, then leveled again as the machine settled down to the music.

"Billy, quit kicking the jukebox, goddamnit," said Sally.

"I'm sure Merle needs this fifty cents," Billy said. "He's got more greedy ex-wives than I do."

"And don't play 'All My Ex's Live in Texas' again neither," said Sally. "I'll dream them words tonight."

"When Maurice puts a quarter in this machine," Billy said, "you can hear whatever the hell you want to. I'll play hymns for you if Maurice is paying." He curtly pushed Q12, "All My Ex's Live in Texas."

"I wish to hell they did," Billy muttered as the song started up. "Unfortunately, they're all right here in Mattagash, Maine."

"I'll play you a game of cribbage," Pike Gifford offered from the bar. "A penny a point." He wore a Band-Aid on his temple. Despite Lynn's worry, the cut had not required stitches and was now on its way to healing. A basket of stale popcorn, like some forgotten still life from the 1880s, sat bleakly by Pike's vodka and tonic.

"You cheat too damn much," Billy said. He was slowly reading titles, choosing his next selection with more care than he had administered in choosing wives.

"Better to cheat at cribbage than at marriage," Pike said. He smiled broadly, several dark cavities emerging as he did so. It was good to be with Billy, as always. Billy was his closest kin, not counting Pike's own children. Billy was better than that. He was the big brother Pike never had. Billy's father, Tom Plunkett, was a half brother to Goldie, Pike's mother. Things had changed when Goldie Plunkett Gifford threw out the elder Pike and got herself that job at the J. C. Penney store in Watertown. She'd met and married a man, way back in 1971, who took her and all her children off to Connecticut, where they'd started their own carpet-cleaning business. All except Pike junior, who refused to go. Instead, he stayed on in the old house with the senior Pike. And every year when Goldie and those siblings made their migration to Mattagash, like birds unable to stop themselves, Pike had ignored their big Cutlasses and their stylish clothes and Goldie's earrings, which reached almost to her shoulders.

"Our little company is doing great, Pikey," Goldie would say to her son at first. "It's doing so good that you can have yourself a wonderful job. And we'll all be back together again."

"I ain't cleaning the shit off people's rugs," Pike told her. And he gave away every goddamn shirt and pair of pants she ever left lying on the sofa, in a bag with some fancy Connecticut store name on it. He refused to keep any of it, not even after the Cutlass pulled out of the driveway in a big shower of dirt, like wonderful confetti coming down in their wake, like fistfuls of dollar bills falling. When the elder Pike died two years later, Little Pike was still only thirteen. Billy Plunkett's family took him in. He slept in the same room with Billy, ate at the same table, shat in the same toilet, made first love to the same girl. Billy Plunkett was Pike's real family, even if Pike did cheat him at cribbage.

Billy settled on "'Til I'm Too Old to Die Young" for his last selection.

"Ain't that the truth, though," Billy said, agreeing with the title. He punched the appropriate numbers, then returned to his barstool next to Pike Gifford's own.

"I was just thinking," Pike said. "When I retire, Maurice ought to give me this stool, you know, the way they give them fancy chairs to university professors."

"You'd only pawn it," Billy said. He finished off his own vodka, then motioned with the glass to Sally for another. He knew that the girls from St. Leonard had watched with interest as he selected his songs, rocking his ass a bit to the beat, running a quick hand through his hair. He might be thirty-three but, by Christ, he still had *it*. Although he was two years older than Pike, his nose was just beginning to sing of a redness beyond the natural genetic intent for the color of his skin, and the little pockets beneath his eyes, swollen, puffy, could have been a lack of good sleep. Ten years down the road, no one would be confused at the telltale signs Billy's body was shoveling up to the surface. But it was still young enough now to repair some of the damage, disguise it, repackage it. Billy knew it was no accident that young girls in their early twenties, young St. Leonard girls, were looking his way. He had seen an adjective once in a magazine in a dentist's office, the horrible day he was waiting to have a wisdom tooth extracted. And the word had jumped up at him, as if all the little letters were living things: *cocksure*. God, Jesus, but Billy had come to love that word, the slinky coolness of it on his tongue, the stiffness of the *k*, as though it were a little gun going off. No matter that in the magazine story it had been a young marine out on patrol in the Mekong Delta who was being referred to, no matter that it was his brashness, his overconfidence that were being pointed out. Billy had stolen the word, as he had stolen so many chain saws over the years, and he had given it the only meaning such a word could, respectfully, be given. And on his tombstone, when the day for that came, he hoped to God they'd use it. *Billy Plunkett: Cocksure.*

"Wanna go sit with them young things?" Billy asked Pike, and then motioned with his head to that oasis of fleshy fruit growing out of a cold Mattagash landscape, between the stuffed grouse and the rotting lynx. "I'm feeling pretty cocksure," Billy added, and winked at Pike. Pike surveyed the girls evenly. No pretenses with Pike. Marriage had taken the pretense out of him. Now even courting was filled with an urgency. It was a little like jacking deer to Pike Gifford. It was illegal, so you did it fast, planted your bullets accurately (but in this case prayed they were all duds), covered your tracks, and didn't forget your hat.

"We'll probably have to buy them their drinks," Pike calculated. "And I only got twenty dollars or so, just enough to carry myself through the rest of the night. Maybe you could lend me a twenty. I'll give it back to you when my check comes." Pike never considered the tip. That was a social pressure that bothered few customers at The Crossroads.

"I only got about ten bucks myself," Billy said. "I was hoping you'd carry *me* until *my* check comes." Billy's disability, like Pike's, had something to do with those mysterious little disks in his back. He didn't know much about them, but he knew they were best friends to the fake compensation claim. Billy had long ceased to mention the stick of pulp that had supposedly jarred against his back, leaving him partially disabled. Now that his checks were arriving safely, he preferred to elaborate, instead, on the poetic effects of his disability. "Them disks in your back work just like the shocks in a car," Billy often lectured the women he dated, before lovemaking. "President Kennedy had to put all *his* girl-friends on top too."

"You stay away from that jukebox," Pike said, "and we'll man-age. Who do you think you are anyway? Some big-time lottery winner like Paulie Hart?"

Pike didn't really mind being down to his last twenty. His check would arrive any snowy day now, from Augusta, if he could count on Lynn to send the damn thing over to Billy's. He thought of Lynn then. He had missed her earlier, in those lonely waking hours at Billy's, the sun prying between his crusty eyelids, his head thrashing back and forth as though someone had plugged it into a wall socket. He had missed the soft swell of her body curving against his, the way it did on the nights when he came home sober enough to climb the stairs. And he remembered another climbing, remembered the uneven scuffle of his father's boots on the creak-ing steps, on their way up to Goldie's room, and then Goldie crying softly, the springs of the bed squeaking as if in pain, until suddenly there was just pure silence and all the kids could let out their frozen breaths and go back to sleep.

"Liz Taylor took off with a strange man on a motorcycle," Sally said. She was still reading *People* magazine. "On her most recent visit to the Betty Ford Clinic," she clarified, when she saw that several of her listeners had raised their eyebrows.

"I wish they'd leave that poor woman alone," Billy said, sympathetically.

"She's gained all her weight back again," said Sally, scrutinizing the magazine photo of Liz.

"Just the same"—Billy leaned over to survey the picture—"if it wasn't for my Kennedy back, I'd take my chances with her. But them disks can just take so much pressure, especially when Liz is overweight."

"Oh, Billy," Sally said, and shooed him away with the magazine. "As if Elizabeth Taylor would give you the time of day."

"She might," said Billy. "Who knows? One of these nights she might end up here, at the Betty Ford Clinic Northeast." He waved his arm at the surroundings. Pike smiled heartily. Let Lynn say what she wanted. Pike had a right, goddamnit, to sit in a bar and enjoy his friends. He had one of those *inalienable rights* he remembered having to salute the blasted flag for back in grammar school, in Mrs. Fennelson's class. That was before those atheist parents—those freethinking hippies from St. Leonard—had complained to the authorities that flag allegiance was being secretly carried out in Margaret Fennelson's fifth-grade class. Someone from Augusta came up and put a stop to it. Margaret Fennelson had cried so hard that ten-year-old Pike thought she, personally, was responsible for the separation of church and state.

"Course, I'll have to take the thin one," Billy whispered in Pike's ear. He nodded in the direction of the girls. "Doctor's orders," he added, and punched Pike on the arm.

"Then you'd better come up with some money," said Pike. "They'll expect you to buy them drinks." He felt very content suddenly, there at The Crossroads, at the Betty Ford Northeast. Pike had never been a man to ask for too much. There were days when he felt honored just to have electricity. But now he was in the country he knew best, a land filled with good Nashville music, a warm well in his stomach slowly filling up with vodka, snow flitting down under the old bluish pole light. Pike had it all. He could even imagine it was summertime if he wanted to. He could imagine mosquitoes and June bugs banging like tiny alcoholics on the screen door. He could hear Maurice's bug zapper outside, the frantic *zap zap zap,* as though it were music, fiery little drums and guitars and pianos. Let others yearn for green grass and tarred roads. It was the magical bug zapper Pike Gifford missed most during the long Mattagash winters. Ever since Lynn had installed one a few years back, he had been enthralled as he listened to it spit out the toasted bodies of June bugs, and garden tiger moths, and millions of mosquitoes. And in his studies, he had come to realize that the bigger the body, the bigger the *zap.* But he never knew just when he'd hear a big *ZAP* or a little *zap.* Pike imagined that's what those jazz musicians on PBS were talking about when they said *improvisational.*

"Well, partner?" Billy asked, and Pike remembered that it was November, that it was snow now silently zapping around the pole light, and that a lot of vodkas would come and go before Maurice saw fit to stoke up the old bug zapper. Billy loudly ordered them another round, eyeing the girls as he did so. He hoped they heard. *Big Spender* had almost the same musical clang as *cocksure.*

"And one for you, too, Sal," Billy offered magnanimously, knowing full well Sally didn't accept drinks while working. She scrunched her face at him.

"Why don't you just beat your chest and make gorilla sounds, Billy?" Sally asked. She rinsed glasses in water that looked like pea soup.

"Speaking of chests . . ." said Billy. He reached mockingly for Sally's top button. "Yours seems to have disappeared." Sally snapped some of the pea soup at him.

"One of them girls is Pierre Latour's daughter," she whispered. "The little thin one."

"The sheriff?" Billy asked, and Sally nodded.

"Shit, I didn't think he was old enough to have a girl that big," said Pike. He had had to consider Pierre Latour's features enough the night of the fight, and the morning after, to know them well. "He don't look that old," Pike added.

"Oh, he's old enough, all right," said Sally. "How do you think your back might feel, Billy, with Pierre Latour on top of you?"

Billy gave the girls one last loving scrutiny. "At a time like this," he said, "a man has to think of his disks first."

"I got it through the grapevine," said Sally, her hands still immersed in the dirty water, "that Pierre Latour's got a thing going with Amy Joy Lawler. And there he is a married man."

"Shame on him," said Billy. "Imagine."

"I didn't realize he was old enough," Pike repeated as though in response to Sally's remark.

"Well," said Billy. "You might say that puts the kibosh on my evening."

"Too bad," said Pike. He had refused to tell Billy how he got

the cut on his temple, too embarrassed to let it be known that
Conrad had hit him. And he hadn't told Billy about his night in
jail. They were close, but there were some things Pike had to
keep to himself. The Crossroads was a place where a man could
be teased unmercifully. "Too damn bad," Pike said again. He
swung around on his stool, relieved that his last twenty dollars,
until tomorrow, would go toward his own necessities and not some
young girl's frivolities. Besides, the thin one was the only decently
pretty one, and Pike had learned years ago that, bad disks or no
bad disks, Billy got the gold egg while he, Pike, held the goddamn
goose with the bloody ass. The other two girls were porkers, and
Pike couldn't see burrowing into all that fat tonight, even if it *was*
freezing outside.

As Billy badgered Sally to feed the jukebox with some of
Maurice's quarters—marked with a big black X so he could reclaim
them later—the door flew open in a small gust of wind mixed with
snow. Billy turned halfheartedly to view the arrivals. He was expecting his brother, Ronny Plunkett, at any moment, but there
stood Claudette LeClair, her sister Ruby shivering at her side.
Claudette was Billy's old flame, the one just before Rita, his most
recent ex-wife. The women began unbuttoning coats, as if to fight.
Billy paled.

"Mayday," he whispered to Pike, and then turned his back to
the women. "Hold on to your testicles," Billy warned. "The Gabor
sisters are here." An ex-girlfriend, Billy knew, could be a lot more
trouble than an ex-wife. They weren't as well paid.

"Hey there, ladies," Pike said, and waved gingerly at Claudette,
who had already waved a plump hand at *him*.

"Don't wave, for Chrissakes," Billy whispered. "I tell you,
you're courting death."

"She waved at me first," Pike whispered back.

"You sure?" Billy asked.

"Yes, I'm sure," said Pike. "You expecting trouble?"

"With Claudette you never can tell. The Avon lady can ring
the doorbell the wrong way and Claudette will beat the shit out
of her."

"I always wanted to yoke up with that sister of hers," Pike

said. He was trying desperately to rub the indentation out of his hair, the one caused by the constant band of his felt hat. He looked at Billy. Billy had a ring around his head too, like a black halo. If a ring around the head was okay for Billy, it was okay for Pike.

"What do you see in *her?*" Billy asked, remembering Claudette's sister, recalling the immense reach of her overbite. "She looks like she fell outta the ugly tree and hit every branch on the way down."

"Don't spoil this now," Pike said. "Her ugly tree ain't that tall. I was wanting to put the bejesus to her the whole while you was dating Claudette."

"Don't *spoil* it?" Billy whispered. "What? My funeral? My life may be in danger, Piko. I didn't leave that woman on good terms. She even sugared the gas tank of my old car."

"The sister didn't do you any harm, did she?" Pike asked. "Now be fair." He was thinking. Twenty dollars. Claudette only drank beer, so the sister probably did too. And while The Crossroads didn't demand the monetary pound of flesh that places in Watertown did, twenty dollars could go just so far, especially with Billy being short as well. They could probably have a couple rounds, Billy could even play "All My Ex's Live in Texas" to his heart's content, and then they could pick up a couple or three six-packs at the Gas and Go in St. Leonard. Pike's ultimate plan was to convince everybody that a party at Billy's would be the proper end to a perfect evening. The rest would be *histoire d'amour.*

"Maybe I can peace-ify things between you two," Pike offered, magnanimously enough, although it was his own immediate future he hoped to brighten.

"Henry Kissinger couldn't peace-ify Claudette," Billy said. "Are they looking this way?" His head hovered an inch above his vodka.

"Hell, Bill," Pike said. "You put me in mind of the dog that shit on the rug."

"You might say I did," said Billy. "On Claudette's rug. Are they looking over here?"

"No." Pike cleared his throat, put on a neatly ironed smile. "They're *coming* over here."

"Thundering Lord," Billy squeaked. "The jig is up." He stared meekly into his vodka.

"Hey, Billy the Kid," said Claudette. She clasped her hands on Billy, one on each shoulder, and began a rough massage. "How's it hanging?"

"Hey, Claudette." Billy turned to face her, instantaneous surprise to see *her*, of all people. "When did you get here?" he asked, as if the place were so full of people how would he know who came and went.

"Just a second ago," said Claudette. "You remember my sister Ruby? Ruby, this is Pike Gifford, Billy's cousin, and trouble since day one."

"Hi," said Ruby. Her mouth was full of gum. "Want a piece?" she asked Pike, who nearly toppled from his chair. Was it going to be this easy? But then Ruby thrust a big pink pack of sugarfree bubble gum into his face.

"Not just yet," said Pike, imagining the bubble gum a prize he would ask for in the morning, Ruby at his side, his mouth full of hangover shit. He was thankful that Ronny Plunkett hadn't arrived yet, his pockets full of retired navy dollars, his tales of espionage enough to turn a country girl's head, such as the one Ruby sported on her bony little shoulders.

"And how've you been?" Billy asked Claudette.

"Thinking about you a lot," said Claudette. "I heard you just got divorced again, and I figured, knowing the Wild Bill, that you'd be here." She ran a finger around the dark, indented halo of hair on Billy's head, his hat mark. "You're still just as cute as a button." she said.

"You too," said Billy, stupefied. The worse he treated women, it seemed, the more they loved him. All except this last one, Rita. But maybe even Rita, like Claudette, would air her anger like some dirty old bloomers, and then come around again to rub the top of his head.

"We're going to the bathroom to brush the snow out of our hair," Claudette said. She blew Billy a kiss.

"AIDS," Billy thought. Could you catch AIDS from a blown kiss? Hell, Claudette didn't have AIDS anyway. She had a shitload of condoms all over her house, in the medicine cabinet, in the cupboard next to the sugar bowl, on the top of the television, in her laundry basket. And she carried a bushel of them in her purse. She never knew when she might need one, at the grocery store, in church, at a funeral. Claudette often said that the only way she'd have another baby would be an immaculate conception. Billy blew a kiss back.

"Order us each a beer," Claudette said, before she and Ruby disappeared through the shaky door of the ladies' room.

"Wahoo!" said Pike. "If I'd knowed this was gonna happen, I'd have changed the oil in my hair. I told you I'd get that sister, sooner or later."

"I still think she looks like fruit of the ugly tree," Billy insisted.

"But she's got a nice ass, and I appreciate that in a woman," said Pike. "Yes sir. I plan to get a real boot outta that Ruby."

"Well," Billy said, and held his two feet up for Pike to witness. "I wore my boots too. Let's see. That's four boots divided by two sisters." Billy scratched his ear and did some invisible calculating inside his head. "Sounds to me like a job for a couple of good mathematicians with bad backs."

New England in Winter:
Meeting at Twenty Below

> . . . A tap at the pane, the quick sharp scratch
> and blue spurt of a lighted match,
> And a voice less loud, thro' its joys and fears,
> Than the two hearts beating each to each!
>
> —Robert Browning, "Meeting at Night"

Sicily Lawler sat in her nubby recliner with the kick-out footrest and did her damnedest to get a single piece of thread through the god-awful eye of a needle—a job she could, in her youth, execute with chilling accuracy. Now threading a needle had become as much a chore as finding the same in that blessed haystack.

"I'm just like a three-year-old dabbling with tying its shoe-laces," Sicily muttered as the thread buckled again, reared back like a reluctant little white stallion, and refused to enter the eye.

"Darn you," Sicily said. She needed to drag out plan B. At the big wooden kitchen table, which George Craft had made from real cherry that grew far back on McKinnon Hill, and for which he had charged Amy Joy only three hundred dollars, Sicily scattered her tools: needle, spool of thread, dress, button, Bible, and magnifying glass. She held the needle sturdily between thumb and index finger, and then, gently so as not to break it, she stabbed the needle into the wood of the table. It stood steadfast, a straggle of after-the-storm sunshine lighting it up as if it were a little silver icicle.

"There now," Sicily said. "That'll teach you to wiggle in front of my poor old eyes." She readied the thread, moistened it with a dab of spit, then shaped the end into a little pointed lance.

"Okay now," Sicily told herself. She held the big black magnifying glass in her left hand, thread in her right.

"Let's go in there and get the job done," she urged, as though she were addressing an entire troop of fumbling seamstresses. The thread inched in slowly until Sicily's eyes caught it beneath her Super-Magnify glass—a tiny birch log making its way to the eye, which was now large enough to have its own pupil.

"Steady," Sicily said. "Very, very steady," she coached herself, knowing that at any minute the old hand could start shaking back and forth. And it did just that: a millifraction from the needle's gape, began its involuntary wobbling, as if Sicily were shaking a thermometer to clear it, or a can of tomato juice to mix it up. *Shake well before using.*

"Oh Lord," said Sicily. She felt some tears of frustration doing their best to ease out of their ducts, little needle holes themselves. Tears were faster and surer than thread. Sicily plunked the heavy Super-Magnify glass down on the table and rested the wobbly hand holding the thread. Little spears of electricity seemed to be vibrating beneath her skin, no doubt sending out those tiny messages from the brain: *Too old, too old, too old.*

"Good gravy," Sicily said, still waiting patiently for the hand to resume its dignity and get on with its work. Surely these weren't *her* hands, were they? Surely some thief had come in the night, some youthful Gifford playing a prank, and had taken her real hands away, had left her an old pair of hands, a used pair.

"If they was gloves," Sicily thought sadly, "I'd throw them out." But they weren't gloves, although purply-brown patches had begun to inch like a lacy pattern across her skin. A pretty design almost, if you didn't know what it was, what it meant. When frost comes to the vegetables, no matter how artfully it disguises itself on windows and doors and garden gates, when frost and something alive get together, it isn't a two-sided victory. Frost wins.

"They say you're only as old as your arteries," Sicily consoled herself, although Amy Joy had told her that wasn't true anymore. What did Amy Joy know anyway? What did *anyone* under sixty know? You learn a few things, Sicily knew, just about the time you hit seventy. You suspect a few truths about that body's-wear-and-tear business which used to float above your head like gossip. Pretty soon you start to feel the truth about it in your joints, your knees, your elbows, your neck. Sometimes the truth is even bigger, more colorful, three-dimensional as all get-out. Winnie Craft was a good example, with her new chain of pigmented warts, all beaded around her neck as if she were wearing a necklace. No matter that she kept that scarf twirled around her, even in summer, to hide them. Sicily had seen them well enough. Oh, but that nursing home where Winnie was, and Albert Pinkham, and all the others, was a regular hotbed, where warts and moles popped up like little mushrooms, and purple patches spread like so many cucumber vines, a place where things *grew,* awful things. And Winnie wasn't so lucky as old Zsa Zsa Gabor, who had the money to have all *her* old-age warts removed. All Winnie could afford was that scarf.

Sicily was about to try plan C, the elbow of her right arm pushed snugly against her big thick Bible for support. She was just setting her props in place, imagining that one day she would be fooling with *plan Z,* when she heard Amy Joy, back from her walk, stomping snow at the kitchen door. The magnifying glass flew with well-calculated speed across the table until it slipped off with a heavy clunk onto a chair. The little silver needle was whipped up instantly—Sicily barely had to look for it—out of its posthole and slammed back into the stuffed tomato pincushion with the big green leaves. The dress was wrapped into an instant ball and tucked away beneath her apron, the button dropped deftly into the apron's pocket. Wear and tear, her foot. Sicily knew that when it came down to *survival*—when it came right down to being placed against her will into a *terrarium of warts*—tissues and brain messages and corneas, the whole shebang, stood at attention and got the job done. Sicily quickly opened her large-print Bible and stared down at it with a deep, pious interest. She had by chance turned to St. Luke, and was thankful for that bit of luck from Providence. St. Luke had lots of dialogue from Jesus, which was blood-red before her eyes, easier to read than the black, wavy words of mere mortals.

"Hi," said Amy Joy as she unzipped her boots and left them in a pool of melting snow by the kitchen door. She hung her coat and scarf in the kitchen coat closet, then laid her mittens on the counter in a swath of warm sun. They were crusted with little beads of snow, white and glassy as pearls.

"God, it's beautiful out there today," Amy Joy said. "The trees are all coated in snow, just like the flocked Christmas trees you see in magazines."

"I almost got all bundled up and followed you," Sicily lied. "But then I thought of something in St. Luke I wanted to read, just to see if I remembered it correctly, and I did, word for word. Lines I memorized during my teenage years, at our old summer Bible school. My memory's sharp as a tack."

"What was it?" Amy Joy asked. She was filling the teakettle with water.

"What?" Sicily asked. Who would've believed for a second that Amy Joy would want to hear Bible talk? She bordered, as Sicily had often told her, on being a freethinker.

"What was it you remembered?" Amy Joy said. "Recite it to me." Sicily glanced hastily at Jesus' scarlet words. Would he help her in a pinch? She read the first red paragraph her eyes fell upon.

" 'And no man putteth new wine into old bottles; else the new wine will burst the bottles, and be spilled, and the bottles shall perish.' " Sicily grimaced. Not only would this convince Amy Joy that she was senile, but as a fundamentalist she had always hated to read about the boisterous drinking parties in the Bible, Jesus sometimes at the vanguard.

"You memorized that?" asked Amy Joy incredulously. "Stuff about putting wine in bottles?" Sicily was about to panic. Sometimes you couldn't even pick up the Good Book without wishing someone had had the foresight to censor it further. Maybe Jesus would leave the drinking behind and move into smoother territory. Anyway, she was stuck. Amy Joy was still waiting for some sort of explanation, or at least Sicily imagined that she was.

" 'But new wine must be put into new bottles; and both are preserved.' " Good heavens, but couldn't the man have spent that much time talking about the blind, the lame, and the stupid? Sicily flicked a look of theosophical sincerity about her face. "They had no water to drink back then, you know," she said. "The Dead Sea was dead even in them days. That's the only reason they drank so much wine."

"Does it mention The Crossroads anywhere in St. Luke?" Amy Joy asked, a delicious little smile curling about her mouth. Sicily was always up to something these days, she knew. What, was another matter. "So you memorized all that in summer Bible school, huh?"

Sicily plowed on, determined to find some biblical logic to the paragraph somewhere, a moral perchance. She was feeling more than a little bit like the prodigal *fool*.

" 'No man also having drunk old wine straightway desireth new,' " said Sicily, " 'for he sayeth, The old is better.' "

"Who taught the class?" Amy Joy asked. "Orson Welles?" That was it, Sicily realized, for she had come to the bottom of the paragraph and only black words followed, probably a description of how the disciples raised their glasses full of old wine and toasted the Dead Sea, thankful for its demise. She slapped the book shut with a resounding thud.

"We always memorized stuff that wasn't real well known," Sicily said. "To test how good a memory we have. I had a real good one. Still do."

"I'd say," said Amy Joy, "that wasn't exactly 'Our Father Who Art in Heaven.' " She was taking bread from a Sunbeam wrapper. "You want a cucumber and cheese sandwich?" she asked Sicily.

"Yes sir," said Sicily. "My memory's just as good as in my teens. I never dreamt I'd remember that wine-ology parable."

Amy Joy spread two slices on the counter, then went for the Miracle Whip. "You want one or not?" she asked again.

"Don't put cucumber on mine," said Sicily. "Cucumber don't go with cheese."

"Why?" asked Amy Joy. "Did St. Luke say that, too?"

"Don't make fun of the Bible, Amy Joy," Sicily said, quite somberly.

"Well," Amy Joy, admitted. "I guess cheese really doesn't go with cucumber. I just like something green when it's winter. It's so white out there it hurts your eyes."

"Sitting here eating like this gives me an idea," said Sicily. "If we ain't going to the Thanksgiving Co-op Dinner, why don't we bring Winnie over here to eat with us?"

"I told you already," said Amy Joy. She plopped tea bags into two mugs. "I'll gladly drop you off and then pick you up. Winnie too." Couldn't a single day go by without Sicily thinking up some outrage?

"Oh, by the way," said Sicily. "I was just about to sew a button onto my dress, when I remembered what Selma Craft told me last week."

"What was that?" Amy Joy asked. She put a cheese sandwich in front of Sicily, and then reached for the whistling teakettle on the stove. She fixed them both tea.

"You remember Ernie Felby died of cancer a few months ago?" Sicily leveled a nice squirt of Carnation milk into her tea. "Well, Mary Felby's been taking in sewing and altering to make ends meet, and when I got to thinking about that poor woman, I had to pull the thread right out of my needle and put that dress aside. It's the least I could do to help. She's got all them kids, you'll remember, and one strung to the high heavens on dope."

Amy Joy poured milk into her own tea and eyed Sicily with interest. "I thought you didn't like Mary Felby," she said. "I thought because the Felbys came from Massachusetts or wherever, you said they were hippies and should be run out of town. Didn't you and Winnie used to go on and on about the Felbys? Remember how you used to say that the city was getting rid of all their trash when folks like the Felbys come and settle in the country? And have their babies in old barns, like cattle? And they don't even believe in mowing their lawns? And they probably grow more dope than they do potatoes? Remember saying all that?"

"Did I?" Sicily asked vaguely.

"Yes, you did." Amy Joy railed on. "You said folks shouldn't be allowed to even move here from out of state, that they'd never be accepted here, even if all their kids were born here. You said them kids should be considered out-of-staters too, remember? You said just 'cause the cat has kittens in the oven don't make them biscuits. Remember?"

"Will you quit saying *remember, remember,*" Sicily mocked. "Besides, the Bible says to love your neighbor, regardless of what state they moved from." Sicily was serene with altruism. Amy Joy pulled a chair back from the table and sat down on it.

"Ouch!" she said, and felt with one hand under her rear. Out came the Super-Magnify glass. Sicily pretended to be interested only in the cheese sandwich.

"Where did this come from?" Amy Joy asked. "And what's it doing on this chair?" Sicily looked up and registered surprise to see it there, in her daughter's hand, turncoat that it was.

"Oh, *that,*" Sicily said, as if to pooh-pooh its very existence. "I ordered it," she said, then paused to think. She looked quickly at the bulging Bible on the table before her. Should she lie, what with Jesus staring her right in the face? You bet. Jesus was only thirty-three when he died, but if he'd lived to be older, if he'd had kids of his own, especially one like Amy Joy, he would have done the same darn thing, probably even had a few parables about it. Sicily rested assured of this; now if she could only think of what to say. The last thing she wanted Amy Joy to know was how bad her eyesight had become. She needed a little help with this lie. *Please, Jesus.* Suddenly the stuffed tomato pincushion loomed before her eyes, its green cotton leaves growing limply from the stem. She'd forgotten it on the table, but there it was, blood-red as the words in St. Luke, the red letters of truth. *Tomatoes.*

"I bought that Super-Magnify glass this past summer," Sicily said, idly, unconcerned. *Thank you, Jesus.* "To check our tomato plants for aphids."

By nine o'clock, the snow lay packed upon the earth, thick with cold, with the tonnage of its own weight. The trees stood stunned above their roots, beaded with shards of frost, while the river was at work with its silent process of freezing over. A pale November moon poked its face out of some scraps of cloud, then rode free in the sky. A cold, silvery moon, but, as the old-timers liked to say, it was the same one shining over Florida. A coyote sent a volley of short rapid yaps down from the frozen slope of Mc-Kinnon Hill. He had come into the clearing, where the deer had been earlier to eat at the frozen cedar buds, and he stood there in the moonlight, a shaggy wild dog, his mate for life trailing a few cold feet behind. He had made a hard, slow comeback, the little wolf had, his numbers growing slightly in the milder winters that had come to northern Maine. A mournful howl echoed now, an eerie report that beat upon the tombstones of the Protestant graveyard, on the carved names of MCKINNON and MULLINS and CRAFT—the old settlers, the old ghosts, asleep in their icy bones beneath the snow.

When Bobby Fennelson came into the kitchen, the cold had settled upon the land with such force that a crackling seemed to resonate up from the river, down from McKinnon Hill, a fiery cold, snapping and popping like so many birch logs set to flame.

"Christ," he whispered. "It must be ten below already, not counting the windchill factor." Loose snow from the last storm had caught up in a loud, brisk wind and swept down off the roof. It had dusted his hat and shoulders while he stood waiting for her to open the door. Now she was brushing it away.

"I need to get Conrad Gifford to come shovel that roof," Amy Joy whispered back. She was already in her flannel nightgown. She reached up quickly and took his hat off. It said *Maine, A Northern Paradise,* several of the letters beginning to come loose, trailing little tails of red thread about them. He leaned forward, into the breath of her words, and left a small cold kiss on her mouth.

As they inched along the corridor, Amy Joy put a finger to her lips and motioned to Sicily's closed door, a ghostly yellow light hovering beneath it.

"I don't think she's asleep yet," Amy Joy whispered. She took Bobby's hand and pulled him toward the stairway. He left his work boots at the foot so that the climb would be quieter, but, noticing the dinginess of his socks, the little bits of wood chips embedded in the wool, he was suddenly embarrassed.

"Sorry," he said.

"Never mind your socks, silly," said Amy Joy. She nuzzled his neck warmly and he looked at her again, as though she were a wild little colt come out of the storm, mane flying, nostrils trembling with frost. "It's *you* I've missed," she added. "Not your socks."

"I'm coming down with a cold," Bobby said, and ran a hand through his hair, messed with the constant ridge where his hat had been. "A real bad cold."

"It's going around," Amy Joy whispered. She lodged a cool finger beneath the collar of his work shirt, along the neckline of his T-shirt, tugged at the Fruit of the Loom tag.

"I'm tired," he said, and coughed into his hand to squelch the noise. Amy Joy glanced quickly at Sicily's door. There was no sound. If she heard the bed creak, she would still have a minute or two to hide him. The truth, and it even saddened Amy Joy, was that Sicily wasn't as fast as she used to be in keeping an eye on her daughter. Amy Joy couldn't have gotten away with anything of this magnitude just ten years back. But what was her alternative? Put Sicily into Pine Valley with Winnie and Albert and all the rest so that she could live her own life, have her own privacy? Sometimes it seemed to Amy Joy that she was caught between a solid rock of ice and a hard wall of frozen pine trees, with Sicily in the middle of it all with her, and both of them were drowning, choking on snow and trees and mosquitoes, and the truth of their aloneness: a widow and a spinster.

"Did you take the spring path up from the river?" she asked, and Bobby nodded. He'd been parking his four-wheel drive far down the old road that fishermen followed to the river. From there all he had to do was trace the well-beaten path Amy Joy made during her daily walks for exercise, to fill the bird feeders hanging from the cold birches, and to gather dead winter foliage for study. She had bought a book called *New England in Winter,* and now the woods fascinated her, all the bulky little secrets of the cankers on the branches, the hair-filled feces of the coyotes and foxes, the certain lay of a mink's track. She had even learned to estimate the size of a whitetail buck by measuring the tree where he left a "buck rub," his territory marker. A tree four or five inches in diameter meant a very large buck had passed that way.

"Dorrie and Lola have been cruising by most nights," Amy Joy said. "I put my light out upstairs and just watch them."

"Toody and Muldoon," Bobby said.

"I don't know how they think I can miss them," Amy Joy mused. "They got that big yellow plow of Booster's. You'd have to be blind. Do you suppose they'll ever think to look down the river road some night? If they see your truck—" She stopped, imagining.

"They ain't that smart," he said. "Besides, that's where the plow turns, so there's always tracks there. They'd be afraid to drive such a narrow road, late at night, all the way to the river."

"I hope so," Amy Joy said.

"The Snoop Sisters," Bobby said. "Ignore them."

"It's hard when they're turning ten times a night in my yard." Amy Joy heard a long sweet snore from Sicily's room, followed by several short zappy ones.

"We'd better go up," she said. "I don't want to wake her."

They made their way up the wide stair of the old McKinnon homestead, the house that Reverend Ralph had built before he left his family behind and went off as a missionary to die in China. It had been a real showplace in its day, especially when the visiting missionaries had come from all corners of the globe to tell their stories of heathen salvation. The reverend's wife, Grace, had died in that house, up in Amy Joy's very bedroom, had died giving birth to Sicily. And Marge McKinnon, the oldest of the daughters, had given in to death during one of the rainiest autumns anyone could ever remember. Marge had died in the downstairs bedroom, Sicily's room. And of course, the inimitable Pearl McKinnon Ivy, the second of the sisters, had taken her last breaths in the upstairs bedroom, again Amy Joy's bedroom. It seemed to be their destiny, these McKinnon women, to outlive their men, outlive their own legends, until they found themselves in one of the fated bedrooms with the high ceilings and old-fashioned wallpaper, waiting for death to gingerly tuck them in.

But some different activity was taking place in the bedroom now. It was not new, this activity. It had been going on between men and women for so long that probably no one even remembered where it all began. In caves, most likely, Amy Joy guessed when she thought about it, although ten below zero in a cave gave mating an entirely different wrapper. But Amy Joy did assume it was new for the old McKinnon homestead. She imagined that the Reverend Ralph—and probably only three times, as he had three children—was the only male to have caused the headboard to bang against the old-fashioned wallpaper. Amy Joy did not know that Marcus Doyle, Marge's beau in her youth, had spent the autumn of 1923 in the old summer kitchen, where Marge visited him on those special nights when the leaves raged all around them like a fire painted up and down the hillsides. And she didn't know that her own mother, Sicily, had sneaked her father, Edward Elbert Lawler, up into her room one night, while Marge and Pearl dreamed innocent little dreams in their own beds. And it was in this very house that Chester Lee Gifford had climbed through a window in 1959, the night he died in a rainy car wreck, and tried to seduce the bony Thelma Ivy. That was thirty years ago. And Pearl? Maybe Pearl's secret was that she *didn't* sneak a lover into the lofty chambers of the old reverend's house. And who knew what secrets the reverend himself had buried beneath the floorboards? Or his wife, for that matter? It was no family secret that she despised her husband as much as he loved the Lord. Maybe someday—like those bodies out in Lake Mead Amy Joy had read about, those drowned corpses dancing around in an underwater current—maybe one day it would all surface.

"The sheets are cold," Amy Joy said as she turned back the blankets. He had already put his shirt on the chair and was unbuckling his belt. She stood looking out the window, waiting for him to undress. The river lay blue as a bruise in the moonlight, the ice beginning to take hold along its edges. It had seen a lot of traffic, that old river had. Amy Joy's ancestors had followed its course, one summery day in 1833, and had founded the entire town of Mattagash, Maine. And a lot of folks had used it since then, a lot of dreams had poled up and down, a lot of lives had gone under, a lot of chances drowned. Those people were all gone now, but the river was still there, waiting, making its soft music in the moonlight.

The sound of belt buckle against wood as his pants were flung upon the chair reminded her of Bobby's presence, this lumberjack, this man of the woods, smelling of spruce and fir and tamarack. *New England in Winter* told about some of the happenings in the wild north woods, but Amy Joy knew, as she slid beneath the cold blankets and snuggled up to him, that there were other wild happenings yet to be recorded.

The Fennelson Curse

FOSTER FENNELSON	*marries*	MATHILDA ANNA
b. 1879		CRAFT
d. 1960		*b. 1882*

WALTER	*born 1897*	*died September 1918, in combat*
MARY	*born 1899*	*died October 1, 1903, sulfur matches*
LUCY	*born 1900*	*died 1937, in childbirth*
ESTER	*born 1902*	*died 1924, in childbirth*
GARVIN	*born 1905*	*died 1957, woods accident*
WILLIAM	*born 1906*	*died 1918, drowned on log drive*
WINNIE	*born 1910*	*at Pine Valley*
PERCY	*born 1912*	*died 1930, went through ice*
MORTON	*born 1917*	*died 1947, in his sleep*
CASEY	*born 1919*	*died 1968, woods accident*
JUSTINE	*born 1921*	*died 1975, hit by truck*
ELIZABETH	*born 1922*	*infertile, New York City*
LAST BABY	*born 1923*	*male child, misbirth*

Mathilda Watches the Wall: Purple Trains in Northern Maine

In the long, sleepless watches of the night,
A gentle face—the face of one long dead—
Looks at me from the wall, where round its head
The night-lamp casts a halo of pale light.

—Henry Wadsworth Longfellow,
"The Crosses of Snow"

When you want to remember only childhood, only the sweet things, you can't do it. It's as if something pulls you forward, like you're on some old wagon you got no control over, and it just rolls wherever it wants to. Memory's driving that wagon, and when you're as old as I am, you just kind of hang on tight and try your best to enjoy the ride.

I was fourteen when I married Foster Fennelson, and fifteen when Walter was born. After that, there was a lot of kids. Some of them I hardly remember. You can say that ain't motherly, but it's true. They was just kids, like everyone else's kids, nothing to make them stand out. But there's some of them children I won't ever forget. Some stood out real good. I remember Mary a lot, maybe because she was my first girl. She was born second, right after Walter. Maybe I like to remember her because I was still young myself, and things still meant something to me. After a lot of years of life go by, you get kind of like an old badger. You get a shell-like heart, and you back your way into a corner and show everyone your teeth. But Mary—no, I hadn't shut any doors to my heart until Mary died.

She was born in 1899, and didn't hurt me none at all, not like Walter. She was a girl, and tiny, and she didn't hurt me. All I remember about her birth was my water breaking, and then her crying—that's how fast and simple it was. Water, and then Mary, like they belonged together. And she was like a little sprite, all pranks and strange giggles, or silent and staring off across the river as if she could see something no one else could. And you can tell you got a special child when that happens. You can just tell.

It was right in the heart of autumn and, oh, them days around Mattagash Brook in the fall, well, there ain't another place on earth like them. They turn over before your eyes all red and yellow and orange, and over your head, and under your feet. Some days it seemed like you could *trip* on the colors. Some days it seemed like the colors was bees all buzzing around your head. And then there was the land, pulsing, getting itself ready, the birds packing up, the squirrels filling their cupboards with hazelnuts. It was in the fall, and that's the saddest time of year, you know, the fall. Everything's harder then. Longer.

She'd gone out on the front steps, had been out there with her little book, hers and Walter's book, the one the schoolteach give them. It was a real little book with hard covers and pictures of trains. There was all kinds of locomotives, panting and puffing across the pages. It was a wonderful gift back then to give a child, especially a child living and growing up so far from the rest of the world, but with a big wide curiosity about that world. When Mary looked at the pages of that little book, it was good as magic before her eyes. So there she was, out on them steps, the leaves on fire all around her, just looking at pictures and sucking her thumb. At least I thought it was her thumb. She'd had that habit, and I meant to break her of it, but she was still only four. And it was all color that day, God in every leaf, in every bird that flew. You don't see that anymore. There's no real color left these days. Maybe in heaven you will, but you don't see color here no more. So I let her be, let her sit out there on the steps, humming her little tune and sucking her thumb. Only it wasn't her thumb. It was my sulfur matches, the *sulfur* on my matches! When I saw what she had, well, I dropped everything and ran to take them from her. But she had already eaten too much. "You won't even eat potatoes!" I remember I yelled that at her. "You won't eat potatoes, yet you eat my sulfur matches!" She was such a fussy eater, who would have ever dreamed? Walter, on the other hand, ate anything. He ate bark, so help me, and many's the time I caught him eating *dirt*. There was a doctor at St. Leonard in them days, and he told me Walter needed potassium was why he did it. Can you imagine that? Medicine for the body just laying there in the ground.

When it hit, her forehead caught on fire, like she'd been lit up. And her little hands curled into balls. I bundled her up like she was kindling, light as a wish, and we took her in the canoe. We had twenty miles of river before a doctor. It was night and only moonlight. Well, you got to see it to know. You can travel by the moon, just like you can the sun, so we knew our route. We knew, I suppose, our destiny even, and it all lay downriver. Sam Gifford, the old half-Indian with cat's eyes, he took us. He steered us by the moon. And them rapids looked like silver, like you could spend them if you had the time, all froth rearing up at us, like fish spawning. I closed my eyes, but I could see right through my lids, could *feel* how it was all moving around me. Real fast rapids. And I was moving too, like trying to get out of a bad dream, me and little Mary, pulled by the moon. She began clutching at my breast, like she wanted to nurse, but she'd been weaned by then. I give it to her anyway, but she couldn't keep her mouth on it. Then she tried to sit up, as if she was well, and remember all them rapids beating against that canoe. Foster and Sam Gifford was just outlines to us, one sitting, the other standing straight up in the night. And night birds cried out from all along the shores, sounds you'll never hear again in this life, on this earth. They was real wild sounds, to match the way things was back then. And then

Mary said—and it was like all the sound died away when she said this, like only *her* sound was important. Or was it because I could hear nothing else but the words of my sick child? Her little mouth made an O in the moonlight, like she was a little fish washed on shore, and she said, "Trains, Mama. Purple trains, and tracks." And then the fit came upon her. I held her down. What would *you* do? What could anyone do? I held her down like you hold a kid you're gonna whip and they squirm to get away. That's just how it was. And white, spitty foam came out of her mouth, like the kind you see along the river near the bank. Frog spit, the kids call it. I could see her mouth full of it in the moonlight, like the white rapids all around us, like a little river was in her mouth. I dug it out with a finger so she wouldn't choke, but her whole body shook. It looked like she was going under the power, if you believe in that kind of thing. Or better yet, she shook like a little sheet out on the clothesline, a pillowcase maybe, flapping with no control. When I saw that light at St. Leonard Point, the lantern they kept hanging all night on the ferryboat, it was as bright as the star in the east. We could have been three wise men, that's how bright that light was. But we wasn't very wise, and the only gift we brought was little Mary, not ready but willing to go to God. Still, autumn ain't a good time for things like that. That's what I kept telling myself. I'd want a little more of earth when it's autumn.

The doctor had to be stirred up from his bed, and he seemed to want no part of a sick child in the night. I heard his wife, her voice coming down from upstairs, like she was some kind of god. "Tell them to come back tomorrow," the doctor's wife said. "But she's sick right now," Foster said, in one of them voices the poor use. I used it too back then. And like all the others, I hunkered down in clothes I was ashamed of. And like all the others who ain't doctors, or schoolteaches, or store owners, I suppose I thought I didn't have as much right to breathe the same air as them folks. Maybe I thought the doctor's wife owned the air. "Please," I remember Foster said. "She's sick *tonight*." So the doctor give her a red medicine, for growing pains. "But she sucked all the sulfur off them matches," I said to him in a quiet little voice, the voice of a mouse. It was then that Mary sat right up and looked at the doctor. She looked him right in the eye and said, "Trains!" It was like she was accusing him of something. And when I put my arms around her, a shiver shot up both of them. I can still feel it when I remember. It was like I'd been hit by lightning. It was like I'd got the shock of my life. It was her soul passing through me, is what it was. Mary's sweet little soul. And I knew then that she'd gone off to where little children go. "She won't suffer no more growing pains," I told the doctor.

Foster and I sat up with her all night. We watched dawn come in through the downstairs curtains of the doctor's house, listened to him and his wife snoring upstairs. Foster put a few dollars on the table. He said we didn't owe anybody for Mary's birth, and we wasn't gonna owe any son of a bitch for her death. And we was glad, then, that she'd be going to a place where money don't matter to anyone. Then we put on our coats and left, left them nice snores rattling like Mary's little trains up in that warm bed, up in that place where little children are made.

My sister Laddie lived in St. Leonard, before that Spanish grippe come through in 1912 and took her and a parcel of her children with it. I went over to Laddie's house and woke her up and said, "Mary's gone. We lost Mary." That was about all I could say. We didn't have a long time to dwell on things back then. We always had other kids. We always had things that needed doing. You don't stop for it, but you carry it in your heart forever. You carry it around, silent, like a germ. We didn't make no graveclothes for her. We left her in the little calico dress I'd made down from an old one of mine. But I had to take her coat and boots, and, oh, how I wanted her to have them. Mary's little blue coat. She wore it all winter like it was a piece of sky. But I had three little children back at Mattagash Brook, one barely walking. Them other babies, them babies waiting for me at home, they could still feel the cold. And all them babies still in me not born, they'd need something to keep them warm until the little coat wore itself out. Until the little boots scuffed themselves to death. So I took them off her, think about that. I pulled them stiff little arms out of that sky-blue coat. Then I took them tiny feet out of them boots. I did this just like a grave robber. It's a difficult thing to get folks nowadays to understand how hard times was back then. Nature weren't always your friend. Sometimes it seemed that nature was out strictly to get you.

Sam Gifford had spent the night making up a coffin. He's good at work like that. It's the Indian in him. He makes baskets, too, the old way. He goes off into the mountains before dawn to find the right ash tree, and then the right cherry, and from the cherry he makes a stick to beat the ash. But the sun has to come up just so on them trees or Sam won't do it. Ain't that something? The sun just so on the cherry tree or he'll turn right around and come back home. But that ash beats out so fine it's like yarn. He makes good snowshoes, too, and I was glad he made the coffin, because I think he put a little bit of his heart into it, the Indian way. He was all drawn inward from building it, like his heart was pulling him inside his chest, so there must have been a lot of Indian went into that coffin.

We took Mary to the graveyard at St. Leonard, up on the high pretty bank where you can see the river. I wanted to bring her back to Mattagash Brook, bury her on the edge of the blueberry patch. But Foster said it didn't matter which part of the earth took her. What mattered is that she was gone. And he was right. So we buried her next to Albion, my sister Laddie's oldest child, who built a snow tunnel and it fell on him. He was always building something, Albion was. Anything his hands touched, he made something out of it. I often wondered if Albion would've gone off to the city one day and built some of them tall skinny buildings that seem to scratch the sky. The weight of the snow suffocated him. Laddie said she looked out and saw a red arm sticking out of the snowbank, just one red sleeve, like it was blood seeping out. We buried Mary next to Albion, aged nine. Maybe with Albion there beside her, she could go on dreaming her train dreams. Maybe Albion could build her some little snowy tracks. And I remembered how she had looked that doctor right in the eye, not one little bit afraid of him. Maybe death gives you some courage, allows you that extra edge. I know it taught me a big lesson. I started looking at everyone real different after that.

We poled back up the river, back up to Mattagash Brook, back up to where you could fall off the edge of the world if you wasn't careful. I sat in the middle of the canoe, holding that little blue coat and them boots. I could still smell her in them. I could *smell* her, like she was spruce. Like her soul was all fresh pine. Foster sat in front of me, in the bow, with his head down. Once in a while I'd see a shudder run through him, a little memory, I suppose. "Cough syrup," he kept muttering. "That weren't nothing but cherry cough syrup he give her." And we went on upriver like that, with me holding that coat and them boots, me sitting up like the prow of some old ship.

And there was a door slammed shut that day. I heard it, above the rapids and the birds—I heard it. And everything went quiet for it to be heard, like it did the night before, when Mary sat up in the moonlight and said, "Trains, Mama." There was a real banging noise. I looked at Foster, to see if he heard it, but he was far off, turning that bottle of syrup in his hands like it was blood. It stayed on a shelf in the cupboard, that bottle. I never used it, but I couldn't throw it out. It's still back at my house, and think of *that*, having a house and knowing where things are in it, and not being able to go there. Someone will when I'm dead. They'll go in like crows to throw things out, to keep what's shiny and interesting to their eyes. That bottle's so dusty and sticky you can't even read it, so they'll toss it out. No one will remember that cold autumn night, October 1, 1903. No one will remember the softness of a sick child against my breast, her head full of angry trains and empty tracks running nowhere. I think that's why I never liked Winnie, the way she always sported that little coat like it was nothing. After Ester got too big for it, I put it away for a few years, for Winnie. How many times did I see her take it off and throw it down, like it was just a *coat*. And for years I'd come fast awake, out of a dark sleep, and ask, "Are you cold, Mary?" I'd ask this so soft that no one ever heard me. But all I could hear her say back was, "Trains, Mama. Purple trains." So I'd lay back and try to sleep, until dawn came in the window, until I heard the first kid put a foot out of bed and onto the floor above me. And I got to be honest with you. For a lot of years there I didn't care which kid it was.

Exits and Detours: The Wife of Mattagash's Prologue

> I feel it on my ribs, right down the scale,
> And ever shall until my dying day.
> And yet he was so full of life and gay
> In bed, and could so melt me and cajole me,
> What matter if on every bone he'd beaten me!
> He'd have my love, so quickly he could sweeten me.
>
> —Geoffrey Chaucer, "The Wife of Bath's Tale,"
> *The Canterbury Tales*

Lynn Gifford slid into her jeans and then sat for a moment on the side of her bed, thinking. Pike wasn't on the other side. And he wasn't asleep, as usual, on the sofa downstairs, too bewildered with booze to bother with a climb. Even though the kids had begun calling the living room "Daddy's bedroom," he was not asleep down there now. He'd been forbidden, after the last fight, to darken the threshold. But as dawn was beginning to take hold of the morning, Lynn had felt her way quietly down the dark stairs and peered at the sofa, just to make sure, before she went back to bed.

Lynn found the sweatshirt she'd worn the day before, crumpled at the end of the bed. She pulled it over her head. It said *Aroostook County: The Crown of Maine.* Pike had given this braggadocio a great deal of thought the first day he saw Lynn wear it. "If we're the *crown* up here at the top, what's that make Portland?" he had asked. "The asshole?"

Minutes passed, but still Lynn sat. She tried to breathe deeply, to collect her emotions. She looked at her Woolworth tennis shoes, flopped on their sides on the rug, and wished she had the energy to reach for them. But they looked miles away. They looked as if they weighed tons. She gazed down at her Timex and discovered it was only seven-thirty, earlier than she had thought. The kids wouldn't rouse on a Saturday for another two hours, and that was fine with Lynn. Maybe they could find some comfort in their dreams.

Pike Gifford had been told, most unceremoniously, by the St. Leonard sheriff that if he came banging on the door, harassing his wife and children, he would be just as unceremoniously arrested. Lynn had filed for divorce, the third time in her eleven-year marriage.

"It ain't like he's broke any of our bones or anything," Lynn told her sister Maisy. "Although this last time, he come close." It was the first time she'd ever admitted her mistake so freely to her family, and this was a good sign. "It ain't like he's broke our bones," Lynn said. "It's what he does with our minds that hurts so much."

"If you find yourself even considering taking him back," Maisy had advised, "I want you to use the same technique I learned at Weight Watchers. It's called HALT. Alcoholics use it too. Just don't make a decision when you're *h*ungry, *a*ngry, *l*onely, or *t*ired. HALT."

"What does that leave?" Lynn asked. Maisy thought about this question deeply.

"Dead, I guess," she answered.

Down in the kitchen Lynn lingered at the sink, waiting to summon the energy she would need to make the coffee. She stared vaguely out the window at the only road that wound its way through Mattagash. In the sunshine, it was silver with ice, dangerous. Only one road left so few choices for people living in a town. Even for people passing through a town. Some lives, it seemed, were like small towns—only one road, only one choice.

Exits and Detours: The Wife of Mattagash's Prologue   131

But Lynn had left the single path of her fate. She'd blazed a trail in the past week. She'd taken an exit. Now she was just sitting, waiting to determine what new directions she might be headed in. So why then didn't she sense a hopefulness in it all? Why didn't she sigh a large, wintry sigh of relief that her children would now be safer, happier?

"Something like a cloud is hanging over my head," Lynn thought as she tore open a sack of Mr. Coffee. While the coffee was brewing she took another quick peek, out of habit, into the living room, to make certain she hadn't missed Pike, snoring among the throw pillows and the children's winter coats. No sign of him, of course. Once, that would have brought on a sharp pain of fear: *Where was he? Was he all right?* Then fear would be replaced by jealousy and anger: *Was he asleep in some other bed, the son of a bitch?* And then fear again: *What if he's dead!* Because she had managed, like a fine trooper, to love him, in spite of it all. Now all she felt was dread, dread and that big black cloud that followed her.

"He come back, Mama?" Conrad asked from the kitchen table. He had slid into a chair there without his mother hearing him. He rubbed sleep from his eyes. He had asked this question every morning for the past week.

"Dammit, Con," she said. "You scared me so bad I almost shit."

"I don't see his car in the yard either," said Conrad. He opened a packet of sugar he'd brought home from school and emptied it into his mouth.

"Conrad, I keep telling you all that sugar's bad for you," Lynn said. "So why do you do it?"

" 'Cause it's sweet," Conrad replied. Lynn looked at him. Why had he suffered so much more than the rest of them? Shouldn't the oldest son be closest to the father? Was it always like that in messes like these? Conrad had been treated the most bitterly, there was no doubt about it.

"I just like the sweet is all," he said, and Lynn turned away to stare off again, out beyond the packed banks of snow, so glassy in the sunshine it hurt to see them.

"I got two houses to clean today," Lynn said. "That old bitch Gloria Craft's, and Amy Joy Lawler's. You're gonna have to keep an eye on things till Maisy gets over here."

Lynn hadn't used a baby-sitter since Conrad turned nine and took the job over for a dollar or two. No one knew how much he'd managed to save, with that and the chores he was forever scouting around Mattagash. "Little Silas Marner" his teacher called him, when he pestered her for odd jobs. And Lynn had trusted Conrad just fine. She was always the first to say that he was a sixty-year-old man in a twelve-year-old's body. But ever since the new warrant had been sworn out, Lynn had asked Maisy to come by whenever she herself had to be away.

"You think he's coming back again?" Conrad asked. "Like he done the last times?"

"Who the hell knows what's going on in that brain of his," Lynn said. She poured Conrad a cup of coffee, along with her own. "Why? You miss him?"

"Hell no," said Conrad. He opened another pack of sugar and dumped it quickly into his mouth.

"Here," said Lynn. She passed him the cup. "You might as well have some coffee with your sugar."

When Lynn heard the thumps over her head, the music of her children's feet hitting the floor, she took the box of grape Pop-Tarts down from a cupboard and popped two into the toaster. In no time Reed was at her side.

"We got any more Pop-Tarts?" he asked sleepily.

"Sit at the table," Lynn told him. "You can have the first one if you do. Are the little ones coming?" she asked, and then heard the twins, in a fight at the bottom of the stairs.

"They usually don't make it down that far," Conrad said dryly.

The twins were quarreling over the ownership of a talking Big Bird.

"It's mine!" Stevie shouted as Julie grabbed the bright yellow legs. Stevie held on to the string that led to the voice mechanism, and one of the striped arms.

"Mama gave it to *me*," Julie insisted, and yanked at the stuffed toy.

"Hi! I'm Big Bird," the toy announced. "What's *your* name?"

"You little bastard!" Julie screamed. "Let go!" Stevie refused. Julie pulled again.

"I love you very much," said Big Bird magnanimously. "Do you want to play?"

"You stupid, you," said Stevie. Still holding the string, he dropped the floppy arm and roughly slapped Julie's face. "You let go!" he screamed. Julie began to cry, but did not relinquish her grasp. Hanging tightly to the bird's legs, she pulled it to her chest.

"Do you want some birdseed?" Big Bird seemed to be inviting them to lunch.

"Stop that, goddammit, this minute!" Lynn shouted from the kitchen. "If you want a Pop-Tart, I'd get in here, *now!*"

"Mama, it's mine," Julie cried. Mucus descended from one nostril, then retreated with a quick sniff. But not fast enough to elude Stevie's eye.

"Snotface," he whispered as Julie gave Big Bird one last, forceful yank. The string snapped, then dangled in Stevie's hand.

"She broke it, Mama!" he yelled.

"I live on Sesame Street," Big Bird announced, a foolish piece of evidence for a victim to offer his attackers.

"Give it to me," said Lynn. She was towering over her two children, who were surprised at her quiet arrival.

"*He* broke it," said Julie, and pointed at her twin so that there would be no confusion.

"I don't give a damn *who* broke it," Lynn snapped.

"I live on Sesame Street," said Big Bird.

"We heard you," said Lynn. "Now shut up."

"He can't, Mama," said Stevie. "Julie broke him."

"He was mine anyway," said Julie, mucus now descending without any possibility of being retracted.

"I bought him for you *both*," Lynn said curtly. "I could only afford *one*. Now you have *none*, so get into the kitchen before I get out my Ping-Pong paddle." Julie and Stevie dropped their petitions instantly and raced to the kitchen table.

"I live on Sesame Street," Big Bird insisted again.

"Not anymore you don't," Lynn said. "You live in Mattagash, Maine, like the rest of us." She heaved him by a leg up the stairs, toward the twins' bedroom. He tumbled across the hallway and bumped into their battered toy chest.

"And you'll probably die here too," Lynn added. A muffled voice floated down to her, Big Bird mournfully repeating his past address, Sesame Street, that place where little kids got up in the morning and said pleasant things like "Good day" to their parents, unless they were Spanish or French. Those little kids awoke with shiny faces and said things like *"Buenos días,"* or *"Bonjour."* And letters of the alphabet were large and colorful and sang songs about themselves. The numbers wore hats and talked about the importance of correct addition. And Muppets made more sense than politicians. Muppets even made movies. Lynn had seen it all on *Sesame Street.*

"Ain't nobody I know lucky enough to live there," she thought.

"I wanted to be Miles Standish," Reed was saying as he ate his breakfast. "But Christopher Craft is gonna be. I think he's too short to be anybody." The twins were quiet at the table, anticipating a repercussion from their mother. Conrad had taken their Pop-Tarts from the toaster and was cutting them in half with a knife. "So Miss Kimball asked me to be the narrator, and that's the longest part of anybody," Reed said.

"Stevie's gonna be a Indian," said Julie, "and I'm gonna be a turkey."

"That's 'cause you *are* a turkey," Stevie whispered.

"Ain't you even gonna be an Indian or anything?" Reed asked Conrad. "Miss Kimball says she still needs four Indians." But Conrad wasn't listening.

"I got me two hundred and fifty-three packets of jam now," he bragged to Reed. "One hundred and twenty is strawberry. Sixty is grape. Fifty-two is marmalade. And twenty-one is honey. I'm on my sixth shoe box." Reed was impressed.

"What you gonna do with them?" he asked, chunks of Pop-Tart turning up between the words in his open mouth, like little chunks of soil clinging to a plow. "Keep them stashed upstairs?"

"I dunno," Conrad said. He tossed a hot Pop-Tart, quickly, onto each of the twins' plates. "We might need them someday."

"I don't want no more of them fights," Lynn said, coming back into the kitchen. "I've seen and heard all the fights I care to. What's the matter with you two anyway? I thought twins were supposed to be closer than just regular brothers and sisters. I thought they dressed alike and *shared* the same gifts. I can't get you two to wear the same color, much less the same outfit."

"There's two twins in England," announced Reed, turning his mind away from the shoe boxes that held Conrad's jams and sugars, to the plight of twins. "They think so much alike that they don't even have to talk. They burned down a lot of buildings, though, so now they're in a mental house."

"Holy shit," Lynn said. "Knock on wood." She rapped the cupboard door with her knuckles and the kids laughed. But above her own knocking on wood, she heard another knocking, another rapping. She saw the faces of her children freeze within their smiles. Only their eyes told the truth: fear.

"Let it be Maisy, please God," Lynn thought. But Maisy was usually late, never early. The knocking sounded again, and the drumming of it drummed into Lynn's temples, beat harshly upon them. Maisy wouldn't knock, for crying out loud! When, in her whole life, had Maisy ever knocked?

"Don't say a word," Lynn whispered to her children. They sat stunned before their breakfast plates, rigid as goldenrod stalks above the glassy snow.

"Is it Daddy?" Julie whispered. "Is he back?" Julie—and her mother knew this to be true—dearly loved her father. So did Stevie. Pike didn't seem to mind the twins so much. He'd already had two small men to dominate, as well as a small woman, by the time they came along. He didn't need the burden of two more victims.

"Sssshhhhh!" Lynn warned, and held a trembly finger to her lips. She could read nothing in Conrad's eyes, a habit of his lately, but Reed's were so large that Lynn thought they might pop suddenly. She looked at the grape jelly around his mouth and felt a quick impulse to laugh.

"Nerves," she told herself. She heard footsteps crunching on the snowy porch, on their way to the kitchen window. She was about to whisper, "Quick! Hide under the table!" But she didn't whisper this. And she didn't hide herself behind the refrigerator. She simply couldn't move. She looked, instead, into Pike Gifford's pained, bleary face as he cupped sunlight from his eyes and peered into the window, where his entire family had gathered for a Saturday morning breakfast without him. He and Lynn locked eyes.

"He looks like an old dog, out there on the porch," Lynn thought. "He looks just like a poor old dog someone left out in the cold."

"He sees us, Mama," Conrad whispered.

"I know he does," said Lynn. "No need for you to whisper now."

"Hi, Daddy!" Julie said, and waved a hand. *Bonjour, Papa. Buenos días.*

"This ain't *Sesame Street,* that's for sure," Lynn told herself. "Let's go on upstairs. Right now," she said to the children.

"Bye, Daddy!" Julie waved again. *Au revoir, mon père.*

"Bye," said Stevie.

"You gonna call the sheriff?" Conrad asked her as they stood huddled at the top of the stairs, where Pike Gifford could not spy on them. "He said the minute Daddy turns up here, call."

"I don't know," Lynn answered truthfully, for she didn't know, *feel,* what was right. "Seems like he's got enough problems without having the law on his back too." A loud blast of horn, the horn on Pike's old Chevy, sounded from the chilled driveway. The echo of it carried on the cold air, far out across the Mattagash River behind the house, and was lost in the thickness of white pines.

"He's gonna run his battery down," said Reed, after two solid minutes of horn blowing. Lynn moved to an upstairs window and peeked out cautiously.

"I'm surprised the fenders ain't fell off," she observed, "much less the battery run down." Reed, Julie, and Stevie crowded around her, stealing their own peeks.

"Stay back now," she warned them. "Don't let him see you."

"You gonna call the sheriff?" asked Conrad again. He hadn't

moved from the spot at the top of the stairs. Even curiosity had gone out of his eyes. "He said the minute Daddy turns up, be sure and call," he repeated.

"No," said Lynn. She ushered her other children away from the window. "I better go out and send him on his way. We get the sheriff involved and there ain't no telling how mad your daddy'll get. It might be better if I just talk to him a bit and then maybe he'll leave. You kids don't move from this upstairs." She slid past Conrad, who had noticed in a brief instant something on his mother's face, something in her eyes. What was it? Love? The curiosity he himself could no longer muster? He knew one thing. It was no longer hate. There might be some fear there, amid the other things, but the hate was gone.

As Lynn grabbed her winter coat from the sofa downstairs, Conrad went into his room and got out one of his shoe boxes, the one that held the fifty-two marmalades. For almost two years now he'd been saving jams and jellies and sugar packets daily from the school cafeteria. Each child was allowed one packet with a dinner roll, so they were rightfully his. Sometimes he traded his milk, or his chocolate cake, for a honey, or a strawberry. Honey was hardest to collect. Conrad hated sick days and snow days, when all you could do was sit around the house and miss out on a grape, or a strawberry. One day Mr. Hatteras, whom nobody liked, had caught him pocketing a honey.

"Eat it here or not at all," Mr. Hatteras said, and Conrad had lost a precious day of collecting. The sugar packets, on the other hand, were so plentiful at school, or around the diners in Watertown, that he allowed himself five or six daily, usually with meals but not always.

While his brothers and sisters stood in the hall and spied out the upstairs window at their parents down in the yard, Conrad sat on his bed and counted his marmalade packets. He wished they were like baseball cards that he could trade with other kids, share his hobby. But his was an isolated calling, he knew, one to be ridiculed by his classmates and unappreciated by his family. There was a straining in his eyes, a pressure, as though tears might come of this knowledge if he let them. But he did not. Instead, he put the marmalades away, safely counted, and picked up the honey. *Hickory Farms Pure Orange Blossom Honey* he read, over and over again, as if it were a little mantra. He counted each packet.

"They're just talking," Reed said loudly from the window, for Conrad to hear. But Conrad went on counting and said nothing.

"Daddy's giving her something," said Julie.

"Move, stupid!" Stevie said, pushing against her. "I wanna see too!"

"Mama's crying, looks like," Reed announced. He glanced toward the bedroom, and saw that Conrad was still taking inventory of his booty.

"They're fighting!" Stevie said.

"Daddy's gonna slap Mama," said Julie. Reed looked away from Conrad and back to the car down below, where two people sat as gingerly as though they were on a first date.

"They ain't fighting," he said. He abandoned the window to the twins and ambled on into the bedroom he shared with Conrad. He threw himself onto the bed, flat on his stomach.

"They're hugging, for Chrissakes," Reed said.

"Stop it!" Conrad shouted angrily. "You've knocked down all my honey packets!" He struck out at Reed's legs, pushed at them with his fists.

"You and your old honey," Reed said sullenly. He got up from the bed. He would sprawl instead on one of the twins' bunks. "What do *you* know about anything anyway?" Reed asked as he left the room.

"I don't know what it is you expect of me," Lynn said to Conrad. She was sitting on the edge of his bed, still wearing her navy-blue coat. Conrad didn't look up from the tier of strawberries he had just begun to stack, then count, but he could *smell* winter on her. It was the same smell as when he was littler and she'd come in from the mailbox, or from shoveling the front porch. A clean, fresh, cold smell of winter. He kept on counting. He could smell something else, too, besides winter on his mother. He could smell his father lurking there, the cigarette smoke, the after-shave Pike wore on Sundays—not Saturdays. Oh, he smelled a lot of things besides winter. He went on stacking and counting. With all these interruptions he would probably be there counting until dooms- day. He wished they'd just leave him alone.

"It's real hard, Conny, for me to try and take care of this big family alone," Lynn said. She rubbed her hands to warm them. Conrad said nothing, but he knew better. What had his father ever contributed but trouble? Now he could no longer recognize the truth about the family. He just knew better. What was it Reed had said? *They ain't fighting. They're hugging.*

"He wants to try it one more time," Lynn told him. "He says the third time will tell the story. He wants just one more chance to show us he's changed, and this time I think he really has. He even bought me a great big box of candy. Lord, it's been years since he done something like that. He didn't even do that the last time, and you know how close we come to divorce *that* time. Here. I brought you a piece." She prodded his hand with some- thing in green cellophane. Conrad ignored it.

"He ain't drinking no more neither, Conny," Lynn added.

Conrad finished a tall tier of ten strawberries and then began construction on another. He could no longer smell winter on his mother's coat. Winter had gone quietly away. Maybe his father even controlled the seasons, for Conrad could smell nothing at all.

"He says he knows it was you hit him with the bat, but he forgives you anyway. Give him another chance, Conny," Lynn went on. "Talking back to him's what gets you into trouble. Maybe if you could just try to ignore him or something. Reed says he'll try if you will. What do you say?" Conrad could hear her sniffing. He knew she would go into the bathroom and cry a bit if he refused to answer. And his answer didn't matter anyway. It wouldn't keep his father away. It would just make his mother unhappy. He could hear the twins' laughter rising up from down- stairs as they scrambled happily about their father's lap. Reed was now sitting at the top of the stairs, his shoulders drooping, waiting for his own kind of answer. It seemed that, being the oldest, Conrad was in first place for a lot of things, whether it was a decision or a slap.

"Well?" Lynn reached out to run a hand through Conrad's thick, Giffordish curls. He stacked more packets, little Towers of Babel. *Seven. Eight. Nine.* The strawberry packets were red as blood. He heard his mother's sniffing grow louder. How he hated to cause her pain. It was even worse than seeing *him* mistreat her. The jams and honeys and the sugars melted into a sweet, syrupy mass before his eyes. He would give in to *her*, but not to *him*, not to that son of a bitch!

"Okay," said Conrad without looking up. Lynn sighed deeply. Reed sighed too, but there was little relief in it.

"Look what he brung you," Lynn said softly. She put a VHS tape of *Rambo III* into his hands. "It's only been at the Movie Factory two days."

Conrad felt some of the excitement now—*the latest Stallone!* —and he hated himself for it. He looked down at the tape box, still aware of his mother quivering like a little rabbit beside him.

"Wasn't that sweet of him?" Lynn whispered to her son. Then she went downstairs to find her husband.

Fires in the Wood Stove:
Fires in the Head

> I went out to a hazel wood because a fire was in my head.
>
> —William Butler Yeats,
> "The Song of Wandering Aengus"

*I*t was Prissy Monihan on the phone, blathering away angrily without even saying hello. Charlene Craft listened patiently, one ear to Prissy's rantings, the other to a woman on *Geraldo* who had been involved in satanic worship, but no longer was. Every so often, Charlene had to stop and remember which conversation was which: Prissy sounded as evilly driven as Satan's ex-groupie.

"They're lucky we don't burn the damn place down," Prissy threatened. It was The Crossroads issue again. The wet-versus-dry debate was raging so fiercely that some old-timers were speaking of two Mattagashes, of dividing the town in the same way the old country of Ireland itself had divided. It was civil war all over again. It would be brother against brother, cousin against cousin, father against son. But then it had always been like that anyway. There were families in Mattagash whose members hadn't spoken for years because one had voted Republican, the other Democrat, one had inherited the family's pastureland, another the swamp. Those old Irish genes were a contrary lot.

"What is it you're trying to do anyway, Priscilla?" Charlene asked. She was struggling to catch the last bit of information from Geraldo about a magazine from which one could order human bones, skulls, and other sundries.

"We got us a petition to have an emergency town meeting," Prissy said. "So far I got twenty female names on it. And Thornton Carr, the new minister, has signed it too. But we intend to get plenty more."

"Is it really such a bad thing?" Charlene asked. "I mean, as long as Maurice doesn't serve any minors, shouldn't it be up to the adults?" Prissy undertook a long, frustrated sigh.

"Is that what we're teaching our children?" she asked Charlene. "Do you want Christopher and James to end up on them barstools?"

"Chris and James are only ten and eight," Charlene said.

"The Bible says—" Prissy began, but Charlene stopped her.

"Priscilla, I wish you luck with your petition, but I don't feel strong enough about The Crossroads to join you."

"You wasn't born here," Prissy said hotly. "You don't understand our ways. We come down from a long line of God-fearing, abstaining people. My own father had the common decency to drink out in the barn where no one, not even Mother, would see him." Charlene closed her eyes. *You wasn't born here.* Well, she could be thankful for some things.

"Priscilla, thanks for calling me," Charlene said, but Prissy hung up before she could finish. That's all Charlene needed, to be labeled as a Crossroads sympathizer. She imagined heavy pine crosses burned on her lawn the minute the snows receded and the wood was dry enough to ignite.

Charlene heard Tanya cough, a soft little garbled sound floating down from her bedroom. It had been a full week now and still no news. The neurological tests had turned up negative, much to Charlene's relief, but she was anxious for news of the latest blood tests. She had phoned the St. Leonard Clinic every day, but every day the black-haired receptionist, the one who started the talk about Amy Joy Lawler's pregnancy, had told her the same thing.

"Not yet, Mrs. Craft," she had said, her French accent barely noticeable. "Dr. Brassard will call the minute he has the results. We have to send these tests off, remember."

But Charlene couldn't wait for phone calls. Instead, she continued to phone every day, just before lunch. That way she didn't feel so out of control, so dependent on some stranger's whim as to when to pick up a telephone and phone a tiny patient's mother. And every day at lunchtime, what Mattagash called "dinner," Davey had been coming in and staring heavily at his plate, wishing for word about Tanya first, then for news of some kind, from some Providence, that the bank had quit calling, that the bank had, magically, forgotten that Davey Craft and his red-orange Timberjack skidder had ever existed.

Charlene snapped *Geraldo* off when she heard Davey's pickup churning its tires across the crisp snow of the dooryard. She watched from behind the kitchen curtains as he got out, lethargic, his body heavy, and slammed the door. He stared up at Tanya's bedroom window suddenly, as if an afterthought had hit him that she might be sleeping and the door had made such a large, metallic sound in closing. But then he looked away from Tanya's bedroom to the river, which had nearly frozen over during the past few days. A cold blue channel ran in the center of it, but if the temperature dropped further, the channel, too, would disappear. In Charlene's three Mattagash winters, the channel had always frozen over. She had hoped that this year it would remain open. At least there would be some blue around to ward off all the boundless white. There would be a gurgling, a rippling to fend off the silence of December, the somber monotones of January and February. There were days when Charlene walked on snowshoes along the riverbank in those wintry months, seeking out the purple-black winterberries that still clung to the alder bushes. Amy Joy Lawler had told her once, when they bumped their carts together two Christmases ago at the IGA in Watertown, that winterberries made lovely decorations. So Charlene had gone in search of them the next year, and that's when she realized how still with snow the woods could be. And the long white riverbank lay so quiet that she had been too nervous to enjoy the outing. One expected, in the heart of such solitude, that a catastrophe would bound out of the hardwoods, a frightening truth would rise up suddenly from behind a snowy boulder. But it looked as though the channel would freeze again this year, taking the safety of its music along with it.

Charlene watched as Davey walked around his pickup, pausing at each tire to kick away the black snowy slush that had hardened and clung there. The mounds dropped beside each tire, dirty icy lumps. She wished he had done it elsewhere. When he drove away after lunch, the filthy lumps would remain, perfect for the boys to stomp on and then track into the house. But he needed something to do, Davey did; as Charlene watched, he finally thrust his hands deep into the heavy pockets of his work pants, and then made his way to the front door. She was busy at the stove when he closed the door behind him and tossed his Monkeyface gloves onto the floor by the kitchen register.

"When did *you* drive in?" Charlene asked, stirring a pot of macaroni. "I didn't hear a sound."

Davey stood with his cold hands out over the heat blowing up from the register, fingers spread nicely to catch the warmth. "There ain't no other kind of heat as nice as a hardwood fire," he said. "It can warm your bones quicker than gas, or electricity. Just good old rock maple and beech set on fire. It can warm you in places where you didn't know you had places."

"That might be true," Charlene said. "But a wood stove certainly makes the ceiling and walls and curtains smoky."

"We could probably put in a bigger wood stove," Davey said, "and stop using oil altogether. That'll save us a big bill during the winters." *Winters.* That meant more than *one* winter. That meant more than *this* winter. Charlene stirred the macaroni and said nothing.

"I got nothing but idle time until we figure out what to do

with the skidder anyway," Davey kept on. He was washing his hands in the sink, some of the greasy water filling up the dishes Charlene had put there after Tanya's early lunch. She left her pot of macaroni to move the glasses and plates and silverware over to the second basin of the sink. "I could be out cutting enough hardwood in the afternoons to get us through all the way to spring."

Charlene began to set the table, quietly, so that the rattle of Melmac plates against Formica tabletop wouldn't rattle its way upstairs and waken Tanya. She wished Davey would hush, would just sit and eat, talking softly with her about Tanya, about the skidder even, but not a lifetime in Mattagash, Maine, not a wish for them to wind up old and bent, leaning like question marks over the heat of a wood stove. But there was no stopping him now. She knew, when his nerves were in a big bundle in his stomach, there was no halting the rush of useless conversation that would fall from him. And these days the past seemed to be a place of refuge for him. It was almost as if he were thinking of the days before Charlene, and the kids, and expensive lumbering equipment, before responsibility, when life was a free easy swing on a country birch tree. As long as he didn't talk about Benny and the stick of wood, she would be okay. It used to be his favorite story to tell the kids, but that was before Bennett Craft shot himself.

"When I was a kid, we were always ready for a long winter," Davey said, and spooned plenty of macaroni and hamburg onto a mound of mashed potatoes on his plate. "Daddy would back the old Mack truck up to the cellar window. He'd already have sawed the trees into hardwood blocks, and them blocks would be piled high on the old truck."

"That must've been a big job," Charlene said jauntily. She sensed that he was on the verge of telling the Benny story, and she was afraid for him if he did. "I missed the weather report today," she added. "Do you think it'll snow?"

"Petey's job was to roll the blocks off the truck where Daddy could split them into firewood," Davey said evenly, as though he hadn't heard her question. "Kevin's job was to toss the firewood down into the basement through the cellar window. Me and Benny was already down there, and our job was to stack the firewood into long tiers against the wall."

Charlene ate her own macaroni in silence as Davey prattled on. She knew there was nothing more she could say. He was talking as if the boys were there, eating with him, listening with the keen ears of youth, wishing they had a cellar window and a truckload of firewood to tend to. But today Davey's audience consisted only of his wife and so he kept his eyes on the sugar bowl as he spoke, on the Chinese design that laced like a crack around its circumference.

"And during the winter, Petey Junior and Kevin and Benny and me would all take turns splitting them bigger sticks into kindling, as we needed it. That old wood stove was the size of this table," Davey said, and he held his arms out to emphasize—empty arms, nothing in them but the static air of another Mattagash winter, of another charged conversation with his wife. His eyes teared suddenly, and the sugar bowl design snaked like a living thing.

"Didn't you hit Benny on the head?" Charlene asked quietly. She could almost feel Davey's desperation to talk again about his younger brother, to remember the old days without remorse. "Didn't you just let him have it across the head one day with a big stick of firewood?" Davey closed his eyes, and Charlene knew he was remembering that smoky afternoon in the old Craft basement, when neither boy could stoke the fire well enough and then, in the catalyst of smoke, Benny had called Davey a name, and Davey had swung a stick of firewood and nailed his younger brother against the wall. Charlene wished suddenly that it was snowing again and the boys were home from school, so that James could say, "Really, Dad? You actually walloped Uncle Benny with a stick of pulp? Wow!" And Davey could answer, "Not pulp, son, *firewood*," and the boys could whistle softly, and Tanya could twirl her hair on her finger and giggle, and Charlene could feel quite safe to hide her own feelings about it all.

"I did," Davey said, his words a whisper. "I hit Benny on the head." Charlene couldn't count the Thanksgivings and Christmases and Fourths of July that Bennett Craft had felt happily obliged to peel off his lumberjack's cap and reveal to the whole family the thin white scar inching across the back of his scalp, bonelike and hairless, some proof of Davey's masculinity. And then Davey's mother would say again how surprised everyone was at Davey, the quiet one, the gentle one. "If they'd told me it was Petey or Kevin did it, well, that would've been a different matter, but *Davey?*" How many times had Charlene listened to the family talk about that smoky winter's day, smoky now with the passage of time, when Davey Craft showed the whole world a new side to his personality.

"That scar on his head was *this* long," Davey said suddenly, and held out his thumb and index finger to measure off an inch or more.

"Who is he talking to?" Charlene wondered. She had been staring down at her plate of macaroni, sorry now that she'd asked the token question, the question that belonged to Christopher or James. She glanced quickly at Davey's hand, still extended, still measuring out the bloody gash, the mark of childhood's unpredictability, like some terrible mark of Cain. The fingers were trembling awfully, the whole hand and arm shaking pitifully. Charlene reached out and clutched the hand in hers.

"Don't do this to yourself," she said softly. The family story, the oral history of that moment in time, of one boy's act of brotherly defiance, had lost its meaning with Benny no longer there to jerk the greasy hat off his head and expose his skull, like some kind of happy jester.

"Why'd he do it, Char?" Davey asked suddenly, and all Charlene could do was shrug. It would seem that it wasn't just the leaves that were raging and fiery the previous autumn. Something was raging in Bennett Craft's head, some kind of fire that no one had been able to put out. So he had taken a rifle and gone out to the back mountain, to a spot where the maples had already begun to drop their red and yellow leaves, and he had put the rifle into his mouth and pulled the trigger. He had done, finally, what no psychiatrist, what no loved one ever could do. He had put out the fire in his head. He had done it himself, and, Charlene imagined, Benny Craft's hand had not trembled at all. And she knew that Benny's was far from the only suicide, or near suicide, to occur in Mattagash, Maine. Everyone still talked about Ed Lawler, the principal from out of state, but there'd been plenty of others since the turn of the century, and the ratio was way out of proportion to the rest of the world. Charlene had come to believe that little towns were like big families. Sometimes the child prospers in the family. Sometimes the child suffers. And it's the suffering child, the child who can hear and see things that other children, happy at play, can never see and never hear, it's *this* child who holds the gun to his or her own head. And when the gun fires, it isn't just a mother or a father, a sister or a brother who must share the burden. The whole damn town has helped to put that needed pressure on the trigger.

"Why don't you go lie down?" Charlene asked Davey. His hand was moist, and Charlene could see sweat beaded heavily on his forehead, too. Sweat in the deep cold of winter! She wished now that she had never mentioned Benny. Oh, if only Christopher or James had been there to ask for themselves, then Davey would be okay. He would never break down in front of his sons: it was something Mattagash men could not do, and that, Charlene sensed, was part of the problem. If only good news would arrive about Tanya, if only money would fall like snow from the sky, if only Benny would turn up at the next Thanksgiving dinner, his scar still white and pure and innocent, hiding all those other scars, those inner scars, those hurts which cannot be stitched and then admired.

"Daddy, I dreamed of Santa Claus," Charlene heard Tanya say, a little voice filtering in through the cares of adulthood. "I dreamed Santa brought me a Li'l Miss Makeup doll and a Little Tikes Party Kitchen." She was teetering in the kitchen doorway, weak on her feet, her hair matted and messed from napping, her flannel pajamas twisted about her.

"Come here, sweetie," Charlene said, and scooped the child

up onto her lap. "It's not even Thanksgiving. What are you doing talking about Santa Claus?" Davey had pushed his chair back at the sound of Tanya's voice and disappeared into the bathroom. Charlene heard water running.

"Daddy'll be back in a minute," she said to her daughter, and settled her comfortably on her lap. "Want some macaroni?"

By evening, any number of phone calls had poured into Charlene's house concerning the Crossroads petition. Had she heard of it? What did she think of it? Did she intend to sign it? By the time she had the children ready for bed, the calls, like early labor pains, seemed to be twenty minutes apart.

"Mama, it's for you," Christopher said. He plunked the receiver down on the kitchen table and vanished before Charlene had a chance to ask him who it was. She had decided, after her first long year in Mattagash, that it was not morally wrong to ask her children to lie about whether or not she was home. Jesus would forgive her. If Jesus lived in Mattagash, he'd have an answering machine.

"Hey there." It was Lola, breathing heavily into the phone. "You'll never guess who left town today." Charlene heard a long intake of cigarette smoke and breath on the other end of the line. Lola was waiting for the drama of the statement to register.

"Eileen," Charlene said, and the word cracked in her throat. How did she know it would be Eileen? She was just about to play Lola's little game and ask who, when the name came rolling out of her subconscious. She'd known all along, hadn't she, that Eileen wouldn't make it, that Eileen wasn't trooper enough.

"Who told you?" Lola asked, genuinely disappointed. There was not a plethora of good romantic happenings in town.

"She did," Charlene lied. She felt an instant urge to bite her fingernail. That was a habit she'd given up years ago.

"She drove herself and the kids to Presque Isle this morning," Lola added, "and caught an airplane back to Arizona." Arizona. Charlene could almost hear the sweep of sand in each lazy syllable.

She imagined herself flying on a plane, just across the aisle from Eileen, her own children in tow, Davey in a seat nearby.

"I know you two was friends and all," said Lola. "But that wasn't a very nice trick for her to play. Bobby didn't even know about it until she phoned him from the airport to come get the car."

"It isn't a trick," said Charlene. Did they think it was magic? Some kind of disappearing act? Eileen had been dropping all the hints she could. They all should have known. Especially Bobby.

"I was just talking to Dorrie about it," Lola continued. "And Dorrie says that if Eileen Fennelson wants to decorate a cactus this Christmas, good riddance. I don't suppose Bobby'll follow her out there. There ain't no trees to cut in Arizona."

"You know what I think?" Charlene asked. She was remembering the cute little two-story house, about two miles from Charlene's own at a lovely spot overlooking the Mattagash River, where the mailbox read *Bobby and Eileen Fennelson*.

"What?" Lola asked. Charlene had rarely been so talkative in the past, and quite frankly, it was a habit that had always irked Lola and Dorrie. Maybe now, with Eileen gone off to the winds, Charlene would think twice about who her real friends were. "What do you think?" Lola asked again, sincerely.

"I think Paulie Hart ain't the only lucky son of a bitch in this town," Charlene said. "And Eileen only had to buy one ticket."

Charlene thought Davey was asleep when she went into their bedroom with an armload of clean socks and underwear, but he was awake, his arms locked beneath his head, eyes on the ceiling.

"How much does that doll cost?" he asked. Charlene looked at him blankly. "The one Tanya wants."

"Oh," she said. "About twenty dollars at Service Merchandise. I already looked it up." She opened Davey's underwear drawer and began neatly stacking his shorts on the left side, T-shirts in the middle, and socks on the right.

"And that kitchen thing she wants?" he asked.

"That's a bit too much," Charlene said. "Nearly a hundred dollars. I already told her it's too much."

"Is it something I could make?" Davey asked. Charlene saw his fingers working beneath his head, as though they were already in the act of building the little refrigerator, the facsimile stove.

"You know, maybe you could," she said brightly. She knew Davey badly needed to feel that he was still in control. She'd seen enough goddamn Geraldo shows to know that. And he *was* good with his hands. "I could probably stock it with stuff from the kitchen I don't need any more. Old pans and dishes. Worn pot holders."

"Come here," Davey said, and held an arm out to her.

She lay in the crook of his arm for the longest time, remembering all the work she had left to do in the laundry room before bedtime, mentally tidying up the kitchen. Just when she was certain Davey must have fallen asleep, he spoke, his voice young, a voice of childhood.

"Char?" he said. "Do you think the day I hit Benny with the firewood, do you think I did something that day, you know, jarred something around, that never got right again?"

"Oh no, honey," Charlene said, and put her lips against the warm skin of her husband's face. "I don't think that for one minute, not one little second."

"He was only eight years old, Char," Davey said, his voice full of longing, full of a wish, a *need,* to put the piece of firewood back where it belonged, to never, ever swing it.

"Ssshh," Charlene whispered.

"I can still hear the sound of it," Davey said, and as Charlene held him, he began to weep.

It was eleven o'clock when Charlene picked up the telephone. She knew that her parents were always in bed asleep by that time, that the sharp, rude phone would at first frighten them. They would sit straight up in their beds, hands reaching for each other in the darkness, certain a child of theirs was dead. But she didn't care. She was frightened herself. And once they heard her voice, once she reassured them no one had been in an accident, they would be relieved, happy to settle back on their pillows in the Connecticut darkness and chat with their only daughter. News that a daughter is okay is wonderful news, something Charlene herself was still waiting to receive. And surely her father, when he finally took the phone away from her chatty mother, would tell her that, yes, of course, now that she'd brought herself around to asking about it, there *was* a nice job opening down at the plant that Davey would just love.

Outside the warm house where Davey Craft and his children were sleeping quietly, where Charlene was waiting patiently with the phone to her ear, waiting for her parents to answer, the river was writhing with cold. The Crossroads petition might be picking up momentum, but the river was losing an old battle. And during the bitter-chill night, like an open cut that has finally managed to pull its edges together and heal, the thin blue channel of the Mattagash River closed in on itself, and then disappeared.

El Pid Comes Up with a Plan:
It's Carpe Diem for Pike

> I hail from Mattagash, Maine,
> The land of the gun and the rod,
> Where the Crafts speak only to McKinnons
> And McKinnons speak only to God.
>
> —Graffiti, The Crossroads bathroom wall, 1989

*B*illy Plunkett had already played "All My Ex's Live in Texas" several times before Rita Plunkett, his real-life ex-wife, whose mailing address was Mattagash, Maine, and not Houston, turned up at The Crossroads in search of him. Even if Billy had seen her in time to duck out the back door, his red-lettered *Damn Sea Gulls!* hat was dangling guiltily from the deer antlers.

"Don't hit me, that's all I ask of you," Billy said loudly, happily entertaining a small group of listeners with his antics. His brother, Ronny, was with him. They had just made a bet on whether or not Pike would amble in at any minute, looking dapper as always beneath his green felt fishing hat. Lynn had taken him back and he'd been on his best behavior for a few days. Billy bet it wouldn't last, that Pike would show up at The Crossroads. Ronny bet he wouldn't. Billy obviously knew Pike better.

"Billy Plunkett, the only times I hit you was when I was suffering from premenstrual syndrome, and you know it," Rita said hotly. She had a small child in tow, a little boy no older than five or six, whose round face peered out of a hooded winter coat.

"Hi, Cooty," Billy said to the child, and the child smiled a quick little smile and then went back to tugging on his mother's arm.

"I wanna go play my Nintendo," he whined, and yanked at the big misshapen sleeve of Rita's sweater. Like the proverbial cold molasses in January, snot was inching its way down from one of his nostrils.

"You will when I finish here and not before," Rita said sharply, and shoved the child to one side. "Nintendo can wait but this can't."

"You get that Ghostbuster gun I left for you, Cooty?" Billy asked, and the little boy smiled again.

"It weren't nothing but a bribe, that Ghostbuster Zapper, and you know it, Billy." Rita wiped the child's nose with a tissue from her sweater pocket. "You just did it to get Cooty to tell you if I was seeing someone else."

"You find the GI Joe X-Wing Chopper I left for you?" Billy asked the boy. He nodded shyly, his eyes milky blue in a pale, milky face.

"I been calling you twenty times a day and leaving message after message," Rita said to Billy.

"Oh really?" Billy said, and motioned to Maurice for another beer. "My secretary musta forgot to give them to me."

"Don't you move," Rita said to the little boy, and then lighted up a cigarette from the pack in her other pocket. "I got a long-distance call to make."

"You want an orange pop, Cooty?" Billy asked the child, but the little boy hid his round white face behind Rita's thigh. Rita picked up the phone that was sitting on the end of the bar.

"Put your eyebrows down, Maurice, I ain't charging this to you," Rita said. "This is Rita Plunkett," she said into the receiver. "Calling for Carl Hileman, and this here is a collect call." Billy winced. He recognized the name, a lawyer from Caribou, but worse yet, the kind everyone referred to as "a woman's lawyer." Many a Mattagash divorce had ended up on the desk of Carl Hileman, a place strewn with the broken, bankrupt bodies of Aroostook County males.

"Christ," Ronny leaned over and whispered into Billy's ear. "She done hired Marvin Mitchelson."

While Rita waited, tapping her foot excitedly and smoking her Winston 100, the door opened slowly and two more children bounded in—a small thin girl, eight or nine years old, pushing in front of her another little boy, this one a toddler.

"Dammit, Ramada, I thought I told you to stay in the car," Rita said angrily. The girl blinked, her pupils growing large in the sudden dimness of the bar. She tugged the little boy along behind her and then propped him up on a barstool.

"He woke up," she told her mother, "and he didn't want to stay in the car. It's cold out there." The toddler grabbed the glass ashtray from the bar and promptly threw it on the floor.

"I left the engine running," Rita said.

"Here," said Ramada. She handed the baby a plastic toy. "I brung your Mickey Mouse train."

"Goddamnit," said Rita. "I won't be able to hear my lawyer for that train." The baby pushed the train about the bar as Ramada balanced him on the stool; it hooted and clanked loudly. Rita slapped the other little boy's hand away from his nose, which was running wildly again.

"Stop that!" she ordered, then: "Mr. Hileman? It's Rita Plunkett. I finally found the gentleman of the house." The Mickey Mouse train gave off a wicked volley of chugs. "Ssshh!" Rita warned the toddler. She raised her right hand menacingly, a potential slap. Billy would've offered to baby-sit while Rita conferred with her lawyer, but none of these children were his. They were Rita's from previous and different marriages, although Billy had legally adopted them.

"Mama, let's go," Ramada pleaded. "The baby's got a dirty diaper."

"Well, you told me we needed to find him before we could give him a warrant for nonsupport," Rita was saying. "And I done that. All I expect now is to be maintained in the manner to which I am accustomed." She exhaled a spiral of smoky rings.

"You been spending too much time with Phil Donahue," Billy told Rita, and offered the baby a peanut, which he threw on the floor. Billy smiled at the child, and then at Ramada.

"I'd ask for *more* than I was accustomed to, if I was her," Ronny said. Ronny had been around the world.

"The hell," said Billy. "You see that trailer I bought her? It was a corker. I wouldn't be surprised if it turns up on *Lifestyles of the Rich and Famous.*"

"That's Mama's favorite show," the little girl said.

"How'd you ever get a name like Ramada?" Ronny leaned back and asked her.

"That's where Mama and my daddy spent their honeymoon," the girl said. Her eyes were dark, narrow almonds. "At the Ramada Inn in Bangor," she added, seeing the puzzlement on Ronny's face.

"That's a real pretty name then," he said. "Lots of family history behind it." Ramada ignored this attempt at friendship. She looked past Ronny's eyes to the colorful array of bottles behind the bar.

"You want an orange pop?" Billy asked her. "Like Cooty over there's got?" Billy pointed to a table behind Rita where the boy sat, an orange pop before him, an orange ring around his mouth.

"That ain't Cooty," said Ramada. "That's Buddy."

"You're kidding," said Billy. "Where's Cooty?"

"He's sick," said Ramada.

"Are they twins?" asked Ronny.

"No, they ain't twins," Ramada said, and shook her stringy hair from her pointed little face.

"No, they ain't twins," Billy agreed. "But they look a hell of a lot alike. Them two musta had the same daddy."

"What would you know anyway?" Ramada asked Billy. "You're just an old drunk."

"Out of the mouths of babes," Ronny said, and nudged Billy's rib cage. A small volley of hoots rang out from the two tables of spectators, and above that the child's train whistled plaintively. Billy looked at the thin little girl with the witchlike chin and smiled.

"I'll tell you one thing, bucko," Billy said. "You ain't on my Christmas list neither." Ramada stuck her tongue out as the baby reached for the baggy arm of Rita's sweater. Ramada caught him before he toppled off the stool. Rita was taking notes on a tiny yellow pad and looking like a paralegal.

"No wonder Cooty seemed so tongue-tied," Billy noted. "That one must be the five-year-old. I get along great with Cooty. Cooty's six and he talks up a storm." Ronny took in this genealogy, nodding agreeably.

"He's here right now," Rita said, and gave Billy a look of wintry indifference. "He's right here sitting up in broad daylight, with a wad of bills in front of him. You'd swear he was the last of the big spenders." Billy smiled, remembering what it was he saw in Rita in the first place. *Big Spender. Cocksure.* Rita had class, damn her.

"So why can't you send the sheriff up with a warrant right now?" Rita was saying. "Quit that, goddamnit!" she added, and slapped the hand of the toddler. The Mickey Mouse train came to a halt, but the baby broke into fierce wails. Ramada lifted him off the stool, and he grabbed her skinny neck and buried his plump face there.

"Be quiet," Billy said to the baby, a finger to his lips. "Your mama's right in the middle of an important conference call."

"Ain't that baby really yours?" Ronny asked, and Billy hunched his shoulders.

"According to Rita, it is," Billy said. "But me and Cooty's got our doubts."

"Send the sheriff *now,*" Rita said again, shifting on the tired balls of her feet as though she wore roller skates. "Well, what in hell did I hire you for? This ain't *L.A. Law,* you know. It's Mattagash, Maine." She slammed the receiver back onto its cradle and then stubbed out her cigarette.

"Give me his coat," she said to Ramada, and reached out to take it. Ramada stood the baby up, each one of his fat feet on one of Rita's winter boots, and held him there as Rita dressed him again in his ski suit.

"Well?" Billy asked Rita with what seemed to be genuine sympathy. "What did he say?"

"He said the sheriff's got a stack of warrants the length of his arm." Rita sighed. "And some of them's for people even worse than you, Billy. Believe that or not." She pulled the baby up stiffly to zip the ski suit.

"Whatever made you think I'd stay sitting on this barstool," Billy asked his ex-wife, "waiting for a sheriff to drive all the way up here from Caribou to arrest me?"

"I know *you*, Billy Plunkett, better than you know yourself," Rita said. She had pulled mittens from the baby's pockets and was stuffing them onto the chubby hands. "You'd rather go to jail than let your pals see you run when you heard the sheriff was coming with a warrant." Billy smiled warmly. Correct-o. It was all a matter of honor. *Cocksure,* that was him all right. Rita did, indeed, know him well. Better than any of his other wives.

"Looks like she nailed you," Ronny said. He cracked another peanut from its shell and tossed the husk onto the wooden floor. Peanut husks would carpet the floor by midnight, two inches deep around some tables.

"Well, I gotta be going," Rita said absently, as though she'd been attending a Tupperware party. "See ya." She picked the baby up in her arms and bounded across the room, husks crunching like brown snow beneath her feet, the other two children in tow.

As the little boy tramped past, Billy reached out a hand and stopped him. "If you got Cooty's new Ghostbuster Zapper, you give it back to him, okay?" The boy nodded his head slightly. "You tell Cooty I said hello," Billy added. "And tell him to keep his eyes open."

"Come on, Buddy," Rita said, her voice tired of kids, of old rattling cars that break down, of marriages that break up.

"Hey, Rita," Billy turned on his stool and shouted after her. "You get a sheriff lined up, call me. I'll try to work him into my schedule."

"He'll get to the bottom of that stack of warrants one day,

Billy," Rita said. She pushed Ramada along in front of her. "And when he does, it'll be your turn. Your license plate might say *The Kid,* but you ain't no Old West cowboy. Your jig's gonna be up one day." As the door banged behind Rita and her gaggle of children, wind rustled the dead peanut husks. They twirled in little eddies, then lay still, like the toasted bodies of June bugs in summer.

"You know," Billy said to Ronny. "I *like* that woman. Maybe I ought to try it again. She's got her good points, you know."

"It weren't her good points used to bother you," Ronny noted, hoping to jar his brother's memory. "Remember them other points?"

"Ah," said Billy. "You're too hard on the woman, Ron. It ain't easy being a single parent these days."

A freezing wind was loping down from McKinnon Hill and rattling the heavy Crossroads sign by the time Pike Gifford arrived in his floppy fishing hat to announce that a petition was circling the town, like some misguided dove.

"They aim to close The Crossroads," Pike announced, as though he had just stepped from a *Gunsmoke* script.

"Over my dead body," Maurice Fennelson promised. He thumped his fist onto the horseshoe bar.

"I think they've already taken that into consideration," Pike said. "Prissy Monihan is at the head of it."

"Oh well," Maurice said sadly, as if to retract the offer of his life. "In that case." He knew all too well that there'd been a heap of dead bodies over which Prissy Monihan had daintily stepped in the pursuit of some noble ideal. The spindly frame of Maurice Fennelson would be no obstacle.

"In that case," Maurice said again, and raised both hands into the air, "I give to hell up."

"That woman needs a hysterectomy," Booster Mullins pronounced loudly. He sucked up the foam from around the rim of his newest glass of beer. "That's where the word *hysterical* comes from. It's short for hysterectomy. Her hormones has gone crazy."

"Then she must've needed a hysterectomy when she was seven years old," Maurice said. "She was in my class, and I remember well how hard she cried when Mrs. Fennelson read us *Charlotte's Web*. We listened to a chapter a day, and by the time that spider died, Prissy was stretched out on the floor in the back of the classroom, her coat made into a pillow, and a hot-water bottle on her head. I tell you, she's a real emotional ticket."

"*I* couldn't live with her, that's for sure," said Booster Mullins, Maurice's cousin, as he cracked another peanut. "I feel sorry for Theodore." The rest of the men stared at him silently, respectfully. Here was a man who lived with the bulbous, ubiquitous Dorrie, and yet he felt sorry for another man's wedded predicament.

"What a guy," thought Maurice, and his eyes grew a bit watery as he realized such compassion in his own family tree.

"What are we gonna do?" Billy asked from the jukebox.

"For one thing," Pike said, "*we* can stop playing 'All My Ex's Live in Texas.' That'd be a start. I'm so sick of that song I hear it in my sleep."

"Too bad Prissy didn't live there," said Booster.

"Naw," Maurice said. "Don't wish that on Texas. They already got enough scorpions out there."

"I ask this again," Billy said impatiently as he selected his last song. "What are we gonna do?"

"There ain't much we *can* do if Prissy gets the Holy Rollers up in arms," said Maurice. He rubbed the stubble on his chin. "You know that bunch. They tend to drink in barns and bedroom closets. They'd sign her petition."

"There has to be a *plan*," Billy insisted. "This is right up there with your basic taxation-without-representation shit. This ain't no democracy if a little bunch of women can tell a man whether he can or can't have a drink."

"I ain't been open but six months," Maurice said mournfully. He poured himself a frosty little shot of Yukon Jack, and then gave a free round to the small gathering that clung to the lucky shape of the horseshoe bar. The men were stern and silent, as they must have been at the signing of the Magna Charta, the Declaration of Independence, at some Super Bowl where they had bet a fiver on what appeared to be the losing team.

"Never you mind," Billy said. "We'll think of something. I've dealt with women who could make Prissy Monihan look like Mother Teresa. My license plate don't say *The Kid* for nothing."

"That lobster we got on our license plates nowadays spoils the looks of it," Ronny said. "The way its claws stick up, it looks like your plate says *The Pid* instead."

"Speaking of one of them women you just mentioned," Pike said to Billy, "Rita's been calling all over town for you. She called my house alone five or six times. She's driving Lynn crazy."

"*You're* driving Lynn crazy," Billy replied. "Which reminds me. What are you doing here?"

"I heard a Michelob calling my name," Pike said, and smiled his wide Gifford smile.

"I heard that you quit drinking," Booster Mullins said. The women of Mattagash might demand social restrictions, depending on one's family name, but the sad cabal that gathered at The Crossroads was of one brotherhood, and now that brotherhood itself was in danger of being disbanded, their rituals scattered, their magic destroyed.

"Yeah?" Ronny said to Pike. "Didn't you quit drinking?"

"I did quit," Pike answered, "but then I reapplied and got my old job back."

"You're a hoot," said Billy. "Lynn ought never to have took you back in the first place."

"Wait till Rita catches up with you," Pike said. "She's wanting money, but I figure she'll settle for a few front teeth."

"I'm like that gingerbread man we read about as kids," said Billy. "I rolled away from a whole bunch of people, including the man at the bank, and I can roll away from Rita, too." He dug another quarter off the bar and headed back to the jukebox. "And I still got all my teeth."

"Maybe," said Pike, and winked at the others. "But if I were you, Mr. Gingerbread Man, I'd be afraid of Rita taking a great big bite out of me."

"From between the legs," said Ronny Plunkett. He turned to survey the group of giggling girls from St. Leonard who had just filed in the door. Jailbait, Ronny suspected, and none he knew by name. He watched as they busily brushed fresh snowflakes from their hair and shoulders.

"Hey!" Ronny shouted. "It snowing out?"

"What's it look like?" the tallest girl, obviously the leader, said sharply. The others giggled.

"Maybe that's dandruff," Ronny answered them, and now it was time for his group, his compadres, those old soldiers of the barroom, those sheets in a snowy wind, to back him up with a sweet splash of warm laughter.

The phone rang suddenly.

"Any of you here?" Maurice inquired, and all the well-bonded males shook their heads. They listened as Maurice said hello.

"I ain't seen him," he told the caller. "But if *you* do, send him over here. I need all the business I can get." He hung the phone up and began wiping away the beer spilled on the bar.

"Who was it?" asked Booster, a bit nervous that Dorrie might be on his trail. She'd be furious that he lied.

"That was Prissy," said Maurice. "She wanted to know if I'd sign her petition."

"You lying dog," said Ronny, and popped Maurice an innocent punch on his frail little arm. Maurice poured himself another shot of Yukon Jack. Sally would be in at any moment to take over for him anyway.

Pike Gifford looked at Maurice, studied his face a bit. "Was that Lynn?" he asked, and Maurice nodded.

"Whoops!" Ronny shouted. "Man overboard!" It would seem he *had* learned something useful during his twenty years in the navy.

"What do you mean, man overboard!" Pike demanded. "I got no intentions of getting off this ship."

"You sure?" Ronny teased. "What if Lynn comes down here to fetch you home?"

"She'll need the Jaws of Life to get me outta here," Pike said. "That's one thing for sure." Laughter swirled up around Pike Gifford, a good warm blanket. All the crazy lights from the beer signs were blinking like soft, beautiful Christmas lights. And on the jukebox was that old swell of country music, written about the *real* things that happen to folks. "She'll need a tow truck," Pike said. He looked at his buddies corralled around him, his glass of vodka sitting like a slippery ad in some magazine, his Michelob chaser beaded with perspiration. It was good to be alive at times like this. Pike Gifford had never known a better feeling, not even in childhood.

"Hey, Pike!" Billy yelled. "Was it you who wanted to hear 'All My Ex's Live in Texas'?" he asked just as the song began. Pike smiled. It was worth the price of Lynn's anger, a moment like this, when life seemed speeded up, exaggerated, bigger than it should be. It was all worth it, for those times when life seemed *smaller* than it should be, when Pike himself felt so insignificant that he barely seemed to exist—those times when he walked into Blanche's Grocery only to have Fennelson and Craft women shrink back as they passed him in the doorway, afraid they might rub against him. For those times when he went into a Watertown restaurant and folks stared at him as though he were some kind of wild mountain man. And a few vodkas could make up for all those unpleasant chats Pike had had with the man at workmen's comp.

"I got it!" Pike heard Billy shout.

"What?" Maurice asked. Sally was filling in for him now behind the bar. The changing of the guard.

"If they manage to get the wet vote changed, Maurice sweetheart," Billy said, "I know what we can do." He was very excited. Even the girls from St. Leonard stopped their chattering to listen.

"What?" Maurice asked again. Sally stopped mopping the bar. The last song ended on the jukebox and it sat idly, quietly. Booster, Ronny, and the others held their drinks in midair and waited. E. F. Hutton never got this much attention.

"Who owns that patch of land just beyond the Mattagash town line?" Billy asked. "Over in St. Leonard? That little flat piece by the river?"

"I suppose it's old Jack Bishop's flat," said Maurice.

"Poor old Jack," said Ronny. "He's got a real bad drinking problem."

"Yes, it is," said Billy. "It is indeed old Jack Bishop's flat. Now, who is your best customer?"

"Present company excluded?" asked Maurice, looking around.

"Present company excluded," said Billy.

"Well, I guess it would be old Jack Bishop."

"He's got himself a real *bad* drinking problem," Ronny noted, and motioned to Sally for another vodka.

"He keeps saying he's gonna raise Christmas trees on that patch of land," said Sally. "One of these days." Billy looked at her in disbelief.

"That land's so poor he couldn't raise hell on it with a fifth of whiskey," Billy said.

"I suppose this place is probably like home to him," Maurice added. "He ain't got a family."

"Correct-o," said Billy. "And now I ask you, is St. Leonard wet or dry?"

"Wet." The entire group answered the loaded question.

"Well, there you have it," Billy said. He flipped a quarter into the air. It turned silver over silver in the light before landing back in his hand. There might be a goddamn embarrassing red lobster on his license plate that some little son-of-a-bitch clown down in Augusta—where such creatures existed, lobsters as well as clowns—decided on, and now, because of him, grown men were forced to drive around with a big ugly crustacean, for shitsakes, on their cars instead of a sensible pine, cone, and tassel. Billy imagined all the poor lobsters growing cold outside, shivering and frosty in the northern climes, climes they had no damn business in. The little shits in Augusta thought the road dead-ended a foot north of Bangor. Good. Thinking like that would keep the sons of bitches downstate where they belonged. He might have big red claws intruding on his license plate, but he was still The Kid.

"There you have it, Maurice darling," Billy said again. Maurice was getting more like a whiny old woman every day.

"What?" asked Maurice.

"What?" asked Pike.

"What?" asked Booster and Ronny in harmony.

"What?" Billy echoed. He was astonished at how blind they were. "We move the goddamn Crossroads, that's what."

Availability at Pine Valley:
No Expectations for Amy Joy

> "You will have no objection, I dare say, to your
> great expectations being encumbered with that easy
> condition. But if you have any objection, this is the
> time to mention it."
>
> —Charles Dickens, *Great Expectations*

*A*my Joy Lawler laid her shovel against the lower side of the house, where the snow would not bury it, and then removed her mittens. They were heavily beaded with small glass balls of snow, so she beat them nicely against one of the porch posts. The sky was thick and full with flakes, and the town plow had been busy all morning. Amy Joy had shoveled a path just wide enough to drive her little brown Cavalier onto the road. If the snow didn't stop soon, however, there would be no journey out of the Lawler yard. Amy Joy planned to go shopping while Sicily was getting her blue-gray locks trimmed at Angelique's Hair Factory.

"I wish she wouldn't call that place a factory," Sicily had been saying for years, ever since Angelique had graduated from some kind of hair-trimming class in Montreal and moved stateside to buy out the aging Françoise of Chez Françoise Hair Styles. "It's as if we're all going around on conveyor belts, to call a salon a factory."

"Do you like the cut?" Amy Joy would invariably ask, biting the inside of her cheek. Angelique claimed to have gained some knowledge akin to mysticism while in Montreal, when it came to senior citizens' hairdos. She also gave them a ten percent discount and hinted that—knock on wood it would still be years away— when God called his children home, she would also be available to respectfully and appropriately attend to their coiffure down at Cushman's morgue. But Sicily's aversion to Angelique's naming process was not the only habit that had caused Amy Joy to develop a raw spot on the inside of her cheek over the years. Lots of other things had added to the nervous habit.

A vehicle came around the turn, a swirl of snow spitting itself off the back tires. It was Booster's maroon Bronco. The big plow was snugly on the front, as yellow as sun. The Bronco tooted loudly. Behind the wheel, the massive Dorrie Mullins waved a chubby hello to Amy Joy, who grabbed the outside broom and began briskly sweeping snow from the front steps. In the passenger seat, Lola Monihan was bouncing lightly up and down, like some kind of carnival duck. Dorrie didn't have a prayer when it came to bouncing. The Greeks, or somebody, had discovered laws about such things. There would be no doubt in the women's minds, Amy Joy knew, that she had seen them, had looked up at the sound of the horn, as any human being would do unless she was from New York City, where no one is surprised at anything.

The Bronco disappeared in a wake of snowflakes. The stores in Watertown and Madawaska would be defiled all day, with Dorrie plowing about in the long johns and pot holders and Clairol hair colors, Lola tagging along like a thin afterthought. Dorrie might even find a new phone shape. Everyone in Mattagash knew that Dorrie had a motif phone in every room of her house, including one shaped like a frog in her bathroom. Alexander Graham Bell would never know the damage he'd managed to create. The advent of the telephone in Mattagash, Maine, had speeded up gossip immensely. Old truisms such as *slower than a turtle coming ass-first* were out of work in Mattagash, what with VCRs, piles of telephones, and lottery numbers speeding up the mythology. All the old slow notions had turned, seemingly overnight, into lightning-fast ideas.

Amy Joy found Sicily napping sweetly in the recliner. She tiptoed past to leave her mittens on the register to dry, and to plug in the teakettle. The phone rang softly. Amy Joy had remembered to click it over to the quieter ring before she went outside to shovel, knowing that Sicily would fall asleep watching her afternoon game shows, and that a large jangling would only frighten her awake.

"Miss Lawler?" a woman asked, her voice still holding a slight trace of French accent. It was Patrice Grandmaison, from Pine Valley.

"Oh, yes," Amy Joy said, remembering. She cast a quick glance in at Sicily, who was still sleeping in her big recliner, her face twitching with the remnants of some little, fleeting dream.

"Yes," Amy Joy said again. Pulling the long cord of the phone behind her, she stepped into the kitchen, where she could conspire in peace.

"I'm calling in reference to our conversation last spring," Patrice Grandmaison explained. "There's availability here now for your mother."

"I see," said Amy Joy. A sharp twitch of tension clutched at her insides. She felt her stomach muscles tighten in anxiety.

"We'd like for you to make a decision as soon as possible," said Patrice Grandmaison. "We do, as you know, have a long waiting list." Of course they did. There were only two facilities this side of Caribou. "Mrs. Lawler has been expecting the move, hasn't she?"

"Ah, well," said Amy Joy. "We've discussed it a few times, but haven't really come to a decision."

"Take another week then," Patrice offered. Another week! "Tell Mrs. Lawler we're all anxious to welcome her aboard." Welcome her aboard! If Sicily heard that, Amy Joy knew how she'd respond. "Welcome aboard what?" Sicily would say. "A sinking ship, that's what. The ship of death, that's what."

It was only minutes later, while Amy Joy sat at the kitchen

table snacking on Philadelphia Cream Cheese and crackers, that she heard Sicily stirring in her chair. Then the muffled tones of the television disappeared. Sicily had snapped it off.

"That crazy *Price Is Right*," Sicily said as she came stiffly into the kitchen. "Ain't it a horror what stuff costs these days? You pay more for a can of spray starch than we used to pay for a rump roast."

"Inflation," said Amy Joy. Sicily put a tea bag into a cup. Amy Joy began spreading a few extra crackers with cream cheese.

"I hear they plan on cooking up thirty turkeys for that co-op dinner," Sicily said offhandedly. Amy Joy ignored the hint.

"You have a nice nap?" she asked.

"Nap?" said Sicily. "My mind's too active to fall asleep in the middle of a day. Lordy, even if I *tried* to nap, I wouldn't be able to." Amy Joy said nothing. This day, of all the snowy days they'd been together, *this* day was not the one to contradict her.

"I called and canceled your hair appointment," Amy Joy remarked. "It's snowing too hard to be out on the road today."

"That's good news," said Sicily. "I wish she wouldn't call that place a factory. Makes me feel like we're all on conveyor belts going around."

"I've got some more good news," Amy Joy said. She couldn't look at Sicily. She simply did not want to remember the look on her mother's face upon first hearing the news. *There's availability.*

"What's that?" asked Sicily. She brought her tea to the table and thumped down into a chair.

"A real nice lady just called from Pine Valley," said Amy Joy. She put the extra crackers on a napkin and pushed them over in front of her mother, who took one and bit into it. Amy Joy looked at the bits of cracker clinging around Sicily's mouth. She was growing *down*, Sicily was, the way she had once grown *up*. What a sad, awful process. One should find rewards waiting at the end of a good, long life. One shouldn't find a bladder used up, teeth loosening, eyes cobwebby with age. One shouldn't have cruel surprises from a daughter waiting as the last big gift from life.

"Oh?" Sicily said now, of the Pine Valley phone call. "I hope

Winnie's flu ain't turned into a pneumonia or something. She's got a real bad flu. It's going around."

"Winnie's fine," said Amy Joy. "Probably lonesome," she added, "but she's fine."

"Well?" Sicily finished her first cracker. "What is it then?" Suddenly she knew. Amy Joy's voice held that wisp of drama about it, a controlled tone—the voice you might use to break the news to someone that there's been a death. But Winnie was fine. And now Amy Joy was looking away from Sicily, her eyes on the gleaming kettle.

"You look at me," Sicily said, her own voice thick with emotion. "You got some bad news, then you look at me when you tell me." She knew what it was, all right; in the marrow of all her bones she knew. Amy Joy could save her breath, except that Sicily had given her breath, given her *life,* dammit, and she deserved an eye-to-eye contact. Amy Joy looked at her. Sicily could see tears forming in her daughter's eyes. Let them flow, the crocodile things that they were. Let them drown Amy Joy in remorse if necessary. Sicily wasn't going to feel one little speck of pity. "But I'm already forty-four and life is passing me by," Amy Joy liked to whine, but she didn't know the half of it. How'd she like to be almost seventy-seven and have no one else in the world but a daughter who's only forty-four and thankless? A crocodile-tear daughter?

"There's an availability now at Pine Valley." Sicily watched her daughter's face as Amy Joy said this, watched how easily her lips formed the words, looked deep into Amy Joy's eyes, the way only a mother can. But her daughter turned her face away. *Availability.* What in hell did that mean? There was availability at the dump, too. They might as well send her packing out there. Suddenly Sicily could no longer hold it back. First it had been her eyes that turned on her, then her hands shaking like old flags, and her knees so arthritic that some mornings it was a chore just to walk. And her back was stiffening up too, her spinal cord tired, like some old door that's been opened and closed too many times. But now this, a daughter turning on her. Her only daughter turning on her like a little Benedict Arnold. Sicily swooped all the crackers and cups off the table and onto the floor, swinging her arm with the swiftness and strength of a woman half her age. Anger could do that. Anger could call back the sweet bird of youth.

Amy Joy pulled back in surprise. "Mama!" she said.

Amy Joy stood on her snowshoes at the top of McKinnon Hill. Far below her, spread out like dots of paint and nearly lost in the falling snow, lay some of the houses of Mattagash. Little lights, small as the lights on the bellies of fireflies, had begun to color all the windows with a dull yellow. Mattagash lay before Amy Joy as though it were a dream she was having instead of a life there, and she turned away from it before tears could fill her eyes. She turned to the canker knot on the cherry tree, to the tracks beneath it where a whitetail deer had passed in the deep snow, each foot leaving behind two thin, separate troughs. She listened to the music offered up in a lonely wood as a slender fallen tree grated against another in the wind, a rusty fiddle fiddling.

Suddenly she saw the sleek body of an F-111 cut through the snowy patch of sky overhead, followed by the raucous sound of its jet engines, the plane so low she could almost see the pilot. The bastards! How many times had it happened, when she was lost in the peace of the forest, that these metallic nuisances had swooped overhead and disturbed her? It had been going on for years now, these jets taking off from Plattsburgh, New York, and buzzing Mattagash before they went back to where they belonged. There had always been planes doing weird things up there, but it had never been this bad before. Amy Joy remembered that as a child she was forever finding long shiny strips of aluminum foil in the fields, tossed down by the air force to test their radar equipment. It was as if the air force didn't care at all that what they threw out was bound to come down to earth somewhere. But the silver falling from the sky had been no large problem. Amy Joy collected it into a large ball, and birds made shiny, colorful nests, until the air force got tired of that. Then they started breaking the sound barrier over Mattagash, as if the ears on the ground, the occasional broken window didn't matter a whit. Now they were sending F-111s, those sleek jets that ran ahead of their sound and were forever catching Mattagashers off guard in the forest. Arthur Mullins had been threatening for years to shoot one down with his old .30-.30.

"Just as a little message to the rest," he always added. And local word was that he had indeed taken a few shots, only to miss. Ten-year-old Tommy Monihan had sat up nightly for over a year trying to orchestrate the jets into an accident by flicking out all kinds of signals with several Black & Decker flashlights. His father finally put an end to what Tommy was calling the Mattagash Code.

"If he don't stop that, we're gonna get up one morning and see about fifty of them air force Jeeps driving into our yard," Tommy's father once said, at Craft's Filling Station. "It's a shame too," Ben Monihan added. "If he'd managed to bring one of them down, he was gonna use the Mattagash Code as his science project."

Amy Joy listened as the large sound of the plane disappeared over the lump of Haffey Mountain, chasing the jet that had caused it. Off in the distance, down the swoop of McKinnon Hill, she heard another sound as a flock of snowmobiles started up at The Crossroads, the excited voices of the owners rising like smoke above the engines. More noisy creatures, these snowmobiles, bursting through the quiet of the woods, disrupting nature at work, despoiling the white blankets of snow in all the fields with their tracks. Amy Joy watched the line of snowmobiles inch, like a little train, across the white field beyond The Crossroads and then disappear into the forest of black spruce, and white pine, and the leafless maple and birch. Maurice Fennelson must be smiling nicely behind his cash register. Every Saturday, the snowmobile club stopped by for a couple strong shots to ward off the cold. Sometimes a rum and Coke, or a frosty Tom Collins, could do more to keep the blood circulating in fingers and toes than could mittens and socks.

Amy Joy's own toes were growing stiff in her boots. She'd worn only one pair of socks, so eager was she to get away from the warm, unhappy kitchen where Sicily had strewn dishes into a broken heap on the floor. It wasn't fair to Sicily, and Amy Joy knew this to be true. It wasn't fair to anyone to be asked to give up all they know and love best, and to be led into a foreign place just because it would be easier for the young to cavort with life. But wasn't Amy Joy entitled too to go off in search of whatever her destiny might be? She asked this of herself again, there with the snow piling up on the stump of the old cedar, a stump Amy Joy remembered sitting on as a child. But its roots had held it in place, supported it, so that even after the loss of its limbs, its leaves, the full concept of *tree,* even after all that had been taken away from it, it was still there, providing a comfortable place for her to sit. Amy Joy sat on the cedar stump and asked herself lots of questions. She had done this in summer, when little green mosses grew up the sides and across the top of the stump. She had done it in autumn, when she was forced to brush away the crinkly orange and yellow and scarlet leaves thrown down by the red maple. Now her questions were heavier, fuller, harder. Bobby Fennelson was in her life now, a large looming question himself. Would he ask Eileen for a divorce? Would Amy Joy even want him to? Sometimes she did. Other times she didn't. And then there was Mattagash, the biggest question of all, lying next to that twisting, looping question mark of a river. How did two people start their lives over again in Mattagash, where no one forgot anything, for generations? Amy Joy thought of the cups lying broken on the kitchen floor, like snowflakes, as if a storm had occurred there, too, a bigger storm than what was raging all around her.

A gray jay, that old Canada jay, called from above her head, a lilting *whee-ah,* downy as the wind that had found its way up the trail of McKinnon Hill. Amy Joy smiled. She reached into her pocket for the doughnut remnant she had stuffed there after breakfast. She brought it out, unwrapped the cellophane, and then let the doughnut rest on her mitten. She held her hand up, arm outstretched. The gray jay flitted about on the branch overhead, sending down a small flurry of snow. Then it gave another call, a loud one this time, the echo of it filling the wintry wood, before it flew down and landed on Amy Joy's mitten. In a second it had the doughnut scrap and was gone, off to the top of a balsam fir, where more snow sifted lightly down.

"You're welcome," said Amy Joy. She had always heard that gray jays were the ghosts of lumberjacks, too attached to the woods to leave it alone. Maybe she was like these reluctant souls. She had no training of any sort. All these years she had done nothing more than keep house for herself, for Sicily and Pearl. Then Pearl died and now she was keeping house for herself and Sicily. Or was the house keeping her? It seemed she knew more facts about the old McKinnon homestead than she knew about herself. It had been built in 1899 by the Reverend Ralph C. McKinnon, who had married his bride in June, then moved her into the new house before the leaves had gone crazy with color that autumn. When the parlor, the same to which the reverend had brought the visiting missionaries of the world, had been torn down in 1970—Pearl saw it as a useless, costly addition—the most incredibly large pieces of birch bark anyone had ever seen came out of the walls. These were white, virgin birch—sheets four feet wide and four feet long. They had kept the blustery snows from beating the old house to pieces for seventy-one years, natural insulation, and Amy Joy fell asleep at night glad to know that the rest of the old homestead was being protected by these ancient, blessed trees. Of course, back in the late forties Marge had added a layer of plainer shavings to the walls to update the insulation, but beyond that the same old birches were keeping the house warm, as though they were still growing in the forest. As if they still had roots. It was this whole notion of roots that had begun to plague Amy Joy, the kind that attach themselves to people. There was something in her blood, in her genes that tied her to the old ways of life. Pearl had said it herself.

"There's one in every generation," Pearl had said, "whose job it is to remember the old stories, the histories. Just like all them colored folks did in *Roots*." Now who would Amy Joy pass the torch to? Was it too late to have her own little torchbearers? Amy

Joy had even gone to the doctor in St. Leonard, at the health clinic there, to ask about the possibilities of conceiving a child, just in case she wanted to. And he had told her she would have to go to Caribou and have a test done there, let technicians fill her fallopian tubes with a red dye, colored little rivers in her tubes.

"We can tell if they're blocked," he said to Amy Joy, but she hadn't gone on to Caribou. She had said good-bye to the friendly girl behind the desk, Dr. Brassard's receptionist, and had gone out into the leafy autumn day. She would let Mother Nature tell her what was what, if she ever made a decision to start her own family. In the meantime she swallowed her birth control pills daily, as though they were a school of dreadful pink fish, swimming nowhere inside of her. And she carefully guarded her nest egg, her legacy from Pearl, so that it would keep her nicely in case she did nothing more than live on in the house, die in the house, finally pay that last visit to the Mattagash Protestant graveyard. But each time her eye spied an advertisement about overseas employment, no experience necessary, she clipped it out and read every word over and over again while she pondered filling out the form. Now even her precious nest egg was beginning to seem awful, like something that needed to *hatch,* but couldn't possibly do so in the long cold winters that wrapped themselves so harshly about Mattagash. Life had grown stale, without any hope of expectations.

Up on McKinnon Hill, named for the old reverend Ralph, who had no trouble himself getting out of town, Amy Joy Lawler watched another trickle of lights come on in the houses below. Supper lights. Just as in the morning, before dawn, although she wouldn't be there to witness it, breakfast lights would dot the valley like pointy stars, the houses swirling like universes around the lives of the folks inside them. Amy Joy sat on the old, well-rooted stump, beneath the dull, dark eyes of the gray jay, and felt the heavy weight of the snow come to rest on her weary shoulders.

After a good long cry, longer than any of her daily naps—yes, dammit, she took a little nap every day, and who was the worse for it?—Sicily opened the top drawer of her dresser and looked down at the contents. There were pictures, plenty of them, of ancestors long gone. Some were of Amy Joy leaning jauntily in the door of her little playhouse. Nowadays it seemed that Amy Joy was leaning jauntily in the door of the old McKinnon homestead, barring Sicily's way.

Sicily picked up the last photo ever taken of her husband, Ed, who had killed himself, who would never have to grow old. He was standing in front of the Mattagash Grammar School, in his gray suit, with the sun splaying about his shoulders, his eyes squinting a bit. The year was 1959. Sicily knew this because the photo had been taken right after Amy Joy's eighth-grade graduation. Sicily had snapped the little button on the camera herself, and had captured Ed three months before he would fire a bullet into his brain. Were his black thoughts swirling in his head even then, Sicily wondered as she held the picture up close to her eyes. She had framed this picture, and had kept it on her dresser, where she could say hello to it each morning and say her prayers within earshot of it each night. That way, she hoped, God might let a few of her prayers rub off on Ed. It was a terrible thing to die a nonbeliever. Sicily at least had her God waiting at the end of her earthly travails, and it hurt her deeply to hear Amy Joy make atheist statements. "Man invented God," Sicily had heard her daughter say often, and it made no sense at all. Man invented things like Tupperware. But Sicily knew that Amy Joy had inherited that notion from her father. Atheism, and Sicily had said this many times, was in the Lawler family's DNA. "There isn't a single freethinker in the McKinnon family," she always reminded Amy Joy. She didn't mention Cousin Flavie, who had turned Catholic right in the middle of her change of life. Why should the McKinnons own up to Flavie when she wasn't right in the head anyway? Now Sicily feared that Ed's lack of religious leaning meant she might not meet up with him in the hereafter. And along with all those "Good morning, Ed"s and those "Amen"s, something else had happened. She had grown shockingly old and Ed hadn't changed a bit. Here she was, moving forward in time, however reluctantly, and there was Ed, not moving a single inch. It got to the point where Sicily had to put the picture away, in the darkness of her dresser. She still said good morning to him, and earnestly recruited him in her prayers, but looking at him had become unbearable. She felt like his mother, his grandmother even, an old, gray-haired, foolish woman still thinking married thoughts about this younger man. Sicily stood the picture back up on her dresser, so that Ed squinted his eyes out at her from an eighth-grade graduation that had taken place over thirty years ago, on a dusty June day in the little town of Mattagash, Maine.

"I got Amy Joy a pretty little vanity set," Sicily said. "With Green Stamps." And she was glad she had given Reginald Monihan a card with two dollars in it. He was a very nice boy, and he died a hero in Vietnam in 1968. Sicily wondered what Reginald had done with the money, wondered if he ever thought of it while he was over there in the jungle, lying on his bunk, waiting to go out on that last maneuver. His family had been very poor and Sicily remembered that Reginald's face had lighted up when he opened the card. *Good Luck, Graduate,* it had said. Everyone was sure Reginald would do great things one day. And he did. He risked his life to save others. He was a very, very nice boy. He deserved every penny of that two dollars.

Sicily put Ed's picture back into the dark drawer, where he could continue to lie in limbo. For the first time in ages, maybe for the first time ever, she went to bed without saying her prayers. Lately it seemed that there was very little to be thankful for. And as for Ed's spiritual salvation, well, it looked like he might have to fend for himself.

Mathilda Fennelson: Pitfalls of the Wish Book

The mail-order business in the United States began in the late 19th century and became one of the chief sources of supply to rural areas. The early catalogs usually advertised only a few items. The mail-order giants that emerged from that era (Montgomery Ward, founded 1872; Sears, Roebuck and Co., founded 1886) now feature almost every type of consumer item—from automobile parts to knee socks.

—Academic American Encyclopedia

I used to think of catalogue women. I used to look at how smooth their hands was, used to envy their pearly faces. I used to wonder what it'd be like to just do nothing but let someone make your picture. The day after my wedding, I was slopping the hogs. I didn't have no time to look at a catalogue, let alone be in one. Ivy Craft, daughter to Marsh Craft, wanted to be a catalogue woman. You'd see her coming along the road practicing. She'd curtsy and stick out one hand, beckoning, I suppose, to the cameraman. And then she'd twirl the skirts of her dress. She hardly ever saw you when she met you, that's how caught up she was with the catalogue. Her daddy, Marsh, said it was the Devil's curse, that Satan uses what he has to work with. He worked on Eve with that shiny red apple, Marsh said, and he works on good country girls with the catalogue. That might all be so, but Ivy Craft died before she saw the dream she was always dreaming come true. So maybe it *was* a curse to want to be in the catalogue. But a bigger truth was that she died of the same cancer her grandmother, Sadie Craft, wife to John and mother to Marsh, died of. Sadie was my grandmother too. And our aunt Persia and our uncle Thomas died of the same. A long, lingering cancer, like it come invited. Like someone asked it to stay. And it's a sad thing, you know, to realize one day that you've given your child something in their blood that is so bad as a cancer. So I suppose it's a good thing Marsh had the catalogue to blame.

Death was a hard reality back then. We didn't have no merciful needles, or hospital beds. I tell you, you sat up all night long with Death. You knew him like you knew your own family. And you saw how he could twist and turn bodies, break spirits. Oh, he's an old geezer, Death is. But nowadays it's all a drug, this going out of life. It's all tubes and liquid food and pain shots. I don't know but what the old way was better. Maybe the pain was at least something, some little hope to hang on to. If I remember correctly, all Ivy could do at the last of it was to sit on the front porch wrapped in a blanket. The heat of July'd be all around her and there she would sit, full of chills, shaking in her little yellow blanket, yellow like a buttercup is. That's when someone realized they had no picture of her, not a single one, much less a catalogue full of them. Ivy's mother said she couldn't bear it, that she wanted to remember the early beauty Ivy had, and not this Ivy, not this ravished beauty. But Marsh wanted it, something to hold in his hands, I suppose, after Ivy was finally gone. And you know, I think Ivy wanted it too, after all that practicing for it. By this time there was big dark rings under her eyes, and her cheekbones stuck out just terrible. She'd gone down to seventy pounds. You almost wanted to laugh at the poor little thing rather than feel sorry, that's how much she looked like a tiny raccoon. But somebody borrowed a camera somewhere and snapped her picture. She made a weak little smile for them, but she was too far gone to curtsy, or even stick out her hand. She just pulled her blanket in tight, and sweated, and waited. Ivy Craft curled into a ball one night and took her catalogue dream up to heaven. She was my cousin and my best friend.

Foster, the man I come about to marry, was courting Ivy until she got too sick. When she come down fully with the cancer, she just asked him to stop coming by. She didn't want to be seen much by folks, especially by a sweetheart. Just her family and me saw the last of Ivy Craft, saw her go downhill. I know that caused a pain in Foster's heart. I remember he'd go down by the old pine tree on the south end of Marsh's field, and he'd wait there for me. He'd be sitting there in the rope swing. I'd see him as soon as I turned the bend in the road. I'd see the shadow of a man swinging, and then Foster'd jump up and catch the swing in his hand to stop it. He'd say, "Any word on her?" and I'd say, "She's the same, Foster. Now you go on home and get you something to eat." And I think that's when he begun to hate me, all them long years ago, waiting on Ivy's rope swing for a single word of news. He hated that I was privy to the dying. It must've seemed like I was courting his sweetheart for him. And the next day Ivy'd say, "Did Foster ask after me?" and I'd nod that he did indeed. She'd draw that blanket about her and smile that weak little smile. I don't think she ever loved Foster. Oh, I think she liked him all right, like you do someone you growed up with, but remember, she never gave him considerable thought when she was practicing to be a catalogue woman. It was only after she first got a little sick that Foster took on new meaning for her. Maybe she envied the life in him. Maybe he was her last grasp at something real, the notion of a husband and a home and a family. Maybe she was trying to convince God that she didn't care anymore about the catalogue so he could go ahead and lift the curse.

I know she was scared. In them days you knew you were gonna die long before the doctor hitched his horse up to a wagon and come to tell you. In the country, in them days, you kept one finger on nature's pulse, and the minute it started to flutter, you didn't need no medical books. You'd be the first one to know, and sometimes the doctor wasn't even the second one. Sometimes other folks knew too. Sadie Craft, wife to John, mother to Marsh, grandmother to me and Ivy, she come into Marsh's kitchen one morning, just a day or two before Ivy started feeling bad. She come into that kitchen with her hair all aflutter. She'd run the whole half-mile down the road to Marsh's with a tin dipper in her hand. And she took Marsh down to the river and showed him the tea leaves in that dipper. She explained all the fancy little patterns to him. "It's a long funeral line," she said, "with a windrow of horses and mourners." Marsh knew, anyone would know, the longer the funeral line in a teacup, the younger the deceased. Well, he sat right down on the river rocks, Marsh did, and he didn't move from there until the next day. He knew his mother was never wrong. She was born with a veil over her eyes, Grandmother Craft was, and when that happens, you can tell the future, even if you don't like what you tell. She even knew ahead when it was her own turn to die of the same cancer, a few years later. Marsh knew he was hearing the truth about Ivy. "I'd rather lose her to the catalogue," Marsh said. And the next day he come up the hill and told Ivy to leave the dishes be. He said he'd give her the money to go off and be in a catalogue. "Next year," he promised her. Keep in mind, Marsh didn't have no money. But he paid for Ivy's dream aforehand. You might say he got it on credit out of his head and give it to her. And how she talked of that train out of Watertown to Bangor, and then on to Boston! She talked about that train like she'd ridden it all her life. You could almost smell the smoke of it, just listening to her. It was only when she started to get sick that she closed up the catalogue for good, and put her interest in Foster. "You get tired of even dreams sometime," she said to me. It was when she got so sick she could hardly move that she closed the book on Foster, too.

I'd packed up a few things and come over to stay with her until she was gone. She wanted me there because she knew the end was near. The rest of us did too. I was sitting up late with her on that last night. She usually got tired right after supper and would sleep until one or two in the morning. Then she'd be awake and in pain until six or seven, trying her best to fall asleep again. My mother said it was the sleep of the dying, that time stops its foolish meaning for things like that. So I packed up some stuff and went over to watch Ivy Craft die. There was no more talk of Boston by this time. She had held on to that notion all she could, until she couldn't close her fingers around the idea of it no more. This one night, this last night, she'd been off in that little sleep of hers, that half-pain, half-waking sleep. All of a sudden she sat right up in bed and tugged at the sleeves of her nightdress. It looked to me like her nightdress was choking her. I was sitting in a chair by the bed, humming to her, humming "Rock of Ages" to her. The lamp was turned down low, but it was flickering on the walls. No one had real wallpaper back then, remember, so the walls was covered with old newspapers. And that lamplight was flickering on the walls, lighting up all the faces around us, lighting up all them old people in the news. This was real *old* news, keep in mind, important the day it happened, but no longer of matter to anyone. And I suddenly saw myself that way. And I saw Ivy Craft that way too. Important for a little flick in time, but then not really worth mentioning. That little flick would be our lives, I suppose. And Ivy felt this too. She looked around at all them line-drawn faces of yesterday like she wanted to grab them. She looked at a picture of our president so long that I thought she was gonna ask him something. Then she reached out her hand to me, the way she'd practiced for the catalogue, reached it out and said, "What do you suppose the news is where I'm going?" And I said, "No different than here, I'd bet." And then Ivy said, "It's all secrets out there, Tildy. No one, not even President Cleveland, can tell us the answers to them. *I* can't even tell *you*." That's just what she said. "*I* can't even tell *you*," she said, "to help you when it's time for your own self." Her little hand was like a piece of string in mine. I just went ahead and held on to it, because there was nothing I could say. Keep in mind we were both thirteen then. "I'll be the news soon," Ivy Craft said to me. And we held each other for a long, long time. Then I went back to my chair, and I fell asleep there.

It was two hours later that I come wide awake. But Ivy was gone. She'd hemorrhaged from the mouth. Her mother was leaning over her, wiping off her sad little face. Marsh had gone back down to the Mattagash River. It is true that a river or a mountain is the best place to go when you got a problem, when something big is breaking up inside of you. I hear of people going to doctors, in their fancy offices, paying a week's work for every hour of talk. The best place to go is a river, or some little spot under a birch, where the birds can listen to your grief. And the crickets. They'll do this for free, mind you. So Marsh went back down to his river, and I stood there looking down at the last of Ivy Craft, my best friend and future catalogue woman. "Ain't she pretty as a picture?" her mama was saying as she wiped that bloody spittle from around Ivy's bony little mouth. "Ain't she the loveliest child God ever made?"

I wanted to name my first girl Ivy, but I knew Foster wouldn't want me to. So I went ahead and called her Mary, but I always thought that child was Ivy come back again, Ivy come back for just another taste of it all. Mary was such a little elf, a child full of giggles and dark, brooding looks. It was almost as if she knew secrets, like maybe she'd learned some answers somewhere, the kind of answers Ivy went looking for. And then there was that little book of trains, the one the schoolteach give Walter. That little book was like a friend to Mary. "Ivy's still trying to get to Boston," I'd find myself thinking as I watched Mary. And you know, I think Foster sensed it too, that Mary was no ordinary child. When she died, I think he felt like he'd lost Ivy twice. I know that's how I felt.

It was only a year after Ivy died that me and Foster got married. The most god-awful, rainy, dull day you would ever want to wake up to. That was June 19, back in 1896, a Friday. I don't think we ever would've gotten married if it hadn't been for Ivy. Me and Foster joining up was just a means of being closer to *her*. There's no way I can relate just how much we both missed her. It was as if we'd lost someone who could see and hear things the rest of us couldn't. It's like you're a snake and then someone goes and cuts off your head, and so you just go on and wiggle through life, knowing the whole time that a real big part of you is gone. Marsh Craft died six months after Ivy did. You can think what you want to. You can listen to a doctor tell you it can't be done. But I'll tell you the exact truth about it. Marsh Craft died of a broken heart. It was like his heart turned into a tumor, turned on the rest of him. Maybe he saw *that* in the tea leaves too, that day, down by the river. Maybe that's what made his soul too heavy to get up and come on back to the house. Maybe he knew.

Me and Foster lived with his folks for a few months after we was married. But I got it into my head I had to be under my own roof by the time Walter was born. And I was, too. We made a down payment on Luther Monihan's house, the one sitting up on that little knoll that teeters above Mattagash Brook. It was just like new when we bought it. Luther built it himself, and then moved his wife, Jennie, into it, and they set about building up a family. But their first baby was born dead, and then Jennie died a couple days later. Complications, they said. I guess it was one of them things in a woman's body that can go wrong. Luther went a little crazy. There's no other way to put it. He couldn't stay in the house no more, so he sold it to Foster and me for a lot less than it was worth. And Luther went off downstate, or out of state maybe, looking for work, looking for *something*. And no one, not even his family members, ever saw that man again. It was as if the large places of the world had opened up and gulped him down.

I had a pile of doubts about the house. People were saying they could see Jennie's ghost during a full moon. She'd be all dressed in white, like she was in her wedding gown, and she'd be rocking nothing at all in her arms. She'd be rocking back and forth like she was cradling a baby in her arms. She'd be all decked out in her wedding dress, just peering out the window. I suppose she was looking down the road for Luther, waiting for him, knowing he'd come one day, sooner or later, knowing he *had* to. We all do. I never seen Jennie, but she was in my house. I felt her there. And some of my children saw her, when they was real little, too little to make stuff up. Walter, my firstborn, come in one night from the garden with a little button in his hand. "Where'd you get that button?" I asked him, and he said, "From the lady." I says, "What lady was that?" and that's when he told me. He'd been out in the garden catching up lightning bugs to put in a mason jar, when he saw a woman digging up the ground like she was looking for something. When she saw Walt, she stood up and come toward him. "Are you my baby?" she asked him. "No ma'am," he told her. "I'm Walt Fennelson." That's when she reached out and give him a little button covered in white satin. It was the prettiest thing, almost like a little white pearl. And Walter said her hands were cold as ice, but she give him the biggest, nicest smile. And then there was light all around her. "Like she was all lightning bugs, Mama," he told me. He was about five or six years old then. I took that button up the road the next morning. I took it right up and I give it to Jennie's mother. I never said a word about what it was, or where it come from, or nothing. I just put it flat out in her hand. She looked at it for a long, long time, turned it over and over careful as could be, like it had a little life of its own. She looked up at me then, and I saw the tears in her old eyes. "I just wish she could find some peace," she said. And then she went inside her house and shut the door, took the little button with her. And many times over the years, some of my children talked about me covering them up in the night, kissing their foreheads, whispering nice things to them. I knew all the time I hadn't done no such thing, but I never let on it was Jennie. She wasn't hurting them. They were as close as she could come to her own baby, and if you ask me, she must've wanted that dead child real bad. That's a sad thing, you know, when a woman wants a baby so bad that she hangs on to earth looking for one. It seems to me it might've been better for Jennie to let go of all that unhappiness, to go on to something better. But over the years, she become like a friend to me. I guess she might be like them imaginary friends children have when they're little. I couldn't see her, but she was always there. When Mary died, it was Jennie helped me to get through it. All them special children I lost young in their lives, it was like Jennie lost them too. And I believe to this day that Jennie showed my babies the right way to go when they left this life. And I bet she's still there in the old house, wearing her tattered wedding dress, watching, waiting, a little satin-covered button in her hand to give to a special child.

I won't be no ghost after I die because I've seen enough of this life. I been a ghost already, you might say, for more than thirty years, hovering on the outskirts of life, haunting my children with my old age. I had enough babies for me, and Jennie, and my daughter Elizabeth, too. I had babies enough for a dozen women, so you won't see me hanging on to life, not when I been hanging on so long just to leave it. I don't know where I *will* go, but after I die I'm going straight there. You won't catch *me* lingering on the dusty road to the hereafter.

Rod Serling as an Alibi:
The ABCs of Reconciliation

"Don't Come Home A'Drinkin', With Lovin'
on Your Mind"

—Loretta Lynn

*P*ike Gifford awoke on his living room sofa, in the early gray light of his living room, and tried his damnedest to remember where he was. For a second he felt sure he must be at Billy's, maybe even in bed with Ruby, overbite or not. But he was not at Billy's, he realized, noticing Reed's ice skates before him on the floor, and a coloring book belonging to one of the twins. And there was Lynn's big old winter coat puffed up on the recliner, as if spying on him. Pike rubbed his eyes, and then shook his head vigorously, as though he might make the dull ache between them disappear with just a bit of earnest exercise. Jesus, but Lynn was going to be on the rag about this. He'd managed for almost a week to toe the mark, even to drive past The Crossroads with a load of groceries from Watertown and pretend that it was just another establishment, no better or worse than any other establishment.

Pike had not always been able to do this. He could recall one incident that had given Lynn great pause as to whether she should forgive him. It was shortly after The Crossroads opened. Lynn had stayed on with her sister Maisy in Watertown and sent Pike home with that week's grocery supply, so that she could have her hair permed at Angelique's Hair Factory without him coming in a hundred times and asking how many more goddamn minutes he would have to wait out in the car. Pike had done a fine job of zipping past the three drinking establishments in Watertown and felt almost akin to a man in control until he saw Billy's Dodge Ram pulled happily up to the front door of The Crossroads. Pike decided he would go inside and pop down a couple of quick ones—Lynn would be another two hours at least—and maybe catch Billy in the mood for a fast game of cribbage. He drove his car around to the back, nestled in between Maurice's Ford pickup and Sally's old Bonneville with the missing fender. That way there would be no need to upset any of Lynn's relatives should they drive by and, seeing Pike's car there, feel a great need to interrupt the course of their own lives in order to fill Lynn in on some details. But those two beers had gone down even quicker than anticipated, so he'd had another, this time adding his usual vodka. God intended beer to be drunk as a chaser anyway. And what do you know but Pike gave Maurice one of the few shellackings in cribbage he'd ever given him. Maurice died in the shit hole, of all places, only one peg away from winning! Pike *had* to hang around just a bit longer to bask in that glory. And Lynn was supposed to do a bit of shopping in Watertown—a dress for Julie—and that meant she'd probably be longer than two hours and, well, nobody ever said a barroom was the place for a man to do his most logical thinking. Before it was all over, Pike had several sacks of groceries spread out on the bar and folks were making themselves a variety of late-night snacks. Even a couple of canoeists from out of state found the opportunity to down a Devil Dog and some Vienna sausages.

That was in June, and it had seemed to Pike that Lynn was honest-to-God going to leave him. She even had papers served on him, as though he were some kind of dog the Watertown pound needed to know about. But, like the slush of spring, like the mosquitoes of summer, the snows of January, it had all passed, had gone downstream in the river of Lynn's mind. Then Conrad had hit him with the bat—the little trickle of piss—and Pike had gone to convalesce at Billy's house, which was not exactly an intensive care unit. But before the lump had time to leave Pike's head, Lynn had served him with *more* papers. With that kind of workload heaped on him, Pike Gifford would have to start carrying a briefcase. Oliver North had never seen so many documents, and *he* had one of those shredders. Not to mention that secretary.

But Pike had come back with a big box of candy, and had gained admittance once more into the realm of his family. He had actually bought the candy at LaVerdiere's Drugstore in Watertown, when he'd gone in for a pack of cigarettes. He was on his way to visit Ruby, knowing that with her generous overbite she'd have an easy time on the hard-filled type he'd selected. But when he'd driven over to Ruby's house in St. Leonard, he discovered her husband's pickup in the yard, its tan nose pointing proudly at Ruby's front door. It reminded Pike of a dog that had just peed on its territory in hopes of keeping other dogs away. Pike had watched the windows of Ruby's house for a few minutes, for a sign from the female in heat. When none came, he knew without a doubt that Ruby had taken her old man back. It was another one of those *left-out* feelings that overtook Pike then. He thought of Lynn, of the twins, of the television blaring out and the wind whipping about the windows. There was a family over there at his house, his own family, going on without him. Billy could help ease that feeling, but then, Billy was in bed with Claudette, and Pike didn't want to sit on the sofa with Claudette's two kids until she got up and took them home. The Crossroads wouldn't be open for a couple more hours. So Pike took the candy and went on home. He didn't know at the time if Lynn would accept the candy or have him arrested. Sometimes Pike saw his marriage as a kind of lottery: it was anybody's guess.

And now here he was on the sofa, his head pounding, his mouth dry. But it wasn't his fault. There had been something about the snow the night before, about the way his wipers whisked it off the warm windshield that hypnotized Pike. *Michelob, Michelob, Michelob,* the wipers whispered. As he approached The Crossroads, it was all he could do to remember his promise to Lynn. By the time he saw Billy's Dodge Ram and Ronny's Volvo lounging in the front yard, Pike was no longer driving. The old Chevrolet was steering itself.

"Just like one of them cars on *The Twilight Zone,*" Pike thought, but he knew he couldn't say that to Lynn. He'd already used a similar excuse the time he disappeared for three days without a trace, unless one counted the lingering smell of cheap perfume. "I musta stepped right into one of them other dimensions," he'd said to Lynn. "Remember that little girl and her dog who disappeared right through the wall on *The Twilight Zone?*" That was Pike's favorite rerun. "Well, you can step right back," was all Lynn had said. "You're probably more welcome in that other dimension anyway."

Pike sighed heavily and kicked at Lynn's coat. It rolled off the sofa and onto the floor, stiff as a body. He looked at his watch. Four-thirty. It had been sometime before two when Billy dropped him off. He should have made a move *then* to get on up the stairs. He'd have been two and a half hours less in trouble. But the truth was that he was a little too woozy to have attempted a reconciliation at that point. Pike wondered what his chances were now of sneaking up the stairs and perhaps slipping unnoticed into the warm bed beside Lynn. He would love to know the exact time she had last lifted her head and looked at the clock; he would add twenty minutes to that time, and then declare that that was when he'd gotten home. Goddamn, but there were booby traps everywhere when a man took it in his head to keep his marriage together. He could slip in with one of the twins, in one of those narrow little *twin* beds, and pretend he'd been there all night. In Julie's bed, maybe. She didn't spread out and kick as much as Stevie. She had a mouth as big as Lynn's, though—but maybe if he fitted a tightly rolled dollar bill into Julie's little palm, she would keep her tiny trap closed. Pike pulled himself up, decided the trip might be worth it. It was at the top of the dark, creaking, tell-all stairs that he ran into a body standing there, waiting for him.

"Jesus!" he said to Lynn, and flung himself back against the wall. "You scared the shit out of me."

"I'd rather beat it out," Lynn whispered, her teeth clenched. Then she went back into her bedroom, without slamming the door. The children were still sleeping. Pike heard her click the lock on, and took the hint. He went back down to the sofa, where the lengthy shape of his body was well known among the cushions, and stretched out there. He sighed again. Sometimes he didn't know what Lynn expected of him. He understood, suddenly, men like Jimmy Swaggart. With so many pious demands on a fellow to be good, he's just bound to go out and do something awful. But Pike wasn't as well financed as men like Swaggart and Jim Bakker. He wouldn't mind getting his mitts on that little Jessica Hahn, though, now that she'd renovated herself. What more did Lynn expect of him? He'd been toeing the goddamn mark for almost a week now, so much so that his toes hurt. His toes were *stubbed*, you might say. He hadn't even stopped by The Crossroads when he knew it was his cousin Ronny's birthday, and Sally would be baking a cake, and Maurice would send a free drink all around the horseshoe bar.

Pike heard one of the kids get up to go to the bathroom, heels hitting the floor roughly over his head. *Conrad.* Conrad walked on his heels, just as Pike did. A flash of anger swelled up inside Pike. He'd almost had to have stitches put in his head at the emergency clinic in Watertown because of Conrad, and he could still feel the disappearing lump, even though it had been almost two weeks. What was it about Conrad that rankled him so? Lynn had asked him this often, had asked this very question. Why did he seem to hate Conrad? It was like looking at a picture of his childhood self, wasn't it, to look at Conrad? Lynn had even gotten out an old school snapshot of Pike and put it next to one of Conrad. If it hadn't been for the dates below, not even Pike could've told them apart.

Pike heard Conrad flush the commode and then water rush up through the pipes of the house. How many times had Pike told him not to flush in the middle of the night, unless he had diarrhea, because the noise of it usually woke up one or more of the household? The little three-legged faggot. He had to do the opposite of every single thing Pike told him. Pike hadn't been so liberal with his own father, had he? If he so much as opened his mouth to protest, he'd have felt Big Pike's hand bash across it. But Goldie, his mother, had never hit him. So why hadn't he gone off to Connecticut with her, when she'd taken the other children and left Mattagash? Connecticut was a place where you could put on a new life, as though it were a skin you'd just picked out. In Mattagash, your life was like an old winter coat you were forced to wear until it wore out. So why hadn't he gone with Goldie? This was what Pike had asked himself a million times now that his childhood was over, the way a Christmas comes and goes, so fast you don't even know it's happening.

Now he heard Conrad, the picture of his childhood—his childhood self kept alive in the blood and bone and muscle of this oldest son. Conrad's steps came quietly now, tiptoeing to the top of the stairs. Pike could hear the measured, labored breathing coming out of the boy's chest. He opened his eyes and looked up the stairs, saw his son silhouetted there at the top, the dark outline of a boy. Conrad was checking to see if Pike was home. The little snoop. Pike had left the old Chevrolet back at The Crossroads. It simply wouldn't start, not even after Billy dragged out his booster cables and tried to jump it. And in the midst of his happiest, booziest moments, Pike didn't give a damn what Lynn might say about his abandoning the car. She could keep her opinion to herself or tell it to the priest the next time she went to Mass. Now he wished he'd figured out a way to bring the old clunker home. Conrad leaned farther down the stairs, his eyes trying to adjust to the shapes of the room. Pike lay motionless, quiet, watching his son. Conrad tiptoed down three steps and peered about the dark room, his eyes searching out the contours of the recliner, looking to find a body of some sort, his father's body. Pike moved his arm, ever so slowly, down to the side of the couch. His hand felt about the floor until he touched one boot. He locked his fingers around the neck of it and waited. Conrad crept down another two steps, his hand against the wall, balancing himself in the gray light of the morning. Pike saw the outline of Conrad's head turn away, toward the door of the kitchen. This was Pike's chance. In a flash he flung the boot against the stairway wall. He saw Conrad jump, a finicky rabbit's jump, heard the scared gasp for breath rattle in the boy's throat.

"Boo," Pike said softly, from his frozen position on the couch. He laughed sweetly as Conrad beat a crooked retreat back up the stairs and into his bedroom. Pike didn't even care if Lynn heard the racket. She was already pissed at him. And besides, what business was it of Conrad's if Pike was home or not? That little fairy faggot had opened up a gash on Pike's skull with a baseball bat, and it would be a damn long while before Pike forgot about it.

Lynn zipped up Julie's ski suit, found Stevie's mitts, and told Reed not to let the twins go too far out on the pond. Reed was taking them sliding down by the old sawmill hill, where the sleds would not come to a halt until they'd glided a bit out onto the frozen swamp.

"That ice is thin out there in the middle," Lynn said. "And there's just enough water in the pond to freeze your feet off, so be careful." She held the door open and let the three of them tromp past. They found their sleds beneath the porch, where Conrad had pushed them when it started snowing the day before. Now it was a bright, gloriously sunny afternoon. The snow shimmered with a blue-white sheen, hard on the eyes, sharp as glass. The temperature was a superb twenty-five above, but as Lynn watched her children tugging on the ropes of their sleds, she could see their cheeks already turning red with cold. She answered their good-bye waves with a feeble wave of her own. From the kitchen window, she watched until she could make out only the color of their jackets moving against the white expanse of forest; then they disappeared into the pines bordering the swamp. She went back to folding towels out of her laundry basket.

It was half an hour later, after the towels had been neatly stacked away in the bathroom, when she heard Pike's footfalls upstairs moving from the bedroom to the bathroom. He'd gone on up to bed at nine o'clock, after Lynn started a noisy breakfast in the kitchen. Forks and knives and pans banged together in such a metallic cacophony that Pike had taken the culinary hint and dragged himself upstairs. He had flopped, fully clothed, across the mattress of the matrimonial bed. There would be no peace down on the sofa, not with the twins wanting to watch some damn rented movie about aliens, and Lynn slinging her wifely anger about the kitchen. Pike wished, on these lazy, painful, hangover mornings, that Lynn would just go on ahead and slap his face, air her grievance, get the show on the road. It was the silent treatment he hated most, accompanied by things being thrown instead of placed. Pike hadn't gotten off the bus to Mattagash yesterday. He knew the sights and sounds of a woman with her dander up.

Lynn was at the sink, rinsing the plates from lunch, when she heard Pike coming down the stairs.

"Nice mornin'," he said sheepishly. He was standing at the door to the kitchen, waiting for a response. Lynn said nothing. It wasn't morning anyway, it was twelve-fifteen. And even if it were, there was certainly nothing nice about it. It was the typical Sunday after the hangover, no more, no less. It meant Pike sleeping until the late hours, missing another morning of his children getting ready for church. It meant she and the kids were expected to tiptoe like mice while the tomcat slept.

"I'm gonna sign that damn petition that Prissy Monihan has got," Lynn thought. True, Pike and Billy were famous for cruising in the Dodge Ram, a beer between their legs and a bottle of vodka on the front seat, a kind of liquid Meals on Wheels. Closing The Crossroads wouldn't stop them, but it *would* inconvenience them. She heard Pike shuffle into the kitchen behind her, but she went ahead and wiped the counter, pretended not to notice. Pike put his hands on her waist, pinched her rear playfully.

"Come on, Lynnie," he coaxed. "You know how Billy can be.

I'd no sooner finished a beer but what he had another one waiting for me."

"Did he cut your hands off and pour it down your throat?" Lynn asked angrily.

"As a matter of fact," Pike said in good humor, "he did."

"If Billy told you to jump off the Empire State Building, would you do it?" Lynn asked. Pike had to think about this. He had never been to New York City. Who knew what caper he might pull once he was cavorting beneath all those lights? Billy had once dared him to jump off Albert Pinkham's barn, when Pike was only ten years old, and he had done it. That was the interesting thing about being Pike Gifford. You just never knew what you might do.

Lynn pushed him away and moved to the stove, where she began furiously washing it with her dishcloth. Pike waited, wondered what his best next move might be. At least she was talking, no matter that her words were as cold as the temperature outside. Spring was happening somewhere in Lynn, he could sense it. Pike let a minute or so pass before he made his way over to the stove and tried his luck again with placing his hands on Lynn's waist. She brushed them away quickly and turned to face him, the dishcloth clenched in the fist she shook in his face.

"Enough is enough," Lynn said. "I'm tired of watching you drink yourself into an early grave." She pushed her way past him and went back to her sinkful of soapy suds.

"So I spent a Saturday night with Billy," Pike said. "Who's the worse for it but me? I'm the one with the hangover. Didn't you get the kids that outer space movie? They probably didn't even notice I wasn't here." He waited to see how this would settle in. Lynn stopped washing the frying pan to look at him.

"Is spending an evening with your wife and children such an awful thing?" she asked. He could hear panicky emotion behind the words, a threat of tears. A good sign. This meant that the dam of anger had burst.

"You're gonna end up like Big Pike and you know it," Lynn said. "Drinking's gonna kill you."

"Don't you bring him up," Pike said, and now *he* was angry. He had been trying to apologize, to heal the wounds, and here she went and doused them with alcohol, if you could pardon the expression. She knew damn well how he hated for her to mention the elder Pike's death. It was none of her business. "Shut up now," he said, pointing a warning finger at Lynn.

"Oh, I don't give a shit anymore," she said. She threw the dishcloth into the water. Soap bubbles flitted like snowflakes into the air. "You can stay out every damn night. I've had it." She stomped out of the kitchen. Pike listened as her feet hit each step on her way upstairs. Then her bedroom door banged shut. This was step A in the pattern of her forgiveness, and he recognized it easily. Step B was for him to leave her alone for a few more hours. Step C was sliding in to home plate with a big sorrowful smile on his face.

Pike went on up to the twins' room to sleep away a bit more of his Crossroads hangover. He ignored the door to his own bedroom, knowing Lynn had locked it anyway. Let her sulk. He had seen the quick flash of remorse in her eyes. She would come around by evening. He pulled off his boots and settled down nicely onto the pile of blankets on Julie's unmade bed.

A few minutes into his sleep, Pike heard footsteps on the stairs and opened his eyes. From Julie's bed he saw Conrad's head appear, then the narrow shoulders, and soon the full body of his oldest son. Pike knew Conrad had been baby-sitting for his aunt Maisy. He'd heard Lynn on the phone yesterday, before he ambled off to The Crossroads and into a heap of trouble, discussing Conrad's availability for the next day. A *boy* baby-sitting. Lynn was turning that kid into a little faggot. But it seemed Maisy had an Avon brunch she had to attend or she would simply die. A brunch, for Chrissakes, one of those things folks were forever having on *Dallas* or *Dynasty,* but had no business bothering with in Mattagash, Maine. What a lot of foolishness some women could think up, and so early in the morning! Pike used *his* brunchtime to get over a serious hangover.

Pike saw Conrad linger at the top of the stairs. He was looking at Lynn's closed bedroom door, his head canted like some little bird's, listening for sounds. Pike considered reaching down casually for a boot and heaving it out into the hallway. Conrad was turning into a regular little eavesdropper and spy, always trying to size up the relationship between Pike and Lynn. But Pike decided not to. He'd gotten him real good that morning on the stairs, and he didn't want Conrad to become immune to these surprise attacks. Two, three times a month had always been enough. So he lay peering out of half-closed eyes as Conrad gave up his vigil and went on into his own bedroom. Reed was still off sliding with the twins, so he had the room to himself. Pike watched as Conrad fumbled around with the articles on his dresser. He hadn't closed his door because, Pike imagined, he'd assumed his mother and father were in their bedroom asleep. Pike smiled. This was better than a shoe hitting a shin, or a boot tossed against the wall. He liked being the spy for a change. He saw Conrad reach into his pocket and pull something out, money it looked like, a few wadded bills, no doubt his baby-sitting money from Maisy. He squatted in front of the dresser, and while Pike watched, he pulled the bottom drawer out of its grooves and put it quietly on the floor. Then he reached a hand into the darkness and brought out a brown envelope. Pike wondered what the little pack rat was up to this time. He was always hoarding something, this kid, always looking over his peaked little shoulder. Conrad opened the envelope, stuffed the bills inside, stashed the envelope again, and hurriedly fitted the drawer back in place. Pike smiled lazily, his headache gone suddenly in the midst of this new discovery. He'd just seen where the little faggot squirrel was hiding his winter nuts.

Maine as a War Zone:
The Flash of White Gloves

"Hunting is just God's way of telling us that he
created too many animals."

—Paulie Hart, Lottery practitioner
and avid hunter

Dorrie and Lola had caught Charlene
Craft off guard, appearing out of no-
where, silhouetted in the bright sun on her front porch. Charlene
had hoped to dig her snowshoes out, now that it had stopped
snowing and the sun was brilliant on the white fields. She needed
the outing badly. Her legs could use the exercise and her mind a
peaceful, woodsy rest. But they had caught her, face-to-face, when
she'd opened the door to let Otis the cat out to pee.

"We'll only be a second," Dorrie said as she unbuttoned her
bulbous winter coat—her stadium coat, although she'd never set
foot inside such an edifice—and hoisted it off. It kept its shape
stiffly, too padded to bend or lie low. Instead, it stood upright on
the sofa, waiting for its owner to come back again. Charlene was
reminded of those statues on Easter Island. She wondered what

Dorrie's winter coat weighed, and if one lone truck had transported it to the J. C. Penney store in Watertown.

"They claim we're gonna have some male strippers in Watertown next spring," Lola said, her peaked little face a mouse's next to Dorrie's large red beach ball. "Prissy Monihan says that if they bring them to the Acadia Tavern, she's gonna picket, just like she did *The Last Temptation of Christ*."

"She might picket, all right," Dorrie said, and began the job of arranging her bulges onto Charlene's narrow kitchen chair. "But you can be sure she'll get a real good look before she sticks her sign up in her face."

"I wish she'd leave this Crossroads thing alone," said Lola. "She gets that place closed down and we're stuck with our husbands home every night, although Raymond has yet to admit he goes there."

"And it's real helpful to have a close-by place to get a take-out pizza, or have a microwave sandwich," Dorrie added, her mind strolling upon the familiar field of food. Charlene decided she might as well thaw some cobs of corn for supper, might as well accomplish something during her entrapment. She found the plastic bag in the freezer and took it to the sink.

"That's what I like about frozen corn," said Lola, watching. "You don't need to pull them silky little threads off it, like you do the fresh."

"Booster claims that God put them strings on corn to keep women busy," said Dorrie. "Ain't that a hoot?"

"Did you hear the latest about that shooting incident downstate?" asked Lola as she helped herself and Dorrie to the remnants of that morning's coffee. Charlene shook her head. She hadn't heard. Lola put the coffeepot back on its burner. If they wanted fresh coffee, Charlene decided, let them go to a restaurant in Watertown. Let them drive Booster's big yellow pickup/plow on down to Colombia, South America, and get themselves some real fresh coffee.

With the corn on to boil, she leaned against the sink and waited. Why couldn't they at least have called ahead, asked if she was busy? But that was Mattagash for you, or St. Leonard, or Water-town. Your privacy was a shared thing. And there were worse things than people bursting into your kitchen at any hour. The shooting was one of them. Charlene shuddered still to think of it: A woman down in central Maine had been shot less than three hundred feet from her house by a man who claimed he saw a deer in his scope. She'd been wearing white gloves, the warning signal of a whitetail. She'd been feet from her own house, on her own land, and someone had shot her! She was young. She had two little babies, a husband, a family. Now she was dead. Some hunter wanted to bag a deer that badly, to hang it by its hind quarters, to show it to his hunting buddies. He had bagged a hundred-and-twenty-pound woman, thirty-four years old.

"She ought to have known better," Dorrie said, "than to wear white gloves like that during hunting season."

Charlene was dumbfounded. "Are you saying this was her own fault?" she asked Dorrie.

"Well, if you're gonna move here from out of state, you gotta learn to adjust," Dorrie said. "You know. Do as the Romans do when in Rome."

"She should've been wearing bright red," Lola broke in to say. "They got some gorgeous hunting vests at Woolworth's marked down to just a few dollars. They even got funny ones that say *Don't Shoot, I'm a Man* on them."

"What good would that have done?" Charlene asked. "She obviously needed one that said *Don't Shoot, I'm a Woman*."

"They say the man who did it is a pillar of the community," Dorrie said.

"He's going through a lot of pain because of this," said Lola.

"It's too bad she had to wear them white gloves," Dorrie said, and twisted her own gloves on the table before her. No wonder Dorrie felt safe in Maine, Charlene thought. Only a safari hunter anxious to murder an elephant for its tusks could mistake this woman for game.

"Wait a minute," Charlene persisted, hoping to gather a grain of sense out of this insanity. "Are you saying she didn't have the right to walk on her own land, much less just feet from her house?"

"Basically," said Dorrie.

"So to speak," said Lola.

Charlene was hit suddenly with a picture, one she'd seen on the news, of the twin babies, of the husband, of the young woman herself. "Then this is as bad as those gangs in Los Angeles," she said. "This is worse than people shooting you at random on the interstate, if they can shoot you at random on your own damn land!"

"Nevertheless," said Dorrie.

"When in Rome," said Lola.

Charlene felt anger rising up in her face, flushing it. They couldn't have gotten this notion from their husbands. Charlene knew that Mattagash men disdained careless hunters. She remembered Davey discussing the event with old Walter Gifford, the best damn shot in Mattagash before he gave up hunting for good. "The sons of bitches," Walter had said. "They get out there in the woods, and their adrenaline gets pumping, and they claim to see all kinds of things. There ain't no excuse for any of them." Charlene wondered about the white gloves. Had the young woman knitted them herself, not knowing that she was knitting up the final days of her life? Had someone given them to her, a mother or good friend, wrapped them lovingly for her birthday? Had she misplaced them just that morning, almost gone out without them before she remembered them on a top shelf in her closet? It wouldn't have mattered. "He had a license to shoot a buck," old Walter Gifford had said to Davey. "Was she wearing a three-foot set of antlers, too?" Charlene thought of this woman's children. What if they'd been playing only feet from the house, tiny white woolen caps on their heads. Would they deserve the bullet too?

"Well, I just heard on the news where they acquitted him," Lola said.

"Acquitted him!" Charlene was stunned.

"I suppose it'll be some time before he gets over the nightmare of it," Dorrie said, and Lola nodded in sympathy.

"Get out of my kitchen," Charlene said softly, and at first her guests giggled nervously, thinking it a joke, thinking it surely the most foolish social mistake a Mattagash woman could ever possibly make, almost as stupid as wearing soft, delicate, white gloves on a chilly autumn day in your own backyard. What was the woman doing out there? Charlene now wondered. Bringing in some of the children's toys? Hanging things to dry in the frosty air? Cutting down dried flower stalks for winter? Most likely her mind would have been on the babies, on the dishes in the sink, on what to fix for dinner. Then *bang!*—that noisy rude sound which must have made her think a jet had broken the sound barrier in that last lifetime of a second. And then she was dead. Charlene imagined the snow-white gloves drenched in blood before it was all over— soiled, wasted.

"Get out of my house," she said, and saw the shock register on their faces.

"Well, I never," said Dorrie.

"No?" said Charlene. "Then it's about time. Get to hell out."

Lola followed on Dorrie's heels back into the living room and on toward the front door.

"And take this tent with you," Charlene added, picking up the huge burgundy stadium coat and pushing it into Dorrie's red face.

"You just made the biggest mistake of your life," Dorrie said, and believed that statement to be true. Mattagash was a social club. You paid your dues and you kept your mouth shut. You didn't kick the president of the club out of your house when she came to visit, especially if she was accompanied by the secretary/treasurer. But Charlene thought suddenly of the wasted days, the glorious Mattagash mornings that had been ruined by visits from this dynamic duo, the wonderful soft evenings interrupted by the roar of Booster's pickup in her yard. Why hadn't she done this ages ago? She felt a tremendous surge of relief.

"You always thought you was a peg better," Dorrie snapped, angry now, fuming like a big old furnace. Charlene was about to counter, when the phone rang suddenly, a welcome bleat. She quickly picked it up, thankful for something to hang on to, a little job for her trembling hands. It was Dr. Brassard, not his secretary, not anyone else but the good doctor himself, in person. Dorrie was ranting at Lola now, about how city people are just as rude as the folks you see on *The People's Court*. They wear white gloves. They make white-hot statements.

"I'd like to put Tanya in the hospital for just a few days," Dr. Brassard said. "I want to run some more extensive tests. I know this will be tough on her, and on you, but I'm afraid it's the only way we can finally determine what's wrong."

"I'm afraid too," Charlene wanted to say. "Okay," she said instead, as though she were talking to someone at the bank. A doctor of *money* maybe, but not a doctor of children. Lola was searching now for her purse. Dr. Brassard had said his good-bye and hung up the phone, but still Charlene clung to the receiver, could not put it down. It grew firmly on the side of her head, an extension frozen to her ear, bad news solidified.

"You ain't heard the last of this," Dorrie said, buttoning her coat. She pointed a sharp, plump finger at Charlene. "This ain't Connecticut." Upstairs Tanya coughed, a feathery whispery cough that rose up out of her little chest and floated on wings down the stairs to her mother's ears. On angel wings maybe, white as gloves. No one heard it but Charlene. Dorrie and Lola were too noisy with anger to have heard. Only Charlene caught it, as though it were a tiny ball tossed to her, thrown into her motherly hands, and at first she thought it had come out of the telephone and into her ear that way.

"My God," thought Charlene. "What if my baby *dies?* Not like Elvis, who will never, ever die. What if my baby goes away soon, maybe when spring comes and the land will be soft enough to take her back, take her home. What if my daughter *dies*."

"You come up here from New Milford with your nose in the air," Dorrie was saying now, "and how long did it manage to stay up? The whole town knows Davey is going under." But Charlene was no longer paying attention. She hung the phone up softly, placing it in its cradle as though it were a fragile, sleeping child. Above her head, Tanya coughed again and said, "Mama?" It came down to her, this little word, the first word her child had learned to say, it floated down to her from another world, apart from the cold, heavy snow of Mattagash. Listening to it, Charlene did not hear the front door slam angrily.

"I'll tell you one thing," Lola said. "I'm cooking one of them turkeys for the Co-op dinner, and Charlene Craft better not sink her teeth into one bite of it. I don't care if she does pay the four ninety-five."

"It's a damn shame," Dorrie said. She had Booster's bright yellow plow aimed straight at the stores in Watertown, following it as though it were the proverbial ear of corn. "Davey could've married Tina Trudeau straight out of high school. You remember her? She was a Miss Watertown and she come this close to being a Miss Potato Blossom Queen runner-up. She got some kind of award as it was."

"I think it was for being the contestant who'd traveled the farthest," said Lola. She had taken her hair comb out earlier, when Dorrie first stopped in her yard to pick her up, and had scraped the snow on the windshield away enough to allow her a square-foot peephole. Now she was leaning forward on the seat, trying desperately to peer out at Dorrie's careless maneuvers along the snaky highway. It was at times like this that Lola missed the dark smelly tar of summer. She clutched her purse and said nothing. Dorrie had been contradicted once that year, and once was enough.

Dorrie barreled on toward Watertown, her knuckles white as little banks of snow, her thoughts sizzling. How dare that puny little sandwich-eater treat her thusly? Just who did she think she was? Charlene might like to place herself on the uppity shelf next to Eileen Fennelson, who had thankfully gone back to Arizona where she belonged, but it should be remembered that Charlene was, after all, the daughter of former Mattagashers. Her grandmother on her mother's side had had an illegitimate child back around the turn of the century. Dorrie decided it was time to resurrect these old sins.

"No!" said Lola. "Old Natalie had a child out of wedlock?"

"Well, she didn't have it *in* wedlock," said Dorrie, and shifted into third, then second, catching up to the heels of the Mattagash school bus. "She wasn't married."

"I'll be," said Lola, remembering Natalie, dead since the sixties.

"And Charlene's own father, Sidney Hart, got a girl in the family way while he was stationed at Fort Dix. She come to Mattagash with a baby in her arms and went from house to house, like she was the Avon lady, looking for Sidney."

"I remember *that,*" said Lola. "I was only about eight years old. Everybody thought she was with the Gideons at first."

"And there Sidney was, all scheduled to marry Charlene's mother. I tell you, it was a hot time in the old town for a while."

"That girl died, didn't she?" asked Lola. "In a car wreck?"

"The baby too." Dorrie nodded. "Sometime after she went back down to New Jersey. But I bet Miss Charlene Perfect never got wind of all them goings on."

"Someone ought to tell her," Lola said, and looked at Dorrie. Dorrie looked back suggestively.

"Maybe someone will," Dorrie said.

"What say we put this behind us and enjoy the nice, sunshiny day?" Lola asked. She relaxed a bit. Following the school bus had forced Dorrie into a sensible pace. By the time the bus driver signaled the go-ahead for her to pass, Dorrie would regain her composure.

"What's the bus doing out at this hour?" Dorrie asked.

"The kids got a basketball game in Houlton tonight," said Lola. "They must be on their way." She fumbled in her purse for her big double pack of Juicy Fruit. She offered Dorrie a stick. The gum was sweet on their tongues, almost as sweet as the gossip about Charlene's family skeletons, almost as sugary as the words about little babies born marked, of women scorned, of men cornered.

"Sidney's father used to call it Fort Prix for a long time after that," Dorrie said, suddenly remembering old Grant Hart sitting up in front of the big Warm Morning stove at Blanche's Grocery, back in the days when Blanche's father owned the store, and entertaining legions with his puns and witticisms. "That was when

Sidney was stationed at Fort Prix," Grant would say, and a warm volley of hoots would ring out around the jars of molasses and the cloth sacks of flour. In the telling now, in 1989, the same joke found the same home, and laughter bounced again about the cab of Booster's big pickup/plow, its huge yellow lip cutting a bright picture on the road to Watertown. This was a laughter descended, a genetic laughter, a trousseau.

"Speaking of Fort Prix," Lola said. They were just passing Amy Joy Lawler's house and a thought had occurred to her. "Do you suppose it's been Bobby Fennelson that Amy Joy's seeing? Do you suppose that's why Eileen left?" Dorrie thought about this.

"I don't think Amy Joy is Bobby Fennelson's type," Dorrie replied, after a few seconds of pondering. "He's spent all that time in the army, like Ronny Plunkett did, and that changes a man. They get used to them city women with their brash, rude ways. You'll notice Ronny Plunkett ain't dated anybody since he's come home, not to my knowledge, not more than a night or two anyway. I don't think Bobby Fennelson would give Amy Joy the time of day."

"Well, you can just drop your suspicions about Davey," said Lola. "Just because we saw him out driving around last night don't mean he's up to anything. He thinks Charlene hung the moon, *why* I don't know." Davey was, after all, her first cousin, and Lola had always liked him.

"Them's the kind to watch the closest," Dorrie said. "Hey, I got an idea." The earlier humiliation was dying away.

"What?" asked Lola. She had just caught sight of her daughter in a back window of the bus. They exchanged a wave as Dorrie pulled out to pass the lumbering vehicle. It would be a sweet day after all, sweet as Juicy Fruit, sweet as gossip.

"Let's go all the way to Madawaska," Dorrie said. "Just in case Elvis is back at Radio Shack."

A half-mile from his brother's filling station, Davey Craft pulled his car onto an old river road and sat there, engine off, while the outside cold crept deeper into the upholstery, crept into his fingers, into his very bones. The tip of his nose had begun to sting, and yet he could not bring himself to turn the engine back on, to flick the switch that would bring a warm wind of air from the heater into the automobile. If he turned the engine on, he might never shut it off again. He might find himself a length of hose. He might sit there with his car idling, his brain idling, his life idling, as the precious perfume of carbon monoxide swirled up about him and took him off to a bitter end. It was tempting to follow his brother Benny's unwavering footsteps into the abyss, but the terrible truth was that he couldn't abandon Charlene and the kids that way. Davey had read about carbon monoxide poisoning. When it's all over, your blood is a bright cherry red, and there was something enticing about such a brilliant red, as welcome as the first burst of wild cherries on the mountain after the longest of winters. But the vivid memory of his family was like a sharp slap to his face. He had been on his way to ask his big brother, proprietor of Mattagash's only filling station, if he could lend him money. The first time he had ever had to ask Peter for assistance was several months earlier.

"Sure," Peter had said quickly. "Hell yes." And he'd taken out his checkbook and dashed off a check for a thousand dollars, a payment on the skidder and the car. "Never hesitate, kid," Peter had said proudly to Davey. And as much as it had hurt, Davey had appreciated it greatly. The second time was four months ago, after Davey had mortgaged the house. Peter was a little slower in taking out his checkbook that time. But he did, the pen less fluid as he wrote the zeros out in a thick black line. Davey had stared at them, feeling very much like a zero himself. The third time he came to ask Peter for money was only a month ago, and that time Peter was ready for him, had met his eyes firmly and said, before Davey could let the dreaded words fly, "This has been my worst month, kid. My own back is against the wall."

"Hey," Davey had said, his arm waving erratically, his hand trying to shuffle off the notion as unfounded. "I was just coming by to shoot the shit," he lied. But Peter could tell, as most folks can, the bent, beaten stride of a man going under, his eyes heavy as someone who has just drowned, his feet waterlogged. Now he was hoping Peter would be able to help once more—brothers were like lotteries sometimes—but he could not bring himself to drive on. The determination to beg had suddenly gone out of him. He had been the family's shining star, hadn't he? He'd been the one born with the caul over his head, an event that had midwives and other, just plain wives talking excitedly of the truckloads of good luck it would bring him. The good-luck caul, passed down to him from his great-great-grandmother Sadie Craft. The one Benny Craft had not been lucky enough to inherit.

"I had the caul at birth when I had Davey," he could remember his mother saying a thousand times in those long, lazy growing-up years. "It covered his head. Davey was my good-luck baby." Now the goddamn thing was smothering him like some horrible wet shroud.

Davey sat in his car on the old snowbound road to the river and thought about how green money can grow in a man's mind, especially when he's stuck in the white of winter.

Historical Preservation: The Great Pyramid as a Tavern

> O whisky,
> Soul o' play and pranks,
> Accept a bardie's gratefu' thanks.
>
> —Robert Burns, another
> boozer of Scottish ties.

*M*aurice was propped up at the bar, watching his Crossroads sign, his *Where Good Friends, Like the Rivers, Meet* slogan, being dashed about in a frightening, wintry wind. But that was still not quite so frightening as the wind Maurice had been hearing lately about Prissy Monihan and her temperance squad. They had managed to procure enough signatures to entitle them to an emergency town meeting. The wet-versus-dry issue would be aired again, and this time Prissy meant to win.

Maurice ran a winter-white hand through his thinning hair and thought about his rebuttal. Billy and Ronny Plunkett had stopped early for what Billy called "the cocktail hour." A couple of old-timers sat at the end of the bar, gumming whiskeys and remembering the winters of yore, their old voices rising like tired wind above the occasional music of the jukebox.

"The band canceled this weekend," Sally told Billy as she mopped up the perspired beer from beneath his mug. "We would've had a full house. You know how folks get out for a band, even if it's local."

"Which band?" Billy asked.

"Caribbean Magic," said Sally. "From St. Leonard."

"Why'd they cancel?" asked Billy. They were one of his favorite bands, next to The Tennessee Tornadoes from Watertown.

"Paulie Hart is playing bass for them now," said Sally, "and nobody's seen him since he won that thousand dollars in the lottery. I guess he's too high up the tree for us now."

Billy cracked peanuts thoughtfully, his eyebrows knitted with some problem, as he tossed the husks over his shoulder and onto the floor. Ronny was reading a Chilton's fix-it-yourself 1986 Volvo manual, something no real Mattagash man would do. A real Mattagash man wouldn't buy a Volvo anyway. But Ronny had spent twenty years in the navy, and he'd picked up outside notions in places like the Persian Gulf, and the Philippines, and down in the Panama Canal. Ronny claimed he could kick Noriega's ass in a country minute, that he had the testicles to do so, accoutrements George Bush was lacking. In fact, Ronny had such a quantity of ball power that he wasn't afraid to drive a shiny blue Volvo back to Mattagash when his navy stint was up, or to read a repair manual about German parts.

"Your vulva break down again?" Billy asked him, his eyes still on the peanuts.

"Fuck you," said Ronny, *his* eyes still on the manual.

At a corner table, some women snowmobilers from St. Leonard sat with ski suits unzippered to the waist and sipped the foam off beers while they waited for the stunning cold that had infiltrated their bones to vanish. Amundsen, Scott, and Peary would have crumbled at the notion of braving a windchill factor of forty below if they'd been obliged to brave it at sixty miles an hour. Some folks were born to dogsleds.

Sally was putting a large frozen pizza with the works into the new microwave for the hardy snowmobilers. Maurice had decided to begin selling microwave sandwiches, pizzas, and bags of chips after he saw how well the late-night buffet sponsored and thrown by Pike Gifford had gone.

"We gonna do it?" Billy asked Maurice, who looked up, startled, as if he'd forgotten that he was in a bar with other people. It was a quiet, dreamy Friday afternoon that could make a man forget where he was.

"We gonna do what?" Maurice asked.

Sally dumped ashtrays loudly into the big aluminum trash can hidden beneath the bar. One of the snowmobilers finished punching in two songs for a quarter—everyone knew the selections by heart—just as the first began. Billy regarded her rear pensively, a little on the heavy side, her arm muscles loose even inside her sweatshirt. The song was one he hated, the thing about "eighties ladies" by K. T. Oslin. Billy hated it because it was a song about broads with balls, and *they* weren't exactly on his Christmas list. He wondered if he had a prayer in hell that the female snowmobiler had chosen "All My Ex's Live in Texas." Probably not. It wasn't what you would call a women's lib song.

"Are we gonna fight for The Crossroads if they get the dry vote to pass?" Billy asked. He rattled the little wicker basket in front of him against his beer mug, a hint to Sally that he wanted more peanuts. She put another full basket on the bar, and this time Ronny reached out a hand and felt around for some, his eyes still on the Chilton repair manual. He was having a hell of a time with his Volvo. Maybe he shouldn't have bought foreign. Everyone had warned him he'd never find parts in Aroostook County.

"This old house was built at the turn of the century," Maurice reminded Billy. "If you're talking about moving it, forget it. It's hanging together by threads."

"Take a look at this," said Billy, and pulled a folded magazine article out of his pocket. Maurice stared as Billy unrolled it. "The Solved Secrets of the Great Monuments," its heading read, and Maurice saw that it was accompanied by several illustrations.

"Wow," said Maurice.

"Look here," said Billy. He pointed to a picture of a large

bluestone lying flat out on wooden rollers and being pulled by a bevy of little stick men. "Here's how they moved them big stones over in England." Maurice stared in sincere interest.

"But them big stones weigh tons," Ronny interrupted, his eyes still on the Chilton manual. "I know, Bill. I've seen them in person. This old house'll crack in two if you move it."

"And here," said Billy, ignoring his brother's pessimism, "is how one man thinks they moved all them pyramid stones, over two and a half million of them limestone suckers. His name is Edward Kunkel, and he thinks they moved them by pumps, hydraulics, and canals full of water. He even thinks that the biggest of them pyramids is actually one big hydraulic ram pump."

"No kidding," said Maurice, his elbows now on the bar next to Billy, his eyes on the outline of the Great Pyramid before him. Ronny put down his manual. He had visited the pyramids during a stint in the Suez Canal. The mysteries of the pyramids were more interesting than Volvos.

"So?" asked Ronny.

"So we got to use our brains," said Billy. "That's all."

"But I seen the pyramids," Ronny insisted. "It took more than brains, believe me. It took some brawn somewhere."

"You know, Ron," said Billy. "Even when we was kids, I saw the doughnut and you saw the hole. But that ain't my point. What I'm trying to say is that man's been doing the impossible ever since the beginning of time."

"A big hydraulic pump, huh?" said Maurice, and Billy nodded.

"Why?" asked Ronny, a nonchalance in his words. He'd *seen* the goddamn pyramids.

"Because it provided water for the whole area," said Billy, "and think of how cheap it must've been."

"A hydraulic ram pump," Maurice mused. "I'll be damned."

"And there's the Mattagash River running right past our noses," said Sally, waiting for the microwave to announce cooked pizza. "We could make it into a kind of parade."

"If The Crossroads goes down the Mattagash River, you'd have a real float, all right," said Ronny.

"You know who you are, Ronny?" Billy asked. "You're the type who was beating on the door of the ark when the water got up to their chin."

"I *have* seen the pyramids," Ronny muttered. "I've seen fuckin' Stonehenge."

"A big hydraulic pump," Maurice said again. "I'll be damned." He examined an artist's concept of how the Great Pyramid was built, using water locks to float the stones up to the next level of construction.

"This old house'll break in a hundred pieces," said Ronny.

"We could roll it on log rollers," Maurice suggested. "Like that." He pointed to a sarsen stone being pulled on a massive sledge.

"But Maurice, I been trying to tell you," said Ronny. "Them stones ain't exactly the kind you find along the Mattagash River bank." He tapped a large gray lintel, which lay in the photo like a beached whale. "Them suckers *weigh*."

"That ain't it, Ron boy," said Billy, and threw his hands up in exasperation. "The point of all this is that we got *history* behind us. Men have always figured out ways to outwit the odds against them. All them secret chambers in the Great Pyramid, what do you suppose they was for?"

"A kind of bank?" Sally said excitedly. "To keep jewels and stuff?" She had forgotten the pizza and turned her attention instead to pyramids. "Like them little jewelry boxes at the bank where rich folks keep their shit."

"Yeah," Maurice whispered. "A kind of bank." Already he had let go of the handle of his big hydraulic pump.

"Maybe," said Billy. "Sure. Why not?"

"A kind of sawmill," suggested an old-timer who had come to lean over Billy's shoulder. "With all kinds of sluices for the logs to slide down."

"Or maybe they were rooms where travelers slept," Ronny said, staring now at the Queen's Chamber and the King's Chamber, both master suites one would never find at the Caribou Days Inn.

"That's it!" shouted Billy, excitement widening his eyes, the poetry of the moment taking him up in its arms. No matter how far Ronny had traveled, no matter how much he'd seen, Billy knew he could always reel his big brother back home, back to Mattagash, could always lure his attention right into the palm of his hand. "That's the idea!" Billy said happily. "It's whatever you want it to be!"

"A big bar," said Maurice sadly, "where men could go and drink in peace, to get away from women like Prissy Monihan." A large sigh escaped his chest, a henpecked sigh rising up from centuries of beleaguered men.

"Dammit, why not!" Billy exclaimed, and punched his fist down on the bar.

"So," said Maurice. "That's it then? We move the building next spring?"

"No," said Billy. Anticlimax was rampant. "That was my first plan, and you might say it was faulty. Ron's right. This old building ain't stone. It's on the last of its wooden legs."

"What then?" said Maurice. His mind was coming around again, full circle, to the huge hydraulic pump.

"What else do we know about this old house?" asked Billy, his lessons in humanity and creativity still going on.

"It'll break up," said Ronny.

"It's held together by threads," said Maurice.

"And what else?" asked Billy, making them work.

"Well, let's see," said Maurice. He helped himself to some peanuts, sensing one of Billy's magnificent puzzles in all of this. "My grandfather Foster Fennelson built it."

"No he didn't," Sally said. "A man named Luther Monihan, related to all the Monihans around here, *he* built it."

"What else do we know about this house?" Billy persisted.

"Well." Maurice finished off a peanut. "I do know that my father, Casey, was Foster and Mathilda's youngest son, and they give the old homestead to him."

"And after Daddy got killed when that skidder rolled on him," said Sally, "the house went to Maurice." Brother and sister made eye contact.

"Well, I *am* the oldest son," Maurice added. Billy smiled. He remembered the gossip about Casey Fennelson and the skidder. Talk around town had been divided, with the women declaring that Casey was just another casualty of the Fennelson curse, another inheritor of the bad-luck gene. Men, on the other hand, were positive Casey had been more a victim of the stupid gene. He'd been known to drive that skidder through the woods as though it were some kind of orange speedboat. However, Billy had more important issues on his mind.

"But what else?" he asked, impatient with his players.

"It was moved down here from Mattagash Brook around 1950," said Maurice, "and it's been sitting here ever since."

"It was moved here in 1960," said Sally. "All except the summer kitchen and the barn." She looked sharply at Maurice. "I'm the oldest daughter. I should know."

"It ain't my fault the old man wanted me to have the house," Maurice said pitifully.

"Yes it is," said Sally. "You asked him for it."

"No I didn't," Maurice lied.

"There's trees growing out of the windows of the summer kitchen," said Sally. She ignored Maurice's tearful expression. "And the roof of the old barn caved in on itself. I saw it once, on a canoe trip. The house used to be white back then. It's really kind of sad."

"But what *else?*" Billy whispered dramatically. He pushed the basket of peanuts closer to Ronny and then went at his teeth with a fingernail. Peanut bits were hell to pick out of crevices, harder sometimes to move than lintels.

"It's supposed to be haunted," Sally continued. "Folks have said so for years. Maurice is so afraid of ghosts that he won't go upstairs alone."

"That ain't true," Maurice lied again. "There just ain't no reason to go up there, other than the front room where we store stuff. The rest is just old empty rooms and creaky floors."

"Boo!" Ronny shouted, and grabbed Maurice by the nape of the neck.

"Goddamn you, Ron!" Maurice choked, his face berry-red, his heart fluttering. He'd been jumpy since kindergarten, and so most folks in Mattagash had long tired of ambushing his nerves. But Ronny Plunkett had been gone for most of the last twenty years, and it seemed to Maurice that Ronny had a bushel of *boo*s to get out of his system.

"The town was supposed to buy it from Daddy to make a new town office," Sally went on in the same level voice. She was used to seeing Maurice jump. "But everybody fought so much he just left it sit here."

"Goddamn you, Ronny Plunkett!" Maurice sputtered.

"Grammie Mathilda's still alive," said Sally. "She's at Pine Valley."

"She must be almost a hundred," Maurice said, his voice shrill. But he was hoping to regain his place in the conversation and, thereby, his composure.

"She's a hundred and seven," said Sally. "To be exact." She and Maurice made more sibling eye contact.

"Hell, she's that old?" asked Ronny. "How old's this house?"

"It was built in 1906," said Maurice.

"In 1896," corrected Sally.

"Oops," Maurice said apologetically. "Don't you ever do that again," he whispered to Ronny.

"Foster and Mathilda bought it in 1897," said Sally. "I looked this all up for the Mattagash Historical Society."

"Some of it is put together with wooden pegs, instead of nails," said Maurice. "That's how they built things back then."

"Well, Christ Almighty," said Ronny. "This is one hell of an old building then."

Billy jumped to his feet and thrust both arms up toward heaven.

"Bull's-eye!" he screamed. "This is a goddamned historical site!"

"A historical site, huh?" Maurice said.

"It's the oldest house in Mattagash, all right," said Sally. "Maybe even in Aroostook County."

"Ladies and gentlemen," Billy said. "What you missed while you were tramping through the fuckin' forests to find the goddamn trees is the whole point of this little talk." He took another clipping from his pocket, this one from the *Bangor Daily News,* and spread it dramatically on the bar. PRESERVATION TO BEGIN ON STATE'S OLDEST BUILDINGS, the headline declared. Then, while the others read, he began looking for a quarter or two in his pocket. It was high time he heard "All My Ex's Live in Texas" again. He felt good. He had reunited the Druids, had given them hope for a ceremonial clearing in the forest.

"So what should we do now?" one of the Druids, Maurice, asked. "What's gonna happen to my bar?"

"That's just it, Maurice sweetheart," said Billy. "This ain't a bar anymore." He pushed Q12. George Strait had just won "Entertainer of the Year" last month down in Nashville, down in good ole Music City.

" 'All my Ex's live in Texas,' " George Strait sang. " 'That's why I hang my hat in Tennessee.' "

"Amen, George," said Billy. "I hear you." He looked up to see Pike Gifford sauntering in, a big Gifford grin spread clear across his face.

"Just in time for my favorite song, huh?" Pike said as he flung his green felt hat on the deer antlers. Billy returned the smile.

"Well, don't just leave us hanging," said Sally. "What is it you're talking about?"

"This ain't a bar anymore, that's what," Billy said. He pushed B7, " 'Til I'm Too Old to Die Young," his second favorite song.

"It ain't?" asked Maurice, imagining himself the proprietor of a huge hydraulic pump.

"It ain't?" asked Ronny.

"Negatory," said Billy. He looked at his companions. Sometimes it seemed no matter how he taught them, they were destined to remain philistines.

"What then?" asked Sally.

"It's a museum," Billy Plunkett announced, "that serves refreshments."

Another Kind of Snow Job:
The First Supper

> And as they sat and did eat, Jesus said, Verily I say
> unto you, One of you which eateth with me shall
> betray me.
>
> —Mark 14:18

A my Joy had spent a few toss-and-turn nights over the situation with her mother. Sicily had her rights, after all, didn't she? Maybe the best thing would be to find someone willing to move in and care for Sicily, so that Amy Joy could move out and into a little apartment in Bangor, or near her horrible relatives down in Portland. Then she could find one of those "experience helpful but not necessary" jobs she'd been dreaming of for years. Checking out books at a library would be a nice occupation, Amy Joy supposed, an opportunity to run a finger across the covers and titles of nature guides she never realized existed.

But what had occurred to her, during those sleepless nights, was what she'd be giving up in order to dally in city life. Where would she find another McKinnon Hill? Where would she walk in summer fields of sweet clover and cow vetch and forests of thickly sprouted pines if she ended up on the third floor of some apartment building in Portland? Amy Joy wondered if there were any woods left in Maine where it might be safe to walk. The whole state was abuzz with what had happened to Karen Wood, who had had the misfortune to walk one hundred and thirty-four innocent feet from her own back door. Some hunter had focused on her little white gloves in his scope and had put a bullet in her chest. Amy Joy used to think that things like that might happen if you trespassed on someone else's land. But nowadays there were so many trigger-happy, bear-hunting, deer-hunting, moose-hunting, partridge-hunting bastards from downstate and from out of state crawling through the woods of Maine that no one was safe any longer on their own land. But there were issues closer to home that Amy Joy had to contend with first. *Sicily.*

Just when Amy Joy had decided to let the move to Pine Valley rest—and assumed that Sicily had come to the same conclusion —she returned from a windblown outing on her snowshoes to find her mother all packed up. Two small suitcases and a cardboard box were waiting by the kitchen door. Sicily was sitting on the edge of the living room sofa, wearing her coat and scarf and gloves. During the past few days, she had spoken only brief replies to Amy Joy's questions. And she'd spent even more time on the phone to her pal Winnie, talking in soft whispers, quickly hanging up whenever Amy Joy entered the room. Now here she was, ready to go.

"What's this all about?" Amy Joy asked. She pulled off her snowy boots and left them by the door.

"No need to take your boots off," Sicily said. "I need a ride."

"Where, might I ask?" said Amy Joy.

"Yesterday I called that Grandmaison woman," Sicily said. "They're expecting me."

"You what?" Amy Joy was appalled. This didn't appear to be one of Sicily's ploys after all, not if she had enlisted Patrice Grandmaison into the drama. Not if she'd packed up all her precious belongings. She loathed for her things to be trifled with. Yet in Sicily's bedroom, Amy Joy saw the aftermath of some serious packing. Bright squares adorned the walls where pictures had hung. Drawers were empty. In the closet was a huge box labeled *Junk.* On the dresser sat the last picture of Ed Lawler, in his gray principal's suit.

Amy Joy remembered it, recalled the day, her eighth-grade graduation. She had a photo of Ed somewhere in her scrapbook, taken on that same day, in the same gray suit, with the same squinty eyes, with the entire twelve-member class, his arm around Amy Joy in a congratulatory grasp. Reginald Monihan, one of the faces in that same graduating class, had had a sweet crush on her back then. He had carried his crush all through high school, had most likely lugged it across the ocean to Vietnam. Amy Joy still had, in her big lifetime scrapbook, a lacy valentine Reginald had given her, with *Love Always, Reggie* scrawled across the bottom. And she kept his high school class picture on a shelf in her bedroom, with other important faces from her life. Sometimes at night, waking from another nightmare of babies—babies needing her to change them, to feed them, to diaper them, desperate babies she couldn't seem to reach with her dream arms that were grown much too short—Amy Joy took down the picture of Reginald Monihan and wondered about the crooked twist of fate, crooked as the Mattagash River. *See You Later, Alligator* was the inscription. Then he'd gone off to the army, and Amy Joy never did see him later. But he had died a hero. Ed had committed suicide. Yet there was something to be said about both deaths. Most folks simply die.

"Why aren't you taking this picture of Daddy?" Amy Joy shouted out to Sicily, but received no answer. Sicily had decided earlier not to answer her when asked. How could she explain to Amy Joy that Ed Lawler, who was forty-eight years old in the picture, forty-eight years old when he died, was far too young to be dragged off to an old folks' home. Sicily said nothing.

"What's this all about?" Amy Joy asked again, going back into the living room. "You don't need to do this, you know. I was wrong to even suggest it." She noticed suddenly that the lines around Sicily's mouth were more numerous, the gray in her hair more desperate, her eyes sprouting more yellow.

"She's grown older just this past year," Amy Joy thought, and was horrified to realize it.

"My mind's made up," Sicily said. She took her gloves off and then, rather than have them idle in her hands, put them back on again. Amy Joy bit the inside of her cheek.

"At least wait until Thanksgiving is over," she suggested gently. "That'll give you a bit more time to get used to it."

"No," said Sicily, "that'll give *you* more time to get used to it. I don't want to spend Thanksgiving here," she added tartly, and reached out to the geranium on the end table. She snapped a brown leaf off its stalk. Things were dying everywhere, it seemed.

"Wait till after Thanksgiving," Amy Joy said again, her heart beginning to drum a bit. What had she done? What would life be like, after all these years, without her mother? This was a serious Sicily before her. Amy Joy knew her games well enough, surely, to recognize that this was not one of them.

"I got nothing to be thankful for," said Sicily. She placed the dead leaf on the soil of the pot, left it there to become fertilizer, just as she was on her way to becoming fertilizer.

"We'll bring Winnie for Thanksgiving dinner," Amy Joy offered magnanimously.

"Winnie's got the flu," said Sicily, and she pushed herself up out of the cushiony chair, adjusted her legs beneath her, made sure they still worked. She clutched her purse under her arm.

"You'll have to lug that stuff out for me," she said, matter-of-factly, pointing to the suitcases and the box sitting in the hallway. "You can keep my furniture." Amy Joy looked at her mother's belongings. Two suitcases and a cardboard box, all plenty big enough to hold the remnants of a life, not to mention the box full of *Junk*. Tears shot quickly to her eyes.

"Mama, please," she said. She looked at Sicily, her closest relative. "I never wanted it to be like this."

"There ain't no other way to do it," Sicily said, and suddenly she seemed so much more *grown* than Amy Joy had ever imagined. She seemed like the mother again, and Amy Joy the sniveling child.

"There ain't no easy way," said Sicily. "You should've thought of that. Now you put up with it."

At Pine Valley, Sicily was given a room just across the hall from Winnie's. It was a room without a view, but in her secret transactions with Patrice Grandmaison, Sicily had mentioned that she wanted to be as close to Winnie Craft as possible. A Mrs. Gauvin from St. Leonard was only too happy to switch her dingy, viewless room for the sunny one Sicily had offered to trade.

Sicily sat on the bed while Amy Joy unpacked and arranged her things. The conversation between mother and daughter was civil, constrained, the talk that washes between strangers.

"You stop that," Sicily had said to Amy Joy in the car as they made the torturous drive to Pine Valley, past the rickety ruins of Albert Pinkham's old motel. "I don't want to hear it. That's not part of the bargain. If you got tears, you save them for private." So Amy Joy had reduced her crying to the occasional sniffle.

"This is the hardest part," Patrice Grandmaison had whispered to Amy Joy when she saw her blotched, unhappy face. "But each day it gets easier. Pretty soon it'll seem as though it was always this way."

Amy Joy wondered about this as she arranged pictures on the Pine Valley bookshelf in Sicily's room, folded items into the drawers of a Pine Valley dresser, hung coats and dresses in a Pine Valley closet. Sicily sat on her Pine Valley bed and stared at the wall.

"You can come home whenever you want to," Amy Joy was saying. "You just call and I'll come get you. You got your own phone here, remember."

Old faces peered in the door at the new arrival, the new kid on the block. Faces from other generations, those ghostly residents at Pine Valley, paraded slowly up and down the shiny tiled hallway, up and down, up and down, a mindless treading, their footfalls so cobwebby, the shells of their bodies so light as to leave no sound at all.

Patrice Grandmaison appeared in the doorway with a small "Welcome to Pine Valley" basket of fruit.

"In the winter our residents do their walking in the hallway," she explained. "Too much snow and cold outside. And too much slippery ice." Amy Joy watched as the skeletons of old lumberjacks, men who could turn logs beneath their feet like the best of acrobats, filed past the doorway. She watched the passing outlines of aging women, women who had helped to birth small towns, who had baked a million loaves of bread, had knitted up miles of yarn. Like years, they ambled past. Sicily ignored them. She was now one of their numbers.

"Mrs. Craft just woke up," Patrice said. "I didn't tell her you're here. I thought since you girls are such good friends, you'd want to rush right in there and surprise her yourself."

"Damn," Amy Joy thought. "She's making it sound like a pajama party." She peeked at Sicily. Surely her mother would respond to that. *We ain't girls,* Amy Joy could hear her mother inform Ms. Grandmaison sharply. *I'll thank you to remember that.* But Sicily did not rise to the occasion.

"How's her cold?" she asked vaguely, her head rising like a turtle's up out of its slump to look at Patrice. Amy Joy wished she'd look at *her* just once, but Sicily had been avoiding her daughter's eyes.

"Much better," said Patrice. "Dr. Brassard takes very good care of folks here. He makes his rounds of Pine Valley every single weekday."

"I'll try not to get sick on the weekend," Sicily said flatly, and Amy Joy smiled. That was a little of the old McKinnon punch she was used to in her mother. Patrice Grandmaison smiled too.

"Dr. Brassard, or one of the doctors from Watertown, is on call at all times," she said. "And guess what? You're just in time for your first supper at Pine Valley. We're having a nice chicken stew with doughboys." *First* supper. Sicily finally looked at Amy Joy. *One of you has betrayed me.*

"Ooh, does that sound good," Amy Joy chattered, and was suddenly embarrassed at her own attempt to pick up Patrice Grandmaison's condescending pretenses. Her mother knew her much too well to be fooled by an airy voice. Did Patrice ever

The Weight of Winter

manage to convince new Pine Valley residents that their arrival there was a marvelous bit of luck?

"I wanna see Winnie," Sicily said, and eased herself slowly off the bed.

"Well, Sicily McKinnon!" a wavering voice said from the doorway. It was Blanche Henderson, who had operated Blanche's Grocery in Mattagash for thirty years, until a fire in 1975 had eaten the old building up in a swift fury. Now Blanche teetered at the door, surrounded by the silvery aluminum legs of her walker. After a little chat, she inched her way on down the hall, a huge metallic spider.

"I'll see you at supper," she called back.

"We were in the same class, Blanche and I were," Sicily told Patrice. *See you later, alligator.*

"There now," Patrice patronized further. "See? You're going to have all kinds of company here."

They ate in Winnie's room, on that first evening, with Winnie in bed still, although her bout with the flu was nearly over. Amy Joy and Sicily sat in front of table trays at her bedside. Amy Joy was surprised at how tasty the stew was, as well as the nice little salad and the spectacular slab of chocolate cake; but Sicily never touched the food.

"You get used to it," Winnie said weakly to Sicily, who simply shrugged.

"They still gonna give your mother a plaque at the Thanksgiving Day Co-op Dinner?" Sicily asked.

"I suppose so," said Winnie. "That peaked-faced girl of Rose's come back again and told me the Women's Auxiliary's gotta give a plaque to someone every year. They already give one to Walter Fennelson, Larry Fennelson, and Reginald Monihan for dying in wars, and now they're desperate. They can't find anyone else important."

"How's Albert Pinkham doing?" Amy Joy asked. She imagined that one year Simon Cross might be given a plaque for having read and delivered the mail for over thirty years. *Someone important.*

"Alive, I guess," Winnie said. "The ambulance come this afternoon. I was afraid it might be for Mama, but it wasn't. Some woman from St. Leonard took ill. I never knew her. She didn't say much."

"She okay?" Sicily asked, and Winnie shrugged her shoulders, as if to ask, *What is okay? That you get to come back to Pine Valley and try for another month? A year?*

"Patrice tells me they play a lot of Charlemagne here," Amy Joy said. "Didn't you two used to be partners in Charlemagne tournaments?"

"Most of the people who play here speak French," said Winnie. "They bid in French and they joke in French. I think they even breathe in French."

"You could get Blanche," said Amy Joy. "And then you'll only need one more. Surely there's another English-speaking person here who likes to play Charlemagne."

"I'm going to my room," Sicily said. Unlike Winnie, she had yet to grow accustomed to the cheery voice of the family member, a soft drone of guilt wafting in between the invisible bars at Pine Valley. "I'll come tell you good night, though," she said to Winnie, "before I fall asleep."

Amy Joy said good night to Winnie, who merely nodded. In Sicily's room, she sat on the Pine Valley chair and waited while Sicily used her own little bathroom. She was cleaning food particles out of her dentures, Amy Joy supposed, as she listened to water running in the bathroom sink. The room looked very much like a motel room, a space reserved for someone passing through. Would it ever grow to be lived in, comfy, homey? Would newspapers and clothes and knickknacks and dust balls pile up high, as they did in Sicily's old room back at the McKinnon homestead? Amy Joy imagined not. Except for the occasional drawings from grandchildren taped to Winnie's wall, her room looked exactly like Sicily's, and Winnie had been at Pine Valley for more than a year.

"I'm going to call you the minute I get home," Amy Joy offered.

"To say good night." But Sicily unfolded her spare blanket, spread it out on her bed, and said nothing.

"Why are you acting like this?" Amy Joy finally asked, exasperation raising its familiar head. "I told you to forget I ever said the words 'Pine Valley' to you. You can come home with me right now if you want to." Sicily still said nothing. Down the hall, at the front desk, a phone rang loudly several times before someone answered it. Employees came and went in the hallway, their voices flippant, free, rising above the circumstances at Pine Valley. Through the walls of the next room came the wavering voice of an old man as he murmured his rosary in French. *Je vous salué, Marie. Pleine de grâce. Le Seigneur est avec vous.*

"Come on," Amy Joy said softly. "Come on home with me. I'll come back for your stuff tomorrow." Sicily shook her head. She went to her dresser and found her nightdress in the top drawer where Amy Joy had guiltily placed it.

"I'm staying here," Sicily said. She found her slippers where Amy Joy had left them at the end of the bed. "Now I need to wash up before bed, so you go on home," she said, and flicked the tip of her fingers at Amy Joy, as if to make her disappear. "That Grandmaison woman is right. Pretty soon it'll seem like I always been here."

"Mama," Amy Joy pleaded, "I was wrong. This was a mistake. I can see that now."

"Listen," Sicily said sharply. "Even when you was little, you spoke your mind. Like your father spoke his. That's where you got that habit, and it ain't your fault. And you're a lot like your aunt Pearl, too, I'll admit that. She couldn't hold her tongue either, but sometimes, when you let a tongue go, it says some things that need to be said. The whole country does this nowadays. It ain't just you. So stick by your guns the way Pearl would've. I lived my life. It's time you lived yours."

"I'll call you," Amy Joy said. "To say good night."

"You already said it," Sicily noted. "So go on home."

Back in Winnie Craft's room, Sicily was tucking her old friend into bed.

"Just you wait," Sicily was saying. "It's only a matter of days until she's down here begging me to come back home."

"I hope you're right," Winnie said. "If you ain't, that means you're already home."

"I know Amy Joy Lawler a whole lot better than she knows herself," said Sicily. She was brushing Winnie's long gray hair, finally freed from its daytime bun. "Travel, my foot. She ain't even been out of the state of Maine. Where's she gonna travel to?"

"She mighta heard you on the phone," Winnie reminded her. "Talking to me."

"No, she didn't," said Sicily. "All she hears anymore is bird calls. All she sees is them flowers and leaves she pastes into books. This'll just remind her of a few things."

"Well," Winnie said, remembering her dreadful experience with her own daughter Lola. "I hope it don't backfire."

"It won't backfire," said Sicily. "She'll be on her knees in no time. And like I been telling you on the phone, I ain't leaving here without you."

"Do you think she'll take us to the Co-op dinner?" asked Winnie, always one to go for the proverbial yard once the foot appeared certain.

And Amy Joy did call, several times, beginning at nine o'clock, Sicily's traditional bedtime while she was still lodging at the old homestead. But the phone rang and rang without an answer. Amy Joy imagined the rings bouncing off the lime-green walls, pinging off all the silver walkers, ricocheting off the dentures soaking in all those glasses. At nine-thirty she gave up, supposing that she would keep the whole institution awake if she persisted. In all her years of knowing Sicily, there had never been such a coup as this, although Sicily had pulled some whoppers. But something genuine was going on inside of her mother, Amy Joy felt certain, something the daughter had unknowingly set in motion. Surely by morning

Sicily would be her old self, would be on the phone before the first cold rays of the sun cut across the frozen river to light up the crusty trees in the yard at Pine Valley.

It was almost ten p.m. when she heard Bobby Fennelson at the kitchen door.

"It's going to snow," he said as he pulled his boots off by the door. "The weathermen are saying two or three inches but, believe me, we're in for more than that. Do you see what that sky looks like?"

"I don't think I can stand it," Amy Joy told him. Her problem was weightier than snow. "Patrice Grandmaison says it's natural to feel guilt for a while. But I don't think I can stand it. I feel so selfish." He put his arms around her.

"There," he said. "Nothing's final, is it? At least not while everyone is still alive." He rubbed the back of her neck and she jumped at the cold of his fingers.

"Well," she said. "Come on into the house. We've got it all to ourselves, for what it's worth."

For the first time, they sat in the living room before the television, sat like an old married couple and watched faraway people moving around in Hollywood dramas. Amy Joy made popcorn and gave him a beer, and then, when eleven o'clock sounded on the old McKinnon grandfather clock, she nudged him awake. He rubbed his eyes and asked, "Did I fall asleep?"

"You'd better get on home," she reminded him. "It's already eleven, and five o'clock is gonna come early."

"I ain't going home tonight," he said. "I'm staying with you. I don't have to go home anymore. Eileen's gone. Remember?"

"Are you crazy?" Amy Joy asked him. "Do you want the Snoop Sisters to catch you here?"

"Let them." He put his arm around her neck, pulled her closer, edged her head over on his chest. "I don't want to go home." He massaged his fingers across closed eyelids, soothing them. "My eyes hurt," he said.

"Did you get something in them?" Amy Joy put her own fingers where his had been, took up the job for him.

"I had to do some welding today," he said.

"And you did it without wearing a mask, right?" Amy Joy asked. "Why do the men around here feel that they have to punish themselves so much? What's wrong with wearing a mask, for crying out loud?"

"I was in a hurry," he said. "And I couldn't find it."

"Please don't do it again," Amy Joy pleaded. She put a soft little kiss on each of his lids. "Okay?" He opened his eyes and looked at her. She could see that they were very red, sore-looking.

"Jesus, I'm tired," he said. "Winter's just started, and already I'm tired. Maybe I should've just packed up and gone south with the birds."

"You need to take better care of yourself," she told him.

"Yes, Mother," he said.

"Come earlier next time," she reminded him, "so we can spend more time together. Maybe I'll even cook us a nice supper." Being able to sit comfortably in front of the TV, to chat in normal voices, they had not bothered to go upstairs and sink down into the soft mattress of the old bedstead. But he would be back. And now she had all this time alone, all this lonely house.

It did snow that night of Sicily's departure from the big lumbering house her father, the Reverend Ralph C. McKinnon, had built at the turn of the century. Wind-driven snow bombarded the house as if it were being blown out of some big Hollywood machine. But it was genuine as hell as it circled the pole lights of town, swept in over the frozen river, dumped six inches of pure white. In the night, in the heart of the storm, Amy Joy came wide awake to the noise of the town's plow filtering in to her ears, passing the house in a scraping wave of snow, then dying away in its own sound. She'd had a bad dream, hadn't she? But she couldn't pull the threads of it together, couldn't recall what the little terror had been. Outside, it was impossible to see the pole light. The white hump of her car, a fluffy whale, lounged near the front steps. She noticed the outline of what looked like her shovel leaning against the garage. She wished the garage were big enough for her car, but it wasn't. Marge McKinnon had built it for flowerpots, and garden implements, and the lawn mower—more a toolshed really, since she had never come to own a car herself. One of these days, Amy Joy promised herself for the millionth time as she watched the snow covering Mattagash, one of these days she was going to buy up some lumber, hire a carpenter, and make that garage believable. In the meantime she lay back on her pillow and did all she could to count the nighttime sheep that jumped beneath her closed lids, sleek, white, snowy sheep, bouncing through the biggest, worst, deepest storm of 1989, skipping like sacrificial lambs to the inevitable slaughter.

Memories of Home:
The Weight of Winters Past

> To house and garden, field and lawn,
> The meadow gates we swang upon,
> To pump and stable, tree and swing,
> Good-by, good-by, to everything!
>
> And fare you well for evermore,
> O ladder at the hayloft door,
> O hayloft where the cobwebs cling,
> Good-by, good-by, to everything!
>
> —Robert Louis Stevenson,
> "Farewell to the Farm"

You think you know about snow? Well, let me tell you about moonlight nights in the blue of January that come right out of dreams. They're too blue, too crackling with cold to be real. That's when the pines would be all crusted with snow, just like they was baked that way. And all the needles would be glistening like glass. Up overhead you could see Orion shimmering, the buckle on his belt so cold your fingers would stick to it if you could touch it, the way your tongue sticks to a pump handle, or to a frosty windowpane. The thing to do when that happens, the trick of it, is not to panic but just breathe out some warm breath to melt the frost. That way your tongue'll let go with all its skin. If you don't, mind this, you'll carry a sore tongue around in your head for a few days.

I got two important memories of snowstorms, one when I was a child, one when I had children of my own. There ain't been a day of my life, when I've looked out a window and seen the first flake, that these two memories ain't come straight back to me. The first one was of my papa, the night he died, in the heart of that big storm, back in 1890. Winter is one thing. A blizzard is something else. We couldn't see the barn from the house. I tell you, you wonder where God is when he makes his mind up to let it snow like that. It makes you think God has turned his head south, ignoring you. Or he covers his holy, blessed eyes and pretends not to see what he's wrought. In them days you went hungry when the snow trapped you in, like scared rabbits in a hutch. You dug away what you could from the door, and you waited, and you dug away more, and you watched the sky. If you got a sick child it stays sick, unless it dies. There's no getting a sick child out at times like that. That snow comes down so heavy you drag your feet just from carrying it on your shoulders. I'm talking about snow most people only read about.

I was eight years old when Papa died. He had a cancer of the stomach and had been sick a good time. Anything he ate he'd throw back up in a thick yellow fluid. And even in winter he'd break all out in a sweat. Back then you might visit a doctor just long enough to get the medical term for what was killing you, but that was it. He'd been in an awful lot of pain all that beautiful long autumn. So I suppose that when the storm hit that next January, he was ready to lay down the burden of life. And there we were, snow packed right up to the door like we was in a big white prison. Mama wrapped the oldest blanket around him, the one with the yarn-patched holes, because we needed the better ones. Then she broke some pieces of bark off the firewood, shaped a little cross, tied it with yarn, and she put it in his hands, just like he was a Catholic, or something. I remember how Papa's face was all drawed inward, like he was still sucking on his pipe, going for the last puff. My brothers Percy and Oscar, the oldest boys, they dug the door open until it was wide enough to put Papa outside. It was the best we could do. It was five days before they could get to the barn to feed the animals, and then half of them was dead. So Papa sat out in the snow, not taking up any more space than is necessary in death. We could see him through the window, a thin creamy layer of snow covering him at first. Then humps of snow, so that he looked like a snowman. And pretty soon the snow was so deep on him that he could've been a stump, or an old log, or a little hill of rocks. And then he was completely gone. It was like the earth had whisked him into her mouth and took him down to her own hungry belly.

They were long, them nights of snow banging at the eaves, black nights, when the oil lamps had been blowed out to save oil, and the fire snapped. Keep in mind we burned our table, chairs, and part of one wall before it was all over. How do I explain to you how whispery them nights was, snow hanging like a net over our camp, the wind banging and rattling like some runaway train. Me and my brothers and sisters all huddled in the same bed for body warmth. When I was sure they was all fast asleep, I'd sit up in bed and I'd listen real hard, so hard my heart would rise up in my throat like a little Adam's apple. And I'd hear it. So help me, as Jesus is the savior of all things, even things that go unexplained on the earth, I'd hear Papa's voice rising like a song above the storm. Words fluttering like butterflies out of that snowy cocoon he'd become. "He's saying his prayers," Mother would whisper, and the wind would rattle the windows. And the coyote's throat would whine like it was broken, the whine of the hungry. That's when I would imagine I was flying, and I'd look down on our camp from the air, happy I could still see a bit of the stovepipe, the line of the road. "He's saying his prayers," Mother would whisper in the dark, and I'd slide my little house of bones up to hers, sharing our natural heat, stoking them furnaces in our bodies that were keeping us alive. And I already knew, just as she did, that when the thaw come and we took Papa to Mattagash Point to bury him, we'd only be taking an old stump, or a log, or a little hill of rocks. He was already gone off from his suffering body, gone into the smell of pine, into the whine of the coyote. And so it ain't a bad memory to think of him, when it comes to snow, and my mind starts to reeling. When you're eight years old, you lean to the adults for your answers. And my mother got us through all that. She was a great big answer in the heart of all that storm. "Just think," she told us, happy in what she said. "There ain't no pain for him now. Just them warm heavenly streets of gold where it don't ever snow."

So when I married Foster Fennelson and went to live at Mattagash Brook, I was more or less prepared for a blizzard. When it snowed heavy in them days, you could almost go blind from the white of it. All the pines and black spruce were white as angels. Even the bare trees looked like they was dazzled with pussy willows. When I got up before Foster to start the fire, I'd look out my kitchen window and it was always a shock. It was like we'd been picked up and put down on another planet. Like all our mistakes had been erased, all the old familiar markers gone. It was like we'd been given another chance. If Foster got up before me, I'd see his footprints going to the barn, all frozen and blue in that early light, and I hated him for spoiling the freshness of it. But most times it was mine first, and I didn't mind getting up so early if it was. If the snow was done, you'd see the first sun coming up over the barn, and it never come up the same way twice. "Sun's coming to get the rooster," Papa used to say to me. "Sun's coming, and he's gonna get that old rooster." And the gorbies would fly right up to the window, begging for food. That's what the old-timers called them Gray Jays, because they was so greedy. They got the souls of lumberjacks in them, you know. That's why they're so tame. They come looking for crumbs from their descendants. Sometimes they hit against the windows as if they're saying, "Remember me?" If it was me, I'd just go off and leave the living alone. I'd have seen enough of the living. But them gorbies, them ghosts, they can't seem to let go. They follow along with the lumberjacks in the woods. I guess they miss the work. At noontime they fly right up to eat out of a lumberjack's hand. But I rarely had extra to feed the birds in them days. The dog was lucky to get something from the table. Them was the days when if it snowed and then stopped, you didn't mind. But when it snowed and snowed and snowed, you started looking in your cupboard real serious. And at what you'd stored in your cellar. And you measured out your flour, counted your potatoes, thinned the soup. One winter like that, we ate horsemeat.

That's my other snow memory, the winter of 1916, when we had to kill old Nellie. It was a terrible, terrible winter. Even the snow, when it fell, was soiled. Coyote ate deer and deer ate nothing. I remember it clear as if it's happening right now. Foster walked old Nellie out behind the barn. I remember that all the kids were in the windows crying, watching. And Nellie stopped at the corner of the barn and looked back. You could just make her out in the snow, her mane all wet with it, her eyes wet. She knew, you know, that the dance was over. The jig was up. I've seen more animals in my day with a head full of brains than I've seen people. And Nellie was real hungry too, so she knew, all right. And there are folks who claim an animal don't have feelings—well, I'm here to tell you that Nellie had every kind of feeling known to man. She loved my children, all of them, even the mean ones. And I think she was a better mother to them than I was. She tended them all summer out in the lower pasture, let them torment her the way kittens do a mother cat. They climbed all over her back, swung on her tail, put bonnets on her head, made her jump stumps, rode her four at a time. Yes, I gotta say it. She had a patience with them that I never found. So when they cried in the windows that day, she stopped and looked back. Then she went on by herself. Foster only had to poke her once, she just seemed to know where she had to go, what she had to do. That's when Walter—he was already about eighteen or so—grabbed me by the arm. "We won't eat meat is all," he said. "Please, Mama, don't kill Nellie." And I think to this day I was about to run out that door and stop it. I do believe that. "Something always comes through for us," I was going to tell Foster. "It will again."

When the gun went off, they all fell silent, like mice listening for the cat. Walter turned white as a sheet. He looked right at me like *I'd* done it. And then Winnie came down from her chair in the window and said, "Now what'll we ride this summer?" Like it was nothing. She weren't much more than a yard high at the time. Just a little tyke. And she was the only child who ate meat that night, just her and Foster. The only one for a week or more. Then finally Garvin did, and Ester, Lucy and Billy. One by one they come out of hiding, like that table was a magnet and their little stomachs was made of lead. I suppose they was tired of potato soup. But they chewed that meat slowly, and so did I. And when our eyes met, we shared our guilt. It was like Nellie was giving us another free ride. You get hungry enough, you do a lot of things to get unhungry. All except Walter. He wasn't just a special child of mine. He was one of God's special creatures. Every once in a while you hear about someone like that, but you rarely meet them. They're the person who runs into a burning house and dies saving a stranger. Or they starve so someone else can eat. That's the way Walt was. And you can't expect them special people to live out long lives. You just can't. When you ain't thinking of yourself all the time, you just ain't cautious enough. With all them other folks on your mind, you get careless. Just staying alive becomes a full-time job. But Walter's another heartache. I'm gonna let that old wagon of memory roll past him for the time being. I'm gonna remember some of the good times for a change.

And I do need to remind myself that there was some good times. I got to admit that. There wasn't just raging blizzards of snow in my life. I can remember days most people don't even know about, long summer evenings on the front porch with all the crickets alive in the grass. And there'd be frogs down at the swamp blowing their throats into bubbles. Sometimes a moose would wade Mattagash Brook and come right up to the front steps, his antlers all brownish-gold in the sun. Most any day you'd catch a bald eagle soaring on its flat wings over the tops of the trees. Foster put out a salt block for the whitetail deer that come to drink from Mattagash Brook, and they sure liked that salt. We never killed what we didn't need bad. Most folks around did the same. Killing weren't a sport but a necessity. And them days turned over slowly, like the pages flipping on a calendar, all colors and noises and long-lasting. I do have to admit this. And I do have to wonder just how many city folks have ever heard a real barn door swing in the wind. I wonder if they know the song in it, because it is music, you know. Nature's music. And sometimes you'd hear lumberjacks in the woods, cutting down white pines, and that was music too. Them axes rung out for a mile. And you could hear the bells on them horse harnesses so loud it sounded like Christmas all year round. Jingle bells in the wild woods! Ain't that something? So I kind of enjoyed them slow times. I guess maybe when my oldest kids got big enough to help, and I got more time to think, maybe that's when things seemed to sour before my eyes. It's a dangerous thing, you know, too much time to think. It can twist and turn your mind. But I got to say it now—*before* my mind turned, there was some awful good times.

I always had a big garden full of string beans, carrots, cucumbers, potatoes, everything I could get to take root and grow fast. It *had* to grow fast up here in northern Maine. It seemed like half the year was spent getting ready for the snow to come, and the other half was spent getting ready for it to leave. We didn't have no fancy gadgets back then. Nature could be your friend one day, enemy the next. But she was mostly good to us in the summers. When my kids was big enough, I sent them into the woods and the fields and they come back with all kinds of wonderful stuff from nature's store. Tiny wild strawberries, and raspberries the size of quarters, and blackberries so easy to pick they dropped off the bushes into your pail. Blueberries grew good where a fire had passed. And the trees gave us chokecherries, and wild cherries no bigger than a fingernail. And from bushes along the riverbank, or along the edge of fields, they'd find hazelnuts and beechnuts. And beneath trees in the forest grew the little orange bunchberry, what we called pigeonberries. Can you imagine city folks getting all this stuff for free at some fancy store? And we used to pick fiddleheads, with their heads shaped just like the scroll of a fiddle. Them is one of the cleanest, most insect-free plants you'll ever find. We used to pick them on Wolf Island, in the Mattagash River, but they grow all over. Sometimes we'd fill ten burlap sacks with them. Then there's the good old dandelion green, a hard thing to clean but delicious to eat. Best to get them in the spring, when they're young and tender. Cook them with salt pork for thirty minutes, along with a mess of new potatoes. I canned what vegetables I could for the winter months. We put our potatoes and carrots in barrels and buried them in the ground. That kept them real good all winter. And it kept our meats. I'd mince deermeat and moose-meat, mix it with spices, make pies out of it. But all summer long we had fresh berry pies. And we caught rainbow trout from Mattagash Brook in them summer months. And Foster brought home partridge and an occasional rabbit. I even used wild shore onions, summer savory, caraway, and wild mint to flavor things. I let them dry, chopped them up, and kept them in cheesecloth sacks. And I always made lots of jars full of mustard pickles.

The kids loved hazelnuts the most. They used to stake out their own personal bushes and no one else was supposed to touch them. Walter always picked north of the house. Garvin would go south along the shore of Mattagash Brook, follow it out to the Mattagash River. Percy went somewhere—I just can't remember now where the others went, but they all had their own territory. Winnie was the only one who wouldn't pick hazelnuts. She said they was too picky for her hands, like she was some little queen or something. But in hazelnut season she always had her mouth full, always talked the others into sharing. It was too bad, you know, because you got to work hard for hazelnuts. First of all, you got to pick them when they're in their little green husks, snap them off the bush like that. If you don't, the squirrels will get them. It's like picking a little green cactus to pick a green hazelnut. That's nature's way of protecting them, I suppose, until they're ready. So you put them in a burlap sack and beat them real good against the barn, or on the road, so they'll leave them little husks behind. And then you put them up somewhere to ripen. Winnie never could talk Walter out of his hazelnuts. Walter saw through Winnie like she was a ghost. He always had that ability, and I mention this because most folks didn't. Most folks weren't that lucky when they met up with Miss Winnie Fennelson.

I think my favorite thing back then was the rhubarb. It grew wild along the north side of the garden. I suppose some old-timer, at one year or another, had planted it there at Mattagash Brook.

But you'd find it in the strangest places, growing where nobody lived, where you never even *remembered* anyone living. We'd come upon it in the thick of the woods, when we least expected it. "Someone must've lived here once," Foster would say. "Must've been a house here once." And I'd think about that, in them days later, when I had that dangerous time to think. Some man had built himself a home, and got himself a wife, and had himself a family, and all that was left to show for it was rhubarb gone wild. Nothing else. It's true, you know, that nature reaches up and pulls down what you build. I've seen limp little vines bust through stone. I seen grave markers yanked down and covered so thick with vines that you can't read them.

And nowadays I think of my house at Mattagash Brook. I can't help but wonder how things is with it. If moss is growing in my kitchen. If birds are nesting in my bedrooms. If the front porch is breaking up and sinking into the earth. I was seventy-six years old the last time I saw my house. You wonder, you know, if the windows is broken out, letting in the wind and the snow. Is the wellhouse rotted? Has the pump gone to rust? I've seen them houses many times. There was old man Hart's homestead, a haunted place, a place full to the rafters with ghosts. And there was the Margaret Mullins house, the old Mullins place. We always called them "old" back then, when we was still new ourselves, 'cause we never imagined that they was once new. And we sure never dreamed that one day our own proud houses would be pointed out that way by the young. Are they calling my house "the old Fennelson place"? Are weeds growing up in my living room? Are rabbits and mice being born there, the way my kids was once born? These days, most of the old homesteads is gone. And when young folks get married now, they ain't looking to move in and fix an old house up, keep it alive. They build one-story sardine cans instead, and they're content to live in them. But that's what the Bible tells us will happen, that one generation passeth away, and another one cometh, but the earth abideth forever. And here I am, so old I'm going and coming and abiding all at the same time.

The Storm Birds Visit:
Conrad Annoys Pike

"Speak roughly to your little boy,
And beat him when he sneezes;
He only does it to annoy,
Because he knows it teases."

—The Duchess in *Alice's Adventures in Wonderland*
by Lewis Carroll

*I*n the morning Mattagash was buried under two feet of fresh deep snow. Icicles, formed days earlier, still hung from the eaves of Pike Gifford's house, big ones a foot wide at their origin and running all the way to the ground, and littler ones the children knocked down with a broom handle and then sucked at, as though they were lanced Popsicles. The snow hadn't stopped until ten o'clock, so school had been canceled.

"If them kids keep missing school," Lynn had said to her sister, Maisy, who stopped in at nine for a cup of coffee, "they'll have to go all summer to make up for their snow days."

It was noon before Lynn and the children heard Pike's boots clumping down the stairs. A silence fell over them like a little gray cloud, a rain cloud in the midst of so much white.

"Holy shit," Pike said when he saw the faces of his family in a somber circle around the kitchen table. "You look like them Supreme Court judges." And then the twins laughed, a tinkling laugh, fragile as icicles falling. And Reed made a small chortling sound in his throat, his best attempt to second the notion. Lynn smiled, a coloring book smile, too large to fit the circumstances, too wide to be sincere. Conrad looked away, to where a pair of black-capped chickadees had come to the coconut feeder he'd tied to the clothes post outside the kitchen window. And then they all sighed a soft little sigh, a small breeze of relief.

"Lord," Pike said. "You'd swear I was the one killed Bambi's mother." Julie ran to her father and stretched her arms up high.

"We're going to Freddy's birthday party," Julie said. Pike turned away from her. He didn't yet have the strength to pick her up. It was much too early.

"Aunt Maisy made him a birthday cake out of cupcakes," Stevie said. "Each cupcake has a letter of his name on it."

"And there's cupcakes that spell out *Happy Birthday,* too," Julie told him. Her face had crumpled into a little frown when Pike turned away to pour himself coffee.

"Maisy's a genius," Pike said. "You can't take *that* from her."

"Please," Lynn thought. "Don't start."

"Daddy, will you come with us?" Julie asked. Lynn made a quick, subtle movement of her hand, as if to quiet Julie, but then she realized there would be no need. Pike Gifford at a birthday party? He might have attended one or two of Conrad's and Reed's earliest ones, but he had soon asked that his name be taken off the invitation list.

"Naw, I guess not," Pike said to Julie. "My tux is at the cleaners." He popped two slices of white bread into the toaster and stood waiting for them to spring up as brown toast.

Lynn bit her lip. "Just don't say anything," she reminded herself. "We'll be gone in an hour, unless he leaves first."

"You got any money left?" Pike asked her. "From that household money I give you?" Lynn wanted to laugh. It had been such a meager amount—only when Pike stayed true to his promises and avoided The Crossroads did the disability check manage to support them—that she had had to borrow again from her mother.

"That was spent before you give it to me," Lynn said. She had swept a small pile of dirt up with the broom and now she was looking for the dustpan. Pike would never learn about the thirty dollars she still had, every cent intended to go for school lunch money and gas for the car.

"You don't even have a *five?*" Pike asked, and Lynn shook her head, her eyes avoiding his.

"Will you, Daddy?" Julie asked again. "Will you come with us?" She had locked her arms about Pike's leg. Pike now had a bowl of cereal in his hands, milk sloshing dangerously close to the rim. He made a feeble attempt to shake Julie loose, but then he stopped. Putting the bowl down carefully on the kitchen counter, he patted his daughter's head.

"Yeah," Pike said suddenly. "I'll go to Freddy's party, and look at Maisy's cupcakes. Sure. Why not?" Lynn was stunned, her eyes darting quickly to Conrad's, then following his glance out to the chickadee feeder.

"It's in just a few minutes," Lynn said, her tone urgent. Pike rarely rushed anything. "It was supposed to be after school, but since school was canceled, Maisy moved it up."

"She's a social wonder," said Pike. He bit into a buttered slice of toast, crumbs falling onto his chest like brown dandruff.

"There ain't any other men gonna be there," said Lynn. "Just Maisy's kids, and Beena's kids, and these kids here." She made a frail swoop of her hand at the children, as though introducing them to Pike. Conrad and Reed sat like frozen gargoyles, the mirth of the impending birthday party suddenly turned grotesque.

"Freddy's gonna be five years old," Julie told her father.

"No he ain't," said Stevie. "He's fifty."

"He's gonna be *five,*" said Julie. "And he's gonna be a Indian in the play." Stevie reached out quickly and slapped her.

"Stop that!" Lynn said. She turned to Pike. "Don't Maurice open The Crossroads at noon today?" she asked. Pike was busy with a box of cornflakes. "I don't mind if you go looking for Billy or Ronny over there. They're probably over there, wouldn't you guess?"

"Now listen at you," Pike said. "First it's I don't spend enough time with you and the kids. Now it's go to The Crossroads with Billy and Ronny. Make up your mind, woman." Lynn tried frantically to read him, to look beneath the gesture, to rifle through the motives that lay behind his Pike Gifford grin. But she could find nothing. She knew it was always one of two things when he acted this way. Usually it was that he needed an excuse to get out of the house so he could beat a retreat to The Crossroads. Those times, he looked to Conrad as a means of providing him with an exit. Or Lynn. Reed, if necessary. But sometimes it was nothing more than boredom, Lynn had decided. On those lazy days when Billy and Ronny had gone downstate looking for entertainment, or The Crossroads was closed, and Pike had nothing to do but rewatch a rental movie, he was pressed to shape his own entertainment. Pike, on the other hand, saw the maneuver more clearly: it was a game of power, the flesh-and-bone bodies of his family only pieces forced to scuttle unhappily about the large squares of the playing board. *Offense* was Pike Gifford's middle name.

"We were just getting ready to go out the door," Lynn said, and wanted to say more. But her tongue lay limp in her mouth, a piece of recording tape too tired and worn to replay itself.

"I won't be but a minute," Pike assured them as he headed upstairs. "I just need to splash on a little after-shave." Lynn put a finger to her lips, a message for the kids to be quiet, as she quickly rang Maisy's number.

"The only thing I can tell you," Maisy said finally, "is to let him come on. You know he won't be here ten minutes before he'll up and leave. Don't pick no fight with him, whatever you do." Lynn hung up the phone with a major sigh. *Defense* had become an integral part of their lives.

Maisy had decorated the kitchen table with streamers and then arranged the cupcakes neatly in three curved rows. *Happy Birthday*

Frederick, they read in order. Positioned on the ceiling above the table was a white, foldout Hallmark bell, left over from her own wedding souvenirs and now used at birthday gatherings. She was serving spaghetti, with the littler kids eating on metal TV trays in the living room and the adults around the cupcakes on the kitchen table. She'd been expecting only Lynn, and Pike's cousin Beena, but Beena had called to cancel. She was snowed in, with no one to plow her yard, and with a sick child to boot. Maisy had been about to remove Beena's plate when she received the call from Lynn that Pike, of all people, would be coming along. If he stayed long enough to eat, which Maisy doubted, he could have Beena's place.

At first Pike was all smiles, even complimentary, and Lynn began to think he was there for the duration. But by the time Freddy had opened his gifts and the children were given plates of spaghetti, she could tell that Pike's enthusiasm was waning. So could Reed and Conrad. Maisy had seated them at the kitchen bar. Her three small children, and Julie and Stevie, had already filled the tiny living room.

"Here, Pike," Maisy said. "Sit here. This was Beena's plate." It was difficult to disguise the anger in her tone. Lynn might not be sure about the emotions she felt toward her husband, but there was no doubt in Maisy's mind about her own opinion of her brother-in-law. She hated him truly and dearly.

"Is Beena still dating Paulie Hart?" Lynn asked, looking nervously away from Pike and into Maisy's eyes.

"She would if she knew where he was," said Maisy, straightening the *r* cupcake in *Birthday*. "But nobody's seen him since he won that thousand dollars in the lottery."

"I think she's too old for him anyway," said Lynn. She saw that Pike was fidgeting with his napkin, and it worried her.

"Well, she's got them two kids to raise," said Maisy. "I suppose she has to think of that. Mattagash don't have bachelors to pick from. It ain't the best place to be divorced in."

"Ain't this pretty, though?" Pike said, and picked up a paper napkin Maisy had left in a triangular shape beneath his knife.

"Fancy, fancy. When you give a party, Maisy, you really give a party."

"Yeah, well," Maisy managed, and tried not to look at Pike. After the incident with Conrad and the bat, she was quite sure she would never have to see Pike Gifford again, much less discuss napkins with him. Sometimes it seemed she would never figure Lynn out. She glanced quickly at Conrad, but he sat looking down into his spaghetti, waiting.

"Poor kid," thought Maisy.

"Do you know what?" Lynn said finally. She could see a look on Pike's face that she knew too well, a little curl playing up around the sides of his mouth. He was getting ready for some outrage and Lynn hoped she could forestall it. "Priscilla Monihan called me yesterday and asked me if I'd sign her petition to close The Crossroads. I ain't heard a word from that snobby bitch in my entire life, not even a hello when I meet her on the street in Watertown."

"Don't she think she wrote the good book, though," Maisy agreed.

"This sure is pretty, all right," Pike said again. "But tell me something, Maisy." Lynn caught her breath.

"Here it comes," she thought.

"What's that, Pike?" Maisy asked. She put a plate of spaghetti in front of Reed, who, like Conrad, only stared at it.

"Here it comes," thought Reed.

"Why'd you go and put my fork way over here on the left side of my plate?"

"What?" Maisy asked.

"My fork," said Pike. "What's it doing over here on the left side of my plate? I'm right-handed." Maisy looked to Lynn's face for support, but found none there. There was none to be given when Pike was on a roll.

"That's how it's supposed to be," said Maisy. "That's how you set a table." She bit her lip and waited. Pike had picked at her often, it was true, throwing out little barbs about her Sunday brunches.

"I'm just curious," said Pike. "It seems to be a good idea if a fellow's left-handed, but if he ain't, it don't seem like such a good move. It seems like a right-handed fellow is going to drag his sleeve in his food when he reaches for that fork. So I was just wondering why you put my fork over there."

"That's how it was in the magazine," announced Freddy, the birthday boy. He'd come to the kitchen for a glass of milk.

"Oh, I see," said Pike. "A magazine told you to do this. They must all be left-handed then, the folks down at the magazine." Maisy's lip had begun to tremble. Her mother had always told her she'd get in trouble for putting on airs.

"Pike, please," Lynn said, but nothing more. It would only make him worse.

"Now, I noticed," Pike continued, "that you put my glass of milk over here by my right hand. If I'm gonna have to reach over anyway and get my fork, why didn't you put my milk over there too? Then I could take a quick drink of milk before I grab my fork." Maisy had taken her place at the table, and she looked helplessly at her own fork in its neat little position on the left side of her plate. Pike was right. She'd have to reach over her food to get it. She wished now she'd never seen the damn picture in *Good Housekeeping*. But she had imagined that Beena and Lynn would be impressed with the setting as everyone chatted happily over the expensive paper napkins and the well-placed forks. Why was Pike Gifford ever born?

"It would seem to me," Pike said, "that the magazine people ought to rethink this thing. If you ask me," he went on, although no one ever would, "a bunch of left-handed kings and queens over in England, or maybe some Kennedys and Rockerfellers, got together and decided all this, and now they expect poor folks like us, like you, Maisy, to go along with all their foolishness." Maisy's face was suddenly drained of color, as white as the snow in her yard.

"Shut up," Conrad said softly, and Lynn motioned quickly for him to be quiet.

"Go on," Lynn said to Pike. "This here's a birthday party. Go on to The Crossroads and leave us be."

"And everybody knows that all the Kennedys and Rockerfellers is any good for is to put on airs," Pike added, as though his wife and son were not in the room with him. "Them kings and queens ain't done nothing but interbreed, even more than folks do here in Mattagash. That's why that royal family looks like a stable of horses. But us folks up here in northern Maine, we know better than to go along with all that put-your-fork-here bullshit. We know that if you sit too high up on the cow, you ain't gonna reach the tits. If the magazine said to hang by your ankles while you eat, would you do that, too?" A picture flashed suddenly into poor Maisy's mind of Princess Di hanging royally by her dainty feet, a smidgen of cake frosting around her mouth.

"Well?" Pike asked jauntily. "Would you?" Maisy began to whimper.

"Shut up!" Conrad said loudly, still staring down at the heap of spaghetti. Reed kicked his brother's foot, a plea for silence.

"Unless, of course," Pike added, "you invited a left-handed little fag over to eat. Now that would be different. Little fags like napkins and fancy forks and stuff like that."

"You get out of my house," Maisy said suddenly, and Lynn felt a rush of relief. She'd been afraid Conrad would be the one to confront Pike. "I ain't scared of you. I ain't no child you can push around. You get out," Maisy said, her whimpers growing toward sobs. Pike stood, smiling sweetly. He bowed to Lynn. He could hear himself telling her later his side of the story: "I intended to spend some quality time with my wife and family, but Maisy threw me out. It's her house. I can only abide. I'm pretty sure her magazine would say it'd be bad manners for me to do otherwise." But then Maisy made the biggest faux pas of all—something *Good Housekeeping* had yet to write about, but about which Lynn and Conrad and Reed could write books.

"You're a bigger drunk than your old man was," Maisy cried angrily. Pike had spoiled the birthday party she'd been planning for days. Thank God she hadn't gone all out and bought some of those linen napkins she'd seen at the Woolworth store in Madawaska. Who knows what trouble they might have stirred up. Lynn caught her breath, heard Conrad and Reed do the same.

"I ain't ever brought up your old man, Maisy," said Pike,

slowly, deliberately. "I don't like the son of a bitch, but I ain't ever brought up his name to you." Maisy sat silently, her spaghetti growing cold on the plate before her. Lynn had kicked her ankle beneath the table as a signal to, please, above all, remain quiet. "Now I expect you to do the same," Pike said. He started to turn away, to find his green felt hat and beat a retreat, but it caught him, that flow of anger that had been his friend for so many years now. How dare she, how dare anybody, rake Pike Gifford, Sr., over the coals? But Mattagash had rubbed the younger Pike's nose into the mess of his father's life for so many years now that his nose was sore. The sons of bitches! Pike grabbed the gaily decorated birthday table and picked it up several inches off the floor, scattering the cupcakes and turning glasses of milk upside down. Then he put it back down, said nothing to the women who hid their faces in their pale, wintry hands. Clutching his hat from Maisy's kitchen counter, Pike Gifford tipped it politely at the gathered company.

"Thanks for the invite," he said. He pulled his felt hat on and went outside. In a minute the battered Chevy Super Sport rattled out of Maisy's dooryard and disappeared in the direction of The Crossroads.

*

It was only half an hour later that Maisy dropped Lynn and the kids off and drove away in a swirl of snow, the party aborted. Pike's family tromped into the house like a small, unhappy army and then separated into various activities. The twins managed to stop fighting long enough to sit in front of the TV for a third viewing of *Bambi*. Reed lounged at the kitchen table in front of his open history book. He'd been doing poorly since school started, and the teacher had warned him about his bad grades.

Lynn had taken out her sewing basket and was searching the dryer for Julie's blouse, the blue one with the missing button. Conrad had made a quick peanut butter sandwich and then gone on up to his room. In seconds he was back, an empty brown envelope in his hands.

"Look," he said to Lynn. "My money's gone."

"Your money?" Lynn asked, and took the envelope. "The money you been saving?" Conrad nodded. Lynn looked at Reed, who shrugged his shoulders.

"Who knew where you kept it?" she asked Conrad.

"Nobody." Tears were quickly filling his eyes. "I been saving since I was nine," he said.

"I know that," Lynn said. "I know you have." She looked at Reed again, but she knew it would be no use, would even be unfair to ask, "Reed, did you take it?" And she also knew it would be unfair to ask Julie and Stevie, children too young to understand the concept of money. It would be unfair because Lynn knew in an instant where the money had gone, and she could tell by Conrad's face that he, too, knew. So did Reed. They were children of the streets, these boys who had never even been to a city. Sometimes, when you live within the confines of a small town, the circumference of an unhappy family, the streets come to you.

"*He* took it," said Conrad, and Lynn nodded. That was why Pike had attended the birthday party. He thought it would provide him with an alibi.

"When he said he was going up to put on after-shave," Conrad continued, and again Lynn nodded.

"I don't know how," she said, "but I'll see to it that he finds a way to give it back to you. I'll tell Billy. Bad as he is, Billy wouldn't steal from a kid. I'll tell Billy to make him give every cent back."

Conrad spent the next half-hour as restless as anyone in his family had ever seen him, flipping through a comic book one minute, peering into the refrigerator the next, pacing the kitchen floor. Finally he left a freshly opened bottle of Coke behind—Conrad rarely wasted things—and went out to pace the cold back porch. Reed stared at the colored picture of wagons headed west in his history book—a place he wouldn't mind going. Try as he might, and even with his teacher's threat of keeping him off the junior varsity basketball team, he couldn't concentrate. Conrad was more on his mind than the Oregon Trail.

"He ain't wearing his coat," Reed said at last. Lynn put the sewing basket away and pulled on her own big bulky jacket. She found Conrad's coat where he'd left it on the couch and went out to talk to her son.

"Here's your coat," Lynn said, but Conrad shoved her hand away. Lynn sighed. She hugged the coat to her chest. Empty, it felt useless in her arms. "You're gonna catch your death," she whispered.

Conrad watched a flock of snow buntings rise up out of the field behind the house, turn pure silver in the sun, then descend on more hay stalks farther away. He remembered his mother's favorite song, "Snowbird," by Anne Murray. Sunday mornings, when Conrad was very little, he would wake to the strains of Lynn's old phonograph downstairs bringing the words up to him, up to his warm bed, and he imagined he was a tiny bird in a nest, up there above Lynn's head. And then his father's voice would interrupt the lovely melody, the haunting words, a voice of hate, and Conrad would hold his breath and try desperately to fly away in his imagination. *Little snowbird, take me with you when you go, to that land of gentle breezes where the peaceful waters flow.*

Conrad watched as the snowbirds, the buntings, rose again and arced over the field in search of more left-behind grain. Storm birds, they had come with the latest blizzard.

"You cold?" Lynn asked, and touched a hand to her son's cheek. "You must be. Put your coat on, or else come on back in. I promise you we'll get your money back. There's no need to let him spoil the rest of the day."

"Why'd you let him come back in the first place?" Conrad said, and Lynn heard anger in his voice, something he didn't often express to her, although she had always guessed it was there.

"What am I gonna do?" she asked. In her jacket pocket she found her pack of Winston 100's, snapped one out, and lighted it. When she exhaled, smoke mingled with the warm puffs of her breath against the cold air. The rings rose up like smoke signals and then disappeared.

"Don't let him come back," Conrad said. "Divorce him. The sheriff ain't gonna come the next time. You know he ain't. He said so. He said you take Daddy back and you're on your own. I ain't afraid of him. All we gotta do is divorce him." Lynn was startled at the rush of Conrad's words. How long had it been since she'd heard more than a few words here and there, or the occasional sentence? He had stopped talking in long, full paragraphs, hadn't he? Funny, she had just now noticed.

"How'll we live, Con?" she asked. "How'll we get by? What'll we eat, for Chrissakes?"

"I got almost three hundred jams now," Conrad said proudly. He'd been waiting a long time for this event, *saving* for it. "I got more sugar than we'll ever use."

"Oh, Conrad," Lynn whispered. "Oh, sweetie." She held him against her chest, wrapped her arms about him. My God, but he was almost as tall as she was! She felt him sigh, long and hard, and it seemed the very force of it shot into her body like a large pang of remorse. A birth pain, even. She didn't have an epidural for Conrad, Lynn remembered. That was a mistake she didn't make when she had the other three kids.

"If it hadn't been for him," Conrad said, "we'd have money, too. Three hundred and seventeen dollars." His voice seemed to leave, a ventriloquist's voice, and rise far above his body, a hovering voice.

"This is what being *doomed* means," thought Conrad. "This is doomed."

"Oh, sweetie," Lynn said again. "It's so much more than sugar and jam, and what we'll eat, or what we'll wear. It's so much more than any of them things, and if I knew *what* it was, if I could explain it to you, so help me Christ I would. I'd do it this very minute." She leaned back to look at his face. Tears swam in his eyes. "But I can't," she said softly, finally, and she felt him take his sigh back out of her body, felt his remorse reel itself out of her, as if it were a current of sheer electricity. She felt, suddenly, two emotions—one of having just given birth, the other of having lost something irretrievably precious.

Curves and Sparkles:
Miles Standish Visits Tanya

> To have or take on a facial expression showing usually pleasure, amusement, affection, friendliness, etc., or, sometimes, irony, derision, etc., and characterized by an upward curving of the corners of the mouth and a sparkling of the eyes.
>
> —*Webster's New World Dictionary*. Definition of *smile*.

Dorrie Mullins cut a big wide arc as she turned Booster's pickup/plow at the Greater Northern Bank in Watertown, and then headed up Basile Street in the direction of the hospital. In the passenger seat, Lola Monihan braced herself, a hand on the dashboard, another on the door handle, and waited until Dorrie hit the notorious pothole in front of LaVerdiere's Drugstore. Then she relaxed her position.

"When do you think they're gonna fix that hole?" Dorrie asked. "It's been there since last spring, but I can't ever seem to remember it's there." Lola nodded. It was true that Dorrie always managed to head right for that hole, as though it were some kind of treasure pit. If Lola could remember to brace herself each time she saw the LaVerdiere sign, why couldn't Dorrie remember the damn hole? Lola was truly sorry she'd never gotten her driver's license.

"I still don't believe it," said Lola. She straightened the big violet bow on the IGA fruit basket, which rode on the seat between them. "About Tanya having AIDS, I mean. I think that's just gossip from folks who got nothing better to do."

Dorrie took her eyes off the street for a moment to look at her friend Lola. It had been Lola who started the rumor that Booster Mullins had only two months to live, the time Booster had gone into the hospital to have his hemorrhoids taken the rest of the way out. Booster had been too embarrassed to let Dorrie tell the truth about his ailment, knowing the kind of jokes it would generate along Mattagash telephone lines. So Dorrie had been most secretive, suggesting that Booster suffered from an ailment inherited from the doomed Fennelson line, something beyond the stupidity gene and the bad-luck curse. It was all too much for Lola. Before nightfall she had given poor Booster only two months to live. That would have been okay if every last woman in Mattagash, except the Giffords and Amy Joy Lawler, hadn't turned up at Dorrie's house with a casserole, or a cake, or a loaf of homemade bread. Dorrie had the refrigerator and the cupboards full of food before she figured out what had happened. And it had taken her three weeks to return every one of those damn pans to the rightful owners. And then Selma Craft had accused her of denting her new Teflon fudge pan. But Lola was stingier with gossip when it affected her own relatives.

"She'd have had to have a blood transfusion to catch it," Lola was saying now. Dorrie saw the pothole, Watertown's second largest, lurking in front of the post office. She ever so slightly eased the Bronco toward it. Out of the corner of her eye, she saw Lola reach out a pale thin arm and brace herself against the dashboard. Dorrie smiled as the right tire struck the hole, *ka-thunk*. Lola bounced in the passenger seat.

"I wish they'd fix them damn holes," Dorrie said. "They just seem to jump out at a person at the last second."

"I don't remember Tanya having a blood transfusion," Lola went on. "Who told you she had AIDS, anyway?"

"She could've had a blood transfusion down in Connecticut, before they ever moved up here," said Dorrie. She swung into the parking lot of the Watertown hospital, the tires of the pickup spinning musically on the gravelly sand that had been spread there on the icy pavement. "How would you have known about it? I know you try, Lola, but you can't be everywhere at once." Lola felt a sting of warm blush cover her face in an instant. At moments like these, when Dorrie seemed intent on bullying her, Lola was only inches away from signing up for a driver education course.

"I hope Tanya likes this here fruit basket," Lola said idly. It was all she *could* say, from her powerless position in the passenger seat.

"Oh shit," said Dorrie. "Charlene's car is here." She pointed to the aging New Yorker, ice clinging to its mud flaps. It was parked in the visitors' parking lot. "Well, that ends it. I ain't going in to visit if Charlene's here. She'll say we're just dropping by to see if we can find out what Tanya's got."

"We *are*," Lola pointed out, "just dropping by to see what Tanya's got."

"Nevertheless," said Dorrie. She rammed the Bronco into reverse and it shot backward, out of the parking lot and up onto the main street. A horn bleated loudly, from a car that had been about to turn into the hospital until the Bronco came flying out. Dorrie ignored the complaint. She gave the Bronco more gas and it sped forward with great urgency. Lola was rummaging in her purse for a pen.

"I'm just gonna address this card to little Tanya," Lola said, "so we can mail it to her from the post office. Charlene don't control the mail. Not even Simon Craft does." She found the pen and went to work on the envelope. That was when Dorrie hit the patch of ice near the railroad tracks. It had always been a dangerous place, forever in the shade of a cluster of abandoned potato storage buildings. The strip of ice was spread across the road like scattered blue paint. Her heart throbbing with panic, Dorrie went for the brake, something she had promised Booster she would never do again when driving on ice, not after she had driven his last Bronco into the side of the garage. The Bronco spun wildly and executed a perfect cop turn, its nose now pointing in the opposite direction. Lola looked up from her writing.

"You forget something?" she asked.

Charlene remembered thinking that hospitals were havens, and yet even the huge stuffed teddy bear that lounged in the corner of the children's ward at Watertown Community Hospital looked as though he wished he were somewhere else, somewhere safe. In the four days that Tanya had spent there, undergoing more frightening tests, Charlene had been unable to get her to smile. Charlene herself had been exhibiting smiles of all sizes and designs, but by the end of the third day, she wasn't really sure anymore if she was pulling it off.

She'd been prodding Tanya to finish her soup, to drink one more sip of milk, to at least taste the pudding, when she became aware that her facial muscles felt knotted up into some kind of grisly lump. She had nodded at Davey to step outside. In the hallway Charlene had to steady herself by leaning back against the wall. "What's wrong with my face?" she asked. An article she had read in *Reader's Digest* about Bell's palsy flicked through her mind. Her face felt hugely distorted, little tremors lacing across her cheekbones, occasional involuntary tics commanding her left eye to twitch. "What's wrong with my face?" Charlene asked again. Davey hadn't slept much more than she had in the past three days, but he'd pulled her up against his chest, made useless, circular motions against her back with his hand.

"Char," Davey had whispered. "You're smiling. That's all."

That was when Charlene finally agreed to the sedative, and curled up on the narrow bed next to Tanya's, and she had not opened her eyes until the first rattling sounds of breakfast carts in the hallway broke through to her. During the night she hadn't wakened, nor had she dreamed. It had been as if someone had snipped a short piece out of the tape of Charlene Craft's life. All she had cared about when she woke was that Tanya was still there, pale and thin, and that the beaded terror that seemed to grip her own face up in a fisted frenzy—a *smile,* not Bell's palsy—was instantly back. By the start of this fourth day, Charlene knew she had mastered the fine art of smiling. And maybe the smile would never go away. Like little girls who are told their faces will freeze forever into frowns, she might find herself in the saddest of places still wearing that inappropriate mask. On the fourth day of Tanya's hospitalization, on the day Charlene had always believed God had created the sun, and the moon, and the stars, *that* day, Charlene sat up on the cot in Tanya's hospital room and looked at the clock. It was not quite seven. Davey would still be at home. Grandma Craft was probably cooking Christopher and James their breakfast. It was, after all, a school day and the boys were at the beginning of fresh, new lives, with all kinds of things still to learn about math, and verbs, and the history of countries they would never visit. Long lives, Charlene hoped. And when Tanya's test results were conclusive, and tomorrow they would be, surely she would live to learn about the problems of long division, about fresh boys she would meet in the dating years, about the pains and joys of children she herself might bear. Davey answered. He was already up and about—Charlene could tell by his voice. It was drained of vitality, but it was wide awake.

"Bring Christopher and James with you," Charlene said to Davey. She remembered how when her brother was in the New Milford hospital with appendicitis, she was not allowed to visit him because she was only nine, not old enough, and she was certain she would never see him alive again. "And ask your mother to call the principal's office and tell them the boys won't be in school today." She heard Davey cough on the other end of the snowy telephone line.

"Okay," he said.

"How's the road?" Charlene asked. At first Davey hesitated. It seemed like a trick question. It fitted snugly in with a barrage of other recent questions, an entire lineup of hows and whats. What's the prognosis? How did the tests turn out? What did the specialist say? How is she? How is she? How is she?

"The roads are pretty clear," he said flatly, and he meant it.

The man from the bank had already called once that morning. Bankers had to catch lumberjacks early.

"Be careful just the same," Charlene advised—not that she still believed that it made any difference. Careful had nothing to do with it. You could make sure your child always had lunch money, always looked both ways crossing the street, did homework on time, never talked to strangers, never petted strange dogs, always took enough vitamins, and yet it still didn't matter one whit.

On that fourth day, the day before God had made the whales, and the birds of the air, on *that* day, Charlene Craft stood staring down at her sleeping daughter.

"There is no God," Charlene whispered, and then feared that Tanya might have heard her, down there in the coils of her sleep. And she felt somehow guilty, felt somehow that she had lied to Tanya. Just the day before, when Tanya had asked her about heaven, Charlene had been more than eager to promote the real estate of such a place. "It's wonderful," she had said. "Bonkers is there." Bonkers had been Tanya's beloved pet dog, her first puppy. "And flowers never die. They're always in bloom. And there's all kinds of colorful lights and beautiful music." And she had gone on to describe heaven as though it were some marvelous pinball machine into which one need never drop a quarter. Now Charlene felt different. She felt as if that caul, the one that Davey had been so lucky to be born with, had been lifted from her eyes, and now she could see the truth looming before her. *I once was lost, but now am found. Was blind, but now I see.* What if Tanya were to ask her again? She'd lie, that's what. She'd make heaven sound like something Robin Leach would love to document. Jacuzzis for all the angels. Rolls-Royces for everyone. A Bonkers on every goddamn street corner.

It was still an hour until lunch when Davey appeared at the door with Christopher and James in tow. The boys wore big smiles on their own faces, happy to be free from school on a day that was actually sunny, a day they would not have to make up in June.

"Hey," Christopher said happily to Charlene. She'd been braiding Tanya's long hair into a single thick plait.

"Hey yourself," Charlene answered.

James put a paper sack on Tanya's bed. "Grandma sent you a cupcake," he said. "And a piece of mincemeat pie. She said don't let the nurse see."

"Yuck," said Tanya. "Mincemeat pie."

"We tried to tell her you wouldn't eat it," said Christopher.

Davey had moved closer to the bed. Charlene noticed that he seemed to be shielding something in his coat. With a quick glance over his shoulder Davey unzipped his jacket. "Look what else we brought you," he said to Tanya as Otis, the big yellow cat, bounded out onto the bed.

"Otis!" Tanya shrieked. It was the most energy Charlene had seen her muster in the past week. Maybe if she just took Tanya home, where she could be with Otis all the time, and lie in her own bed, in her own room, surrounded by her own things, her own family . . . But it was at home where Tanya had grown so ill in the first place, wasn't it? Charlene sighed. She looked up at Davey's drained face.

"A great idea," Charlene said. At least somebody was still thinking of Tanya. The only thinking Charlene had managed to do in the last few hours was to decide that any true, loving God wouldn't do this to a child, to a family. Giving Tanya a cat to bury her face in was a whole lot more beneficial than taking heaven away from her, just in case she might need it.

As Charlene watched Otis curl up in the crook of Tanya's arm, she thought about the commercials she had seen for years, attempts to raise money for tiny children in Ethiopia whose ribs ran beneath their skin like fragile little rills. Children dying for a slice of bread, a bowl of rice. Mothers shooing the flies away from the dead bodies of infants. Why hadn't she questioned God about those horrible things? Why did she wait for the truth to enter her own house and slap at her own child before she could face it? Now she felt like a hypocrite for having waited so long.

"Otis has a cold nose," said Tanya, and quietly stroked the fur of the big cat. Otis had begun to purr loudly, his throat vibrating with contentment at being back in Tanya's arms.

"Sssshh!" Davey warned the cat, holding a finger to his lips. "Do you want the nurse to hear you, Otis? Keep it down." Tanya laughed, a genuine laugh, not one of her fake little laughs to please Charlene.

"Daddy, look!" Tanya whispered. "Otis has quit purring. He heard you." Otis squinted his big yellow eyes, as if in agreement, and Tanya laughed again, the sweet, pure innocent laugh of childhood. Charlene wondered what Davey had told the boys on the ride down, if anything. It was difficult to say what kind of hysteria his mother may have been planting in their heads for the past four days. But now it wouldn't be long until the newest test results, like uninvited relatives, would be in.

Christopher came back with three cans of Mello Yello from the machine in the visitors' lounge. Charlene poured some for Tanya in her hospital glass and then a bit for herself.

"Yuck," she said, borrowing from Tanya. "How can you kids stand this stuff?"

"You're not supposed to *taste* it," said James. "Just swallow it whole. It's better that way." Charlene looked at Davey and raised her eyebrows.

"*I* didn't give birth to them," he said. "*You* did." It was meant as a joke, but suddenly they locked eyes, and it was no longer funny. Only the children laughed. And then Otis stretched out longer on the bed, a small cat snore escaping through his nose. The children laughed again, and there was a warmth in the room that hadn't been there before. Charlene would tell Davey this when she had the chance. "I want the boys here every damn day," she would tell him. "I want that goddamn cat here every day too. This affects us all."

"Do your Miles Standish," James said to Christopher. " 'I ask you then, John Alden, to take my proposal to Miss Mullins.' " James said this with dramatic flourish, bowing courteously to the empty space before him.

"Make him stop, Mama," Christopher pleaded.

"Stop it, James," Charlene said, although he was quite entertaining. Poor Christopher. He was still so small for ten years old. Smaller now than James, who was only eight.

"And listen to this," James added. "Elaine Monihan is playing Priscilla Mullins, and she's a whole foot taller than Christopher!"

"Ma," Christopher implored, and kicked at the leg of Tanya's bed.

"Was Priscilla Mullins related to Dorrie and Booster Mullins?" Tanya asked.

"God, I wouldn't doubt it," said Charlene.

"Speaking of Priscillas," said Davey. "Priscilla Monihan called Mom and talked her into signing the petition to close The Crossroads. I hear she's getting quite a few names on the list."

"Can't she find more important things to do?" Charlene asked. She looked at Tanya's little round face. There *were* things so much more important.

"You can't make his shoes orange," Tanya squealed to James. She pointed an accusing crayon at James's side of the coloring book they were working on.

"Yes I can," said James. "He's a rock star." Tanya hooted. The kids were being kids, the way they normally acted, and now Charlene wished she could do her part. She wished she had a stove there in Tanya's room. She would make a big pot of spaghetti, the way the kids liked it, with green beans mixed up in it. She would scurry about setting plates, only half listening to the childish prattle. She was a homemaker, after all. It was what she did best, all she had ever wanted to do. Yet here she was, sitting awkwardly on the edge of her cot, watching her children drink Mello Yello and eat candy bars.

Davey had dozed off in front of the television, one arm hanging listlessly over the side of his chair. Charlene would let him sleep a few more minutes before she woke him. Then she would send him over to LaVerdiere's Drugstore for some cat food, a plastic litter box, and some cat litter. The only one who could carry on as if nothing had changed was Otis. Charlene would see that he earned his table scraps. And she would have a little talk with the head nurse. There was no way in hell Otis was leaving the hospital until Tanya left it. Finally, for the first time in weeks, Charlene felt in control.

On Main Street, Dorrie found two empty parking spaces, plenty of room to parallel-park the Bronco and its plow. She zoomed in, jammed on the brake, and came to a thunderous halt in front of the Green Stamp redemption center. The big yellow plow rocked gently.

"This close enough for you?" Dorrie asked Lola, whose thin arm was sore from the day's bracing. Lola was there to cash in her books of stamps for a Deep Heat Whirlpool Hot Spa. "It heats the air to maintain constant bath temperature," she'd told Raymond, who wasn't sure he wanted a Deep Heat Whirlpool Hot Spa. "What in hell is it?" he'd asked his wife. "All you do is put the nozzle in your own bathtub, turn it on, and it beats up the water just like a real spa," Lola assured him. "It even has little pressurized jets. They sell for almost eighty dollars at Service Merchandise, but I'm getting mine with Green Stamps." But if Dorrie continued to chauffeur her, Lola would be putting the damn hose into her coffin, instead of her bathtub. If only one could get a driver's license for ten or twenty books of Green Stamps.

"I'll just be a minute," Lola said, opening her door and then testing a foot on the pavement before she stepped out. She'd already fallen once that spring, on the icy sidewalk in front of Angelique's Hair Factory, and Dorrie had laughed so hard that she'd accidentally tooted the Bronco's horn. "I can't help it," Dorrie had explained. "There's just something real funny about someone falling down." Lola had no intention of giving her best friend further amusement.

"You run into Elvis in there, you be sure to come get me," Dorrie said, and then winked. Lola slammed the door to the Bronco and inched across the sidewalk.

"Like hell," Lola thought. "I meet up with Elvis, and Dorrie

Mullins won't hear from me again until she gets a postcard from Graceland." Lola wondered suddenly if Elvis had a driver's license or if he, too, was always at the mercy of some power-loving chauffeur. And it was true that Dorrie was on a real power trip when it came to chauffeuring Lola around. Half the time Lola came back from running some errand to discover Dorrie gone, and then she had to track her down all over Watertown. Lola always looked first at the food establishments. But surely Dorrie would wait for her today, what with the sidewalks a dangerous sheet of ice. Lola heard the pleasant sound of the bell above the door announcing her entrance, and so she set off down the aisle in search of a clerk.

Dorrie watched Lola disappear into the redemption center before she put the Bronco into first and eased back out onto Main Street. A Deep Heat Whirlpool Hot Spa! What would Lola Monihan conjure up next? Of course, Dorrie had not been able to fit comfortably into her own bathtub for several years. She was condemned instead to taking what was vulgarly called "a whore's bath," sponging herself down with a facecloth she dabbed into a sinkful of water. You could put twenty Lolas into a bathtub, however, thin and pitiful as Lola was. Dorrie slapped her blinker on and veered quickly into the parking lot of David's House of Doughnuts, barely clipping the outdoor phone booth. The man inside dropped the receiver and covered his eyes as she whizzed past. A small group of Watertown schoolchildren saw the Bronco coming, the huge yellow lip of the plow in its usual sneer, and raced for cover.

"Move them little Frog legs," Dorrie muttered as the Bronco screeched to a halt, and the lovely smell of David Levesque's freshly baked doughnuts hit her ready nostrils.

Prissy A. Town:
To Hell with Liberté, Egalité,
& Fraternité

Carry proceeded into the hotel's dining room,
wearing a small pearl hatchet brooch . . . [She] then
bawled across the dining room to Higgins, "I want
you to bring me a glass of beer."

"We have no beer," he replied. "So please be
quiet." One of the men present suggested, "Have a
cocktail," which hardly helped matters.

"Yes," cried Carry, "bring me a cocktail. I
understand you have it here." As guests erupted in
an uproar, she resisted Higgins' attempts to quiet
her, shouting, "You are running a hell house and I
mean to expose you." . . . Unimpressed, Mr.
Chapman (the proprietor) removed Mrs. Nation
from her chair. To the applause of the remaining
guests, he ejected her . . . A struggle ensued to jam
Carry into an elevator and send her to her room.
She manhandled the poor elevator boy, "all the time
storming about the 'hell-den' and using other strong
language" . . . Mrs. Nation went straight to City
Hall, where she called Bangor not a decent place to
live. "Bangor is so rotten, I could not even get a
lawyer."

—Incident at The Bangor House, August 29, 1902,
involving Carry A. Nation, as recalled in
the *Bangor Daily News*, September 1989

*I*t was right after the long yellow Mattagash school bus, Mattagash District
#12, lurched past The Crossroads on its way to turn around at
the St. Leonard line that Sally thought she heard something out-

side. She decided it must be Beena's kids, happy to be free from school for the weekend and now celebrating with loud wild play in Beena's backyard just across the narrow Mattagash road. Or maybe it was the first crowd of snowmobilers, females out on a last crusade before the kids needed supper. Whoever it was, they were boisterous, their voices ringing together like frosty tin cans. Sally had just hung up from talking to Libby, who phoned with a bit of gossip about poor little Tanya Craft. The news had been passed around some before Libby heard it, but it was said to have begun originally with none other than Selma Craft, Davey's mother and a horse's mouth if ever Sally saw one. Tanya was stricken with some horrible disease that rooted no place else but the soil of Connecticut, that Mecca to so many Mattagashers.

"They say she won't live out the month," Libby relayed, her voice breathy with excitement.

"See that?" Sally said. It was her motherly I-told-you-so tone. "And here you been, pestering me to death to let you move to Connecticut."

"Do you think it might be AIDS?" Libby asked. "I kept house for them only two weeks ago. I even kissed their cat."

"What's that racket?" Pike Gifford asked now. He and Ronny Plunkett were seated at the bar and in the middle of a best-of-three cribbage tournament. If Pike didn't hurry up and peg his ass past the skunk point, four holes away, that's just what he would be: skunked. Ronny had first count too, as luck would have it, and he needed only eight points to win.

"Snowmobilers, I think," said Sally vaguely. She now had her arms up to the elbows in the perpetually soupy dishwater behind the bar, and her mind on Tanya Craft.

Ronny played a queen and the countdown began. "Ten," he said. Pike eyed him suspiciously. All Pike Gifford could hope for was to peg enough to get past that embarrassing, invisible skunk line, four measly points away. He had kept small-numbered cards just for that purpose, two aces and two fives, hoping he could score with them. Getting a cribbage skunk at The Crossroads was a serious matter. At other, less discerning drinking establishments, a list of poker or pinball champions might be displayed, and the team winners of the most recent Charlemagne card tournament. Or if cribbage was the favored game, one might expect to see a short list thumb-tacked to the wall naming those rare and lucky souls who'd managed to get a "twenty-nine" hand, the perfect score in cribbage. The Crossroads saw things differently. The Crossroads figured a man could be counted on to do his own bragging. But his worst defeat, well, that was a thing to flaunt in his face as he sat before a much-needed nipperkin. A lined sheet of notebook paper was neatly taped to the front of Maurice's General Electric microwave. *November Skunks,* it was titled, and it listed two names: *Pike Gifford, (by Billy P.)* and *Pike, (by Billy).* Below this a second title in Sally's black marker print read: *Double Skunks,* and beneath that was a single, most doubly unfortunate name: *Pike Gifford, by Billy Plunkett.* Pike couldn't wait for December to roll around, when the sheet would be torn down and a new one pasted in its place to await fresh ignominies.

"Fifteen for two," said Pike, and plunked a five down. He took his two points, jabbing the holes of the pegboard with great gusto and then staring sadly at the two holes he had yet to peg. Ronny quickly played a jack.

"Twenty-five," he said. Pike looked at his opponent, his cousin Ronny Plunkett, with steely, determined eyes. To be skunked by Billy was a different matter. Billy was the best damn crib player in Aroostook County, bar none. But to have Ronny—who was, even though Pike liked him greatly, a bit of a stuck-upper—trounce him thusly would be a shameful thing. Pike might have to stay home with Lynn and the kids until December, when that fresh sheet of paper would flap nicely from the microwave. What hurt Pike even more was the way folks seemed to read his name over and over while they waited for their pizza.

"Thirty," said Pike, and gingerly placed another five on the table. Ronny squinted his eyes and pondered the sum. Pike had seen that look before, usually at the breakfast table, all those years he had spent growing up in Ronny and Billy Plunkett's house. It meant Ronny was about to take the last slice of toast.

"Well?" asked Pike. "Is it a go?" Surely it was. He was merely being ceremonial. The idea was to get as close to thirty-one as possible. Ronny would need another ace. Pike had two of the precious things in his own hand. What were the odds Ronny had one? Pike felt a victorious swell roll up in his stomach. It was a wonderful feeling to be beat badly but not skunked. Ronny might've smoked hashish with strange Turkish women, but he didn't know diddly-squat about cribbage in Mattagash, Maine. Pike was almost surly.

"I don't know," Ronny said, and scratched his head. "Thirty, huh?"

"What do you mean, you don't know?" Pike's voice rattled. He could almost see the last slice of toast disappearing again, and then the words *Pike Gifford, by Ronny Plunkett* appearing on the horrible tally sheet of the damned. "Do you have an ace, or don't you?" Pike pressed. "Is it a go, or ain't it?"

"Oh, looky here," said Ronny, "at what was hiding from me." He produced the ace of clubs. "Thirty-one for two," Ronny announced, and then pegged the two holes he'd just won. Pike stared, flabbergasted, at the pair of aces in his hand. He still needed to peg two holes. If he didn't, he would give Ronny Plunkett an opportunity to hold his nostrils tightly together, scrunch up his face, and utter *pa-yew!* But with two aces in his hand, there was only one way Pike could score now. And that would be if Ronny had the fourth ace.

"One," Pike said solemnly, and let his ace of diamonds drop, like a sad, red leaf, onto the table. Ronny squinted his eyes and stared at it.

"Let's see," he said. "If I played another ace, it would give me two points for the pair, wouldn't it?" Pike's Adam's apple bobbed suddenly in his throat. Was it possible? If by the chance of Providence it was, then Pike would be able to put his last ace down and peg six lovely holes for three of a kind. He would even get an extra, though unnecessary, point for playing the last card. "Please Jesus," Pike thought, even though it was tacky to ask help from a man he barely knew, albeit he had bandied his name copiously about. It wasn't that Pike didn't believe in him. He most surely did. But Jesus was like the man from the bank. You didn't want to really consider him until he was looming in your face. Suddenly Pike was acutely sorry that he had taken Conrad's money. He had planned all along, however, to return it the minute his disability check arrived, and Pike wanted God to know that, just in case the Divine One was there in Mattagash, watching the cribbage game with interest, reading the innermost thoughts of Pike Gifford's mind.

"But I ain't got an ace," Ronny said quickly. "I got a four." He plunked his last card down. "It all adds up to five," he said. "You need a ten to score, Piko. Or another four. You got either one?" Sally giggled softly from behind the bar. While waiting for the ruckus still going on outside to eventually come through the door, she was monitoring the cribbage game.

Pike stared at Ronny's cards. A ten, a jack, an ace, and a four. A four had also been cut on the deck. Pike rapidly tallied his cousin's score. The son of a bitch had ten points, more than enough to win. And since Pike had dealt, Ronny could take his score first.

"But you get a point for having last card," Ronny said, mockery in every word, and Pike recognized it as such. "Here," said Ronny. "I'll take it for you. Oh darn. Look at that. You only needed one more point to get your smelly ass past the skunk line." Pike looked at his little steel peg, teetering so close, one hole away from a scorching embarrassment. He took a very large gulp of his beer, the foam creating a cool ring around his lips. Screw Conrad and his money. Pike should have known better than to offer any pact up to a God who obviously didn't play crib.

"What's that awful smell?" Ronny asked suddenly, straightening up. "If I didn't know any better, I'd swear it was piss à la skunk. Can you smell it, Sal? The last time an odor like that hit me in the face, I was lying headfirst between a Turkish whore's legs." Pike kept his eyes on the cards before him. The beautiful aces and fives ran together, but he didn't see them. Instead, he imagined the letters of his name shaping themselves once more on Sally's list, followed by the coup de grâce: . . . *by Ronny Plunkett, World Traveler and Whore Expert.*

Sally wiped her hands on the bar towel she kept pinned to a belt loop on her jeans. "Where's my marker?" she asked, searching behind glasses on the bar. "I'd better beat the rush hour." Outside, the raucous sounds seemed to be building. Sally expected a group of snowmobilers to come piling through the door at any moment in a crinkling rush of snowsuits and stomping feet. Now they'd have some new entertainment to stare at while they waited for their pizzas. Pike watched thoughtfully as she scrawled his name for a fourth time on the skunk sheet. He felt as though he himself were dangling there before curious spectators, his ankles and wrists firmly bound in Sally's stock. Just as Sally finished the last *t* in the surname of Pike's nemesis, another Plunkett burst through the door.

"Jesus!" Billy cried. He was cradling his *Damn Sea Gulls!* hat in his hands. It appeared to be red with blood. "Don't you see what's going on out there? Lock the goddamn door!"

Sally had just added a third strip of Scotch tape to the skunk list, securing it further, lest a breeze, especially one from Pike's mouth, should blow it away. She tossed her marker aside and hastily abandoned her position behind the bar. Maurice, napping on a cot in the back room until he relieved Sally at six o'clock, heard Billy's distress signals and came wide awake. Ronny jumped off his stool, propelling it several feet behind him. He grabbed a full bottle of Miller Lite beer from the bar, a killer instinct picked up from twenty years in the navy. Pike armed himself with the pegboard—an inch-thick, foot-wide board that some decorative genius in Taiwan had cut into the shape of a large, solidified 29 —then abandoned it for a Michelob. Like whales about to beach, the group headed for the door.

"What is it?" Maurice cried. "Is that blood?" He pointed to Billy's dripping hat and then turned a medium snow-white.

"No, it ain't blood," Billy groaned. "Didn't any of you see what's out there?"

"We was playing some crib," said Ronny, proof that they hadn't been just sitting around idly.

"Maurice," Billy said. "You better go out there. We got trouble." He stepped back so that Maurice could peer out the frosted window in the front door. Sally crowded up on his left shoulder, Ronny and Pike to the right of him. It was Prissy Monihan they saw outside, with a small horde of demonstrators huddled about her.

"What's that they got in their hands?" asked Pike.

"I can't tell," said Maurice, and his warm breath melted a small patch of frost from the window. *The better to see you with, my dear.*

"Get off my foot, Maurice," Ronny advised.

"Looks like Windex bottles," said Sally, her female expertise kicking in. More of the winter's frost evaporated from the pane, enlarging their view. "That's just what they are," Sally confirmed. "Windex bottles."

"Well it ain't Windex *in* them," said Billy, still wringing out his hat. "It's red food coloring."

"What?" said Sally. "Why?" Then she knew. The new minister, Thornton Carr, promenaded into view, a placard strapped to his back which declared: *The Blood of Our Children Drips from This Building.*

"What's that mean?" asked Maurice. "I know this old building is on its last legs, but it don't have a leakage problem."

Thornton Carr walked at a mournful gait across the dooryard. Prissy, Elsa Carr and her two teenage daughters, old Sarah-Tom Fogarty, and Wilma Fennelson, who was a distant cousin to Maurice, belted out what sounded like a solid hymn to the listeners behind the paned glass. Then Thornton cut an attractive pirouette and began the march back. The front of his placard warned: *We'll Spray Anyone Who Enters.* Sally read the words slowly, and looked down at Billy's hat. So did Maurice, then Ronny, and Pike.

"Correct-o," said Billy. "They blasted me." It would seem the damn sea gulls were not the only creatures capable of dumping on Billy Plunkett's head.

"What'll we do?" Sally whispered, her face pressed closely to the window.

"Friday night is my biggest night," said Maurice, a hollow ring behind his words, the sound of an empty cash register spitting up zero.

"You're gonna have to go out there and see what they want, Maurice," said Billy. He hung his hat on the usual deer antler, the brown plaster of Paris spill now speckled with bloody spots, an apparent signal to the sea gull responsible that a visit to some ornithological proctologist might be in order.

"Me?" Maurice asked indignantly. "Why the hell does it have to be me? Why can't somebody else go?" Pike Gifford slunk back, away from the group, hoping to escape notice. He imagined the others spinning around at any moment, pointing accusing fingers at him and chanting, "Him! He's the only one on the skunk list! Let's sacrifice *him!*"

"Because it's your cash register, Maurice sweetheart," said Billy. "You're the man who pays the bills."

"Just barely," Maurice said meekly.

"You're the only one who can handle the problem," Billy added. Maurice highly doubted this, but he opened the door and inched out into the cold afternoon. The afternoon sun was casting a fine golden sheen on the snow, the automobiles, the telephone wires. It even bounced nicely off the pinkish frames of Prissy Monihan's glasses, warmed them a bit. Maurice heard the big thick door to The Crossroads close behind him, as though it were the door to the blessed ark. He took an invigorating breath of cold air and smiled sweetly.

"Nice day, ain't it?" said Maurice.

"You ought to burn in hell, Maurice Fennelson," Prissy announced. Scenes of being bombarded with countless streams of red food dye unfolded in Maurice's vision of things to come. Whatever he did, he needed to avoid getting shot. With the wind-chill factor what it was, he would be something akin to a large cherry Popsicle by morning. Maurice eyed the Windex bottles warily. Remembering the rattlesnakes he'd seen on *Nova,* he decided to stay a body's length away from Prissy, and judged her to be about five feet long.

"You're gonna have Satan's pitchfork jabbing you in the backside for all eternity," Priscilla added.

"Other than that, what can I do for you?" Maurice asked.

Actually, it was probably nice and warm in hell, the thermostat rarely dipping below eighty. In Mattagash, it was already well below freezing and not yet dark.

"You can close this den of iniquity!" shouted Prissy. "That's what!"

"I'm making a living here," said Maurice.

"No you ain't," said Prissy. "You're making a killing, and it's our children who will pay the price." A soft smattering of applause broke out around her. It had often been said of Priscilla Monihan that her personality problems began the day she missed out on Mattagash's only social protest, one her mother had helped launch. The ladies had ousted a downstate stripper, an event that was still spoken of with pride in some circles, reverence in others.

"I ain't ever sold a drink to a minor," Maurice said, which was certainly not true. "Now why don't you women just go on home where it's warm, and knit something?"

"They made livings in Sodom and Gomorrah, too," Elsa Carr shouted. "And you might say they got closed down in a big way." Maurice stared at Thornton Carr, a most henpecked man indeed, and pitied him the scrawny little dark-haired wife and the buck-toothed daughters. Thornton looked as though he agreed with Maurice that knitting somewhere warm would be a grand idea.

"The Bible ain't against a man having a drink," Maurice tried to reason, forgetting that he was dallying with the unreasonable. "You just name me one place in the Bible where it says drinking's bad," he challenged, an act of folly. Maurice would be hard-pressed to even find a Bible. Prissy, on the other hand, slept with a well-worn copy under her pillow. And it was Maurice who had always been so fond of saying that if a man bets you fifty dollars he can make the jack of clubs jump out of the deck and spit tobacco juice in your eye, don't bet him. It's *his* trick. "You'll get an eyeful of tobacco juice every damn time," Maurice liked to add.

" 'Be not among winebibbers,' " Prissy recited. " 'For the drunkard and the glutton shall come to poverty.' You'll find that in Proverbs, chapter twenty-three, verses twenty and twenty-one." Maurice cast an even-eyed look at Prissy.

"Name another place," he said, and then listened sadly.

"One Corinthians," Prissy quoted. " 'Be not deceived: neither fornicators, nor idolaters, nor adulterers, nor effeminate, nor abusers of themselves with mankind, Nor thieves, nor covetous, nor drunkards, nor revilers, nor extortioners, shall inherit the kingdom of God.' " Maurice looked behind him at the faces in the window. She'd nailed them all with that last one. There was so much tobacco juice in Maurice Fennelson's eye that he was obliged to lean back against the ancient wood that had gone, years ago, into the making of The Crossroads, wood cut by one man and, most probably, hauled by one horse. A faint spell overtook Maurice and he closed his eyes.

Prissy had gone on to recall other biblical books, but above her voice Maurice heard an approaching sound. It could have been those hay wagons of yesteryear, or a single old workhorse twitching out a white pine that would become a beam in someone's living room until it rotted with time. But Maurice opened his eyes and saw that it was none of these things. It was Booster Mullins, in his maroon Bronco with the sun-yellow plow. Maurice wished suddenly that Booster would lower that plow and clean the driveway in much the same manner that Jesus had seen fit to clear the Temple. A bucketful of biblical riffraff would make a nice thump when tossed into the Mattagash River. But all Booster did was pull into the yard, kill the ignition, and jump out. Maurice winced. Without the Bronco, Booster was fair game. Maurice looked up at his sign, the one with the two beautifully bluish rivers arching up to join themselves. *Where Good Friends Meet.* A bitter irony, if ever Maurice saw one.

Booster edged past the pacing minister and stood back to read his message.

"We'll . . . spray . . . anyone . . . who . . . enters," Booster read, and was immediately hit in the face with a blast from old Sarah-Tom's container.

"Not unless he enters the bar!" Prissy said loudly, grabbing the old woman's wrist.

"What's that?" asked Sarah-Tom.

"NOT UNLESS HE GOES INSIDE," said Prissy.

"Okay," said Sarah-Tom. "Why didn't you say so?" Maurice thought old Sarah-Tom had died years ago. Prissy really *was* digging them out of their graves, even in the wintertime.

"You do that again, you old biddy," said Booster, wiping the cold red wash off his face, "and I'll stick that Windex bottle so far up your ass you'll squirt ammonia every time you open your mouth."

"It ain't Windex," said Maurice, a muffled voice from the rear.

"What'd he say?" asked Sarah-Tom. Just then Billy Plunkett opened the door to The Crossroads and stepped out.

"What are you doing, Maurice dear?" Billy asked. Maurice Fennelson would be a full-fledged woman when it came time for him to die. Billy was certain of it. And he shouldn't have tried to send a woman to do a man's job.

"Resting," said Maurice. Pike and Ronny filed out the door with Sally, now in her jacket, behind them. Billy turned to survey the crowd. The minister, a new arrival from Virginia or some other clime southward, had begun to shiver noticeably in his boots. He was bearing his heavy placard as though it were the very cross that had caused all this trouble in the first place. His two daughters, their buckteeth pearly white, seemed dazed by it all. Then there was old Sarah-Tom, named for her husband Tom Fogarty and therefore distinguished from the other Sarahs in town. Behind Sarah-Tom stood the gangly Wilma Fennelson, a Mattagash spinster, known since childhood as "cucumber face" because of the elongated shape of her head. The minister's pigeon-faced little wife rounded out the picketers.

"Ladies," Billy said, and made a gesture to his head. "I'd take off my hat, but then one of you has already done that for me."

"You're a drunk, Billy Plunkett," snapped Prissy. It was true that she'd missed out on the campaign against the stripper, the way some young men miss out on a war. Her mother had promised to wait for her, that autumn day thirty years earlier, but Prissy had come home from high school to walk through an empty house, to hear the sounds of being left behind—the tinkling chimes on the back porch, the gush of water rushing through the pipes, the sudden squeaks in a floor. She had stood and listened to the heart of the house, steady and dull and lonely, and had promised herself that, from that day forward, if ever a Mattagash boat was launched toward some righteous cause, it would be *her* foot that pushed it from shore.

"You're a drunk, Billy Plunkett," Prissy said again, and then cast a paranoid eye down the road toward Watertown. Where *were* they?

"Now, Priscilla," said Billy calmly. "I'm gonna try to forget you said that. As a matter a fact, there's a whole lot about you I'm gonna try to forget. So why don't you go on home and do the same thing?"

"Not until the photographer gets here," said Priscilla. "I called up the newspaper." She had, indeed, phoned the *Watertown Weekly*. A good article about her plight, if it had just the right heading, could do miracles for her mission. CHRISTIAN CONFRONTATION AT THE CROSSROADS was one alliterative suggestion Prissy had scrawled earlier and would gladly give to any interested reporter.

"The newspaper?" asked Billy. "Why do that, Priscilla? There's only seven of you. Six and a half, really, when you consider old Sarah-Tom who's partially dead."

"What'd he say?" asked Sarah-Tom.

"And all you're doing is standing out here in the cold aggravating folks," Billy continued. "You got a minister there who ain't used to snow and cold and would probably be better off with a vodka in him. You got his spindly-assed wife and two gag-toothed girls. Old Sarah-Tom's bound to get pneumonia and finish dying. And there, behind you in the puke-tweed coat, you got Wilma Fennelson, so frigid herself she don't even know it's cold out here."

"What a vile mouth," Wilma Fennelson said, but Billy ignored her. He was in the midst of his *cocksure* act, well aware of the appreciative spectators behind him.

"Now, we all know that nature was cruel to Wilma," Billy went on. "So I'll say no more. But you, Priscilla, tell me the honest truth. When was the last time you took a laxative?" Prissy's face was already red, one of those Scotch-Irish faces you see in advertisements for soap or booze. But Elsa Carr blushed deeply.

"We never had a watering hole in this town before," said Prissy. "And the only reason we got one now is that Maurice here is too lazy to get a real job." Maurice's face was still pale enough to show chagrin. His honorable profession was being attacked.

"It's a living," Maurice said weakly.

"Pssst!" Wilma Fennelson leaned from behind Prissy and hissed at Sally. "I'm in charge of turkeys for the Thanksgiving Day Co-op Dinner sponsored by the Women's Auxiliary," she whispered. "Can I put you down for one?"

"What?" asked Sally. "Are you crazy? You're trying to close me down on behalf of one organization and asking me to cook a turkey on behalf of another? What can you be thinking of?"

"Two birds with one stone," Wilma said meekly.

"Well, someone needs to take that stone away from you," said Sally. "You're dangerous."

"It's too cold to stand out here arguing with these poor lost sheep," said Booster. "I'm going inside for what I come here for in the first place, a drink. And now I intend to have me a double."

"Go on home, Priscilla," Billy urged, "and take this ragamuffin group with you. You'll be the laughingstock of the county if the newspaper shows up."

"No we won't," said Prissy. "Seven people will more than fill out a little newspaper picture." But the darn paper hadn't turned up for the *Last Temptation of Christ* picketing either, since only Prissy and the minister's girls had managed to make the protest. Prissy knew that scores of people were willing to sign things, but when it came to marching for the Lord, her army was small. That was fine. Prissy had been keeping notes for years, and when Judgment Day finally arrived, she would be most happy to turn the list of earthly shirkers over to their Maker.

"You might end up on the same page where they advertise them strippers from Canada," Billy said. "How's that gonna look?"

"The blood of our children drips from this building," Prissy said vaguely. She raised her red Windex bottle as if she might shoot. Billy shook his bottle of beer vigorously, thumb squeezed over the end, and aimed back. Behind him he heard Ronny and Pike prime their own bottles, backup guns.

"We ain't just gonna spray these at you," said Billy. "We're gonna make you drink them." Prissy stared at him. She'd heard the stories of what sometimes happened to nuns in lonely convents when barbarians raped and pillaged, although, when you consider the Catholics, those nuns had probably asked for it. But Priscilla didn't believe any of them had been forced to drink beer.

"Come on, Mrs. Monihan." The minister finally spoke, a thin sorry-to-be-here voice. "We'll settle this at the town meeting."

"Yes," said Elsa, and blew on the ends of her fingers. Billy was surprised. Didn't these southerners know about frostbite? He could tell they weren't used to picketing in cold weather. And all that Bible stuff took place over there in the Holy Land, where it was two thousand degrees at noon, and so they had no guidelines. Billy wondered suddenly if Ronny had porked any Jerusalem broads while he was double-dating with Uncle Sam.

"You been like this ever since Mrs. Fogarty read us *Charlotte's Web,* back in the second grade," Maurice said to Prissy. He had retreated to a safe position beneath his Crossroads sign. A cold wind rustled his flannel shirt and bit through the thermal underwear inside. Maurice trembled. Prissy lowered her Windex bottle.

"Mrs. Fogarty shouldn't have read us that story," she told Maurice. "God's spiders don't talk." A little lump caught up in her throat as she remembered Charlotte's inevitable death, her spiderlings gone off on the wind.

"No, they bite," said Billy. Ronny and Pike lowered their weapons and drank from them. Prissy cast one final glance down the road to Watertown, but there was no sign of newspaper people with eager cameras. She made a mental note of the editor's name, *Julia Bayly,* so she could add it to her snitch list on Judgment Day.

"I'm Friday's paycheck," said Billy Plunkett. "I'm gone." He and Ronny and Pike disappeared back into the warm womb of The Crossroads, that forgiving maternal belly of the bar.

"The Bible says to 'drink wine with a merry heart,' " Sally shouted at Prissy's narrow back. "So there!"

"Bitch," Maurice added, a tidbit not found in I Corinthians.

"I still say someone should give Prissy Monihan a hysterectomy," said Booster Mullins, and shook a generous amount of salt from a shaker into his glass of beer. It foamed up nicely. "Whether she wants one or not," he added.

"She'll be okay for a while," said Billy. "She got a lot out of her system out there today."

"Speaking of female plumbing," Sally said, putting the salt back in place next to its spouse, the pepper shaker. Some of her customers liked pepper on their microwave pizzas. "I got some fibroid tumors in me the size of tennis balls. Dr. Brassard says they grow on the womb and that the womb oughta come out." Booster grimaced. Billy Plunkett decided this would be a good time to play "All My Ex's Live in Texas" again. Pike stared at the stuffed Canada lynx and tried not to think of his genitals, which had begun to ache sympathetically. Maurice decided to wipe down the bar. Didn't Sally realize that this kind of talk belonged somewhere other than in the sanctity of a country barroom?

"Oh, come on, you guys," Sally went on. "Why do you get all uncomfortable with female talk? I've heard you discuss other parts of the female body in words that weren't exactly medical. What's the matter with talking about tumors and wombs and periods?" Maurice himself blushed deeply over this last one, the menstrual jab. Sally was *his* sister, after all.

"That'll be enough now," Maurice said. His wiping grew erratic. What had become of women who once had the decency to walk into stores and ask for a box of cornflakes when they really wanted Kotex? Maurice had seen a sea of changes among the females in Mattagash, Maine. And that Gloria Steinem woman, he felt quite sure, probably had a New York hand in most of it.

"Yup," said Sally. She was clearly enjoying her one-upwomanship. "I told him we might as well take out the ovaries while we're in there. Get the whole shebang."

Billy had played his quarter's worth and was now back at the bar.

"I'd be careful," he said, remembering just what he believed to be the start of his and Rita's marital problems. "Taking the ovaries out of a woman is the same thing as taking the spark plugs out of a pickup truck. You might say it douses the fire."

"I ain't afraid of dousing my fire," Sally said. She zipped up her jacket. The bar was now officially in Maurice's hands. "Besides, I got plenty of coals to start another one."

"You know what else can happen to you when you lose your ovaries?" Billy asked.

"What?" asked Sally.

"It's a little-known fact," said Billy.

"What?" asked Ronny.

"Something I saw on *Nova*," said Billy.

"What?" asked Maurice.

"It's been scientifically proved," Billy added.

"What?" asked Pike. Billy smiled. Good old Piko. You put a bone in front of a dog and he's bound to jump for it.

"You start getting skunked at cribbage," Billy said, and bobbed his chin at the infamous skunk list.

No Skills Necessary:
The Miranda Act

"He never would've been a drinker if he hadn't
got hooked young on that darn Vicks Formula
Forty-four."

—Prissy Monihan, explaining
her brother Fred's addiction. Amway
presentation in her home, 1987

*D*uring the first days following Sicily's
departure, Amy Joy had gone into a
whirlwind of what should have been spring cleaning, boxing up
clothing she hadn't worn in years, washing curtains, putting the
basement in order. She had even attacked all the cabinets in the
house, emptying drawers that held pencils with no erasers, pens
that had dried up years ago, old keys that seemed to unlock nothing, not even the memories of what chests they might belong to,
what doors. With the panicky cleaning over, she was finding it
more and more difficult to relax in the big old house. Not even
the *Bangor Daily* crossroad puzzle gave her its usual pleasure. Guilt
washed over her each time she picked it up and realized that she
now had it as she'd always wanted it: pristine, without Sicily's hen
marks and erasures, free of the foolish answers. *Five-letter word
for 'insect genus': scary.*

The local weatherman, his voice scratchy on the old tube radio, was promising a light snowfall as Amy Joy sat with a cup of tea and stared out at the gray jays, the evening grosbeaks, and the blue jays. They were busy popping open sunflower seeds she had scattered at the base of the old white birch. Amy Joy was restless, but she'd already had her outing on snowshoes, had filled all the bird feeders on the back mountain and at the edge of the field.

"All right," she said. The cat looked up at her and meowed softly. "Even the cat agrees. I can't put it off anymore. Either I get a job and leave Mattagash, or I don't. But I have to decide now."

She went upstairs to her bedroom and found the empty cigar box, one of her favorite souvenirs from Ed Lawler, and opened it up. There were her precious pamphlets, some ordered from magazines, some from newspapers, some a year old, some nearly twenty years old. Amy Joy unfolded the most recent and read the words again. "You Too Can Be a Nanny in the English Tradition," the headline promised. "Let us train you in a mere six months. Both English and American openings with prominent families." Amy Joy folded the paper back into its neat little square and sighed heavily. What could she have been thinking of when she ordered it from that magazine at Dr. Brassard's office?

"Mary Poppins I'm not," she decided. And what of the other brochures she had been so sure would provide her a gateway to the world? She thumbed through them quickly, stopping at "Agency Seeks Live-in Companions for Invalid Professionals." Amy Joy had called an 800 number for this particular advertisement, and before she had time to slip it into the cigar box, Sicily had pounced upon it. "It's a sin to live with someone and not be married," she had warned, waving the brochure. "Invalid or not. Besides, this is nothing more than dirty old men chasing their so-called companions around the house in wheelchairs." Amy Joy smiled. Sicily had her moments. But now, with her mother gone, the brochures did seem silly. "Secretarial Jobs in Saudi Arabia." What would the climate be like? The few times the temperature in Mattagash had risen to ninety degrees, everyone had conniptions. Electric fans were the hottest item going at LaVerdiere's Drugstore in the heat of July. Amy Joy wished suddenly that the indomitable Sicily were shuffling about the kitchen at that very minute, muttering some gossip. Her mother's presence had always been such a large incentive, had made even the nanny job, even wiping the snotty noses of little brats, sound like work at NASA. With Sicily gone, it appeared that Amy Joy Lawler had to face one large, terrifying fact of her life which had never presented itself to her before.

"I'm scared to death," she whispered, but this time the cat lay curled in a warm ball and ignored her. But Amy Joy knew it was true. Three days earlier, she had phoned the *Bangor Daily News* to place an ad: "House For Sale. Built at turn of century. Spectacular view of the Mattagash River. 50 acres of pure country." Twenty minutes later, she had called back and canceled it. Whatever she did, she needed the old house, with its birch bark insulation, its family histories, its river beating along outside the back door. She needed a place to come back to, if she ever did get up the nerve to leave. And so much of it depended on Bobby Fennelson, didn't it? Would he and Eileen get divorced now? Would he and Amy Joy take up the notion of life together? Would Bobby want to live in Mattagash?

Amy Joy closed the cigar box. Maybe if she took a little trip, it would help her decide what to do with her life. She had always wanted to go to Boston, because Boston had such a nice ring to it. That's where the old loyalist ancestors were, in the 1700s, before they crossed the border into Canada, before they came to found the town of Mattagash, Maine. After Amy Joy became interested in genealogy, thanks to Aunt Pearl, the name of one of those ancestors had always swum around in her head, like an anxious little fish hoping to spawn somewhere. This was Sarah Bradford, who married John Webster Diamond in 1775, down there in Boston, right in the heart of the new colonies. But no one knew anything more about her—just the name, like a soft, sad, musical song. If Amy Joy visited Boston, maybe she could spend long evenings poring over facts in some dusty archives;

maybe she could bring Sarah Bradford's life back out of obscurity if she only looked hard enough. Would some future genealogist, a niece or nephew many generations removed, look for an Amy Joy Lawler, in some distant 2089, only to pencil in *spinster* and then *barren* next to her name on the family tree, on a branch that ran nowhere, a dead-end nodule? Genealogists could be so cruel.

"Amy Joy?" It was Priscilla Monihan on the phone, and Amy Joy was almost glad to hear her voice, to hear *someone's* voice, until she remembered why Prissy would be calling. For the third time in a week, Amy Joy Lawler politely told Prissy Monihan that she was not interested in signing her *Christians Versus The Crossroads* petition.

"Just because you're childless," Prissy said, and then, remembering the latest gossip about Miss Lawler, "at least for the time being," she added, "don't mean you shouldn't take an interest in this issue. Next thing you know, Maurice will want to put a lottery machine in there to encourage gambling. People like Paulie Hart will go broke in a week. First the lottery, next bingo. You mark my words. We'll be as bad as the Catholics before this is all over. We're living in the shadow of Sodom and Gomorrah now."

"We're living in the shadow of six months of snow, Priscilla," said Amy Joy. "And that makes Sodom and Gomorrah sound like nice little junket cities in the Caribbean." Amy Joy suddenly imagined what their slogans might be: *Sodom and Gomorrah Welcome Students for Spring Break. Christians Also Welcome.* Maybe they would need nannies there too, and live-in companions for dirty old men in shiny wheelchairs.

"So you won't sign?" asked Prissy. She had always known that Amy Joy Lawler, like her father, Ed, before her, was living right next door to blasphemy, on the corner of Atheist Street.

"There's the teakettle whistling," Amy Joy said quickly. What were the excuses she'd used for Prissy's two other phone calls? *Someone's at the door* and *There's the teakettle whistling.* Though Prissy sniffed hotly to hear the same old excuse proffered, there was little she could say. She had gotten the teakettle excuse twice already that day. But rather than come right out and accuse the falsifiers, she resolved instead to add their names to the burgeoning list of religious shirkers she would turn over to the Supreme One on Judgment Day. Their teakettles would whistle in hell, whether they wanted them to or not.

Hoping to forget Prissy and her nonsense, Amy Joy settled into Sicily's big armchair and opened the newspaper to the classifieds. She had to *do something*. She couldn't just sit around and fret her days away. She could at least circle those jobs in the paper that sounded interesting. But the *No Skills Necessary* section seemed to cry out for dishwashers and motel chambermaids. The only ad that remotely answered Amy Joy's expectations was for a driver of the Aroostook County Bookmobile. She wondered if she should cut the ad out and save it. Sicily would die of embarrassment, it was true, to learn that a McKinnon descendant was peddling books as easily as loaves of bread up and down the roads of northern Maine.

It was when she went into the kitchen to find the scissors that Amy Joy heard a soft knocking at the door. Too bad Prissy hadn't waited five minutes. Amy Joy could've truthfully used the *Someone's at the door* excuse. She glanced out the little window over the kitchen sink and saw a tall woman, her head lowered, standing on the front porch steps. It looked like Mary Felby, Ernie's widow, the hippie woman from the back settlement. There was a small splatter of wet snow falling lightly, something the weathermen had predicted would dissipate shortly, amounting to nothing. But Amy Joy saw that it had accumulated on Mary Felby's thin shoulders, and on her dark stringy hair. Mary wouldn't have any organic vegetables or fresh berries to sell at this time of year. Maybe she was selling something she'd canned. Amy Joy imagined chaos in the Felby family budget with Ernie gone.

"Mary, what in the world are you doing out on such a day?" Amy Joy asked as she opened the door. But when the thin figure lifted its face, it was not Mary Felby after all but a young girl, nineteen years old, maybe twenty, but no more. The face seemed familiar, except that Amy Joy knew she had never met this person.

"Hello there," the girl said, and stepped a bit closer to the kitchen warmth that had rushed out the open door. A wind was sweeping around the chimney, leaking its way beneath her collar, and she obviously wished to avoid it.

"Come on in," said Amy Joy, "and get out of that wind." The girl clutched a small bag that had been resting near her feet, a tan grip Amy Joy had not noticed, and stepped quickly into the big warm kitchen. Sicily would've claimed this girl might be a Moonie, but some things had yet to reach the Mattagash town line by 1989 and Moonies were among them. Winters in Maine were far too cold for selling roses on roadways, or for the bare bald pates of Hare Krishnas. Religion had its own sense of geography.

Amy Joy shut the kitchen door on the cold and turned to appraise her visitor.

"It's nippy out there," the girl said, and rubbed her red hands together. "I walked from the grocery store." It occurred to Amy Joy that, of course, there was no vehicle sitting outside in the yard, keeping itself warm like some loyal old dog while its mistress did a bit of business.

"From Marshall's Grocery?" Amy Joy asked. This was the new grocery, built back after Blanche's fire in 1975, and run by her son-in-law. But it was almost three miles away.

"It's not too bad until the wind blows," the girl said. "It's a short ways, really." She did not have the Mattagash brogue in her speech, Amy Joy noticed, but an out-of-town sort of accent. She had assumed that this was some young Fennelson, or Craft, or Monihan, out selling tickets for a chicken stew supper or a hand-made quilt. Hadn't she seen her somewhere before? One could usually recognize a family resemblance in the youngsters of town, their eyes, their noses, their foreheads. Mattagash lines held well, with kids always looking like newer, brighter pictures of their parents. Yet Amy Joy couldn't quite place those familiar eyes, that small aquiline nose, that broad forehead. And there was the accent, so alien to town, a Down East accent that clipped away the *r*'s. She had said *shot* instead of *short*.

"Well?" Amy Joy said. "Is there something I can do for you?"

"I'm Miranda Vanwarmer," the girl said, and then waited, a

soft smile curling the edge of her mouth. Amy Joy knew that she was expected to know the name, so she filed through her memory. *Vanwarmer. Vanwarmer.* It was such an unusual name, and yet it sounded familiar to her, although not as familiar as the large round eyes looking out of such pale, snowy skin. But nothing.

"I'm afraid you'll have to tell me more," Amy Joy said. "I just can't place you."

"Cynthia's daughter," Miranda explained.

"Cynthia?"

"Cynthia Ivy from Portland. Your cousin Junior's daughter. Junior is my grandfather." Amy Joy said nothing for long, full seconds. Of course, now she could easily place the eyes, the proud nose, the queenlike brow. It was like looking at a young Pearl McKinnon, at any McKinnon from out of the old family scrapbooks. As a matter of fact, there was more McKinnon in the girl's face than ever could be found in Amy Joy's own mixture of McKinnon and Lawler. There was more of the McKinnon face in Miranda Vanwarmer than there was in Sicily McKinnon. This was Pearl, this little girl, not stocky yet, not big-shouldered, but those haunting features, the proud flip of her head as she spoke. Except for the accent, it was as if she had just stepped off the ship from the old country, from the days when cultures and religions married within their own kind, held their own lines well, as though they were castles or battlefronts. This was the face before the McKinnons married into the Mullins camp, the Crafts, the Lawlers, the Ivys. Pearl McKinnon Ivy's *great*-granddaughter!

"I'll be darned," said Amy Joy. "No wonder you looked like someone I should know." Amy Joy had known that Pearl had great-grandchildren somewhere. The token birth notices had winged up the state over the years, but they had been filed away in some drawer or under some plate in the cupboard and forgotten.

"I'm sorry I didn't call first," Miranda said, "but I was hitchhiking and I didn't really have any loose change."

"What?" Amy Joy was sure she must be mistaken. "Hitchhiking? From where? From Marshall's Grocery?"

"No," the girl said. "From Portland. I walked from the grocery store." She was shivering, her long thin fingers still weaving themselves together, still seeking warmth from each other.

"Oh, listen to me," Amy Joy chided herself, "asking you questions while you're standing there freezing to death. Take your coat off and stand over the register. That's not a hardwood heat coming out of there—it's gas. But it's still nice and hot."

"A what heat?" Miranda asked. Shed of her coat, she was thinner than Amy Joy had imagined, and taller—as tall, she could see now, as the McKinnons, majestic almost with her sure, swift movements.

"A heat that comes from burning wood," Amy Joy explained. "From a wood stove. Don't people you know have wood stoves in Portland? I thought they were all the rage again among city folks who never grew up with them."

"A friend of mine has one," Miranda said. "It's at her father's lake camp, though. They burn some kind of tree in it."

"Are you hungry?" Amy Joy asked, and Miranda shook her head.

"Did your car break down? Is that why you're hitchhiking?" Again the response was negative. "Well, the water's hot for tea. Surely a nice cup of tea will warm you up a bit."

Miranda stood on the warm register, her thick dark hair, the younger Pearl McKinnon's hair, floating about her shoulders like wavy water. Amy Joy wondered if anyone had ever told Miranda how much she looked like Pearl. She put a cup of tea on one of the place mats on the kitchen table and then motioned for Miranda to sit. What in the world was the girl doing here, at the other end of the state from Portland, wearing what looked like hiking boots?

"You're probably wondering what I'm doing here," Miranda said, and put sugar in her tea, a practice frowned upon in Mattagash.

"I guess you can say that," Amy Joy said.

"I'm here—" Miranda said, and paused. "Could I have a sandwich? I guess I *am* hungry."

"Cynthia Jane's daughter," Amy Joy said as she made a quick cheese sandwich. "I'll be darned." She had seen her second cousin

Cynthia Jane Ivy three times—at Marge McKinnon's funeral, at Marvin Ivy's funeral, and at Pearl's funeral—and it was enough to make Amy Joy hope that everyone else they knew mutually would end up immortal. Cynthia Jane suffered from what she herself termed "long-waistedness," and was forever cranking clothing down out of her privates.

"How *is* your mother?" Amy Joy asked.

"Busy at the moment," Miranda answered. "She's living several lives, and one of them happens to be mine."

"Ah," said Amy Joy. "I see." It was beginning to fall together the way pages of an old family scrapbook should. Blood will out.

"And your uncle Randy?" Amy Joy put the sandwich on a plate and passed it to Miranda, who was watching the snow swirl outside the window. Marvin Randall Ivy III had terrorized Mattagash during his last visit, bringing with him both marijuana and a severe case of *Phthirius pubis,* the latter affecting a much larger portion of town than the former. When Randy failed to appear for Pearl's funeral in 1987, Junior Ivy had announced that his son was on some special mission from God, in some steaming tent in the middle of Africa.

"I hope they got blue ointment there," was all Kevin Craft had said. "Otherwise, I pity them poor natives." Kevin Craft had been one of the recipients of Randy Ivy's premissionary zeal.

"Uncle Randy's still preaching," said Miranda. "Saving African souls. Married to a saint. Has saints for kids. His pets are saints too. At least, if you listen to Grandpa Junior talk about him."

"That's Randy, all right," said Amy Joy, and smiled. Miranda needed to rummage through the skeletons in the Ivy family closet, the majority of which belonged to Randy Ivy the missionary. Maybe she'd find the family a little more interesting.

"And Aunt Regina is still a bookworm, and is married to a bookworm. They're both too bookwormy to have children." Amy Joy smiled again. She couldn't remember what Regina Beth had done at Marge's funeral, but she had read through Marvin's and Pearl's.

"Does your mother know where you are?" she asked.

The Weight of Winter

"Not exactly," Miranda said, then: "No, she doesn't." Not one to mince words, Amy Joy noticed. She had more than the sturdy dark looks of her great-grandmother. She had the old McKinnon backbone.

"You've run away then?" Amy Joy pushed a jar of dill pickles closer to Miranda's plate.

"Not really," Miranda said. "I was eighteen last week. It isn't that it's illegal or anything."

"Where does your mother think you are?"

"Somewhere on the streets of Portland, I suppose," said Miranda. She decided against the dill pickle and pushed the bottle away again with her long slender fingers. McKinnon fingers! Amy Joy thought. How often had Sicily remarked on the potential musical genius that lay dormant in those magical fingers of Ralph McKinnon's three daughters after Flora Gumble, grammar school teacher and pianist extraordinaire, died back in the 1920s. "A lot of raw McKinnon talent went down the drain that day," Sicily liked to note sadly, staring at her hands.

"I don't want to sound impolite," Amy Joy said. "But we don't even know each other. I'm curious as to what you are doing up here."

"It's the last place she'd look for me," Miranda explained. She scooped her shiny dark hair back from her face with both hands, making a temporary ponytail, then let her hair fall freely once again. How did it happen? How did kids learn things from people they'd never even met? Amy Joy wondered. She had seen Pearl, a million times, scoop all her heavy gray hair into a ponytail, a girlish gesture really, and then as fast as she'd made the thing, she'd throw all that hair to the winds again. Amy Joy had watched a special on TV once that talked about just such things, about male twins being separated at birth but thirty years later driving the same cars, wearing the same style clothes, the same horn-rimmed glasses, enjoying the same hobbies, both married to women named *Betty*. And she knew how little boys who'd never seen their fathers walked like them, slung their arms the same way, held their heads as though they belonged to their *grand-*

fathers. How many times in Mattagash alone had Winnie or Sicily or Dorrie or Lola mentioned a certain child's habits as being most unlike his so-called father's?

"I don't care what Eppie Hart tells the world," Winnie once said as she and Sicily rocked on the back porch, "but that child walks and talks just like Henry Fennelson because that child *belongs* to Henry Fennelson. Did you ever know a Fennelson that didn't kind of spring up a bit on their left leg as they walked? That child has the Fennelson gait, I don't care if it does have Howard Hart's name." And here at Amy Joy's kitchen table, with another November storm trying desperately to happen, with soft wet flakes beating down at the old Mattagash River, at the slopes of McKinnon Hill, at the old McKinnon homestead, another generation was using the same old-settler blood to keep alive, was making useless ponytails, was tapping fingers long as batons on the thick cherry of Amy Joy's handmade table.

"My mother hates Mattagash, Maine," Miranda said.

"That I do know," said Amy Joy, recalling all three of Cynthia Jane's visits. Even for folks who did happen to have bright and sunny dispositions, funerals were not camping trips.

"So I figured that if Mother hates it so much, it can't be all that bad," Miranda went on. Her face had warmed itself again, was blush-colored now, had beaten the storm. "We've never agreed on anything since day one."

"Still," said Amy Joy. She paused to listen as the wind picked up fiercely off the river, then died away again. "You're going to have to call her. She'll be worried sick."

"I doubt it," said Miranda. "Why is it so difficult for people to understand that some parents just don't like their kids and would prefer not to have them around? It happens, you know."

"I'm sure she'll be worried," Amy Joy said, although it was easy to imagine the long-waisted Cynthia Jane more concerned with short-waisted pantyhose than with a runaway daughter. "It's common for mothers and daughters to squabble." She thought suddenly of Sicily, her own mother, the Squabbler Divine.

"We've been *really* fighting since I graduated from high school last spring," Miranda said. She had cleaned each of the tiny bread crumbs off her plate as she talked, slowly, wetting a finger and snagging each one. Amy Joy watched her thoughtfully. "She and Daddy won't help me with college unless I go to the one *they* picked. And besides, I don't want to go for a couple of years. I want to travel around Europe first, Canada, Mexico." Amy Joy's breath caught for a second in her chest. "How wonderful it must be to be that brave," she told herself.

"It's not a good school?" Amy Joy asked Miranda. She had to stop her from reeling the poetic names of the world off her tongue so easily. Wasn't she even a little afraid?

"It's an all-girls college," Miranda said. "And I've got bigger plans than that." She was done with the crumbs and began to rattle the saltshaker softly against the pepper. Pearl's nervousness, too. Amy Joy remembered Sicily reaching over one morning, during breakfast, and taking a spoon out of Pearl's large hand. The *tap tap tapping* had been driving Sicily and Amy Joy crazy.

"And what are those plans?" Amy Joy asked, listening to the irritating tinkle of the little glass shakers.

"I'm going to be an artist," said Miranda as Amy Joy stared at her hands and wondered if any superb concertos were lying dormant in those long, piano fingers.

"Mama?" Amy Joy whispered softly to Sicily. Sicily had fallen asleep in the TV lounge in front of *Cocoon,* the rental movie for that Saturday. Patrice Grandmaison must've thought it would cheer the seniors up to watch a film in which others of their ilk fared so spectacularly. But Hollywood scripts with aliens who could make you young again only depressed the more realistic Mattagash senior citizens. Most of them had left the room even before Sicily fell asleep.

"What is it?" Sicily said, sitting up. She rubbed her tired eyes. "Did all them old fools go to Mars yet?" she asked, and nodded her chin at the VCR and its unreeling tape. "What a stupid picture."

"Did you fall asleep during the movie?" Amy Joy asked. She

noticed that Winnie was not in the room. Sicily squinted her eyes up at Amy Joy, and then past her to where Miranda stood. Miranda smiled, a wide McKinnon smile, a dark swath of bangs sweeping in over her left eye. Sicily stared.

"Pearl?" she said, shaken, thinking maybe she was still asleep. It wasn't an easy task to come out of a deep snooze, still cobwebby with the dreams of the subconscious, only to be confronted with tricks like this. She clutched at the little scarf someone had knotted prettily about her neck. Amy Joy frowned at such foolishness: Sicily hated scarves.

"Don't be upset now, Mama," Amy Joy said as her fingers quickly undid the scarf around her mother's neck. She pulled it free. "This is Pearl's great-granddaughter. Her name is Miranda. Can you just imagine us meeting one of Pearl's great-grandchildren?"

"Pearl was a fool to leave Mattagash," Sicily said, shaking her head and making her little clucking sound of disapproval. "But you couldn't tell her anything." She looked again at Miranda, who said nothing.

"How was the movie?" Amy Joy asked, but Sicily would not be deterred.

"This is what's wrong with the whole world nowadays," she sputtered, her index finger attacking the air. "Everybody wants something that lies just down the road," Sicily said. "And nobody ever comes to any good who goes off looking for what was already under their own nose. What did Pearl gain, I ask you to tell me, by traipsing off downstate? She wanted to be a hairdresser, but she ended up marrying into a parcel of pallbearers and half-wits. That's just what she did. And then she come dragging herself home like an old dog, just so she could die in peace." Amy Joy considered this.

"It wasn't exactly in peace, Mama," she said. "*You* moved in. Remember? Now you've got company here. Can't you even say hello?" Miranda stepped in closer, her dark McKinnon eyes amused by Sicily.

"I agree with you about the pallbearers and half-wits," said Miranda. "But you've really made me mad with what you said about *Cocoon.* I think it's a great film." Sicily stopped clutching at her nubby sweater to give Miranda a swift look of disapproval.

"That picture's nothing but a cruel lie," Sicily said. "The closest any old people in *this* place will ever get to going on a flying saucer is Saturday, when they ride the senior citizen bus to Watertown to pick up their dentures. And in the meantime all we do is sit around here like faded roses someone brung us, or carnations, or stubby green plants. We're all sitting here like a bunch of old wilted Mother's Day bouquets." She flung her sweater off her shoulders and onto an empty chair. It was so alive with electricity that she'd suddenly felt incapable of controlling it any longer. It was as if the sweater wanted to do things Sicily, riddled with age, simply could not do.

"Can I get you anything?" Amy Joy asked. "I'm going to Watertown for a few groceries. The snow didn't amount to much. The weathermen were right for a change. Do you need toothpaste, or shampoo, or a new large-print *Reader's Digest?*" If she stopped talking, Sicily would begin. She could see her mother's mouth now as it rounded up words, corralled them until the moment was right.

"What age are you?" Sicily asked the tall girl with those old McKinnon eyes. "About one fourth of being as old as I am? No wonder you think that's a good picture."

Miranda shrugged. So this was where her mother, Cynthia Jane, had managed to pick up her award-winning personality. It was obviously in the fateful genes.

"So what pisses you off the most?" Miranda asked suddenly. "Is it that I'm so young, or is it that you're so old?"

"Yes," said Sicily. "Well then." She reached again for the sweater and took it up in her hands. "That's fine talk," she said. "Fine talk indeed, this language of the new generation. What can young folks be thinking of these days, that's what I'd like to know." Amy Joy had said "pissed off" so many times that Sicily could no longer count them. Still, it was different hearing it from an out-of-towner, a Down Easter, with their little birdlike way of talking, forgetting all the blasted *r*'s.

Amy Joy panicked. "Can I get you something?" she asked

frantically, imagining that she would bring a whole year's supply of *Reader's Digest*s back from Watertown as an offering to placate Sicily, the letters three feet high in each of them.

"Yes," said Sicily. "You can get out of my face."

Winnie came back into the lounge and stared idly at the television screen. She was still recovering from her bout with the flu, a virus that seemed to circulate perpetually at Pine Valley.

"You ain't watching that out-of-space nonsense, are you?" Winnie asked Sicily, who was now wearing her sweater.

"No," said Sicily. "I just had visitors. The earthly kind."

"Did you?" said Winnie. "Ain't that nice? Who was they?"

"Relatives," said Sicily.

"Has Amy Joy come yet?" Winnie asked. "If she doesn't do what you said she was gonna do by tomorrow night, you owe me twenty dollars." Winnie fitted a white Tic-tac onto her tongue and then reeled it into her mouth.

"If I owe you twenty dollars, Winnie Craft," said Sicily tartly, "you'll get your twenty dollars. In all the years you've known me, have you ever known me not to pay my debts?" Amy Joy was right. Winnie could be a handful. Sicily had only been at Pine Valley a week and Winnie was beginning to bob and chafe upon her nerves.

"Well," said Winnie. She hesitated. Best not, she decided, list several gin rummy debts Sicily had allowed to lie delinquent over the years of their friendship.

"If it turns out I owe you money by tomorrow night, you'll get it," Sicily snapped.

"No need to get mad," Winnie said. She had forgotten, in her year's stay at the home, how her old friend Sicily could annoy. "You was the one who wanted to bet. You was the one who said Amy Joy would be begging you to come home. You was the one who said she could only stand to live with herself for a week before she'd go stark raving crazy. And you said you'd take me with you when she does come after you. It don't matter to me if

I win or not." Winnie was now clearly hurt. "All I was trying to do is tell you I know daughters better than you do. Who would've ever thought Lola would've stuck me in here like I was some kind of hobo?"

"I would've," Sicily thought. She bit her lip. Winnie was lucky Lola hadn't put her in years ago, while Lola was still in the fourth or fifth grade.

"But here I am," Winnie continued, her voice trembly. "Living proof of what can happen. I should've took Lola down to the river when she was a little girl and drowned her."

"Sssssshh!" one of the movie watchers in the lounge, a woman with a stern white pug atop her head, warned Winnie. Winnie didn't know her well. She was from St. Leonard. "I'm try to watch dat movie, me," the woman said, and pointed at the television.

"Instead, I'm living with Frogs against my will," Winnie sobbed.

"There now," said Sicily, and squeezed Winnie's wrinkly hand. "I told you we'd both be out of here by Thanksgiving, and I meant it." Winnie stopped weeping instantly.

"Really?" she asked. Sicily handed her a barely used tissue.

"Well, there's definitely a cog in the machine now," Sicily said, remembering Miranda's defiant eyes, *Pearl's* eyes. "Amy Joy has company and that's sure to keep her mind on the wrong things."

"You don' want to watch dat picture," the pug lady said loudly, "you go to your room, you."

"They all get killed in the end," Sicily shouted back. "That spaceship crashes into the Statue of Liberty."

"Come on," said Winnie. "Let the Frogs have the swamp." She took Sicily's arm up in hers and they left the TV lounge behind them, two old women rocking against each other.

"What if your plan backfires?" Winnie whispered. "What if Amy Joy finds out she *can* live alone? What if she won't let me come live with you? What if she don't ever beg you to come back home?"

"In that case," Sicily said to her dearest friend, "I'm gonna be really pissed off."

Stopping the Blood:
Hands over Hearts

> "Mother! Mother! Why does the minister keep a
> hand over his heart?"
>
> —Pearl, to her mother, Hester Prynne,
> in *The Scarlet Letter* by Nathaniel Hawthorne

Just between you, me, and the bedpost,
I never cared very much for religion.
But I believed in God, so every Sunday I dressed my children
just as good as anybody else's and then I took them to church.
This was providing the weather was good enough that Reverend
Ralph McKinnon, my first cousin, could make it himself. Nowadays folks around here grumble if they have to drive to church
in a fancy car on a sunny day. God ain't changed, but people has.
People around here has changed a whole lot. But back then we
walked two and a half miles one way just to worship. We made
quite a little parade as we went. It started with Foster carrying
Walter, when he was all we had, and church was in a little log
cabin. Then Walter walked and Foster carried Mary. By the time
most of the family had come, before the war, we had a pattern to
it, though we was lacking Mary by then. We looked like birds

going south, like a great big V going to church. And on them days when the wind was gusting, we did break the way for the little ones. Like the birds do. They say birds can fly farther when they fly that way. You learn things from Mother Nature when you live in the heart of her. You got to survive, and nature can teach you how. One way she helped out was with flies. It ain't a bad idea, if you can't get to a doctor for a few days, to let flies light in the wound and lay some eggs. When the eggs become maggots, they eat up all the dead, rotten flesh. That's what they like best. They'll eat a wound nice and clean. You just got to abide the tickle of the maggots, and the idea of them on your leg. That way your relatives won't be visiting the graveyard on your account.

Nature can give you powers, too, just like you're some kind of witch. There's some folks who can stop your blood if you need them to. There's a charm to doing it. It runs in families, but men got to pass it on to women and women to men, or it won't work. No one could stop blood like Uncle Frank. He was a great uncle to me. He could stop blood like he invented it. Men working way back in the woods felt a little safer if Uncle Frank was at the same lumber camp. They had a better chance of making it if they got an ax in the foot or the calf of a leg. And when Uncle Frank stopped their blood, it was like he'd hit them over the head with a hammer. Their knees would buckle and down they'd go, that's how fast that blood would stop! I've seen it. I've seen men and women knocked out of the chairs they was sitting in. And the doctor we had down at St. Leonard in them days laughed about all this. He said it was in a person's mind, is all. That they do that to themselves, and that it has nothing to do with Uncle Frank. But we was the ones who laughed at that doctor. It must've been in old Nellie's mind then, I said to Foster. And there she was, a horse!

I recall the day Nellie was twitching a log behind our house, dragging it up the slope there. Foster had cut some cedar to make the front porch, so I put Walter and Mary to sleep in the wagon and come to help him. That's when Nellie fell and drove a pointy sapling into her side. Well, blood come out of that little hole like she was a faucet! Foster went as fast as he could for Uncle Frank. Uncle begun right away working something in his hands that you couldn't see. He'd never let you see. That was part of the charm. Then he started saying some words to hisself, saying the charm words. When that blood stopped, it was like the little Dutch boy had stuck his thumb in that horse's side. Nellie's front legs wrinkled up like they was cardboard. She went down *plop!* And she didn't get up till an hour later. Foster and I put tar pitch onto the hole to seal it and Nellie was back at work the next day. So don't let a doctor try to talk you out of what you know to be true. That blood stopping sure wasn't all in Nellie's head. I'll tell you something else, too. Folks couldn't stick a pig if Uncle Frank was leaning on a fence watching them. The pig just wouldn't bleed.

Uncle Frank finally taught me the charm before he died. "My dance is almost up," he said. And he give me the charm, sort of like a good-bye gift. For it to work, you need two sticks or such to make a cross. Uncle Frank used to carry matchsticks, but you can pick up twigs if you need to. And then you make a cross out of them. By the time he showed me the secret, his hands was so old they shook. But I can't tell the rest of the charm. It'd ruin it if I did. I can only pass it on to a male in my family, and I don't even know if there's any males left alive. Nor do I care. But them charm words are between Uncle Frank and me. And Walter. I told it to him before he went off to war in France. But I will tell you this. When God intends for blood to run, *it will run.* And then there's no stopping it. Take Martha Craft's little boy. He was born a bleeder, and when he started bleeding that last time, there wasn't enough crosses from here to China to stop him. And I guess Walter's wound over in France was too big to plug up with charms.

When you know the blood charm, you're cursed with seeing things most folks don't ever see. All the important days in my life has had to do with blood, it seems, now that I think back to them. There was the blood of my children being born, my children dying, of folks I saved with the charm. But I'll never forget the day I decided to give up the blood charm for good. That was the day one of the McKinnons come after me to stop blood. Keep in mind, the McKinnons—and I say this being descended from them—thought God made the world in six days and on the seventh he asked if they'd like him to change anything. But one day Marge McKinnon, my second cousin, come running up the steps to my front porch, banging on my door. That was toward the first of April in 1913, another spring that stands out in my life, and I remember it like it was yesterday.

It was the earliest spring ever recorded in these parts. The ice broke up in the river and run itself out by the time April 1st come. And little limp flowers, the first flowers of spring, had begun to poke up about the roadsides. In all my days I never saw such an early spring in northern Maine. You'd have swore it was the middle of May. Porter Craft had poled Marge that seven miles upriver by canoe, to the mouth of Mattagash Brook. She was all in a tizzy. Keep in mind she was only about twelve and her mother was bleeding to death. I tell you Grace McKinnon was one of the kindest, softest souls ever to tread this earth. So I tore off my apron and yelled for Ester to watch the littler kids. It was a half-mile, maybe more, down to the river where the canoe was waiting. I run all the way. You can do things like that when you're scared. I could still smell the snow laying quiet in the woods. Spring cress had sprung up along the road, and I remember thinking how I'd rather be laying on my back in that cress, looking straight up at them April clouds. They was slow-moving across the sky that day, like big puffy horses. And I could hear a crow calling out from his watch, warning his flock. There's a woman coming on the run, that's probably what he told them. Here comes a woman and a girl and something's up. And all the time I'm running, I'm thinking. My thoughts are running with me, down that road to the river. I was wondering just what God was up to. That's what I was thinking. My feet was hitting the ground and my mind was saying *Please God* each time they did.

The truth is that Grace McKinnon didn't deserve to have *me* stop her blood. I only met her a few times in my life. Folks was always so busy back then, and there we were, all them miles from Mattagash settlement, up there at Mattagash Brook. But I read her through and through the few times I met her. She was a very good woman. I said before that God takes the special people home right away. That's why Mary and Walter and folks like them is long gone. That's why I'm living enough time for two lives. This is my sin. But I wasn't the only woman who lay down with the Reverend Ralph McKinnon. I may not even be the last. There's a good chance he's now laying down with angels. He could talk you out of your soul. He could use the Bible to turn your head. He could strike just when you've lost a child, and I had just lost Mary. And here's something else. I'd do every heavenly bit of it again. He was my first cousin. You tell that to most folks nowadays and they'll cover their ears. But in my time it weren't at all unusual for first cousins to marry and have big healthy families. What ain't healthy is that Ralph McKinnon had one family and I had another. What ain't healthy is that Ralph McKinnon was a minister, and he preached a strong sermon every Sunday, which always mentioned sinfulness. What ain't healthy is that after Mary died, and I knew what it was like to lie down in bed with a man I loved, I went to church mainly to see him. I hardly ever went to see God in them days. I pulled my kids out of bed on some of the rainiest Sundays ever to fall on Maine. We had no church in the winter, those of us from Mattagash Brook. It was too far away. But in the blessed summer, when the elms rattled their silvery leaves, in them wonderful summers, years of them, I knew a little bit of what it feels like to love. That's when Ralph McKinnon come by the house after church, after being so kind as to hitch a pung up to a horse and come preach a sermon in the wilderness. And Foster was— how can I remember where Foster was, all them times? Even then I didn't much care.

So this is what I'm thinking, all the time I'm running through the woods with little Marge McKinnon, his daughter. I'm thinking this ain't the way it should be. There should be someone else in Mattagash, Maine, knows how to stop blood. But Uncle Frank was long dead, and I was on my own. When Porter Craft brought the canoe to shore, just behind the McKinnon house, I saw Reverend Ralph standing on the bank. He was whittling. He could shape the most beautiful crosses out of wood that you ever saw. I climbed that hill, him standing on the top of it like he was a cross himself, and I went past him and into the house. The curtains in the bedroom was all drawed up, the windows shut tight. I could barely see to move, so I pulled the curtains back in one window and then opened it. You could almost see the stench of death waft its way out. I looked at the woman in the bed. "Gracie," I said to her. "It's Mathilda Fennelson. I'm here to help you." And then I put my hand on the bed, just rested it there. She'd had a baby, she'd had Sicily three weeks earlier, so I figured some of the afterbirth had stayed in her and was causing her to hemorrhage. "I'm gonna help you," I said again to her. "I'm gonna stop your blood." And she smiled, the sweetest, weakest smile I ever saw. I brought my hand away, so I could reach into my apron pocket for the two little sticks I always carried with me, and that's when I saw the blood. My hand was wet and sticky with it. And it was a different color blood than afterbirth blood. I lifted the blankets and saw a bed full of it, Grace's blood. And it didn't seem to be coming from her womb at all. There was no blood on her there. And she said, "You can't stop this kind of blood, Tildy Fennelson. This is a blood has a right to run."

That was when I saw her wrists, cut, the way you take a plum and slice into the red of it. Someone had put bandages around them little wrists, had tried to close them off. It had taken a lot of time, the coming to get me, the coming back. She'd bled an awful lot by then. But I'll tell you one thing. I wouldn't have used my charm even if I'd been there the second she did it. I can't tell you the charm words, but I will tell you this. Them words you use is the words to a prayer. And that wasn't a place for prayers, even though it was a minister's house. It wouldn't have worked a whit anyway. You can't bring God into a room where the Devil's been. And for a sweet young woman like her to take her own life, there must have been a devil in her room. There must have been a devil in her life. And I knew who it was. I'd seen the Devil standing on a hill, whittling his cares away, making another cross for someone to bear. "Who put them bandages on your wrists?"

I asked her. I'd put my little sticks away and I'd started tearing up the top sheet into strips. "Margie," she said in the tiniest whisper. It was that twelve-year-old child who did the wrapping, who did the journey to fetch me. All this while Nero fiddled. I circled her wrists back up in clean, tight strips, and while I was wrapping she said, "Tell me something, Mathilda," and I said, "I'll tell you what little I can, Grace. What is it you want to know?" I expected she wanted to talk about death, you know, like Ivy Craft did, back when we was kids. But she lifted herself on her elbows, that little smile always right there in the same place, and she said, "How many of your children did he father?" If she had riz up them bloody little wrists to slap me, I wouldn't have been more shocked. That's the gospel truth. To this day I don't know how she knew. I never heard a word of gossip about it, all them years I lived in that little town. And not one of my kids come home crying from school 'cause another kid had said something cruel about me. All I can figure is she knew because *he* told her. But no matter, I found I couldn't lie to that dying woman. "Four of them," I said, and I kept on wrapping that last wrist of hers. "Garvin, William, Winnie, and Percy," I said, and it was the truth. I knew my times of month, and I knew who I was with during them. Then I dipped a cloth in the washbasin and put it on her forehead. I loosed up her nightclothes. All that while them two little sticks was bobbing and clinking in my apron pocket. Would the charm have saved her, if I'd give it a try? Your guess is as good as mine. She was a woman who wanted to die, there was no doubt in my mind of that. And sometimes I wonder if three of them children, three of them four tainted children, might have lived long lives if they'd knowed they weren't born with the Fennelson curse. Them notions can prey on your mind, you know. There was other notions preying on mine. I never lifted my eyes again to look at Ralph McKinnon after that sad, bloody day in his wife's bedroom. A decade later, he went off to China and died there.

And I never told them kids that Ralph McKinnon was their father. When Percy started looking at Sicily McKinnon like he might want to marry her, I knew I'd have to say something. But

Percy went through the ice when he was only nineteen and drowned. God must have been keeping a close eye on the family genealogy. And Winnie never knew, in all the years she felt she wasn't as good as Sicily McKinnon, that Sicily was her half sister. It wouldn't have benefited her one bit to know that. It would have benefited Sicily even less. Some folks around here thought Reverend Ralph was a god. And I'll tell you something else. Not all of the women who knew that man as I did owned up to their youngsters when them kids growed up and started marrying. The sins of their fathers was never so true as it is in Mattagash, Maine.

I wish I'd have knowed right then, so I could have told Grace McKinnon, that I would be punished for my sins. That I would watch most of my children die off, one by one, before my very eyes. That's what happened too. When you know the blood charm, it makes you a lot more watchful. You begin to see things other folks miss. Blood on the moon is a real bad sign, when you know how to look for it. I remember clearly the night the moon spoke loudest to me, a night early in March 1917. I'd woke up because of a coyote way off, howling its heart out. It was probably chasing a bobcat, or a lynx. I could hear the old dog whining on the porch, scared, scratching to get let in. When I got up to tend to it, I stepped out on the porch just a second to listen. That's when I saw the moon. I tell you, in all my days I've yet to see another ring like that. It was a big, big ring around the moon, all violet and yellow on the outside but scarlet on the inside. Scarlet like blood. Now, I've seen northern lights bright enough to scare a southerner. But that ring I saw, that cold night out on my porch, was not of this earth. It was red as blood. Blood around the moon. And I knew there was more than a spring storm coming. I knew a powdering of snow wasn't what that moon had in mind. And I knew I was cursed by being able to see it all aforehand.

Sure enough, the next day when Foster come back from St. Leonard Point with supplies, he brung some news, too. The Germans had sunk more American ships. Thirty-seven men had drowned. "So now they'll kill thousands to get even," I said to Foster. But he didn't say anything. Men are quicker to war than women. Women learned, a long time ago, to bite their tongues. But there it was. And it was only three weeks later that Foster come home with some bigger news. He'd seen a paper they was passing around in Mattagash, like it was a collection hat. So he copied down the headlines on a piece of cardboard and he brung it to show me. I took that cardboard in my hands and I saw them big words scrawled on it. U.S. DECLARES WAR ON GERMAN IMPERIAL STATE. I went right out to the front porch, slammed the door behind me. I sat down on the steps and pulled my knees up to my chin. No coat on or nothing, and it was a cold, cold day. If someone shouted out to me, I didn't hear them. I just sat out there and knew, when there's blood on the moon there's trouble on earth. "I can kiss that boy good-bye," I said. "President Wilson don't know him from Adam, but his own mother can kiss him good-bye." And that big front porch fell so silent, like all the boards in it was sad. And the veranda, the one Foster and me built while Walter and Mary was little, seemed to sag more than it should. And the porch swing was so still, and covered in snow. And I realized suddenly that if I ever heard another guitar strummed on that porch, in them long summer evenings, it wouldn't be Walter strumming it.

And the next day, Walter went right down to Mattagash, then on to Houlton, and he signed the papers to go. Then he come back to spend a few days with his family. At least he got that time to say good-bye. All kinds of folks come and gathered at the house. It was a big thing in them days to have our young men go so far away. None of us had a book with a map in it, or a globe of the world, something we could have stared at during them long winter nights. So folks come to say good-bye. Foster got out Grandpa Fennelson's old handmade pung. He'd give it to Foster's dad, for letting him stay on with them till he died. The neighbors come with their own sleighs, and we raced them in the moonlight. Can you imagine that? Sleighs full of people, harness bells screaming, folks singing out the old songs. And it was no secret that Foster and the other men dug down in them hidden places men know about and found a bottle of whiskey or two. And in among all that laughter, I kinda thought Walter might be safe after all. It was as if that crowd might save him. But every now and then, at the crest of some windy hill, while them bells carried their sound across the air, I'd find myself looking right up at that old moon. We shared a secret, the two of us. When there's blood on the moon there's trouble somewhere. Why only some folks can see them things, I never knew. But most people go through life with a veil over their eyes. It's the rest of us who are forced to suffer the truth. Long after that big safe crowd had gone, when there was only sleigh marks in the yard, and dirty dishes in the kitchen, it come down on my head like a rock. That's how hard the truth can hit you. And I looked over at his thick head of hair, all them yellow curls. I looked at them Scotch-Irish eyes, so blue it was like the oceans of the world had poured into them. He was my firstborn, remember. "Ain't nobody gonna save that boy," I said to myself.

The morning he left, I was big with carrying Morton, big and wobbly. But I wanted real bad to look pretty on that last day. I wanted him to remember me young, and I *had* been young once. So I got up an hour before sunup to try to look that way again. I turned the kerosene lamp up—ain't that funny the things you remember?—I turned it up and then I got myself a jar of water and a comb. I put my hair up on the top of my head. I always kept my hair long, all my life, and I believe it still is. I made myself some tiny ringlets on the sides of my face and then I tried to powder myself some, with some old rouge my sister Laddie had give me. I was never good at fixing myself up with the store-bought things like some women. There was a time when I was pretty by nature. But I'd had eight babies by the time Walter went to war, and another on the way. So I took out that powdery rouge—it was all broken in little chunks, and I rubbed one of them chunks on my face a bit. I tried to wear the nicest dress I owned. It was a flowery blue and green one that Laddie had worn on the train trip she took to Bangor, when she went to visit her in-laws. She give it to me when she gained all that childbearing weight. "I'll never lose back down enough to wear this dress again," she said to me. And she was right. She never did. But I was too big with Morton to wear it myself. I couldn't get my belly into it. It was like trying to put something big into a little sack. So I wore Foster's Sunday shirt, left the bottom buttons undone. I didn't care what Foster might say about it. I wanted to wear something nice. When I walked into the kitchen, Walter was already at the table. We was always the first two up, even when he was a little boy. "Mama, you're beautiful," he said. Bless his heart, he said it like it was true. I suppose he knew I'd done it for him. And it made me feel foolish right then, away from the dark shadows of the lamp, the sun coming up full and bright. There I stood in Foster's shirt, with that big belly, with a face covered in rouge, with limp little ringlets trying hard to curl. I never did have a natural wave. So I turned my back to Walter, took some hen eggs from the basket, and put them in the sink. Eggs in the sink! I took down my mixing pan and broke them eggs in it, and that's when I looked out at the barn. The sun was coming up all gold and yellow. "Sun's coming to get the rooster," I said to Walter. "Sun's coming to get that old rooster for good this time." That was a game we'd played when he was real small. "No sun can get little Walt," he said. I hadn't heard him say that in years! "The sun can get the rooster, but it can't get me, Mama." That was the second time I knew for sure he was gonna die. I turned right around and said, "Run, Walter. Run back into the woods and hide." And I felt that baby kick me, and everything went around and around in my head. It was like life and death was happening all at the same time. One baby was going off to die and another was trying to get born. I got so dizzy Walter led me to a chair. He stroked my hand like I was something wild, a horse maybe. He calmed me down. "The sun ain't gonna get little Walt," he said to me.

When I got that telegram, a year and a half later, I was almost pleased. A real telegram, addressed to me like I was someone important. Like someone out there in the wide world knew that I was on the planet. Then I remembered why anyone would want to send an old fool like me a letter. I soon quit feeling important. I remember I'd been sick all that morning. I was carrying Casey at the time. Morton was already sixteen months old, and he was reaching up for the letter. I put it on the table and then wiped my hands on my apron a long, long time. Before I opened it, I remembered my kitchen as it was that morning Walt left. Time is like that, you know. You can reel it back anytime, you just can't keep it. I thought about that pregnant old fool with red cheeks, wearing a man's shirt, trying to hide a belly full of baby. "That's how he must've remembered me," I said to myself. "Just a fat old clown." So I went ahead and read about how Walter had throwed himself on a grenade, over there on some hill in France, in the Argonne Forest, and that he saved a lot of men by doing so. It was one of our own bombs, and think of that, a British Mills grenade, taken by the enemy off one of our dead soldiers and throwed back at us. Life is like that, ain't it? It'll toss everything right back at you sooner or later. They give Walter a lot of nice medals, and the town of Mattagash, Maine, put up a nice plaque for him. He was our first soldier to die in a war.

So this was something I wish I could have told Grace McKinnon on her deathbed. "Life throws everything back at you, like some bomb waiting to go off," I would have told her. It's an awful truth to realize, and yet I been punished with a hundred-plus years to think about it. I been given all this time to ponder clearly about love, and I come up with this thought. I loved two men in my life, dearly. One died in France, the other in China. Ain't that funny, how things can happen? And all them years, when folks would catch me peering way off in the distance, like I was listening to the thunder, it weren't no homey thoughts passing through my mind. I'd be thinking of Walter, all alone in that deep, black forest, with them two little sticks in his pocket he never got the chance to use. And then I'd get to wondering about Grace McKinnon's pale, dying face. "He must have told her," I'd be thinking. "But *why?*" For three quarters of a century I been entertaining myself with the answer to that question, like it's some kind of toy, some kind of top that just keeps spinning and spinning so I can't ever read what's written on it.

I guess I'll be taking the charm with me when I go, 'cause I never told nobody but Walter. But I'll see Walt when I do die. And Mary. And them other children I barely remember. And Uncle Frank. And Ivy Craft. And poor, poor Jennie. And Martha's little bleeder. And when I think about meeting up again with the Reverend Ralph McKinnon, with his strong hands, and his cool, whispery voice, it makes the goose bumps raise up on my arms, and my breath catch up fast. I guess there is still the foolish notions of a young girl growing like moss inside this old fool's body. But I would hope that all is forgiven up there. That Gracie's little wrists will be good as new, with flowers growing around them for bracelets. And we'll all have a real good laugh at earthly charms, and match-made crosses, and them loving Sunday sermons that never seemed to end.

The Bottle Families: HALT

I never knew childhood, like the kids on TV
So I held on to dreams, like a farm boy would do
And I made the bottle, into my family
But that's no way to be, what's a poor child to do?

If I had the money, for the dues that I've paid
Baby I'd have it made, I know just where I'd be
I'd build me a castle, with tapestry walls
And fill up the halls, with lost souls like me.

—J. Lynn Glaser, "I've Been an Orphan"

*I*t had been a long time since Lynn Gifford had gone to so much trouble with her makeup, her hair, and the clothes she finally chose to wear. But then this was a special occasion. The Crossroads had been open for six months and Lynn had yet to investigate the premises herself. It was Pike's stomping ground, a place where he and Billy convened like the members of some sad, distorted family reunion, and there was a tacit agreement floating about in the air that Lynn should never stop by without Pike's permission. The few times Lynn and Pike ever went out socially were to Watertown, where wedding receptions were usually held, or to the Acadia Tavern. But change comes to all things, and The Crossroads was no exception. Lynn had heard news that Pike's favorite bar would very likely be closed. Prissy Monihan, as Pike had often said, watched far too much *60 Minutes*.

"That's where she gets most of her notions," Pike had said. "From that goddamn Diane Sawyer."

It was five o'clock when Lynn called Pike's cousin Beena Gifford Rodriguez. Beena had gone off to Florida, married, had two children, divorced, and was now back in Mattagash, not an easy place to survive as a single mother.

"I'm like them damn salmon," Beena said once to Lynn. "Except there ain't anything worth swimming upstream for, not if you end up in Mattagash."

"So why are you back?" Lynn asked her, and Beena shrugged. Lynn had seen that shrug before, from Mattagashers who had left their well-paying jobs in Connecticut and trudged back home. A shrug. But it was a word, this shrug, in a secret Mattagash language, because everyone seemed to understand what it meant. Everyone seemed to nod in answer. The shrug said: *Who knows why? I guess I must love it.*

"I ain't got nothing better to do anyway," Beena had said, when Lynn asked if she'd go with her to The Crossroads. "Paulie ain't so much as called me. Even his mother don't know where he is. I guess money changes *some* people."

By the time Beena and Lynn drove over the crunchy snow in the Crossroads parking area, there were several cars gathered, Pike's old Chevy and Billy's Dodge Ram among them. Maurice had a respectable crowd for a weeknight.

"He's here," Lynn said, and nodded toward Pike's clunker. They sat there for a few minutes, the car still running, the old heater working hard to fend off the cold, and stared up at the big wooden sign as it rocked gently in the river wind.

"You sure you wanna go in?" Beena asked. Lynn scraped a fingernail against the frosty glass of her window and thought about it.

"I got to," she said. "Conrad's going bat shit. He ain't ever missed a day of school in his life except when he had the measles in the first grade, but now I can't even get him out of bed in the morning. I'm real worried about him, Beena. You know how he's different from other kids. He takes things real serious. Saving up that money all these years meant a lot to him. Kind of like a security blanket, I guess. If it was Reed, I wouldn't worry too much. But it's Conny, and besides, I promised him I'd get his money back."

"Pike's gonna be mad," Beena said. She turned the ignition off and the car, borrowed from her mother, settled down on its tires to wait for the real cold to hit. "Just be prepared."

"Even in my sleep," Lynn said, "I been prepared." She pulled on her woolen gloves, shouldered the strap of her raggedy cloth purse, and opened the car door. Beena followed, their boots scuffing the well-packed snow, noisy as a little army.

It was Ronny Plunkett who saw the women first, his face filling up with a quick rush of unexpected excitement, that old Nam jungle rush, when you could hear the enemy breathing but you couldn't see the little son of a bitch.

"Bogey at six o'clock," Ronny whispered to Pike and Billy. Billy had been in the midst of badgering Maurice for some of the establishment quarters with the black X on them.

"You get them back, Maurice darling," Billy said. "It ain't like you're out any money."

"You just wanna play that damn ex-wife song," Maurice complained. "And I can't, I tell you I can't, stand to hear it one more time."

"Bogey at six o'clock, Piko!" said Ronny again, urgency now lacing his words, and it all suddenly registered with Pike. A problem somewhere on the clock, somewhere in time, and he struggled with his reasoning mechanisms. His mind raced around the invisible face of his old alarm clock back at the house. Six o'clock was directly behind him, at the door to The Crossroads. He spun around on his stool and met Lynn's gaze, over the heads of the two couples dancing on Maurice's small floor. For a moment it was almost exciting, the way it was all those years ago when he and Lynn were dating. Walking into the Acadia Tavern in Watertown on a Saturday night, wondering if she'd be there again with her girlfriends, supposing she just might come home with him if she was. It was all a part of that wonderful mating ritual, the sparks of which had slowly gone out with babies being born, with bills accumulating, with time passing. *Lynn at six o'clock,* as if she were halfway through her life, or his life, maybe. Pike nodded his head at her and hoped it was imperceptible to his comrades at the bar. He mustn't look too agreeable, but still, what in hell was she doing there?

"Seems to me this would be a fine time to play "All My Ex's Live in Texas," said Billy, and Maurice handed him a marked quarter. "Unless there happens to be a funeral march on there somewhere," Billy added, and kicked the rung of Pike's stool. Pike rounded up a weak smile. He saw Lynn dodge the dancers and head directly for him, Beena at her heels. He had always liked his cousin Beena. Why in hell was she down here offering Lynn support? What had happened to all that blood-is-thicker-than-water shit? But Pike supposed that being female was the thickest blood of all.

"Somebody call a priest," Ronny said loudly. "This man's a Catholic." Pike grimaced. What was so important that Lynn couldn't have waited until he decided to go home again? True, he had been gone for three days, ever since he borrowed the money from Conrad, but he intended to go home that very night, assuming the smoke of battle would have cleared. Apparently not, judging by Lynn's smoky face.

"Hey," Pike said to Lynn. She had stopped before him, her hands in her jacket pockets, her eyes unsmiling. "What you doing here?"

"It's a free country, asshole," Beena said over Lynn's shoulder, and this saddened Pike deeply. When blood *doesn't* run thicker than water, it really flows.

"You want a beer?" Pike asked. He shot Lynn one of his fast little smiles, the kind she had singled out years ago as the building block of his charm. His pulse was quivering a bit. "How about it, girls?" Pike said jauntily. He hoped Billy was done selecting his two usual songs and was taking note. Pike felt downright cocky, and to think that just moments ago, he was distressed that his name was now on the cribbage skunk list six times. "Give the ladies a beer on me, Maurice." Pike motioned with a gallant sweep of his arm.

"Don't you mean them beers would be on *Conrad?*" Lynn asked. Pike's smile went away, fast as light, and in its place came the scowl Lynn knew so well. But she was ready for it. "How much of that money you got left?"

Pike said nothing. He was weighing his situation, his position with his good buddies, his place in time. What a bitch time was. Lynn had come in at a six o'clock place in time, and she had looked great in those tight jeans and that cranberry-red jacket, good enough for Pike to try to pick up, as if she were Ruby with the overbite instead of his own wife. Then she had moved to twelve, had climbed up the clock to join him at the bar, and during that move a lot of changes had occurred. The jacket now had spots on it, and a couple of cigarette burns. Lynn's crow's-feet were noticeable to him, and so were the dark roots where the natural color of her hair had sprouted up, and the wheezy way she had of breathing through her mouth. It was all a matter of one's position in time, Pike realized, of observation at a distance.

" 'All my ex's live in Texas,' " George Strait announced smugly from the jukebox. " 'That's why I hang my hat in Tennessee.' " Lord, what Pike would give to have his green felt fishing hat dangling from a rack at the Grand Ole Opry instead of from the jagged deer antlers at The Crossroads.

"I want you to give him back every cent," Lynn said. "You done a lot of low things in your day, Pike, but stealing from your son is the lowest."

"I didn't steal it," Pike said. He canted his head toward Lynn's face, doglike, hoping his words would not drift behind him. This domestic problem was nobody else's business. "I borrowed it. I'll give it back to him the minute my check comes." It was good to have George Strait singing loudly about his own marital woes. The last thing Pike wanted was for the regulars to learn why he'd bought so many rounds lately. He imagined Sally putting up another sheet next to the skunk list, one called: *Fathers Who Have Stolen from*

Their Sons. But Lynn wasn't budging. With Beena's face rising like a wintry moon over her shoulder, she stood stiffly, waiting.

"He'll get it back within the week, for Chrissakes," said Pike. "Am I keeping him from playing the stock market or something? Is he on the phone to Donald Trump? He's a kid. He can wait a few days."

"How much you got left?" Lynn asked again, and this time she took her hands out of her pockets. Pike could see that she had knitted them into fists. Surely, he thought, she wouldn't—but she did. The blow came from a backhand and caught his left temple, knocked the glass he had raised to his lips into a shattering of broken pieces on the bar.

"Oh Jesus!" said Beena. She grabbed Lynn's arms. Pike had risen with his beer bottle snugly in his hand, had lifted it to strike back, when Billy grasped the bottle firmly in his own hand. He spun Pike around.

"All right, Piko," he said. "Calm down. It's all over."

"Shit!" said Pike. "You see what she did? She hit me in the face for no reason at all. I was gonna buy them two bitches a beer one minute, the next minute—*whack-o!*"

"You know what I come down here for," Lynn said. Spears of hair had escaped from the elastic band she'd bound them with, and were now straggling about her face. Her voice was shaking. She'd had no idea until the second it happened that she was going to hit him. Another time, she would have cried then and there. But not now. He enjoyed them too much, her tears, grew strong from them as if they watered him, nourished him. She would cry in the car this time, with Pike safely distanced from her, with Beena steady at the wheel.

"You know why I'm here," Lynn repeated. "Don't make me come back with the sheriff. I'm giving you two days." Pike shrugged, then thrust his middle finger up to the back of Lynn's retreating cranberry-red coat. The movement of her rear in the tight jeans meant nothing to him now. She was just a woman moving away from him in time, a bogey moving from twelve o'clock back to six o'clock, and then out the creaking door.

"Cancel the priest!" Ronny shouted, and laughter rippled uneasily about the bar. The dancers stood frozen, in the middle of their two-step, watching Pike.

"What's the matter?" Pike asked them loudly. "Ain't you ever seen a bitch before?" Now the laughter washed more easily about the room. Time was changing things. Time was erasing and healing with just seconds to do its work. Time was lapping up the mess.

"Here, soldier" said Maurice, and slid a free beer down the bar to Pike. "I treat all wounded veterans to a drink." Billy's second song had started, "'Til I'm Too Old to Die Young," and the words were milky and soothing, *familiar* to Pike. And so was the happy shape of the beer bottle, built like a woman when Pike thought about it, sleek-throated and hippy, the way he preferred them.

"What was Lynn talking about?" Billy asked, when he was sure the rest had found other entertainment. Most of the crowd had gathered around Ronny, who was explaining a technique that involved Oriental girls and baskets with ropes attached to the ceilings over the beds in whorehouses.

"She's crazy," said Pike. The swelling in his eye had all but disappeared.

"She might be crazy," Billy said. He took a quick drink of his beer and then snapped open the shell of a peanut. "But what was she talking about?"

"Conrad lost some money, who knows how," said Pike. "She wanted to know if I'd seen it." He flipped two quarters at Billy. It would be worth hearing George Strait sing about his own good luck with women one more time, if it meant getting Billy's mind on something else.

When Maurice insisted on picking up the drinks, Pike was just getting started.

"It's only a quarter to one, Maurice, goddamnit," he protested. "What's wrong with just one more?"

"Laws are laws," said Maurice, mopping down the bar, a look of stern jurisprudence on his brow.

"Fuck you!" Pike shouted. He slammed the empty bottle on

the bar and laughed to see how quickly Maurice quivered. Billy was right. Maurice was slowly turning into a goddamn woman.

"It's stoked up," said Billy. He had gone outside to start the Dodge Ram so that it would be toasty by the time he dragged Pike off the barstool and headed for home.

"I'm driving my Chevy," said Pike.

"No you ain't," said Billy.

"I gotta go home," Pike said. "I hid me a bottle of Smirnoff behind the couch." Billy thought about this. A couple of shots of vodka would be a warm ending to another boozy night. It was so cold out he'd thought he'd never get the Ram started. It had sputtered and moaned before it finally caught. Now it sat with a heavy gray cloud of exhaust fanning up around its ass, like a spruce grouse, warming itself nicely.

"I'll drive you," said Billy. "But I want your butt in and out of that house in no time flat. And don't bug Lynn. Leave her be."

"That's my house," Pike insisted. "If I want to sleep there tonight, I damn well can."

"No you can't," said Billy. "You got a room reserved at my house tonight." He hoisted Pike off the stool and together they launched themselves across the floor.

"See you tomorrow!" Maurice shouted behind them as he unplugged the Budweiser sign.

"Fuck you, Maurice, you cheap son of a bitch," Pike yelled. "You seen the last of my ass."

"Yeah, yeah," said Maurice. He unplugged the jukebox, giving George Strait's throat a needed rest, and then snapped off the Michelob light. "And the Pope ain't got any money," Maurice added. "Tell me another one."

Pike was on his hands and knees, reaching behind the couch in search of his vodka bottle, while Billy waited outside in the Ram. But there was no bottle. He had put one there, hadn't he, just before Maisy's birthday party? Surely that wasn't the one he and Billy had drunk as they sat parked on the rim of the old gravel pit, watching the sky turn pink with dawn. That had been Monday night. The Crossroads was closed on Sundays and Mondays, and yet Pike and Billy had toasted every goddamn Gifford ancestor in memory on Monday night, while a cold wind sifted the loose snow off the gravel pit's top and then layered it neatly far below. They had drunk a bottle of vodka and Pike had complained that they would die of carbon monoxide poisoning, what with the heater running to keep them warm. It had been easily twenty below that night. Where had they gotten the bottle of vodka? Billy had told him that newer models of automobiles don't carbon-monoxide someone, that you need a faulty leak.

"This Dodge Ram is a goddamn fort," Billy had said, tipping the vodka bottle up to his lips and rapping his fingers on the steering wheel with great emphasis. "You're safe here, my boy." And it was true, Pike did feel safe, but then, any time he got together with Billy and vodka he felt safe. Billy and vodka were family. And Monday night, when the bottle was empty, they had stood outside the Ram in the oppressive cold, solid as brothers, while Pike heaved the empty bottle up toward the silvery moon. There was something about their lives, a clue almost revealed, as the bottle caught the icy light, turned end over end over end, then disappeared into the blackness at the bottom of the pit. All good memories, but where had the bottle come from in the first place?

Pike rummaged a hand flatly along the floor beneath the sofa and still came up with air. His thoughts clouded with doubt. It was just possible he and Billy drank that damn bottle Monday night, toasting the windchill factor and the constellations in the sky over Mattagash. Or, and this occurred to him in a quick flash of anger, someone in the goddamn nuclear family had stolen it from him. He heard Billy toot softly outside, a bleat almost, filtering in from the cold. Pike smiled. Billy sounded like some old cow out there waiting to be milked. Just as he was arranging his thoughts, ideas as to where the bottle had gone, he heard the bottom stair step, that old telltale step, squeak. Pike looked up to see Lynn, wearing pajama bottoms and one of his old thermal underwear tops, peering at him out of sleepy, half-closed eyes.

"What you doing here, Pike?" she asked. "You know you ain't welcome here."

"This is my house," said Pike.

"Not anymore," said Lynn. "You broke the final straw when you took that poor kid's money."

"I *borrowed* his goddamn money!" Pike shouted. "He'll get it back."

"You better mean it," said Lynn. Her hair was still straggling down from the elastic band, the mascara she had applied so diligently beginning to blacken the area beneath her eyes. She looked to Pike like some sleepy raccoon, and he smiled at this. Billy tooted again, a soft little peep.

"It ain't funny, neither," said Lynn.

"Mama?" a voice asked from the top of the stairs. It was Conrad. "He down there?"

"Go back to bed, sweetie," said Lynn. "I'll handle this."

"Maybe he's lying," said Pike. "Maybe he ain't saved any money. You ever seen it? Ask yourself that. All he's ever saved is them stupid jams and all that sugar. He ain't nothing but a little fag."

"You already admitted taking the money," said Lynn. She had left the stairs and was standing in front of her husband, her thin hair flailing about her face. Reed and Julie and Stevie now appeared on alternate steps, their hair tousled, their eyes adjusting to the dimension of light in the room below.

"Get up that stairs and back into bed!" Lynn shouted up at them. "Now!" She pointed a straight angry finger, and the children disappeared, all except their feet, which remained quietly on the top step.

"I want my money back," Conrad said. He had followed Lynn down the stairs, and now he stood in the living room, his pajama bottoms clinging to his thin hips, his T-shirt spotted with purple Kool-Aid.

"Conny, go back upstairs," Lynn pleaded. "I'll take care of this."

"*Conny*," Pike said with disgust. "What kind of name is that for a boy anyway? You ain't nothing but a three-legged little fairy, collecting sugar and jam. Why the hell can't you collect fireflies, or rocks, or something like that?"

"You give it back to me," Conrad shouted. He made a feeble attempt to swing a fist at his father, but Pike caught the thin wrist and held it tightly. He pulled Conrad's arm up over his head, as though he were a champion fighter.

"And the winner is . . . !" Pike announced. Conrad was becoming more interesting as he grew older. And now that he was confronting Pike head-on these days, there was no telling what entertainment waited in the years up ahead.

"Let him go!" Lynn said, and she beat her fists on Pike's back. Billy tooted wildly again, the headlights of the Dodge Ram peering in at the house like the eyes of some indifferent God who preferred to keep his distance. Pike released Conrad and reached for Lynn instead. She had hit him once already tonight, in front of his best buddies, in front of womanly little Maurice, in front of everybody who mattered to him. But she had better think twice before she raised a hand to Pike Gifford, Jr., again. And now that he thought about it, she had probably taken his bottle of vodka. He *had* put a bottle under the sofa, of that he was certain. He pushed her against the wall and held her there, his hand locked tightly about her throat. Conrad might be at an age where he almost winded Pike, but one-handed was all he needed for Lynn. Pike edged his wife up the wall a bit, forcing her to stand on her tiptoes. Julie began to whimper, a soft whine at first, then rising in pitch, like some little northeasterly. Conrad saw his mother's face, a blush of fear spread across it, her eyes wide and darting.

"Quit it!" he screamed at Pike. "You're choking her." He jumped on Pike's back and wrapped his thin arms about his father's neck. But Pike tossed him off easily with a shrug of his shoulder, and then readjusted his grasp on Lynn's neck. She would never, ever steal another bottle of his, and better yet, she would never hit him again in front of the whole goddamn world.

Conrad was frantic. Lynn's face was now a deeper red, her eyes trying desperately to focus on Pike's face. "Please," her eyes were saying. "Please don't." Conrad pushed Julie against the wall as he raced past her, up the stairs, and into his room. Where was the bat? Dammit, he had told Reed to always, always put it back under his bed when he finished playing with it. It had been to Conrad the greatest statement of his life so far, the only safety he had felt among the numbers of his family. Now it was gone.

"Reed!" Conrad shouted. He beat his hand frantically about the floor beneath the bed, spilling and scattering the shoe box of jams. He didn't care anymore about the jams. How could his mother eat them, how could she enjoy them some sunny, happy morning, as he'd always imagined would happen once Pike Gifford was gone forever, if she was dead? The jams scattered like berries about the floor, but still no bat.

"Reed!" Conrad shouted again. "Where's my bat? Didn't I tell you to always put it back?"

Standing in the bathroom doorway in his underwear, Reed was white-faced, ashen, dazed as a patient in some disorderly institution who has been roused up in the night and forced to answer a difficult question.

"I was batting snowballs with it," Reed said. "I left it out in the backyard." His voice broke in midsentence, modulated. If only he weren't already ten, it would be so nice to cry.

Conrad pushed past him, out into the hallway. He had to think quickly. He was his mother's little man, wasn't he, her protector? She had never come right out and said it, but he knew she was proud of him for having stood up to Pike once before. And besides, if *he* didn't, who would? Who could? He heard Julie's scream rising from below, the steady smooth whine of a tiny freight train. He'd never find the bat in time. Reed could have left it anywhere out there in the deep snow. And then Conrad remembered the gun, Pike's automatic rifle he used for killing deer, in and out of season, the occasional moose, and the slew of warm, feathery partridge during bird season. Conrad remembered the gun the way some children remember homework, that unavoidable thing always put off until the last minute. *Unavoidable.* He dashed down the hallway and into Lynn's bedroom. He pushed the clothes in her closet aside, spilling some off the rack, until he found the cool barrel leaning back against the wall. Lynn had insisted Pike keep the gun there, away from Julie and Stevie, who were too young to understand the danger. The bullets, Conrad knew, were in their little box and tucked away in Pike's sock drawer. He grabbed them, shoved one steadily into the chamber of the gun, and cocked it.

Downstairs Lynn had managed to push Pike back long enough to loosen his grip on her throat. She had brought her knee up swiftly, hoping to make contact with his groin. But Pike had arched himself away in time.

"Kick him in the balls," her sister Maisy had instructed her. Lynn thought of Maisy now. Pike's hands were back on her throat, and she was growing dizzy again from want of air. Maisy had been a good sister to her. She remembered Maisy's sweet sincere face as she had explained *HALT* to Lynn.

"Never do anything when you're *h*ungry, *a*ngry, *l*onely or *t*ired," Maisy had said. With Pike cutting off her air supply, Lynn felt adrift from all of it, as though her life and the participants in it had become a hazy, lazy dream. But Lynn had a question for Maisy. "What do you do when you're all of them things, Maise?" Lynn wanted to ask her sister. "What do you do then?"

"Let her go!" a voice commanded Pike. He jerked his head quickly to see Billy standing in the doorway.

"She's got her a mouth, Bill," Pike said sheepishly. "You know what they're like. This one's worse than Claudette and Rita added together. This one's got one hell of a mouth." Pike was a bit embarrassed to be caught in a domestic fight by his best barroom buddy, his near brother, but surely Billy would commend him later, at The Crossroads, for not taking any shit off a damn woman.

"Get away from her!" Billy said. Lynn made a soft little squeaking sound, a mouselike plea for air.

"Bill, I'm telling you," said Pike. He readjusted his grasp on Lynn's neck. "She comes down to the goddamn Crossroads to slap my face, then she hides my bottle of vodka." Lynn closed her eyes. She no longer cared if Pike killed her. Maisy would take the kids. The kids would be better off with Maisy. It was time this craziness stopped. *HALT*. Her head fell to one side just as Billy lunged for Pike.

Even Lynn heard the shot, way down in her hazy dream of a life she used to know. Or maybe it was a life she dreamed of, the kind of life that is lived on *Sesame Street*, where the houses sit in neat rows, with flower boxes in all the windows, where it doesn't ever seem to snow. It was a loud *pop*, and it reminded Lynn of the corn she had popped for the first storm of winter. Pike had wrapped his husbandly fingers around her throat that night, too, hadn't he? And yet here she was, still in the same *defense* position.

"Something awful has happened out there in the real world," Lynn thought, and she came back to it, like a drowning woman coming up to the sunny surface for air. "Something awful has happened," she thought again as Pike's hand left her throat.

"Get up, Bill," Pike said. Billy was down on the floor. What was Billy doing on the floor? Pike was the one who always got falling-down drunk, but not Billy, not "The Kid." Now he saw blood oozing up out of Billy's throat, like a tiny red fountain, a fireworks of blood. Where in hell had the blood come from? How had Billy cut himself in Pike's goddamn living room? They were just going to be there a minute, just going to get a measly bottle of vodka and be off into the chilly night. What was all this blood shit? Then Pike looked up and saw Conrad, on the telltale, tell-all bottom step of the stairs, saw his rifle weighing heavily in Conrad's hands. Conrad raised his eyes from where Billy lay, and looked into his father's eyes. They were so much like his own that he might have been gazing into the mirror at his older self. A gurgling came now from Billy's throat, a musical sound, the kind the Mattagash River makes in the spring when it can finally run free of ice.

"Someone call an ambulance," Lynn said hoarsely. Her throat was already beginning to swell. She scooped the wailing Julie up into her arms.

"Get out of my way!" Reed shouted to Stevie. Reed was the one to make the emergency phone calls now. He had taken over for Conrad the night Pike's scalp had opened up beneath the silver bat, and already it seemed he had inherited the job. As he dialed the numbers, it seemed the job would be his forever.

"Look what you done now, you little bastard," Pike said to Conrad. He was trying desperately to block off the flow of Billy's blood with a dirty thumb. "If you hit his jugular, he'll bleed to death." Pike had seen deer die this way, and die quickly.

"The ambulance is on the way," Reed said. No one mentioned that it had thirty twisty miles to cover before it reached the *Welcome to Mattagash* sign. Billy lifted up a hand, feebly.

"You're bleeding booze, Kid," said Pike, but the joke went nowhere. He pressed his thumb tighter to Billy's throat. If he lost Billy, he lost everything. To hell with Lynn and the kids. Billy was the only real family Pike had ever known. "There ain't nothing coming out but vodka," Pike said, and Billy smiled. He motioned to Pike with his hand. Pike leaned in closer.

"Yeah, Bill?" Pike asked, expecting some famous last words. He could almost hear himself repeating them at The Crossroads, a small tearful crowd gathered around to hear what the great Billy Plunkett had had to say as he rounded the last bend. Instead, Billy slapped him, with amazing force, and Pike pulled back in disbelief.

"What in hell did you do that for, Bill?" he asked. But Billy had closed his eyes and was breathing noises out of his throat again. Conrad still stood, the gun in his hand, stunned.

"This is what being *doomed* means," Conrad thought. "This is *doomed*."

"He'll be okay, Con," Lynn whispered and realized she would not be able to say anything else. Her throat was swelling tighter around all the words she might say. Worse yet, it was blocking off forever the words she *should* have said so long ago. *Something awful is happening, and I'm the only one who could have stopped it.* She motioned to Conrad to come to her, but he turned and went quickly up the stairs. Lynn buried her face in Julie's hair and began to rock them both back and forth, back and forth.

"It's gonna be all right," she lied. When they heard the second shot, that most unusual *pop,* come down from upstairs, come down from Lynn's bedroom where the little box of bullets had waited, it caught them all off guard, all except for Reed. He jumped immediately into action, and was en route to the telephone when he realized that the ambulance was already on its way.

News of Little Nell:
Mattagash Is Off-Broadway

"One would have to have a heart of stone to read about the death of Little Nell without laughing."

—Oscar Wilde

"You know, there is no evidence that Oscar Wilde ever said that."

—*Dickens, A Biography* by Fred Kaplan

A lot of water—albeit frozen water, considering the temperature—had sped under the proverbial bridge by the time Charlene and Davey Craft rounded up their daughter's hospital toys and prepared to take her home. Hope, like snow, was in the air.

"I know you've probably heard of Lyme disease," Dr. Brassard told them. "That's what Tanya's got. I know that word 'disease' frightens a lot of people." They were sitting in fat, comfortable chairs in his office, and feeling most uncomfortable, waiting for the news of Tanya's fate. Tanya was upstairs in her room, waiting for them to take her home. As a family they had done their share of waiting. Charlene didn't even care what kind of hysteria the word "disease" would create in Mattagash, Maine. Davey reached for her hand, squeezed it tightly.

"The first case recorded was in Lyme, Connecticut, but we've never had any cases this far north before," Dr. Brassard explained. Davey looked quickly at Charlene, who knew what he was thinking.

"We spent our summer vacation in Connecticut," Charlene told the doctor. "The kids played baseball in a woodsy little park next to my brother's house."

"It's very likely that she contracted the disease then," Dr. Brassard said. "I think Tanya's going to be okay," he added, and Charlene sighed. Davey squeezed her hand tighter. "But I won't lie to you. There have been cases that were fatal." Now Charlene realized that all along she had feared it was cancer. She put her index finger into her mouth and tugged at a hangnail that had been bothering her. She had begun biting her nails again, something she had not done since the perils of high school dating. Now they were reddened down to the quick.

"*Ixodes dammini* is the species," Dr. Brassard said. "A tick no bigger than a poppy seed that can bite without your even knowing it. It's one hell of an infection. It can hide in the eye, in the brain, a lot of places."

"How is it treated?" Davey asked. He had his legs crossed, his hat resting on one knee.

"Antibiotics," said Dr. Brassard. "And that's what we've got her on. Doctors still don't agree as to the length of treatment because some patients respond well, others not so well. Women seem to need more aggressive treatment than men. No one's really sure why. They think it's hormonal."

"She did have a rash," said Charlene. "And that's a symptom, isn't it?"

"Some people bitten never develop the rash," said Dr. Brassard. "In a way, if this had to happen to Tanya, better now than a year ago, when patients were being misdiagnosed by the thousands. We know a lot more about it now, but we're a long way from home plate." Charlene looked at Davey. Lyme was an expensive illness, she already knew from the Geraldo show. There were hospitals, tests, doctors, medicines, time missed from work. She was thankful she and Davey had reached a decision about all of that at last.

"Tanya is responding well," Dr. Brassard went on. "I think, in a matter of weeks, she'll be just fine." He was leafing through some papers on his desk, ready to dismiss them, it seemed.

"Well, as I've told you," Charlene said, "we're moving back to New Milford, Connecticut, as soon as possible. It's almost certain that Davey will have a job waiting for him at the plastics factory that my dad manages." Her fingernails had begun to ache. She reminded herself that in no time, a month maybe, they'd be grown out again, the painful biting of them a memory, just as Mattagash would be a memory. "Good old Connecticut," Charlene added— an irony to be headed back to the origin of Lyme disease. She looked at Davey, and he nodded his agreement. For a minute Charlene had been frightened Davey might suddenly change his mind. But in all their discussions, they had come to the conclusion that not only would the move be better for Tanya, it would be better for the whole family. And Davey needed that dependable job.

"We'll have no trouble finding someone qualified there," said Dr. Brassard. "Call me tomorrow," he added as Charlene reached out a hand, its fingertips raw, and patted Davey's arm. "I'll have the name of a doctor in New Milford for Tanya."

With Thanksgiving now less than a week away, Charlene was packing frantically. If they hurried, they could be rolling into her mother's sweet Connecticut driveway, a U-Haul of memories tagging behind them, just in time to bite into the turkey.

"I don't care if I have to leave the furniture," Charlene had said to Davey before he drove off to take care of the blasted skidder. "All I know is two things. Tanya's gonna live, and we're gonna get the hell out of Dodge."

She had managed to stop packing long enough to give Tanya her medicine and start a quick lunch for the boys. Tanya was now up in her bedroom snoozing, Otis sprawled at her feet, so Charlene could concentrate on James and Christopher, the latter most unhappy about the rapid move back to Connecticut. James was elated, having missed the Saturday afternoons at New Milford movie theaters, the arcades full of the latest video games, his city friends. "I even miss the ice cream truck," he'd told his mother. Christopher, on the other hand, insisted he be left behind. "I'll live with Grandma Craft," he had pleaded when informed of the moving plans. "That's not a good idea," Charlene had said. "Over my dead body," is what she thought. But Christopher was not appeased. He had thrown himself upon the sofa, dressed in his Miles Standish outfit, from Pilgrim hat to shining boot buckle, and had refused to pack a single toy, a shirt, a book.

"Come and eat," Charlene called softly from the foot of the stairs. She didn't want to wake Tanya, who had finally settled down to sleep. James was in his bedroom, boxing up his prized comic books. He came bounding down the stairs.

"Ssshh!" Charlene reminded him. She pointed to a chair at the table. "Sit, please," she said.

"Where's Miles Outlandish?" asked James. He blew on his bowl of soup.

"Don't start with that Miles Outlandish stuff," said Charlene. "He's in a bad enough mood as it is." She went to the living room. Christopher's face was hidden beneath the Pilgrim hat.

"Come eat, honey," said Charlene. "But you'd better take off that white bib."

"It ain't a *bib*," said a muffled voice from beneath the hat. "That's all *you* know. It's a *collar*." He plunked a booted foot on the coffee table, the other still stretched out before him on the sofa.

"If you eat tomato soup wearing that collar," Charlene told him, "it will be a *bib* before you're done. Now take off that hat, get that Pilgrim hoof off my coffee table, and come out here and eat your lunch." Christopher plunked his second foot on the coffee table, then waited defiantly beneath the hat.

"It might be close to Thanksgiving, Chris," said Charlene, "but there's no law about spanking Pilgrims, not in this house anyway. I'm giving you five minutes."

"Why can't I stay with Grandma Craft?" Christopher whined. "Tell me *why*." Charlene put a hand on her hip and sighed wearily.

"Grandma has her hands full as it is," she said. "She can't take in a young boy and raise him. She just can't. And besides, what makes you think Grandma Craft wants you to stay with her?"

"She already told me she does," said Christopher. "You just don't like Grandma, is why I can't stay." He removed the hat and sat up on the sofa, his little face red with anger. "I'd rather live with Grandma than with you," he said. "You're a damn witch!"

Charlene felt the skin on her face stretch. She assumed it was draining itself of color, as angry faces are supposed to do. She pointed to the stairway, Christopher's room being at the top of it.

"*Now,* Mr. Standish," she said. "Unless you want to end up in the stocks until you're eighteen." She watched as Christopher scuffed angrily past her. At the top of the stairs he stopped. It might have been beneath Priscilla Mullins's window, but it wasn't. It was only a few feet from Tanya's bedroom, and this was what concerned Charlene. He raised a thin arm haughtily into the air. Charlene thought he was about to curse all future Thanksgivings.

"Grandma *said* you'd make me go," said Christopher. "I got no rights because I'm a kid. I should get a lawyer." Then the boot buckles disappeared at the top of the stairs and his bedroom door slammed loudly.

"Miles Standish might've made friends with the Indians," Charlene told James, back in the kitchen. "But if he wakes Tanya up, there isn't a peace pipe from here to Plymouth that'll save him from a beating."

"Can I have his sandwich?" asked James.

"Did you hear what he said about me?" Charlene exclaimed. She was still reeling in disbelief. Christopher had picked up some rough habits lately for such a little boy.

"You oughta hear what he's been saying about poor Priscilla Mullins," said James.

Charlene had washed up the lunch dishes, given the boys permission to go skating, and was back at the packing when she heard car tires crunching into the snowy driveway. It was her mother-in-law, Selma Craft, who was always dropping in unexpectedly.

"Damn," said Charlene, peering out the living room window. "She's brought her knitting with her."

Selma Craft hugged Charlene stiffly, and then slipped her boots off and left them by the front door. Charlene knew Selma would make small talk until she got to the real reason she'd come, and she did. They chatted quickly about Tanya, the Crossroads issue, the long drive to Connecticut, Ella Hart's new grandson, Sicily McKinnon's move to Pine Valley. Then Selma cleared her throat and said what Charlene knew she had come to say all along.

"Who's gonna take Christopher's place in the play?" Selma Craft asked her daughter-in-law. Her thin gray hair hung straight about her face, barely touching her shoulders. Charlene wished Selma would perm her hair into small blue waves, as other old ladies saw fit to do.

"They'll just have to find someone," Charlene said. "This isn't Broadway. There are more important things, such as Tanya needing good medical treatment."

"You know," Selma said slowly, and Charlene braced herself. "I wouldn't mind a bit if Christopher was to stay on here with me. He'd be good company, and I don't think he wants to leave Mattagash for the city." She took up her knitting, a gray sock, and went to work finishing the toe, her needles flashing and clicking with great urgency.

"Christopher needs to be with his family," Charlene replied curtly. "He's too young to make big decisions." She waited to see if Selma would counter. She was ready for it. "You've raised your family, now let me raise mine," she'd tell her mother-in-law.

"I still wish you'd wait till after Thanksgiving," was all Selma replied. "Didn't you promise to cook one of them turkeys for the Thanksgiving Co-op dinner?"

"I didn't promise any such thing," Charlene said. "And even if I did, no one would starve if there's one less turkey."

"Did you promise to make a salad?" Selma asked. "I hear they plan to have some twenty different ones. I'm making my Frozen Cherry."

"No," said Charlene. It was going to be wonderful to see Selma Craft only on the occasional vacation. "I told them I was cooking dinner for *my* family and that we were eating it at home. I don't know why everyone else isn't doing the same thing."

Selma knitted up the last stitches in the toe of the gray sock. "You folks who was raised in the city have a hard time understanding our ways," she said. Her voice was dispirited. Just that morning she'd been awakened early by her irritating bladder problem, and she had lain in bed, unable to sleep, and wondered how many more times in her life she would get to see her son Davey. He was her favorite child, her good-luck baby, born with that blessed caul over his eyes. "Now that we don't have such things as quilting bees and barn raisings anymore," Selma continued, "we find other reasons to gather up in a bunch and take a good hard look at one another. And I don't mean folks gathering up the way strangers do in them big malls down in Bangor and Connecticut, where all kinds of derelicts are waiting behind them indoor trees to steal your purse, or maybe even rape you. I mean folks getting together and saying things like, 'How's Tommy like his new truck?' or, 'What did Gloria's baby weigh?' Or maybe even rolling down your sock and showing someone where a bumblebee bit you, or opening up a kid's mouth and pointing out to everybody where the last baby tooth used to be. There ain't no *big* things in little towns like Mattagash, Maine. I could've told you that long before you ever moved here, Charlene. There ain't no murders and bombs and hijackings. That's why the little things is so important. When they're all strung together, them little things make up the whole of some people's lives."

"Davey should be here any minute," said Charlene. The last thing she cared for was some perceptive explanation of Mattagash and its ways—not now, not while she was experiencing the throes of leaving. "He's gone to get Bobby Fennelson to tow that darn skidder out of the woods. Then the bank can have it." She continued packing her dishes from the creaky old rosewood china cabinet that had belonged to her paternal grandmother. It had once stood in Gertrude Hart's dining room, in the old Hart homestead, which had been renovated and was now being lived in again, this time by Dorrie and Booster Mullins. The china cabinet had been to Connecticut and back, and would soon be on its way out of town again. It had seen a lot of dishes come and go in its day. It had seen a lot of people, trapping their ghostly reflections in its glass, recording their passage as though it were some kind of magical camera.

"Us country people," Selma went on. If her daughter-in-law was leaving, then, by cripes, she'd leave with some of the advice Selma had been dying to give her. "Us country people can go off to the city. We can learn to dress in city clothes, and learn to order out of fancy menus. We can hold down city jobs and we can even learn to talk a different way. I seen it happen with folks from here a thousand times. But *you* people," Selma said, and Charlene was quick to catch the derisive tone. "*You* people come here to the country and you walk around like chickens without heads, and you can't tell a buttercup from a marigold. You can't tell pine from spruce. But you got all kinds of advice to give those of us who can. And while you're looking down your nose at us, we're looking up. We're reading the sky for signs of rain, or snow, or counting the rings around the moon. You take away every single thing man has invented in the last two hundred years and us folks here in Mattagash will go right on ahead and live out our lives. We might miss some things, but we'll survive. It's people like you, city people, who'll be banging your fists on the sides of the ark." Selma put on her coat. Her hands had begun to shake, so she quickly gathered up her balls of yarn, one the soft gray of the sock's body, the other a mixture of red and yellow and green that she had used as a decorative trim around the top. Selma's mother had taught her how to knit. Selma's mother had carded her own yarn. Selma's mother, to her dying day, had never once walked into a store and bought yarn from over a counter. Now women were buying all kinds of stuff at Woolworth's in Madawaska, Maine, and there was talk of plans for a huge mall, bigger even than the mall at Bangor, to be built in Caribou, sixty miles away. Selma had seen a proposed sketch of it in the *Bangor Daily News,* complete with dangerous potted trees and a trickling little waterfall.

"This here is a pair of socks I made for Davey," Selma said. She balled them up and tossed them onto the sofa. "I don't suppose he'll need them down there, working inside all day long, in that factory. But if he ever does, he's got them." She waved a good-bye at Charlene, who had stopped in the midst of wrapping a candy dish to listen to her mother-in-law's lecture.

"You never liked me, did you?" Charlene asked, and Selma paused, stared down at the cardboard box of cooking books and recipe files, packed for a journey.

"You're the one with all the big answers to everything," said Selma. "I'd expect a city girl like you would already know the answer to that." She opened the kitchen door and peered out into the dazzling white yard. She could see the cold rise up, in wavy lines, like a living thing. She reminded herself that she must stop by Wilma Fennelson's house to borrow a container of whipped cream for that Frozen Cherry Salad, one of the assorted twenty to appear at the Thanksgiving Co-op dinner. Wilma bought things in large quantities—toilet paper, bleach, cans of milk, packages of yeast, cake mixes. Selma suspected it was the spinster in Wilma Fennelson that tended to hoard things, but having her for a next-door neighbor was as good as living next to a twenty-four-hour A&P.

"There ain't a sign of snow in that sky," Selma said, and bobbed her chin at the firmament. "We'll see you tomorrow," she told Charlene, who was still fingering the candy dish. Selma went on out to her car. She could have told Charlene that she, too, had some questions that she'd like answers to. She'd like to know why, in this new day and age, mothers and fathers had to live and then die so many miles from their children, and their grandchildren. She'd like to know what had happened to the family unit, and those long evenings spent at home, singing the old songs, telling the old stories. She'd like to know why her son Bennett had killed himself. And Selma Craft would like to know who on God's green earth had come up with some of the unnatural notions folks held these days.

"Indoor trees," Selma thought as she started up her car. "What'll they think of next?"

Davey Craft kicked one of the huge tires on his skidder and watched as a clump of black ice dropped from the hub. Bobby Fennelson had towed it out of the woods for him, and now it sat on the hill below his house, lolling like an orange insect on the riverbank. Davey was almost relieved that the old river had frozen over and could now carry the skidder's weight, should it find itself scuttling about down there on the ice. Just the night before, with the inevitable move back to Connecticut shaping itself in his subconscious, Davey dreamed that he had pushed the skidder over the hill. It went, all slow motion, flattening the hazelnut bushes and bouncing over rocks hidden in the snow. Davey had stood on the bank, without coat or gloves, a wind full of ice and rain beating against his neck. He had watched the orange-assed skidder spin soundlessly on the blue ice of the river, had heard the ice break into long spider-leg cracks, and then the skidder went down, an orange rock sinking, disappearing, until the ice healed nicely over it again. Such was the drama of dreams, but Davey was nonetheless relieved that the ice could now hold a pulp truck loaded with logs, just in case an erratic impulse grabbed him. It was the same feeling he got sometimes while sitting in church, a terrifying realization that he had the power to stand up suddenly and shout obscenities at the multitude. He was always relieved to find himself in control, to sit quietly in his seat and let those dangerous impulses roll by.

Davey kicked another tire, and then fingered its big thick chain, links the size of doughnuts. He leaned back against the heavy winch, crossed his arms, and closed his eyes. From beyond the river he could hear the northern raven sound its anxiety notes. He was having a little anxiety of his own. He would miss it, when all was said and done, and he was safely at a new job with the

Ronder Plastics Company. He would miss the open air, the sound of other men, other machines at work, the flat steady wings of a bald eagle overhead at lunchtime. It would take some adjustments at first, Charlene was right about that. But the Ronder Plastics Company had been known for over twenty years for their high-quality electric curlers. Davey wouldn't be working with the curlers at first, it was true, but would begin with the color-coded clips in an effort to learn the business from the ground up. But in no time, his father-in-law had assured him, he would find himself in the very department where all the excitement was, with the boys who made the inner core of the curler.

"It's a high-energy inner core," Charlene's father had told him on the phone. That was the night he and Charlene had come home from the hospital knowing that Tanya would live, that she was ill, yes, but she would *live*. That was the night, in the wake of such good news, Davey had been willing to work with the color-coded clips forever. "Our Ronder Style Setter is a real seller these days," Sidney Hart had continued, his voice ringing importance all the way from New Milford, Connecticut, the thick sound of traffic in the background. The rat race, in the background. "Now, the Style Setter has four small, ten large, and six jumbo curlers, all with that high-energy inner core I was telling you about. We're talking about a ninety-second heat-up. The unit comes with a nice little travel pouch and twenty color-coded clips, but I guess you'll learn all that once you start. Before long, you'll be able to do this job with your eyes shut. Just like the rest of us."

Davey opened his eyes and looked up at the hazy sun that hung past noon in the sky. Sundogs, he noticed, had positioned themselves on each flank, ice crystals in the upper atmosphere. Colder weather would be coming, if that was possible. A soft yellow sheen swept over the yard and then spread itself evenly on the field across the road. Wind had blown the last snow off the tops of the white pine and the black spruce, turning them green again. A spray of mountain ash berries, crusted with ice and missed by the birds of autumn, still clung blood-red to the mother tree. It appeared to Davey, judging from his panoramic view of Mattagash, that nature had been doing a little color-coding herself. Yes, he would miss it, but the day would roll around—when he'd built back his nest egg, when the kids were grown—that he might find fifty acres or so, a good spot to build a camp on the Mattagash riverbank. And he would come back to Mattagash again, for long lovely summers of retirement. Or maybe in the fall, when one could find no greater color-coding on earth. And it didn't matter this time what car he was driving when he came. It didn't matter how much cash he had in the bank. David Craft had learned some things during his Mattagash exodus, some very important things. Money can buy an awful lot. Money can even buy some people happiness. But, for Davey, happiness was his children, his wife, the things a bank can't take a mortgage on. The things a bank can't take away.

Davey kicked the steel-tipped toe of his boot against a different tire and loosened another clump of dirty ice. It was a bright yellow toe rounding out a maroon boot, easily seen when a man is at work in the snow, or sawing among the green of a fallen tree's branches. A cautionary toe. A lumberjack's boot, something he would no longer need at the Ronder Plastics Company. He was about to abandon the skidder, to pop his head inside the door and ask Charlene how the packing was coming, when he saw Booster Mullins's big maroon Bronco, its yellow plow looking a bit cautionary itself, signal a quick turn into his yard. Dorrie was in her constant spot as driver, her stomach pressing against the steering wheel. "Do you suppose her belly ever gets chafed?" Billy Plunkett once asked the crowd at The Crossroads, when the subject of Dorrie's compulsive shopping trips came up.

In the Bronco with Dorrie, and sitting in that constant spot of her own on the passenger side, was Davey's cousin Lola. They had not been to visit since the little altercation with Charlene over the hunting incident. Now they seemed ebullient with forgiveness. Dorrie swiftly wound her window down and beamed at Davey.

"Look what we brung for Tanya," Dorrie said, and thrust a fruit basket, still bearing its little green IGA sticker, out the window. It was topped off with a large red bow. Lola scowled. It was the third fruit basket they'd bought for Tanya in as many days. Dorrie had eaten the grapes and the kiwis out of the first two while Lola was running various errands. This one Lola had kept safely under her wing.

"We got us the scare of our lives last night," Lola said, leaning forward. "I heard on my police scanner that an ambulance was on its way to Mattagash for a man *and* a child, and I just stood there in my kitchen and started screaming my head off."

"What happened?" asked Davey.

"You ain't heard?" Dorrie said. She reached out a fat hand and fluffed the red bow up a bit.

"I jumped right out of bed the minute that scanner went off," Lola continued. Couldn't Dorrie keep her big mouth shut, just once, and let Lola tell a story? "And when I heard that report come in, I picked up a bowl of pretzels sitting on the kitchen counter and I smashed them all over the floor."

"Ain't that the prettiest bow?" Dorrie asked Davey. Lola leaned ahead farther, her forehead pressing against the rearview mirror.

"That's when Raymond got up out of bed and asked me if I'd gone stark raving crazy. 'Raymond, honey, that ambulance is got to be coming for little Tanya,' I said to him, 'and I bet the growed man they're coming for is Davey.' Don't ask me how I knew, I just did, and I kept right on screeching."

"Yeah, but you were wrong," said Dorrie. "Remember that time you dreamed Raymond was hit by some trash from outer space?"

"That's back when all that satellite stuff was falling down out of the sky," Lola said, defending her visions.

"She always gets the wrong vibes," said Dorrie, and began to flush her muddy windshield with a spray of blue washer fluid.

"Raymond broke his foot a month later," Lola reminded them.

"Sure, but you dreamed that trash hit him on the *head*," said Dorrie. "Wasn't it a big tire or something?"

"Who," said Davey, "did the ambulance come for?"

"Where on earth have you been that you ain't heard?" asked Dorrie. "It's all over town." But then she remembered that Charlene and Davey Craft, by their own desires, had never bought a membership into the Gossip Club of Mattagash, Maine, which had now branched and cobwebbed its way into other states, even other countries.

"I just knew something had happened to Tanya, her being so sick and all, and I just assumed you'd gone and done something stupid to yourself because of it," Lola went on. She wished Dorrie would stop the whirring noise with the damned windshield cleanser button. Davey was *Lola's* cousin. You would think Dorrie might shut up, there in the wintry driveway, while Lola bonded with her kin.

"Girls, please," said Davey. No wonder they tired Charlene. "I been up in the woods since daylight. Now will somebody tell me?"

"Well," said Lola. A *thwacking* started up. "Turn off them wipers while I'm talking, would you please, Dorrie?" Lola asked. She gave her friend a taut little stare. It was Billy Plunkett, years ago, who had called Dorrie and Lola *the fiddle and the bow*. Not only were they built that way, Billy explained, Dorrie being bulbous and Lola rail-thin, but they had similar functions. "All the gossip that comes out of Dorrie's mouth is stuff Lola told her," Billy said, to the nodding heads of his male audience, at the Acadia Tavern in Watertown. "Dorrie wouldn't have a thing to say if it wasn't for Lola. She just don't know it."

"I'm just washing the windshield," said Dorrie.

"And I'm just *talking*," said Lola. She rarely rebelled against Dorrie, but on that particular morning, with Davey so noticeably impatient, it appeared that the bow was growing weary of its partner. The bow was ready to do a little fiddling of its own.

"Conrad, the little Gifford boy," said Lola. "He accidentally shot Billy Plunkett." The wipers stopped thwacking. The windshield was now splayed with mud. "Billy's dead," she added. "Ain't that the worst you ever heard of?"

"And then he went and shot himself," said Dorrie. Never mind if Lola was mad. There were two corpses, after all. What was wrong with friends sharing?

"What!" Davey exclaimed. He felt the muscles at the base of his neck cramp with anxiety. "Oh my God," he said.

"Dorrie, *I* was telling this," said Lola.

"Well, go on and tell it," said Dorrie.

"You just did," said Lola. "How can I go on and tell what you already told?"

"Oh, don't be so childish," said Dorrie. The wipers started thwacking again.

"I told Raymond I ain't a bit surprised something like this happened," Lola said. "Something like this has been coming for a long time over at Pike Gifford's house." But Davey had turned his face away from her. She had lost Davey, thanks to Dorrie's damned interruptions and now the incessant thwacking.

"Where there's booze, there's a short fuse," Dorrie rhymed. "That's what I always say. And for once Prissy Monihan is right. If it hadn't been for the dad-blamed Crossroads, this probably wouldn't have happened."

"Oh my good God," Davey said again. He thought suddenly of Tanya, sick still, but safe in her soft little pajamas with the blue teddy bears on them. Now someone else's child was dead. He thought of Lynn Gifford, whom he knew only from a quick hello. Her demeanor seemed tough and hardened, it was true, the mark of doing time in some prison without bars, the sad tough mark of street people. Yet she lived in a house, right there in Mattagash, not very far from Davey's own little house. So why had this happened, *how* had this happened, right under everyone's nose, right under the enormous, smell-all proboscis of Mattagash, Maine?

"Billy and Pike had been drinking as usual," Lola said. "I wouldn't be a bit surprised if *she* was too."

"That poor kid," said Davey. The fruit basket seemed suddenly fragile, helpless in his arms, like a baby.

"Well, anyway," said Lola. She leaned back against the seat. She would wait until their next stop, which would most likely be at Marion's house, sister to Dorrie. The minute Dorrie started her warm-up, Lola intended to just go ahead and blurt out the news herself. Territorial bonds had already been broken. Dorrie wasn't content to pee upon her own fire hydrant. She had to go and wet everybody else's, too.

"I can't tell you how relieved I was when Wilma Fennelson called and told me the ambulance was on its way to Pike Gifford's," Lola continued. "Wilma's got herself a police scanner too, and she picked up the very first call. I guess I must have slept through it."

"Wilma's a spinster," Dorrie said. "She ain't got nothing better to do all day than sit beside that scanner." She started the Bronco up in a big roar of noise and gray exhaust. Davey stepped back a bit. "There's one of them things, what they call a kiwi, right in the middle of that basket," Dorrie said. "You tell Tanya to get well soon," she added, and gave the Bronco a bit of gas. It spun first, the wheels singing wildly, then caught a good solid strip of packed snow.

"Look at all them kids Isabel has got," Lola was saying. "And she ain't ever missed a call on *her* scanner."

When Davey stepped inside his house, he saw Charlene standing at the kitchen sink, her face pale, a hand in front of her mouth as she quietly bit at a fingernail.

"You've heard?" he asked, and she nodded. She had heard. She had already phoned Lynn Gifford to offer help in any way it might be needed. Maisy, Lynn's sister, had thanked her for calling. Charlene didn't know Lynn, but she had come to believe that nothing could be more horrible than losing a child, and that had happened to Lynn. Now they were sisters. For so many days Charlene had been absolutely certain that *she* would be the one. It seemed that the gods had spared Tanya, but in that sparing, the shadow of fate had fallen upon another child. Charlene Craft felt, in some inexplicable, foolish way, responsible.

"My God," said Davey. "Billy Plunkett's dead too."

"Conrad thought he was shooting his father," Charlene said, and her eyes teared. "There must have been *something* we could have done." Davey shrugged. He wondered what it would have been. It wasn't just in Connecticut that folks could live side by side for years, their lives never touching. Even in small towns people get so busy that the tiny roads and narrow paths leading to their neighbor's house become like interstates and six-lane freeways. Cities or towns, Davey knew, it doesn't matter where you live if you live unseeing, if you live uncaring, if you live *just to live.*

"How'd you find out?" he asked.

"Your mother called," Charlene said. But she didn't tell him about the talk she and Selma Craft had had just hours ago. She didn't tell him how much she had ached to ask Selma now, "Wouldn't you say this is a *big* thing, old fool? Wouldn't you say a big thing has happened in this goddamn little town?"

Life as a Maid:
The Jaws of Mattagash

I thought, my love, that I should overtake you;
Sweet heart, sit down under this shadowed tree,
And I will promise never to forsake you,
So you will grant to me a lover's fee.
Whereat she smiled, and kindly to me said,
"I never meant to live and die a maid."

—Elizabethan song, author unknown.

Amy Joy pulled Sicily's dinner roll apart and then buttered one half. Sicily had been toying with her peas, pushing them deep into the mashed potatoes and burying them there. Now the potatoes were polka-dotted, green and white. Amy Joy tried not to look at them.

"How's Winnie?" she asked, ignoring the fact that Sicily had picked up the unbuttered piece of roll, leaving its counterpart to sit idly by her plate.

"Too much butter," said Sicily. "Of course, if you fill me full of cholesterol you'll get rid of me a lot sooner."

"Now don't talk silly," said Amy Joy.

"Winnie says that Lola sends her all kinds of candy and cakes in hope that she'll die of a sugar high," Sicily went on, and then took a bite of the polka-dot potatoes. "Winnie says that's because Lola thinks she's in her will. But she ain't. The other day Winnie got out a copy of her will and scratched Lola's name off it. She tore a hole in the paper she erased so hard."

"Winnie needs to call her lawyer if she wants to change her will," said Amy Joy. "He must have a copy. That's the one needs to be changed." Then she felt a bit embarrassed to admit how pleased she would be to see Lola miss out on even a tiny windfall. "But don't worry. Winnie will die when she's ready, not from too much sugar."

"That's not how Winnie sees it," said Sicily.

"How's her mother?" asked Amy Joy. "How's old Mathilda?"

"The Women's Auxiliary can't give her a plaque, after all," said Sicily. "The doctor won't let them take her out of here. He says she's ready to go any minute."

"And what does Winnie say to that?"

"Winnie says it's about time," said Sicily. "I mean, with Mathilda being so old, Winnie says she's been expecting it for thirty-some years now."

"I suppose so," said Amy Joy. She was hoping the talk would take an exit down some more positive road.

"Still," said Sicily.

"Still what?"

"I wonder if you're ever really ready to lose a mother." She threw her roll back onto her plate, one bite missing. "After all," she said, "each person has only one." She pretended to look off, past Amy Joy, out the snowy window. Amy Joy had seen this look too many times to mistake it for pensiveness. She pushed the banana pudding closer to Sicily's plate, but Sicily scooted it off the tray. It bounced onto the table with a quick little thud.

"Winnie says they use old bananas for that," Sicily explained.

"That's ridiculous," said Amy Joy. "It's probably prepackaged."

"Who wants to eat prepackaged pudding?" Sicily asked, resting her case.

"You loved instant pudding when you were at home," Amy Joy reminded her.

"Things taste different when a person's home," said Sicily.

Winnie appeared at the door, her walk a bit bouncier, or so it seemed to Amy Joy. "I suppose if they did have the funerals instead of putting them in the morgue, they'd probably have closed caskets," said Winnie. The shootings at Pike Gifford's house, two days earlier, was still the talk of Mattagash, a solid wave of what-ifs, hows, and whys sweeping the town. "There ain't been a closed casket around here since that tractor rolled over my brother Casey," Winnie added.

"It wasn't a tractor," said Sicily. "It was a skidder."

"You gonna eat that?" Winnie asked, pointing at the banana pudding. Amy Joy looked quickly at Sicily. *Winnie says they use old bananas for that.*

"Go ahead and eat it," said Amy Joy, and pushed the bowl in Winnie's direction. "Mama was just saying a few minutes ago how banana pudding didn't agree with her."

"If you ask me, *she* could've stopped it," said Winnie. She was referring to Lynn Gifford. "Some folks are saying now that she was abused too. I tell you, people get away with all kinds of stuff these days, things we never would've gotten away with in my generation. And they go on talk shows and they blame everything on liquor, or them drugs they take. They blame it on the television set, and the radio. They even blame stuff on their poor old mothers." She took a big yellow bite of the pudding.

"What a way for children to have to live," Sicily said quietly, and for once Amy Joy agreed with her.

"I feel sorry for Pike, too," said Amy Joy.

"What!" Sicily exclaimed.

"You can't mean that," said Winnie.

"I do," said Amy Joy. "I remember how lost he seemed after Goldie went off to Connecticut with the other kids."

"He wouldn't go," Winnie argued. "She couldn't get him to go, and she tried everything. Bought him all kinds of clothes. Promised him stuff. He was too much like his father, that was his problem." Amy Joy thought about this. Who *should* a little boy be like? Who would he most likely grow up to become? If given the chance, would Conrad have gone on to be Pike?

"I remember how some of the girls like Wilma Fennelson and Dorrie made fun of him," Amy Joy said, leaving Lola's name off the list for Winnie's sake, although Lola should have headlined. "They made fun of his clothes, his hair, the house he lived in. All through school, they never let up on him a single minute."

"You can't feel sorry for people like that," said Winnie.

"You might save me a bite of that pudding," said Sicily.

"You give people like that a foot and they take a yard," Winnie cautioned. Amy Joy looked down at the laces on her own boots, tied into bows, knotted like tongues. Once, while she had been picking blueberries by Albert's motel, Amy Joy had seen Pike— Little Pee he was called then—coming along the road with an alder fishing pole. Behind him, skipping along like cherubs, was a string of Mattagash maids, all in a row; a Craft, a Fennelson, a Hart, a Monihan.

"A grown man picking on a little boy," said Sicily. "It's too darn bad he didn't get shot instead, like he was supposed to." Pike wasn't much more than six or seven years old, Amy Joy remembered. A little boy with a fishing pole, on his way home—one of those tacky Norman Rockwell paintings—trudging along the road. Behind him came the girls, skipping to the Baptist church, the girls on their way to God.

"All he's ever done in his life," said Winnie, "is drink and chase women and steal and lie. And that Billy Plunkett, rest his soul, wasn't much better." The girls, descendants of the old settlers, had surrounded Pike, had tugged his pole away from him, pulled at his hair, tied his shoelaces up so that he couldn't run.

"And he won't pay the price of any of this," said Sicily. "He's gonna go scot-free. What can they arrest him for?"

"They ought to put both him *and* her in jail," said Winnie. "I'll say it again. She's as much to blame for this as he is."

"We're all to blame," Amy Joy said. She was thinking of the look of terror she had seen on Little Pee's face, that blueberry-picking day all those years ago. They had broken his fishing pole, pulled his hair, tied his laces, rubbed grass in his face, and Amy Joy had only watched them. She had wanted to cry out, as Pike had done, for them to stop, but there was something on their faces, something flushed and breathless and sensual, that enabled them to move apart from the real world, to operate outside its human principles. *They* were protected, not Pike, not Amy Joy. This was what she remembered, and now she wondered if Pike remembered it too—that look on their faces, that privilege they shared, that secret. They might have been pilgrims on some long and zealous crusade to the Holy Land. They might even have been men on the dusty road to war. But they weren't. They were little girls, virgins, on the road to God.

"I hope they take them other children away from her," said Winnie. "No wonder them kids turn out like they do."

"Yes," said Amy Joy. This time Winnie was right. "It *is* no wonder." She had helped Pike up from the ditch, tried to untie the laces for him, but he had pushed her hands away. Instead, he took his shoes off and slung them over his shoulder, picked up the broken fishing pole, and went off down the road, past the tiny white Baptist church where the sermon was just starting. Behind him, half hidden in the grass of the ditch, lay a fistful of shiny dark hair, a wave running through it like a quick shiver. Amy Joy had picked it up and studied it carefully. It was like holding the sad remnant of some animal that has been caught in a trap. The jaws of Mattagash are firm and merciless.

"But I sure can't feel sorry for Pike Gifford," said Winnie, "and I don't see how *you* can." She threw the second half of the sentence at Amy Joy.

"Not to change the subject or anything," Sicily interrupted. For years now, she had believed it was her job to keep Winnie and Amy Joy from falling face-first into an argument. "But who is the Women's Auxiliary gonna give a plaque to?"

"They'll find somebody," said Amy Joy. If the Women's Auxiliary had already bought a plaque, they would, by Christ, give it to *someone*.

"It only takes the trophy shop in Madawaska a few minutes to inscribe a name on it," said Sicily. "They still got some time to decide."

"That peaked-faced girl of Rose Monihan's is in charge of it," said Winnie. "If it was up to me, I'd take that responsibility away from her. I don't think she's up to it, so close to her hysterectomy. I hear tell she wanted to give the plaque to Paulie Hart for winning that thousand dollars in the lottery. But she's been under some kind of medication, the poor thing."

"That's made with old bananas," Sicily said as Winnie finished up the yellow pudding.

Amy Joy was thankful that Miranda was upstairs napping, in Pearl's old bedroom with the lilac-flowered wallpaper, when she saw Bobby Fennelson standing outside on the steps. But it was early afternoon. Why in the world was he not out with his crew, on the wooded section of P. G. Irvine land he had contracted to cut? Why hadn't he telephoned to warn her? Now his truck was sitting in the broad sun of daytime, out in the telltale yard for everyone to see! She opened the door quickly and whisked him inside.

"What is it?" she asked. There was frost in his mustache, little beads of frozen perspiration.

"Christ, it's cold out there," he said. He pounded his gloves together emphatically, stomped his feet a bit on the rug by the kitchen door. "I got grease all over my boots."

"I'll put the kettle on," Amy Joy offered, and scurried to the sink. "A hot cup of tea, or maybe hot chocolate, will warm you up. Does that sound good? It seems like years since we've talked. I've got a guest with me now. My cousin Junior Ivy's granddaughter. She's a little firecracker on the surface, with lots of tough talk, but underneath she's really just a young, smart little girl. It's almost as though I've got Aunt Pearl back again. She wants to be an artist. You should see the things she can draw with just a piece of paper and a felt pen."

"We need to talk," Bobby said, and Amy Joy felt panic grab at her heart. There was something in his eyes, in those dark Fennelson eyes, that frightened her.

"The stuff that's been happening in this little town lately!" she exclaimed. "The funerals are tomorrow. I guess it's more like a service. They won't be buried until spring really, with the ground frozen and all. Are you going to the service? I tried to call you the minute I heard about it, but your phone was busy. It seems like your phone is either busy these days or there's no answer." He had been talking to Eileen, hadn't he?—all those times she'd gotten the busy signal, blaring in her ear like a warning call, a siren.

"Amy Joy."

"Can you imagine all that happening? Poor little Conrad. He used to shovel my roof, you know. And in the summer he mowed the lawn for me. I could've done it myself, but he was such a nice boy, and he seemed to appreciate getting paid. And he was always so polite, not like some of the kids these days. He reminded me a lot of Reginald Monihan. He was a little go-getter. I think his mother is the reason for that. I think Lynn has been through a lot, and now, with this, who knows how she's gonna make out. I called her up and asked her if I could help in any way. She used to clean house for me twice a month. I could have done it myself, but—" Amy Joy's hands fluttered about the teakettle. It took her forever to plug it into the wall. "What does this remind me of?" she asked herself. Then she remembered. This was Sicily. This was the prattle of the cornered beast. This was Sicily talking fast and hard and long, so that reality could not get a word in, so that reality would flounder somewhere in silence. This was Sicily. She pulled the kettle plug out of the socket and turned to face Bobby.

"What?" she said. It occurred to her—seconds before he said anything about Eileen, or the kids, or even Arizona, warm, sweet, level Arizona—that she had always hated mustaches.

Amy Joy lay awake, beneath the extra blanket, and stared at the picture at the foot of her bed, one of Jesus holding a woolly lamb. She had hated it for years until she came to know it, until Pearl told her of the many hours Grace McKinnon had spent painting it. "She was always painting something," Pearl had said. "I was not quite five years old when she died, but I can still hear the lapping

The Weight of Winter

of her brush, that little tune she'd be humming as she worked."
Now, instead of hating it, Amy Joy saw the painting as a kind of
tapestry of Grace McKinnon's life, a piecing together of seconds
and minutes and years into yellows and greens and blues. Sometimes, Amy Joy knew, people don't even have paint-by-number
pictures to show for their lives. Sometimes there wasn't a single
solid piece of evidence to prove that a person had been there on
the planet, loving, hating, laughing, crying, dying.

Amy Joy wondered what she would leave behind besides books
of pressed wildflowers and red maple leaves. What had Conrad
left? Billy Plunkett? What would be the statement of their lives?
And Bobby Fennelson? She supposed that, for some people, their
children remained behind, like pictures and books and wildflowers. For some people, that was the answer. And Bobby would
leave new trails, in the deserty places of Arizona. She had always
wanted to see the desert, long before Bobby Fennelson had cut
her the firewood that soft, sweet autumn, just two months earlier,
and had spent his weekend splitting it into blocks for her. He had
been gone for years in the army, a lifer like Ronny Plunkett, and
had returned just that spring to Mattagash. He had seen firsthand
a lot of the places in the world that Amy Joy had dreamed of
seeing one day.

"Paris," Bobby told her, "is like the inside of a crazy pinball
machine, all cars whizzing and horns tooting and lights flashing."
And she had seen it, just as he described, she had seen the twelve
magnificent avenues spoking out from the Arc de Triomphe, had
listened as the traffic spun around it like a flashing wheel. "Paris,"
he said, "is little cafés where you can sit outside and order all
kinds of wines you can't pronounce." And she had seen the cafés
then, just as they were in her big art book. She had imagined Paris
as a city of little shops, and dancing girls, and cherry blossoms,
with huge red sunsets eating up the waters of the Seine.

Amy Joy lay awake and listened to the mouselike noises coming
from Pearl's old bedroom. Miranda was up late working on a
painting, from a photo she'd found in the McKinnon family
scrapbook.

"I didn't even know that a name like McKinnon was in my family tree," she had said to Amy Joy. In her hands was a photo of Grace McKinnon, a silhouette really, the camera capturing more shadow than flesh. But it was a striking shot, with Grace slim and petite, a wide-brimmed hat covering one eye. Behind her, swimming for the camera, was a swarm of hollyhocks, the flowers in different shades of black and white. Hollyhocks, like the wide forehead and long aquiline nose, had been part of the McKinnon heritage. Grace was standing behind the old homestead, on the spot where Amy Joy now had a lilac bush, and she was looking downriver. She was looking in the direction of the sea from land-locked Maine, one hand shading her eyes, as if she remembered something from there, from the old country, the way eels remember. Miranda loved the picture. "She's flirting with the river," she said to Amy Joy. "I've started a painting of her. You'll see, in a few days she'll be alive again."

Having Miranda in the house for just a short time had been like rewiring the old homestead, taking it from the dark flickering of candlelight, or the soft hissing of gas, to the quick bright flash of electricity. It was alive, the way it must have been when the visiting missionaries came, with their haughty tales of taking a foreign religion into a land where it didn't belong. The old house was living, breathing again, exhaling smoke from its chimney, settling down on its haunches for another Mattagash winter. The old house was a kind of shell, Amy Joy realized now, a hard outer skin for the soft flesh inside. How could she have entertained the notion of selling it? With the house wrapped firmly about her, the Chester Giffords, the Reginald Monihans, the Jean Claude Cloutiers, the Bobby Fennelsons could come and go, like billowy ghosts passing through wind chimes. Sometimes, Amy Joy knew, people are glued to the pages of their heritage. Sometimes people are married to houses. With Miranda's scratching noises filling the old homestead with a soft litany, Amy Joy rolled over on her side and fell asleep.

The Weary Children:
Conrad Learns to Leap

> "For oh," say the children, "we are weary,
> And we cannot run or leap;
> If we cared for any meadows, it were merely
> To drop down in them and sleep . . ."
>
> —Elizabeth Barrett Browning,
> "The Cry of the Children"

*T*he Gifford twins, Julie and Stevie, were in their front yard with Reed, who was knocking icicles from the eaves with a broom's handle, when the Craft car went by pulling its orange U-Haul. Christopher Craft, who had known briefly what it was like to be in the shoes of Miles Standish, waved a quick good-bye. Reed waved back— Christopher had been in his class—but Stevie threw a glassy chunk of ice that had dropped from the eaves. It hit the rear fender of Davey Craft's car with a dull thud. The brake lights on the U-Haul came on immediately, and Stevie dropped to his belly behind Pike's old Chevy clunker and lay low, waiting. But Davey Craft must have decided there were more serious things to contend with. The brake lights went off and the Craft car kept on its way to Connecticut. Stevie got to his feet again, a cold grin on his face. Another successful ambush, the fifth that day alone.

"Why'd you go and do that?" asked Reed. He swung his arm quickly and cuffed Stevie—too slow to duck—briskly on the head.

"Ow!" said Stevie. "Bastard! I'm gonna go tell Mama."

"You leave Mama alone," said Reed. "She's got enough to worry about." He went back to the icicles, their long silver bodies breaking musically into bits and pieces beneath the broom.

"Stevie is a crybaby," said Julie. She was sitting on the frozen snow of the front steps, sucking on the tapered peak of an icicle.

"You can catch a disease from eating icicles," said Stevie. "That's why Tanya Craft is sick and her parents have to take her to Connecticut. She ate a whole bunch of icicles, and now there's a zillion worms living in her stomach and her stomach is full of big holes."

"Yuck!" said Julie, and threw the icicle down. The taper stuck point-first into the snow by the steps.

"He's lying," said Reed. He leaned the broom against the front door and opened it. On the rug, inside, he paused to wipe his boots. That was something Conrad was always telling him to do. Conrad had been worse than an old woman at times.

In the warm kitchen, Lynn was making luncheon-meat sandwiches. "Tell the twins to come eat," she said. She put a plate of sandwich halves on the table, and then found a large can of chunky vegetable soup.

"Sandwiches!" Reed shouted out the door. "And wipe your boots here on the rug, or take them off." Lynn smiled.

"I don't want a sandwich if it's got olives in it," Julie announced. She and Stevie were pulling off their snowy boots. "I want a slice of meat that don't have olives." She threw her coat down by the kitchen table.

"Julie, put your coat away," said Lynn, exasperation in her voice. "Ain't I told you that a million times? Don't just drop it wherever you happen to stop."

"Them ain't olives," Stevie whispered in Julie's ear. "Them is frog eyes." He shucked off his coat next to Julie's on the floor.

"Pick them up, dammit," said Reed. He grabbed up both coats and went into the living room with them. Lynn watched him go.

"He's taking over for Conrad," Lynn thought, and she wondered if that was good or bad. She and Reed had already gone to their first counseling meeting in Watertown, earlier in the day, something they would do weekly. "It's never too soon after a tragedy to seek help," the psychologist had told Lynn. Reed was holding far too much anger inside—that's what the psychologist said. But Lynn knew anyone would be blind not to see that. The psychologist was fat and had a funny habit of squinting his eyes, but he was teaching Lynn and Reed how to grieve. His office had real leather sofas and lots of thick books. His fingers were manicured. He looked to Lynn as though he had never grieved in his life.

"Reed will have to come to terms with his father," the fat psychologist had said to Lynn. *No kidding,* Lynn thought. "He's hurting very much inside," the psychologist said, "for his big brother." *You must have one of them crystal balls!* But Lynn didn't say this. The state was paying this man, not she. And it was true that Reed's anger at his father was a major factor. Pike was still at Billy's house, living on there with Ronny, who seemed perpetually without career plans. Pike Gifford was now enrolled in the AA program in Watertown, orders of the social worker who had come to visit the family two days after the memorial service.

"Julie, you'll eat what I make," Lynn said. She didn't care what program Pike took, as long as he never came back into her house. The children could visit him if they wanted to, but Lynn was finished with his promises.

"I don't care if he's been to the Betty Ford Clinic," Lynn had said when Maisy called her with a message from Pike.

"He says he's learned his lesson this time," said Maisy, who was not convinced. "He says he's in counseling now, and they tell him he's got a good chance of getting well."

"Where's Conrad's chance?" Lynn had shouted. "You ask him that the next time he calls."

"Don't yell at *me*," Maisy reminded her. "I ain't ever liked the son of a bitch. He's a snake in the grass as far as I'm concerned, and always will be. I'm just telling you what he asked me to tell you. He says give him a year and then see. Don't make up your mind yet."

"Tell him I hope he's dead in a *week*," Lynn said. "Tell him never mind about no *year*." Didn't Pike realize that this time it was different? His son was dead! Pike Gifford might as well tell Lynn that he was taking crochet lessons and doing extremely well. It would make as much impact.

"He says he had Ronny drop the Chevy off 'cause he knew you'd need it," Maisy had told her. Lynn had intended to ask for the car anyway, in her latest divorce petition. Now she wouldn't have to fight for it, piece of junk that it was.

"Stevie ain't learned his lines yet for the play," said Julie.

"Stevie!" Lynn said, and he jumped, his sandwich flopping apart in his hand. She put a bowl of chunky soup in front of him. "What did you promise me? You said you'd be sure to learn them lines. That's the only way I let you be in the play. Don't poke at them sandwiches with your spoon."

"All I got to say is, 'I am Chief Mash-ah-something,'" said Stevie, his little mouth full of sandwich.

"It's Chief *Massasoit*," said Julie. "The teacher's told him a thousand times. And that ain't all he's supposed to say, Mama."

"What else you supposed to say?" Lynn asked. She had taken a sandwich for herself, but left it on her plate with just two bites missing.

"Your appetite'll come back one day," Maisy had said. "Just try not to starve until then."

"He's supposed to say, 'I have come with ninety braves and five deer to celebrate this day.' But he's too stupid," said Julie.

"I ain't neither stupid," said Stevie. He kicked at Julie's leg beneath the table. "All *you* have to say is *gobble gobble*."

"Quit!" said Julie.

"Stop it, both of you," Lynn said. She had been watching Reed, who was having his own kind of trouble with his appetite.

"How about you, Reed?" Lynn asked. "Have you memorized your part?" Reed nodded, but he wasn't paying close attention to his mother. He was looking instead at the kitchen window, remembering mere days ago when Pike Gifford had come and peered inside at his family having breakfast. Just as the Indians had first peered at the Pilgrims. It could have all been different—that was the awful thought plaguing Reed. It could have been prevented if he or Conrad had been in charge. But they were kids. The adults called the shots when it came to this crazy grown-up game. *They ain't fighting,* Reed had told Conrad that day, *they're hugging.*

"Well, recite a little bit of it for me," said Lynn. "Ain't you the narrator or something?"

"He's got the biggest part of anybody," said Julie. "He's got a longer part than Bernie Henderson, who's gonna play Miles Standish now that Christopher Craft is gone."

"Say some of it, honey," Lynn urged. She pushed the doughnut box closer to Reed's plate. He would be thin as a rail if this kept up, but then so would she.

"Go on," Lynn urged, in her life-going-on-as-usual voice. But only the twins, she knew, could be fooled.

" 'The year was 1620, and the month was September, when the *Mayflower* set sail for America,' " Reed said, his voice soft and dramatic. " 'The passing was long and dangerous, the ship over-crowded. A baby was born at the height of the storm, and many came close to death. But only one Pilgrim died in the crossing.' " His voice broke. He stared at the box of doughnuts, all chocolate-coated, from a bakery way down in Bangor. He wondered if any little boys down there were sitting at tables right then, with their families, happy to be there, happy they were all alive. Thankful, even. " 'It was November before they dropped anchor, but their troubles were not over, for the land was hostile to them, the plague would soon be upon them, and winter was coming fast,' " Reed continued, his voice barely audible. He stopped.

"It ain't Bernie who's gonna be Miles Standish," said Stevie.

"Yes it is," Julie insisted. "It is too."

"Bernie says he's getting a car for Christmas," said Stevie. "And he's only eight."

"He's lying, stupid," said Julie. "Now ssshh! The part is coming up soon where everybody gives thanks."

"Go on, Reed," said Lynn. She had tears in her eyes. She wouldn't say so to the children, but it would be a long time before she gave any thanks to God. As far as Lynn Gifford was concerned, she owed God jack shit. "It's really pretty," she added. But Reed stood up, his chair toppling behind him.

"If he ever comes back here," Reed said, and at first Lynn thought he was still reciting, thought he was addressing the plague, giving it some human form. "If he's ever allowed in this house again, I'll kill him. And I won't miss neither, like Conrad did. That's what I'm gonna do if you ever let him come back." He threw his spoon on the table—a clattering noise, a sharp period to a long, painful sentence. Sometimes, Reed had come to realize, children are the ones who should make the rules.

"What you doing, honey?" Lynn asked later when she went into Reed's bedroom, the one he had shared with Conrad. He was lying on the bed, his legs spread, his arms beneath his head. Spook, the dog, slept by his side, a mass of cockapoo curls. "You know Spook ain't supposed to be on the bed." She petted the curly fur. It was pretty common knowledge that although Lynn made large statements about Spook's limited territory, he even slept on *her* bed when he pleased.

Conrad's side of the bed was covered with the packets of his old collection: two hundred and fifty-three jams and honeys, who knew how many sugars. Lynn looked away from them quickly.

"Why have you got them out again?" she asked, but Reed said nothing. "It'll only make you feel worse. It ain't gonna bring Conny back." Still he said nothing. He was thinking of Thanksgiving, and of all the people around the world who would have reasons to give thanks, no matter how tough life had been to them. People like the Pilgrims. In the background, New Kids on the Block were singing quietly, on the Radio Shack stereo Lynn had gotten the boys as a shared Christmas present the year before. Now it seemed years ago that she had done such a thing. Lifetimes.

"Don't stay up here and listen to music all afternoon, okay?"

Lynn said. The twins had gone back to school the day after Conrad's memorial service, but Reed stayed home. Lynn agreed that he needed more time before facing his classmates. The twins were resilient; Reed was not. Now Thanksgiving was only two days away. The twins would spend half of the following day in school, and then vacation would officially begin. On the following Monday, though, Lynn was hoping that Reed would gather up his schoolbooks and be ready to try it once again. "Maisy's coming over and we're gonna make a big pan of fudge. The weatherman says it's gonna snow like hell tomorrow, and tomorrow night, and the next day. And even the day after Thanksgiving. If it does, they'll have to cancel the Thanksgiving dinner at the school."

"And the play?" asked Reed.

"Well, if it snows so hard no one can get out of their yards, sweetie, I suppose the play will be canceled too."

"Good," said Reed. "I didn't want to do it anyway."

"Miss Kimball said you didn't have to, Reed," Lynn reminded him. "I think it was awful nice of her to call and talk to you about it. She thinks it'd be good for you, especially since you was looking forward to it."

"No I wasn't," said Reed. "She talked me into it."

"Honey, I thought you loved being the narrator," said Lynn. "And you been practicing that part for almost a month now." She rubbed his belly with her fingers, circular caresses. She could feel his bony rib cage, holding up the house of his body. "I heard you practice them lines to Conrad a lot of times."

Reed said nothing. He turned his head toward the music coming from the stereo. It would be great to be a new kid in a new house on a new block in a new town. Conrad's new house was the tiny cement morgue marking the entry into the Catholic graveyard. He would live there until spring, until the land was ready, as it was when the Pilgrims planted their first crops.

"Is it because Conny's gone that you don't want to do them lines?" Lynn asked. "If that's the case, you can practice them on me."

"I don't want to, Ma," said Reed. He closed his eyes. He hoped the snow covered the whole damn school building, so deep that not even the chimneys could be seen. He wished all the rest of his life would be canceled, not just school, not just a dinner.

"I gotta go keep them little monsters from tearing each other apart," Lynn said. She had heard the musical notes of a fight rising up from the kitchen table, spoons being knocked against glasses, plates vibrating. "Don't stay up here forever. I'll yell to you when the fudge starts to harden."

Reed listened as her footsteps retreated down the stairs, the soft footfalls of his mother. The album finished playing and then started over again, a wonderful little mechanism inside directing it on, instructing it, making all its big decisions. He heard the wind start up strong and fierce, beating around the leafless birch outside his window. On snowy nights, before Conrad grew so silent, the boys used to gather there, at the window, and watch the snow swirl in over the Mattagash River.

Then Reed heard Maisy downstairs, her voice loud and fake with optimism. Freddy was with her, Freddy, whose birthday party Pike had crashed a week and a half earlier. Reed lifted himself up from his bed and the springs creaked beneath him like ice cracking. He gathered up Conrad's jams and honeys and sugars, packed them back into the shoe boxes, then put them under the bed, in their usual safe spot. They might come in handy one day. They might be a kind of windfall, such as the Pilgrims had found in Indian corn.

At the window he knelt, tried to pry it up with the palms of his hands. It would be nice to breathe a cold, sharp breath of river air. But the window was stuck, frozen solid with winter. Reed knew all about early winters in northern Maine. The Pilgrims hadn't been the only unlucky ones, had they? They could have been even unluckier. They could have dropped anchor farther north than Cape Cod. They could have scraped to shore where the Mattagash River meets the St. John, just as the old loyalist settlers had.

Reed watched the gray jays loading up with the bread scraps his mother had tossed out on the frozen snow of the backyard.

Sandwiches neither he nor Lynn could eat. Snow lay on the hills, and in the sky over the trees, threatening to fall. Reed had read in his geography book that Maine is eighty percent forest. Growing up in Mattagash, he had always thought it might be much more than that, maybe ninety-nine—that other percent being given over to the rivers and roads. But whatever the percentage of trees was, snow loomed above Mattagash's share.

" 'After that first dreadful winter of the plague,' " Reed said, his breath warm against the window, " 'after that first spring when half their number had perished, they still found it within their hearts to give thanks to God, for they still had their crop of Indian corn to keep them.' "

Bagels in Mattagash:
The Mayflower as a
Beer Joint

No written record exists to indicate what foods
might have been served, but we can be fairly certain
that the menu included roast turkey, roast goose,
roast duck, roast venison, several kinds of meat pie,
baked fish, steamed lobster, steamed clams, steamed
oysters, Indian-style corn bread, and a large
assortment of vegetables, fruits, berries, nuts, and
jellies. Since their supply of beer was exhausted
while they were still living on the *Mayflower*, the
abundance of grapes gave them an opportunity to
make wine, a not-unacceptable substitute for the
beverage they missed so much.

—Leo Bonfanti, *The Massachusetts Bay Colony*. Details of
the first Thanksgiving (parts bowdlerized for the Mattagash play)

Dorrie Mullins was peering out of Alice
Gurley's kitchen window when the
Craft car and its orange U-Haul came slowly around the turn, past
the ruins of the Albert Pinkham Motel. Dorrie had been checking
the sky for snow, worried that this time the weathermen down in
Bangor were right.

"I'll be damned," said Dorrie. "There they go."

"Who?" asked Lola, and pushed her way in past Dorrie's huge
frame so that she, too, could see.

"Davey and Charlene."

"Who are Davey and Charlene?" asked Alice Gurley, their
hostess.

"I'm getting tears in my eyes," said Lola. "Me and Davey's been close as lice since we was little kids."

"You ain't crying over Charlene leaving, are you?" Dorrie asked, and smiled heartily as Lola gave her a big are-you-kidding look.

"Oh yeah," said Lola. "My heart's broken."

"Davey is a nice man, though," said Dorrie.

"Who is Davey?" asked Alice Gurley.

"He come around and said good-bye to everybody in the family," said Lola. "Real nice and gentleman-like. It's a damn shame he's going back to Connecticut. You know Charlene is making him."

"Well, I got to admit that if my kid had that disease, I'd want to get closer to some of them big-city specialists too," said Dorrie. "That poor little Tanya's got her work cut out for her, getting over a strange disease like that."

"Who's Tanya?" asked Alice Gurley. "What disease?"

"You can go right down to the hardware store in Caribou, or anyplace they sell Hartz dog products, and get you a VHS tape on that disease," said Lola. "That's how common it is these days."

"Prissy told me Lyme disease is a whole lot easier to catch than AIDS, and it's almost as bad," said Dorrie. "Prissy says you can catch AIDS *and* Lyme disease from mosquitoes."

"Oh, but that's not so," said Alice Gurley. "Who has Lyme disease?"

"A little girl from here in town," Lola replied, finally remembering Alice there, in her own house. "That's them moving back to Connecticut." She nodded her head as the ass of the orange U-Haul disappeared for good around the turn.

"What bad luck," said Alice Gurley. Alice was fresh to Mattagash, Maine, having just arrived to spend a few weeks in her new house, getting it ready for the next summer. Like many other retired folks her age, Alice yearned to get away from the six-lane mess of southern California, the thick smog, and the even thicker aura of materialism. She had bought Richard Hart's house, after Richard filed bankruptcy and went off with his family to seek better luck in the want ads of Connecticut. A lot of people like Alice were turning up in Mattagash and other small towns across America, suddenly endorsing nature, hoping for a back-to-the-land philosophy to grab them up and rescue them from the squalor of the city. Mattagashers were polite to these newly landed Pilgrims, but they generally distrusted them, thought them foolish, and sometimes even disliked them. Such was the case with the retired professor from New York who had been imprudent enough to tell Booster Mullins that he, Booster, should return to using a pair of horses in the woods, rather than endorse the technology of the skidder. Booster had floored him, right there in the high school gymnasium, in the middle of a town meeting.

"The little son of a bitch," Booster had later told the men who gathered at Craft's Filling Station for more details. "He put all his kids through school by teaching out of books, and now he wants *me* to go back to horses so I'll cut less wood. Where does he think his books come from? This is the bastard who stands outside LaVerdiere's Drugstore every Monday morning complaining because his *New York Times* is late. Where does he think *that* paper comes from? I'm supposed to hitch up a team of horses while he's driving his ass around in a BMW."

"Fifty thousand trees go into the Sunday *New York Times*," Ben Monihan had mentioned to Booster, something he might use as future ammunition. "I saw that on *Nova*. It's a good thing for him you *ain't* using a team of horses."

"It was impossible to be friends with Charlene," Dorrie said now. "And God knows we tried, didn't we, Lola? But it was like trying to be friends with Queen Elizabeth. You never knew when someone might ring for the butler to come and show you to the door."

"Charlene always complained about the cold anyway," said Lola. "Since the first winter she spent up here."

"Well," said Alice, hoping she sounded as robust as the other women in Mattagash. It was important to fit in with the natives, learn their lingo, adopt their ways. Margaret Mead had taught the intelligentsia that, enabling them to make touristy fools of themselves all over the world. "If they can't stand the cold, they ought to get out of the kitchen," Alice said, and laughed sweetly, that city laugh, the little snicker of a chipmunk. Dorrie and Lola stared at her evenly.

"Ain't it if you can't stand the *heat,* get out of the kitchen?" asked Dorrie.

"Well, yes, it is," said Alice. "I was simply making a little joke."

"Oh," said Lola.

"Oh," said Dorrie. "Warn us next time." Alice was already beginning to miss the thick gray smog of southern Cal, and somehow the traffic jams of her past were not quite so bothersome in her memory. The blaring of hundreds of horns was beginning to emerge symphonious compared to the cacophony of Dorrie and Lola.

"Take you, Alice," said Dorrie. She was now back at the table and finishing the slice of pineapple cake Alice had cut for her. "You seem to understand the personality as well as the *geography* of Mattagashers. They go hand in hand, you know."

"I see," said Alice. "Would you like a bagel?" she asked Lola, and held up a plate of the creatures. Lola looked at the doughnut shape of the bread before her. She had no idea Alice was Jewish, not with that pugged little Irish nose. But ever since Mr. Ornstein, from somewhere downstate, had come north to buy the Watertown IGA, everybody in Aroostook County knew how much Jews loved their bagels. He had opened a tiny delicatessen in the back of the store and had stocked it so full of bagels that it was difficult to find any sensible Protestant bread back there. "What could they have been thinking of?" Lola had asked Dorrie as they hovered over the counter at the deli's grand opening, when the bagel made its northern debut. Bread baked into the shape of doughnuts! "Don't ask *me,*" Dorrie had finally grunted. "They must've lost their recipe book, all them years they spent traipsing around in the desert."

"What would make you want to bring bagels to Mattagash?" Lola asked Alice Gurley. Lola wasn't prejudiced, so long as none of her children married someone who was Jewish or Negro. But maybe she and Dorrie had misunderstood this new city slicker. Maybe Alice was in town looking for a little trouble, an agitator of sorts.

"I happen to love bagels, that's all," said Alice. She broke one apart and then smeared the end with some cream cheese. Lola and Dorrie observed this action as closely as Salem Puritans watching a suspected witch smear chicken blood on the Bible. Alice took a bite.

"We better go," said Dorrie. "If it don't snow like them weathermen say it's gonna, I gotta make a salad and a big pan of carrots for the dinner."

"Me too," said Lola, casting a final glance at the offending bagel. "They plan to have twenty different salads." Who in the world would have known Alice Gurley was Jewish? Sure, she just *happens* to like bagels. And the Pope just *happens* to wear a dress.

"Can I make anything?" Alice asked. "I am, after all, going to be here for Thanksgiving." There she was, a Pilgrim in a strange wintry land, where diseases, like plagues, ran rampant. There Alice Gurley was, needing help, lacking companionship, seeking a place to dine without culinary persecution. It was an opportunity for the Mattagashers, namesakes of an old Indian tribe themselves, to copy Chief Massasoit's generous gesture.

"Oh no, we got plenty," said Dorrie. "Don't you worry none."

"And the tickets is all sold out to the dinner anyway," Lola lied, a practice Chief Massasoit had managed to avoid, even while dealing with the squabbling, bickering Pilgrims.

"Well," said Dorrie, over her bulbous shoulder. "Welcome to Mattagash anyway." The door to Alice Gurley's new house closed behind them in a sweet little suction of air, a natural sigh.

"Oh my Lord," said Lola, on the path to Booster's maroon Bronco, that big self-appointed welcome wagon with the sun-yellow plow. "I thought for a minute she was gonna insist on coming to the dinner. You don't think it was wrong of us not to invite her, do you? It being Thanksgiving and all?"

"She'll be okay," said Dorrie, and cranked open the driver's door, hoisted herself up into the saddle. "The Jews have their own version of Thanksgiving, anyway. That's when they dress up in them little beanies and give each other candles for Christmas."

At the Mattagash gymnasium Dorrie left the Bronco idling, its tail pipe emitting a volley of gray exhaust, Mattagash's own contribution to the overall pollution problem.

"We'll just run in and vote and run back out," said Dorrie. "This ain't New York. It ain't like someone's gonna tow it away."

"I kinda hate to see The Crossroads close down," Lola said sadly. "Now Raymond's gonna be right back under my feet every time I turn around. You know him and Booster only went out on the weekends before Maurice opened up. Watertown's a long way to go for a drink." Dorrie nodded in sympathy. Booster would be back under her own hefty hooves more than she cared to think about. The Crossroads had become like an office to him, it was true, a refuge where he claimed to do his best thinking. And it was also true that his woodsworking business was picking up. Booster even had plans to buy a second skidder. Now the font of his inspirations was running dry.

"Someone suggested what if Maurice sold only beer," said Lola. "And you know as well as I do that a little beer now and then never hurt nobody. I even make pancakes with it, and sometimes I use it as a hair rinse if I'm out of Vidal Sassoon. But Prissy wouldn't hear of it. She wants that place closed down almost as much as she wants her picture in the *Watertown Weekly*."

"Well, there ain't much we can do now," said Dorrie. "It was pretty easy for Prissy to get this emergency vote called, because of Conrad and Billy. And maybe she's right. Maybe it wouldn't have happened if it hadn't been for The Crossroads."

"You ever seen Pike Gifford when he *hadn't* had too much to drink?" Lola reminded her. "This was an accident waiting to happen and you know it. The Crossroads had nothing to do with it."

"Maybe," Dorrie said. "But Prissy convinced the town selectmen otherwise. And we'll stand out like sore thumbs if we don't vote."

"Prissy could talk the Pope into eating a hot dog on Friday," said Lola.

"I think it's okay now," said Dorrie. "I think the Catholics canceled their Meat Act." She opened the heavy door to the gymnasium and a gust of warm air surged out, followed by the stale sweaty fragrance of basketball practice.

"Good Lord," said Lola, plugging her tiny nostrils. "I wish someone would make them boys wash their jockstraps once in a while."

Maurice Fennelson was out scattering more salt in his yard when Dorrie and Lola zoomed past in the Bronco. The women pretended not to see him, or the red-mittened hand Maurice unfurled to wave at them, as though it were some happy flag. They had, after all, just voted to close him down. It would be the pinnacle of hypocrisy, even for Dorrie and Lola, to acknowledge Maurice now. Maurice was a doomed man, waving. And judging from the long line of voters waiting outside the makeshift booth in the gymnasium—Prissy had bought a new shower curtain, pale blue with green sea horses on it, to be tacked onto the booth as a door—Dorrie and Lola were in accordance with a host of others. Like sheep, the voters had gathered at the edge of the cliff, with Prissy jumping first to cast a ballot. But Maurice didn't mind. He'd never liked Dorrie or Lola anyway. And he'd already waved once that day, at Davey and Charlene Craft, as they inched cautiously past, pulling the rented U-Haul like a big round Florida orange, a bright thing against a panorama of snow.

In the Bronco, Dorrie adjusted her rearview mirror with a chubby hand. She caught Maurice's thin frame in it, as though he were in some kind of little mirrored cage, his watery image trapped there. Then he was gone as Dorrie careened the Bronco past the *Welcome to Mattagash* sign.

"You really think it'll snow hard enough to cancel the dinner?" Lola asked. The sky was a dark shield, looming in over the river, banking itself on the treetops like a gray balloon.

"It don't look good," said Dorrie. "All we can do is wait and see. It probably ain't a great idea to go all the way to Madawaska, though, just in case that storm comes out of nowhere. Besides, I think that was just a bunch of idle gossip about Elvis being at Radio Shack."

"Ain't it amazing how some folks can't find anything better to do?" Lola commented.

"You want to stop and check on your Mom?" Dorrie asked, as they zipped into St. Leonard.

"Hell no," said Lola. "The last thing I need today is a lecture. But if you want to stop and see yours, I'll go in with you." Dorrie thought about it.

"I guess not," she said. "She don't know me anyway, and all she talks about is Larry. I'll bet you we buried Larry a hundred times this year alone. Did you know he was the first soldier from Mattagash to ever die in a war?" Dorrie braked for a small bevy of French-speaking children who were crossing the road, skates slung over their shoulders.

"Hurry it up, you little tadpoles," Dorrie muttered.

"Come to think of it . . ." said Lola. She scrounged around for a pack of Juicy Fruit in her bottomless purse. "Mama's oldest brother was the first one from Mattagash to die in a war, over there in that Argyle Forest."

"I didn't know that," said Dorrie, unhappy to give up her own ghastly statistic.

"Mama hardly remembers him," said Lola. "She was just a little girl when he died. But he won all kinds of medals," she added proudly, as though war were some kind of Olympics.

"Is that right?" Dorrie mused. It was apparent that brother Larry would have to settle for runner-up. Why was it that Lola, who was supposed to be Dorrie's very best friend, needed to compete with her on every single issue? If Dorrie said that she, Dorrie Mullins, had an idiot child at home with an IQ of 50, Lola would jump right in and claim *she* had one she used as a coatrack.

"Uncle Walter was the first," Lola rubbed in. "World War One. And then Larry was second in Korea, and then Reginald Monihan in Vietnam was third."

"Good heavens," said Dorrie, irritated. "You sound like you're on *Jeopardy* or something." *Final* Jeopardy *category: Soldiers from Mattagash, Maine, who have died in a war, in proper order, please.* "You're starting to sound just like that Alex Trubeck."

"Really?" Lola thought about this. How many times had she heard Dorrie say that Alex Trebek was a show-off, that he liked to rattle the answers off as though he knew them?

"Not to change the subject," said Dorrie, who wanted to do just that. She could tell Lola was thinking too much, over there in the think tank on the passenger side. "I don't believe Amy Joy Lawler's been seeing *anyone.* There's no way in hell she could hugger-mugger something like that. And she don't really look pregnant to me. Oh, I mean, she's put on a few pounds over the years, but who hasn't?" Lola looked at her enormous friend, at the bobbing chins, all three of them.

"I haven't," said Lola.

Cocoon *in Mattagash:*
Down the Yellow-Tiled Road

> "There's no place like home."
>
> —Dorothy in *The Wonderful Wizard of Oz*
> by L. Frank Baum

Amy Joy had tried to read her newest copy of *Harrowsmith* magazine, but found she couldn't concentrate on organic tomatoes. Television, with its canned laughter, wasn't the answer either, so she snapped it off. Each time a car swept past the old McKinnon house, on the twisty Mattagash road, she felt a quickening of her pulse. But none turned into the driveway, tires crunching on snow. And the river path that Bobby Fennelson had followed to the back door of the McKinnon homestead on all those snowy nights, on all those moonlighty nights, stretched out long and white and untouched by human footprints. Bobby Fennelson was gone to toasty Arizona. Bobby Fennelson was making footprints in the sand now.

With Miranda staying up late to paint, Amy Joy took a warm glass of milk and went off to bed. It came to her at first in the coils of a dream, like a kettle whistling in her kitchen—a loud, piercing sound. She was making tea, wasn't she, and there was Bobby, telling her again how much he missed his kids, how there are sacrifices in most things, how he would miss her, too, miss Mattagash. "The teakettle's whistling, Prissy," Amy Joy said aloud. "I gotta go now." But instead of hanging up the phone, as she had done to Prissy all those times, Amy Joy was reaching for it, and now she was awake, and it *was* the phone, ringing its heart out in the night.

"Mama," Amy Joy thought, and a little fist of fear gripped her. It was Maxine Monihan, now married to a DuPont from St. Leonard, another Mattagasher to cross the French Catholic line. It was well past one o'clock. Why in hell was it *Maxine Monihan?*

"Amy Joy?" Maxine said. In her voice was a wisp of excitement impossible to conceal. "Did I get you up? Yes, I suppose I did."

"What is it?" Amy Joy asked.

"An ambulance just roared into Pine Valley," said Maxine. She lived in the trailer park that overlooked the driveway at Pine Valley. "Since your mom is there, I thought you might want to know."

"It's for Mama?" Amy Joy asked. She was fumbling for the night-light. A tumbler of water tipped, then spilled noisily into the darkness before she found the switch. Light flooded the room. "What's wrong with Mama?"

"Oh, I don't know if the ambulance is for her or not," said Maxine. "Lola's mother is there too. I'm gonna call her next. All I know is that it's come for someone. I can see the blue light from here."

"What!" exclaimed Amy Joy. What kind of deranged Paul Revere notion was this? A warning call *just in case.*

"I gotta get me one of them police scanners," Maxine was saying as Amy Joy slammed down the telephone. She fingered quickly through the book of phone numbers by her bedside and found the number for Pine Valley, with its lime-green walls, its tiled floors. Amy Joy quickly dialed the numbers. So what if Sicily made a mess of the crossword puzzle? What was a crossword puzzle worth?

Miranda rapped lightly on the door, opened it, and peered in. "What's wrong?" she asked. She had taken her contacts out to soak and now she wore large brown glasses. "The McKinnon women have always had bad eyes," Pearl had once said. "But they still don't miss much."

"I'm not sure," said Amy Joy. "Somebody just called and told me that the ambulance is at Pine Valley, but I don't know who it's for. And there's no answer." She hung up the phone and flipped the blankets back. "I gotta start the car so it'll warm up. I'm gonna drive down there."

"I'll go with you," said Miranda, and disappeared back into her own room.

The road ahead of them was flecked with sparkling ice diamonds, those little secrets in the snow.

"It's a good thing I had the block heater plugged in," said Amy Joy. "I doubt the car would have started." But she had planned to drive to Watertown early the next morning for a dental appointment, so the car had been ready, the block heater keeping the antifreeze warm, the antifreeze keeping the engine warm, the warm engine keeping the oil from growing thick with cold.

"At least it's not snowing," said Miranda. Behind the huge lenses, her eyes were round as an owl's.

"It's too cold to snow," said Amy Joy. She was leaning in snugly over the steering wheel, peering through the defrosted hole growing on the windshield. "Try not to think," she warned herself silently. "Just drive." She applied a bit more pressure to the accelerator pedal, and the little brown Cavalier breathed more cold air into its carburetor.

"It's a beautiful night, isn't it?" asked Miranda. "All the tall banks, everything white." Her voice was a soft, even monotone, a reassuring little wave coming at Amy Joy, washing up from the darkness on the passenger side. "Bless her," thought Amy Joy.

They followed the river, which lay like a blue shard of ice, reflected in moonlight, shimmering like a dream. The ancestors' river. The old road.

"The snow is so pretty," Miranda said. Yard lights, scattered along the road to St. Leonard, threw glistening shadows on the banks. Houses were bundled against the cold, their windows black eyes in the night, their chimneys breathing smoke.

"Did you know that snow is made up of different crystals?" Amy Joy asked. The only thing they could do was keep talking, as she had so recently done with Bobby Fennelson in the warm kitchen, she at the sink, Bobby with his sweet, strong hand on the doorknob. "There are seven common types of crystals, and that's what decides the kind of snow it'll be. Whether it'll pile up, or drift, or pack down hard. The next time it snows, we'll catch some flakes and I'll tell you what they are."

"Maybe I can paint different snowflakes," said Miranda. "I don't think anyone's done a snowflake study."

"Sell them in Florida," said Amy Joy. They were rounding the last glittering turn before Pine Valley. "You'll have a hard time unloading them in Maine." She could see the blue light now, still swirling in violet circles about the snowy yard. She would buy Sicily a thousand crossword puzzles. She would listen to the twisted, rewritten parables of the Bible. She would agree that George Bush was the next best thing to sliced bread. She would —yes, she would—take her to the blasted Thanksgiving Co-op dinner.

"That's Patrice Grandmaison," Amy Joy said, and pointed to the woman hovering about at the open doors of the ambulance. Patrice looked up in surprise as Amy Joy's little Cavalier crunched to a halt beside the ambulance. There was no crowd, except for Maxine Monihan from the trailer park next door and a couple of St. Leonard faces Amy Joy could not recognize. Dr. Brassard was there, giving some instructions to the attendants.

"Who is it?" Amy Joy asked Patrice. Miranda had followed her from the car and was now shivering, her arms hugging her own body.

"Mathilda Fennelson," Patrice whispered. "She's had a stroke."

Amy Joy leaned forward before the attendant closed the door, and saw Mathilda's old body on the stretcher. Her eyes were open, glassy blue, and her mouth, while not exactly smiling, seemed content with all the ruckus.

"Poor thing," said Amy Joy. Maxine's flushed face appeared before her, excitement painted all over it.

"Sorry," Maxine said. "I thought you and Lola would want to know, your mothers being here and all. I know *I* would." Her nose was red with a cold, and she sniffed loudly before producing a Kleenex.

"Someone needs to take the telephone away from you, Maxine," said Amy Joy. "The telephone wasn't meant for people like you." *Mr. Watson, come here. I want you.* Amy Joy stepped back as the ambulance pulled away, a small spray of frozen snow spitting up from its tires. Dr. Brassard followed in his own car, its red taillights bouncing out onto the road.

"Your mother's fine," said Patrice.

"I tried to phone first," said Amy Joy. She was watching Maxine's stout silhouette as it moved away, back to the trailer park, back to the tiny kitchen and tiny living room and tiny bedroom of Maxine's own tiny life.

"I wasn't in my office," Patrice explained. "I was in Mathilda's room. We had to wait for Dr. Brassard to arrive before we moved her. He forgot to plug in his block heater and his car wouldn't start."

Miranda and Amy Joy followed her back into Pine Valley. Old faces peered out of doorways, aging men and women in pajamas and nightgowns, hands to their mouths, eyes torn between sleep and panic.

"Go back to bed, everyone," Patrice whispered loudly. There were other residents still asleep, some too anchored in their own minds to care, others too deaf to hear.

On the way to Sicily's room, Amy Joy and Miranda passed number 32, Mathilda's old room. Amy Joy stopped and peered inside at the empty bed. The resident nurse was just cleaning up. Lights blared loudly, reflections from so many silver things:

spoons, thermometers, catheter tubes, suction tubes, oxygen tubes, steel pans and bowls. A container of swab sticks sat quietly, their heads snow-white, waiting for the next battle. Amy Joy picked up a tube of salve that lay on a table by the door.

"For bedsores," said the nurse.

In her own tidy room, Winnie was sitting on one of the two chairs, sobbing, while Sicily rubbed her neck.

"Mama!" said Amy Joy. "I was scared to death." She put a hand on Sicily's arm, but it wasn't necessary. Sicily was in control, kneading Winnie's shoulders with the skill of a masseuse, comforting her in a smooth little lullaby voice.

"You're never ready for it," Winnie sobbed.

"Mama," Amy Joy said again. "I was so afraid something had happened to you. Maxine called me up and told me the ambulance was here."

Miranda leaned in the doorway and watched. At first Sicily seemed to notice only Winnie, working around the little brown moles on her neck, calming her with *shush*es and *there now*s. She glanced up, suddenly, at Miranda.

"You're like looking at my sister Pearl," said Sicily, and Miranda smiled. "Look at her, Winnie. Ain't she the spitting image of Pearly? This here is Pearl's great-granddaughter." Winnie looked up, tears in her eyes, at the lanky girl in the doorway.

"You're never ready for it," Winnie said. "I don't care who you are."

"That crazy Maxine should be shot, that's what," a voice said loudly from down the hallway. A cloud of commotion followed it, people scuttling, winter coats swishing, boots thumping along the tile. From her resting spot in the doorway, Miranda was able to survey the racket.

"A little skinny woman and a big fat woman," she whispered to Amy Joy, who grimaced. Lola and Dorrie.

"Calling a person in the middle of the night for no reason at all." Lola's voice was coming closer. Behind her, Dorrie's thick, heavy breathing was audible, the sound of dead weight being propelled forward.

"Let's go, Mama," said Amy Joy. She was hoping to make a clean retreat before the dynamic duo arrived. "We're going home. I'll come back for your stuff tomorrow." Sicily stopped kneading Winnie's motley neck.

"I ain't dressed," she said.

"Put your coat on over your gown," said Amy Joy. "The car is warm. Your old bedroom is all made up and waiting." Winnie began to sob louder.

"There she is," said Lola, her face appearing like a weed in the doorway. "You okay, Mum?" she asked Winnie, who was still weeping. Miranda stepped back to let Lola pass.

"Excuse me," Lola said. She knelt dramatically at Winnie's knee. "Now, Mama, you got to remember that Grammie Mathilda was a hundred and seven years old. Most folks don't get to keep their loved ones that long. She'll go to heaven now, with all them other old-timers, folks she used to know. She didn't recognize anybody anymore. Don't you want Grammie Mathilda to go to heaven?"

"I want *you* to go to hell," Winnie cried. "When was the last time you come to visit her? When was the last time you come to visit *me?*" She had begun to rock softly on her chair, comforting herself now.

"Listen to you," said Lola. "I ain't been here ten seconds and already you've started. People won't want to visit you, Mama, if you're nasty to them." A huffing Dorrie materialized in the doorway, wearing her bulging stadium coat.

"She okay?" Dorrie asked.

"She's fit as a fiddle," said Lola, and gave Winnie's limp arm a squeeze.

"I don't care who you are," Winnie was whispering again. "You're never ready for it."

"Someone ought to put Maxine on a bus to hell," said Dorrie. "She can claim it's a chemical imbalance if she wants to, but I know better."

"Let's go, Mother," Amy Joy said to Sicily, and motioned with her head toward the door.

"Look who's here," said Dorrie. "Seems like I run into you the last time I was here."

"We're on our way home," said Amy Joy, and with a hand on Sicily's arm maneuvered her out the door. In the hallway, Miranda raised her eyebrows into a question.

"Idiots," Amy Joy whispered.

"You're looking fit and trim, Amy Joy," said Lola. Winnie was now crying loudly.

"You probably been real busy lately, though," said Dorrie. She and Lola exchanged a meaningful look.

"Mama, you're gonna wake up the whole place, sweetie," said Lola. "Now you just calm yourself down. So help me, I'll wring Maxine's neck the next time I see her."

In Sicily's room, Amy Joy found her mother's black boots beneath the bed and pulled them out. "Grab her purse," she said to Miranda. She found a clean towel in the little bathroom and wrapped Sicily's toothbrush, comb, and denture cream in it. In the closet she found Sicily's coat.

"Can't we take Winnie?" Sicily whispered loudly from the hallway.

"Oh, don't start," said Amy Joy. *"Please."* She looked across the hall, to where Lola and Dorrie peered like traffic cops out of Winnie's room. Lola shouldered her purse strap and patted Winnie a final time.

"We'll see you tomorrow, sweetie," she said. "You get you some sleep now. I'll check with the hospital about Grammie and call you first thing." Dorrie followed her back out into the hallway.

"I'm glad *my* mother didn't wake up," said Dorrie. She had passed Claire Fennelson's room on the way in. "They must be giving her sleeping pills again. She misses everything that goes on down here."

"You're taking Sicily home?" Lola asked. She had seen the bundle in Amy Joy's arms. "Dear heavens, but this is the best place for her. She's got company her own age, and lots of good medical attention."

"Mind your own business, please," Amy Joy said curtly.

Miranda had found Sicily's purse and was waiting in the hallway. Dorrie noticed her there, saw the dark eyes looming large behind the glasses. This was not a Pine Valley worker, as Dorrie had originally thought. Yet, this girl looked vaguely familiar. Her stadium coat bulging stiffly, Dorrie maneuvered herself out into the hallway and eyed Miranda intently.

"I don't believe I caught your name," Dorrie said.

"That's because I didn't throw it," Miranda answered, turning her wide McKinnon forehead toward Dorrie, regarding her with a cold McKinnon stare.

"There's no need to be rude, Amy Joy," Lola chided. "But then maybe you're in some kind of emotional state." Amy Joy ignored her by going back into Sicily's room. She had just remembered that her mother would need a change of clothes for the next day. Sicily's bed was now as empty as Mathilda's.

"You're just trying to make one of them statements of yours," said Lola. "You're just taking Sicily home to make the rest of us look like terrible daughters. You always did think you was a peg up the pole." Amy Joy pretended not to hear. She found Sicily a clean dress, some underwear, and a sweater, something she could wake up to find on the foot of her own bed, back at the house where she'd been born. The house where she should die, when the time came. She snapped off the lamp by the bedside.

"I'd think you'd be too busy to take Sicily back home," said Dorrie. She and Lola exchanged another esoteric look. "That you'd have the house just full of company." They clomped off down the hall, the sound of their voices ricocheting off the tiled walls, following them like a sad, obedient dog.

"I'm gonna wait till she ain't expecting it," Lola was saying. "Then I'm gonna call Maxine up and tell her a tree fell on that Frog she married."

Amy Joy stood in the shiny tiled hallway and watched the women go, Dorrie waddling as effectively as any duck, Lola leaning forward as if into an invisible wind.

"Amy Joy's just trying to make the rest of us look bad," Dorrie said, repeating Lola's earlier accusation. They disappeared around the corner, the sound following in an angry echo, engulfing them, until it, too, disappeared.

"Come on, Mama," Amy Joy said. Sicily was standing in her big black coat at the door to Winnie's room. From behind her shoulder, Winnie's sad face peered out, like a pale winter's moon.

"If I'm going, Winnie's going," said Sicily, and pointed to her foot. Amy Joy looked down at what appeared to be a dark brown cord tied around Sicily's ankle. She was about to ask what it was, when Winnie stepped up alongside Sicily, and Amy Joy saw that Winnie, too, had a similar cord knotted about her own ankle. No, it was the very same cord.

"What is that?" Miranda asked, leaning down to investigate.

"It's a nylon stocking," said Amy Joy. And indeed it was, the old-fashioned, rubbery kind, with a heavy seam running up the back. "They've tied themselves together."

"Do you want me to get some scissors?" Miranda asked. Sicily frowned. This little girl didn't only *look* like Pearl.

"You get scissors and we'll scream," Sicily promised. Winnie continued to weep. Amy Joy considered sending Miranda off for Patrice, but then Patrice had been getting ready to drive to the hospital, behind the ambulance.

"That's it," said Amy Joy. "I've had it. Stay here then, if you're going to act like that." She put Sicily's clothes down on the tiled floor, and motioned for Miranda to leave the purse. She had taken only ten steps when Sicily began to cry too, her voice joining Winnie's in a harmonious squawking.

"I don't want to die here," Sicily wept. Amy Joy could hear voices rising up from other rooms, muffled whispers, the tenants of Pine Valley tuning in on the fracas.

"I don't want to die here either," Winnie wailed.

"Shut up!" a male voice down the hall advised loudly.

"You just shut up yourself!" Winnie screamed back.

"I should've had more children," Sicily was now announcing between sobs. "I should've at least had twins. Maybe one of them would take me home to die."

"Shit," Amy Joy whispered. "Shit. Shit. Shit," she said, one for every step she retraced to Winnie's door. "Come on," she said to the two old women. Sicily stopped crying. She had been on the verge of shouting, "Nice talk!" to Amy Joy's retreating back until this new development surfaced.

"We're taking Winnie with us?" Sicily asked.

"We're taking her with us," said Amy Joy. She had knelt and was trying to untie the nylon. The knot held firm. How could such old hands find such strength? "Where are your scissors?" she asked her mother.

"I don't have any scissors," said Sicily. "Only the pair we had at home."

"Do you have any scissors?" Amy Joy asked Winnie, who shook her head. Miranda tried the knot, but it still wouldn't budge.

"You're going to have to walk like that until we get you home," Amy Joy said. Sicily and Winnie nodded like well-trained seals. "Get Winnie's coat, and a few things," Amy Joy told them. She couldn't help but wonder, smugly, what Lola would have to say about this.

"Come on, Win," said Sicily. Together, they hobbled toward Winnie's closet and found her coat. Sicily helped guide Winnie's arms into the holes.

"Let's get my toothbrush and stuff," said Winnie. They ambled off, trussed up like convicts, in the direction of the Pine Valley dresser. Amy Joy picked up the bundle of Sicily's belongings she had dumped by Winnie's door.

"I came here tonight because I was worried about my mother," said Amy Joy. "And now I'm going home with Chang and Eng." Sicily and Winnie had rounded up a few things, and now they hobbled in unison back to the door.

"Are you gonna be sorry for this tomorrow?" Miranda whispered.

"I'm sorry right now," said Amy Joy. But as Bobby Fennelson had said one sunny afternoon in her kitchen, *Things have a way of working out.* Winnie would need to sleep in Sicily's downstairs bedroom; otherwise, she would be forced to climb the steep stairway. Amy Joy would need to change the big four-poster bed for narrow twins.

"This is better than *Cocoon*," said Miranda. She took the articles

Sicily was piling into her arms—Winnie's purse, Winnie's reading glasses, Winnie's big worn Bible. Off they went, Amy Joy and Miranda in the lead, Winnie and Sicily limping along behind, down the tiled corridor of the Pine Valley rest home.

"This is just like being on the yellow brick road," Sicily said happily. Amy Joy, wearing her heavy snow boots and not a slick pair of ruby slippers—which would be hell on ice—considered her mother's comment.

"I needn't tell you which one of us is after the brain," Amy Joy snapped. Sicily pretended not to hear.

"I don't wanna put anybody out," Winnie was saying. "Is Amy Joy sure she wants me?"

"Of course she wants you," said Sicily. "And every morning we'll have breakfast, just the two of us, before Amy Joy gets up. Then we'll sit in rocking chairs and stare down at the Mattagash River." Sicily wondered suddenly, as they passed Blanche's door, if maybe Amy Joy would consider bringing Blanche along too. But the short, swift way in which her daughter's arms were now swinging as she walked changed Sicily's mind.

"I ain't seen the river in over a year," said Winnie. She was still crying.

"You're coming home with me now," Sicily said. The word bounced lightly on her tongue, a sweet, sweet word, *home*. She patted Winnie's shoulder as they tottered on down the hallway. "You just shush now, before Amy Joy changes her mind."

"Praise God for Amy Joy," Winnie noted. Eyes closed, she raised a flat palm up to heaven.

"That reminds me," said Sicily.

"What's that?" asked Winnie, and opened her eyes. She fumbled in her coat pocket for a Kleenex.

"Don't you owe me twenty dollars?" Sicily said.

Mathilda Flies Away:
A Return to Mattagash Brook

> Oh that I had wings like a dove!
> For then I would fly away and be at rest.
> Lo, then would I wander off.
> And remain in the wilderness.
>
> —The Bible, Psalm 55

Tonight I'm all old memories, and they keep picking at my mind, sticking me like they're pins. Me and this town was born at the same time, in the same year, so you might say we kind of grew up together. We been close as sisters. We seen a whole lot of changes come and go, as well as folks. I remember a time when there was a real deep sense of family in this town. We had ways of doing things that you don't see no more.

One of them things we used to do was to burn the dead grass every spring. There was still snow along the edge of the woods, and on the floor beneath the trees, so the fire never got out of hand. You always had the river on the other side to stop the flames. But still we wet down old potato sacks and kept them nearby just in case. You needed to watch out for your buildings, not let the fire catch. It was something to see, I tell you. When dark fell and the grass was fairly well burned up, you could see that ring of fire, just an orange circle of flames around the field. There wasn't anything quite so pretty. And the aroma of it! You could still smell the cold snow laying there in the woods, even though you couldn't see it. That mixture of smoke and snow is something I can smell yet, here tonight, here so many years away from it. Us children used to run the ring of fire, while our parents stood and talked in them soft, old-timer voices. And when no one was looking, we broke off hollow reeds and lit them up like they was little brown cigars! Then the old spring moon would come up, a big white ball, and down below was that dying ring of orange fire. I ain't ever forgot it. Or how the grass come up later, from beneath all that black soot, so green it hurt your eyes. You could turn your horses and your cattle out in it like it was a big painted rug. And before you knew it, that grass'd be dotted with bluebells, and orange and yellow hawkweed, and wild mustard. And we'd find buttercups to hold under our chin to tell if we liked butter or not. I mean *real* butter, that you churned by hand until your arm got sore, butter that made your taste buds pop to life when you put it in your mouth. And sometimes we'd eat the big pink tops of the red clover, little bursts of sugar on our tongues. When bladder campions grew around the field, with flower pods like little melons, we'd squeeze the pods shut, trap air inside, and then we'd pop them on our arms. They sounded like tiny guns going off. And there was other things come back to life in that field after the fire. After the fire, that field was like a thing born again.

We burned the grass every year like that, with little kids growing up to be the parents who stood and talked and leaned on rakes, while *their* little kids run like Indians in among the fire. Then somebody's kid went off to college for an agriculture degree and he come back home in a huff, telling us it was wrong to burn the grass. "You're killing all the organisms in the soil," he said. "You're killing the earthworms, too." I don't know if that's how it started, but folks dropped off burning the grass each spring. You don't see that too much anymore, not since Bradford Fennelson went to college. I suppose some changes is for the better.

And you don't see too many mayflowers anymore, that little trailing arbutus that grows in peaty woods. In the spring my mother took me to look for mayflowers, way back in the woods beyond the field. We'd find them crouching there, small and whitish-pink, like they was little teeth or something. There never has been a wildflower in northern Maine to fill up a house any more with the smell of perfume. I don't know if there still is mayflowers out there. The more that new settlement of houses grew up, full of young people starting families, the more the mayflowers moved back into the woods. It was like they could hear civilization coming for them, and so they run. The last time I went looking for them must have been over thirty years ago. Imagine that. But there they was, way back on the hardwood ridge, crouching like they was hiding from something, their little petals soft as tissue. I tell you, I couldn't pick a single one. They looked up at me like they was pleading for their lives. And all along that hardwood ridge I saw the leftovers of old fences, the split-rail kind, made by the first settlers, people come and gone before even I was born. I could hear the noise of logging trucks, on the roads the P. G. Irvine Company had made through the woods, places no white man had been before. And I could hear traffic down on the main road, cars coming and going. And I thought about them split-rail fences, and them little fragile mayflowers growing in peace, and I wondered how long they had left. I wondered how long any of us had. I wondered how long before there ain't any dark places anywhere.

Nowadays folks has got all kinds of notions in their heads. They ain't looking down at the ground under their feet anymore, at the old-settler soil. They ain't looking to nature for any answers. They're waiting for the weatherman to tell them if it's gonna snow or rain. They're looking to television, and to the telephone, and lottery tickets, and automobiles for all their answers. A kid can't add two and two without a machine telling him it's four. A kid ain't got no imagination anymore. There was a time we'd sit and watch someone make hand shadows on the wall, and feel blessed just to see it. Nobody tells stories anymore. They got movies to watch instead. And nowadays folks are yearning to own more earthly goods than they got need for. There's machines everywhere these days, even machines that keep us breathing, keep pumping food into our worn-out stomachs, oxygen into our tired old lungs, blood into our threadbare veins. They can keep us alive all they want, but they ain't gonna save us. Machines will be the death of us, you mark my words.

Tonight I'm all memories, burning like that orange ring of fire. Tonight I'm all taste and touch and smell. Tonight I have the body of a young girl, light and in love, ready to bear all them children over again. Tonight I been rolling these eyes around in their sockets, looking for new squares of ceiling. I have turned the century of my face up to the doctors. I have turned the years up to them, the babies, the gardens, the snows, the wars, the barrels full of rainwater that I washed my clothes in. I'm remembering the north pasture tonight, the field we always intended to plow. There was a brook there, and an old barn—whose I don't know—sagging in on itself. I'm falling in, too, my ribs breaking up like wood. I'm like fruit that's turned ripe and then rotted, and is useless to everyone. Is this life, when the muscles and bones twist with pain, as though they're trying to snap? Is it life, when it's not death? If it is, then let me go. That's what I want to say to the doctor who tends me like I'm some weedy garden. To the nurses who feed me with tubes. And now I see the reverend—or do I imagine this? I see the curtains with small red strawberries, fluttering in the old bedroom, and the reverend is like a heavy warm blanket pressing me down. I want to give him the last kiss, like it's a little heart. My memories are all fire now, with the snow laying safe at the edges. But it isn't the reverend, is it? It's Foster, come like a dear old friend, a face I've known for over a hundred years. A face like a brother's. A face like a good solid home to me, one with a big front porch, and a summer kitchen with a red roof. A home up by Mattagash Brook, where the crayfish hide under the rocks, and the wild cherry covers the ridge. Old man, the time has come, tonight, to see the horse's mouth foam with work. I want to watch the soil churning up rich and black behind the plow. There's an ax we left rusting in a stump, up in that old north pasture, where there's still so much work to do. Listen, Foster, there's a need now to take up the ax again, to swing it at something, a tree maybe, that'll go into making a house. Now I'm all body, all dead weight. I'm all heart and nerve and memory. Old man, there's a reason to go again to the spot where the hemlocks bend by Mattagash Brook. I need to hear the shiver of birch leaves. I need to smell the sweet smell of pines. My ancestors' pines. Now I can smell the may-flowers again, that rich perfume smell, so thick you could cut it. I can hear them opening their tiny petals. Now I'm all mayflowers breathing on the hardwood ridge. I'm Papa and Mama, and Ivy Craft, catalogue woman. I'm Walter and Mary and Luther's Jennie and the Reverend Ralph. I'm all the people that I ever loved. I'm the last turn in the old river, the last bend before home. Foster, can you smell the thick smell of pine? Listen! The whippoorwill has come back to his tree. Remember how, when the kids was little, we'd stand on the porch and listen? It must be night again, 'cause that's the only time he'll come. He sleeps all day, Foster, all day in the forest. And he looks so much like the leaves that you could step on him if you ain't careful. Now I'm standing on the night porch, holding the lantern up to catch his eyes. His eyes are like the fire that's burning up the spring fields. There's a moon above the fire tonight, a big white ball. Everybody I ever loved is standing out there now, watching that field burn, leaning on rakes. This is it, Foster. This is the part where the fire is over, and the moon is sinking. This is the lovely part where we tell the children good night, then lock the blessed door. . . .

Nimble Mots at
The Crossroads: The Last Bus
to Canterbury

> What things have we seen
> Done at the Mermaid! Heard words that have been
> So nimble, and so full of subtile flame,
> As if that ever one from whence they came
> Had meant to put his whole wit in a jest.
>
> —Francis Beaumont, "Lines to Ben Jonson"

"Holy cow," said Sally as she thumbed through a copy of *People* magazine on the bar. "Pretty soon all that's gonna be left of poor Joe Namath is a big old nose."

"Let me see," said Ronny Plunkett, reaching for the magazine.

"A dollar fifty at LaVerdiere's Drugstore," Sally said, and whisked the magazine out of reach. "Go get your own."

"To hell with it," Ronny said. "I've seen bigger noses than that anyway."

"Yeah?" Sally was unimpressed. "Where?"

"In the Suez Canal," said Ronny. "You ain't seen nothing until you've seen some of the schnozzles over there." Sally turned the page on Joe Namath. Sometimes it seemed that Ronny Plunkett had seen too much of the world for his own good. There were some things, Sally was sure, that you should always wonder about.

"I wish Maurice would get back," Sally said. "Not knowing is driving me crazy." She studied another picture thoughtfully. "Why don't someone tell Donald Trump to prune them eyebrows of his? With that kind of money, you'd think he could hire someone to do that."

"I wouldn't get my hopes up," said Ronny. He was talking about the messy condition of The Crossroads, not the one above Donald Trump's eyes. "The women in this town get an idea into their heads and there's no stopping them. And I hear there was a slew of cars at the gym all day long yesterday, right up until they closed the shower curtain at ten o'clock." He had eaten the bowl of free popcorn until only the unpopped kernels were left. "Can I have some more popcorn?" he asked. "All I got left is old maids."

"Poor Maurice," said Sally. She closed *People* magazine and then slid it down the counter to Ronny. "I bet he tossed and turned all night long. You know how nervous he is anyway. I don't know why they couldn't have counted them votes last night and let us know then. They're just trying to drag it out, is all."

"With that bunch of women in charge of counting votes," said Ronny, "you're a sitting duck. Too bad George Bush couldn't have sent some folks up here to watch the ballot box, the way he did for them Filipinos."

It was just beginning to snow when Maurice sauntered unhappily into The Crossroads, dragging his artistic sign behind him. He had stood outside, in a wind filled with young snowflakes, and watched as his sign teetered on its chains. He'd had grandiose ideas, there where the two rivers met, where The Crossroads loomed. But a handful of women, growing larger every day, women snowballing into a mob, had brought him down. So Maurice had taken the aluminum ladder out of his Ford pickup, propped it up against the old building, climbed it like a Sherpa, hoisted the sign off its hooks, and then lowered it to the snowy ground.

Sally looked up as the sign clunked against the Pac-Man machine, rocking the stuffed Canada lynx to life.

"Hey," she said to Maurice.

"Hey," said Maurice. He looked sadly at the lynx; its marble eyes seemed watery with its own sorrow. Maybe Maurice would give it to Booster as a gesture of goodwill. Dorrie might like it for her living room.

"Where you been all day?" Sally asked.

"I slept in late," said Maurice. "I just went ahead and let them z's rip. I just said to hell with it. Wasn't anything I could do anyway." He took off his gloves and slapped them together, laid them gently on top of the sign.

"It snowing?" Ronny asked, although he wasn't concerned. Now that he was retired from the military, Ronny Plunkett didn't care if it never stopped snowing.

"I shoulda packed up ages ago and moved to Connecticut," said Maurice. "Opened me a little bar down there." He was thinking of the delicious sight of Davey Craft's orange U-Haul as it had bounced past The Crossroads just the day before, headed south, its nose aimed toward adventure and acceptance among the paved streets of Connecticut.

"Not me," said Ronny. "Now that everybody in town's got a satellite dish, Mattagash is just like that Piccadilly Circus I visited over in London, England. We can sit on our asses up here in northern Maine and watch the whole damn world go by." He snapped open the crisp body of a peanut and dumped the meat into his mouth.

"That's easy for you to say," said Maurice. "You got that pension coming in from the navy. But for those of us who try to make a living here, it's a different story." Maurice nodded to Sally when she held up a frozen submarine sandwich and gave him a quizzical look. Sally popped it into the microwave and selected the cooking time.

"Well?" she asked Maurice. She knew, of course, by the presence of the Crossroads sign, now leaning snugly against the wall, that the death knell had sounded among the snowy hills of Mattagash.

"Well, what?" Maurice said sadly. He popped the top off a

Schlitz, early for Maurice Fennelson. "What do you think? Of course, they voted to close us. Would God and Prissy have it any other way?"

"Let me tell you something right now," said Ronny. "And I know this to be a fact. God can't stand that bunch of women. They ever turn up at the Pearly Gates, and there's a real good chance they won't, God's gonna shuffle them right on in, right on through, and right on out the back door. God don't want that muddle of women in his establishment."

"Too bad they wouldn't try to close *him* down," said Maurice. He imagined lightning zags piercing down from heaven with names like *Prissy Monihan* on them. "This is the last night," Maurice went on. "And now that they put the whammy on me, only a handful of folks'll dare stop by. I might as well have one of them big Jewish stars on my door. I'm just running up my electric bill for nothing."

"It's gonna snow like a motherfucker anyway," said Ronny. "You seen the sky out there?"

"I'll tell you one thing," said Maurice. "If there is a God, he'll make it snow so hard there won't be any way in hell them women can have their big Thanksgiving dinner. They'll have to sit at home and eat partial dinners." He could see Prissy trying to content herself with a huge pot of mashed potatoes and a gallon of Jell-O. "Yes sir," Maurice concluded mournfully. "This is our last night." He eyed the lovely sign leaning on its shoulder by the door, keeping the Canada lynx company.

"How's Pike making out?" Sally asked Ronny. All kinds of rumors had abounded, with Pike even doing the shooting at one point, until the newspapers sorted it all out for everyone, and then everyone calmed down, satisfied that no one could add more to the mountainous heap now that it was all in print anyway.

"He's still with me at Billy's place," said Ronny. His voice cracked a little, the *Billy* sounding sharp against the soft music of the other words. "And he's having a hell of a time, needless to say."

"Well," said Sally, "I'll tell you one thing. A great portion of the blame for what happened is Pike's. There now, I've said it."

"The Crossroads ain't to blame, though," Maurice was quick to add. He imagined Carl E. Hileman, the Melvin Belli of northern Maine, hiding behind the boxes of empty Miller Lite bottles, ready to stir up a little legal bullshit.

"No, The Crossroads ain't to blame," said Sally. "We ain't one of them big impersonal city bars where bouncers can tell folks they've had too much to drink. This here is what you call your average neighborhood bar. It wasn't our fault Pike was drinking. Pike is always drinking."

"I heard he stopped," said Maurice. "Beena told me he called Maisy and swore to her he was all done with booze, that he's taking AA lessons in Watertown." Ronny considered this.

"Does AA stand for Alcoholic Always?" he asked.

"You mean he didn't go?" Maurice said.

"He went once," said Ronny, "but some social worker had come around and put the fear in him. By the next day, I guess, the fear had went away."

"Did he stop drinking?" asked Sally.

"Do nuns go into heat?" Ronny answered. Maurice thought about this deeply.

"I don't know," Maurice said. "Do they?"

"No, Maurice, I'm afraid they don't," said Ronny. He cracked another noisy peanut. There were some subtle things, Ronny Plunkett knew, that one couldn't learn from a satellite dish.

"You mean to tell me he's still drinking?" asked Maurice, and shook his head sadly.

"I ain't surprised," said Sally. "Beena's little girl goes to Al-A-Tot in Watertown. That's for the kids of alcoholics. Beena's been reading all kinds of material on it. Her ex-husband was a full-fledged, flaming alcoholic, you know. It's a disease, is what it is, like cancer or anything else."

"Come on," said Maurice. "A man could quit if he really wanted to."

"And it's inherited," said Sally. "That's what Beena says. She says it's passed down from one generation to another."

"Really?" said Maurice. "I guess our family was lucky to just get the bad-luck gene passed on. Almost everybody died young, but at least there was no alcoholics." Ronny looked at Maurice Fennelson. It was obvious that a little of the stupid gene, too, had rubbed off on the past proprietor of The Crossroads.

"You know what I think we ought to do?" Ronny asked. Maurice and Sally raised eyebrows simultaneously, another genetic trait some families pass down.

"What?" said Sally.

"Well, everybody's been moping around here, missing Billy and not saying much about it," said Ronny. "You know we have. We been feeling bad about Conrad, and even Pike, and we been acting like a morgue down here."

"So?" Sally replied. "That's the general idea, ain't it?"

"But listen to me, people," said Ronny, and he could hear Billy's voice, could hear The Kid himself: *What you folks missed when you was tromping through the fucking forest to find the goddamn trees is the whole point of my little talk.* "Ain't our Irish ancestors famous for raising hell at a wake, instead of being all hangdog and miserable? I been to a wake over there in Dublin, an uncle of this girl I met in the Canary Islands. We had a hell of a good time. And that's how our ancestors meant for it to be. But we crossed the ocean, and all our good rituals fell into the hands of women like Prissy Monihan, and now we're sitting with our fingers up our asses and waiting for the enemy's next move. Let's celebrate, goddamnit! Let's say good-bye to Billy the right way. You know that's what he'd want."

"What about Conrad?" said Sally. "Won't it seem disrespectful?"

"To who?" asked Ronny. "To Prissy? You know, in your own heart, how you feel about Conrad. Why care what this town will say?"

"Only Booster will come," said Maurice, his eyes sparkling like the true Irish descendant he was. "And I think if Pike's still drinking, he might as well come too." The phone rang, a sweet long bleat. Sally took her chin off her hands to answer it.

"That's all we need," said Ronny. "Just us. Just our little group.

Let's close the old Crossroads down the right way! Let's see Billy Plunkett go out in style. *Our* way, not Prissy's." Maurice's eyes were now glowing, the sparkle having burst into magnificent flame.

"And let's not wait until tonight," Ronny added. "Let's start right now. Booster's probably home. His skidder is broke again."

"All right!" Maurice said, and pounded his fist on the bar. Ronny smiled. He could hear Billy Plunkett's voice in the soft whine of the microwave, in the blinking little lights of all the Christmassy beer signs, in the old jukebox sitting silent, waiting for quarters.

"That was Dorrie," Sally told them. She had put the phone back on its cradle and was now tugging at the little hairs that grew beneath her lip, something the electrolysis kit she'd ordered off the shopping channel on television had failed to remove, as promised. "Grammie Fennelson died a couple of hours ago."

"Lord," said Maurice, "what next?" He was wondering if the Mattagash hit squad could, in some way, blame him for that, too.

"Poor old soul," said Sally. "It's a sin to say it, but it's only about thirty years overdue."

"And this was her old house, you'll remember," said Maurice. "Built in 1906."

"In 1894," said Sally.

"Both going out on the same night," mused Maurice. "Both going home."

"They say death happens in threes," said Sally. "She'd be the third." A look of relief washed over Maurice's face.

"Well," Ronny said. "I guess you ought to call Booster. We got all kinds of reason for an Irish wake now."

At the outset of the party, when the first round went about the bar, compliments of Maurice, an extra bottle was opened for Billy Plunkett. It sat, in his honor, on the bar in front of Billy's favorite stool, the one closest to the jukebox. Sally had already punched "All My Ex's Live in Texas" and "'Til I'm Too Old to Die Young."

"Here," said Pike Gifford. "We might as well do this right."

His eyes were crimson with the effects of a long drinking binge without much sleep, and he was anxious for the little extra shot of vodka to kick in, to take away in a warm wave the uncomfortable feeling he was experiencing, even among his best cronies. Pike suspected they were less than happy with his role in the deaths of Billy and Conrad. But, goddamnit, all he had done was try to shut Lynn's big mouth. It wasn't Pike Gifford who pulled the trigger, although every face he'd seen in the past week had seemed to say just that to him. Pike had taken to avoiding faces as a result, hanging out at Billy's, sleeping in Billy's bed, touching Billy's things as though The Kid were still in them. And now and then, if he allowed himself to get a bit sober, he felt unfathomable guilt. It was Billy he missed, Billy he yearned for, Billy who spun around in his nightmares. It wasn't Conrad. He had tried, a thousand times, to pull the boy's face up in his mind's eye, but it was never Conrad. It was always Billy—Billy on his first bicycle, Billy picking hazelnuts along the river, Billy sinking a steady stream of quarters into some jukebox.

"Here," Pike said again, pulling Billy's *Damn Sea Gulls!* hat from his pocket, straightening it out a bit, and draping it from the neck of the lonesome beer bottle.

"Where'd you get that?" Sally asked. Pike had reached down and picked up the hat the night of the shooting. Billy was on his way out the door, on a stretcher carried by two strangers, and Pike wanted him to have something familiar to take along with him. But the doors to the ambulance had already closed and Billy was whisked away in a whirl of flashing blue lights and shrieking noise. The ambulance looked like an old Wurlitzer jukebox to Pike as it squealed over the icy yard and out onto the road to Watertown. Conrad was in that ambulance too, but all Pike could think of was telling Billy, at some future date, "You looked just like you was inside an old Wurlitzer, Bill. I guess all them quarters you spent in your day has guaranteed you a spot in jukebox heaven." But he would never get the opportunity to tell Billy any such thing.

Sally tacked Billy's "The Solved Secrets of the Great Monuments" onto the microwave door, next to the infamous skunk sheet. The partyers sat about the horseshoe shape of the bar and stared at Stonehenge. The little group of stick men were all still there, all still busy pulling the large bluestone about on wooden rollers, the air around them no doubt filled with Neolithic swear words and slang. Some jobs never end, just as Keats's bride will always be on her Grecian urn, on the way to her wedding, even if, a hundred years ago, she changed her mind about marriage. Decided the guy was a jerk. Dreamed of a career in the Women's Royal Air Force. Some people are simply stuck doing what they've always done.

"You think there's any chance we might—" Maurice began, his eyes on the huge bluestone, but Ronny interrupted.

"No, Maurice darling," said Ronny. "This old building will crack in two like a glass box if we try to move it. So get that out of your head."

"Maybe I *will* buy that piece of land from Jack Bishop, like Billy suggested," said Maurice. "Maybe I'll just go ahead and build me a new bar."

"That's the spirit," said Booster Mullins, cousin to Maurice, grandson also to Mathilda. Now he and Raymond Monihan were stuck with their wives, Dorrie and Lola, every goddamn night of the week. Watertown was too far to drive for hardworking men, but popping by The Crossroads for a couple of fast ones had been a cinch.

Ronny surveyed the scraggly group. Their faces were longer than totem poles as they listened to George Strait sing, "All my Ex's live in Texas. That's why I hang my hat in Tennessee." This was not Ronny's idea of a rollicking Irish wake. Billy was his brother, dammit, and if anyone missed The Kid sorely, it was Ronny Plunkett. And if it had to be Ronny Plunkett to get the show on the road, so be it.

"You ever hear the story about Billy and the schoolteacher?" Ronny asked. Everyone had, but stories in Mattagash are told many times, embellished by the tellers, appreciated greatly, polished with time, and then passed on into folklore. "It seems Bill had disappeared from class one afternoon and never come back. So the next day she asked him where he'd been." The others sipped their beers, smiling nicely, waiting for the sweet punch line to roll them off once again into a ball of good Mattagash humor.

"Mrs. Dubois," Sally added, with a woman's instinct for clarification, and Ronny nodded.

"Mrs. Dubois asked Bill where he'd been. 'Me and Roberta—' Billy started to tell her, but she stopped him. 'Roberta and I,' says Mrs. Dubois. 'Roberta and I,' says Billy, 'was out in—' Again she stops him. '*Were*, Billy,' she says. 'Roberta and I *were* out in, but yes, go on, out in what?' 'That there old barn at Albert Pinkham's,' says Billy. 'No, no,' says Mrs. Dubois. 'I'm sorry but that's inappropriate grammar. You were out in *that* old barn of Albert Pinkham's.' So Bill says, 'Roberta and I were out in that old barn of Albert Pinkham's.' Mrs. Dubois is so happy she almost pees her pants. 'Yes! Yes!' she says. 'That's it, Billy. Now please go on. What were you doing?' 'Fucking our brains out,' says Billy. 'Or should that be *fucking out* our brains?' " The laughter came up around them in a soft blanket, wrapping them with memory, enveloping them with a sense that some things do last, that maybe death isn't the big deal it pretends to be.

"I better go upstairs and bring down another case of beer," Sally said. It looked as if Billy would get his big happy send-off, after all.

"You ever hear about the time Billy drove all the way to Caribou with one of them automatic garage-door openers?" asked Booster, taking the baton from Ronny, carrying the tradition forward, polishing the folklore like some precious old family silver. "He managed to open three or four doors between here and there," Booster went on, "before a cop stopped him and asked what he was doing. 'I'm with the Neighborhood Crime Watch,' Billy told him." And again the laughter came, the sweet warm wave that must have rolled in at all the best Irish wakes, back in the old country.

"Remember that fisherman from Boston, this past summer, who got me to order him a case of some strange red wine, something French, so it'd be here when he come down from three weeks on the Mattagash River?" Maurice asked, and the others nodded. "And he comes in one night and sits over there by the door, and he signals to me he wants a bottle of his wine. So I get out a nice plastic ice bucket and load it up with ice, stick a bottle of wine in it, and tell Billy to take it over to his table."

"And the fisherman says to Bill," Pike interrupted, taking the ball of the story into his own hands, "he says, 'What are you doing to my wine? This here is expensive French wine and you're supposed to serve it at room temperature.' So Bill looks at him a second—you know that look of Bill's—and he says, 'I don't know about France, mister, but right now you're in Mattagash, Maine. Room temperature around here is usually ten below. You want me to get you some more ice?' "

"What's the matter with *you?*" Maurice asked. Sally had returned to the bar without the case of beer. She had been up in one of the old bedrooms of the house, now a storage room for filled beer cases, as well as empties. Maurice was also using it as a halfway refrigeration area for his microwave sandwiches, leaving it closed off and unheated when the weather turned vicious, hoping to rescue his electric bill from extravagant heights. "You look like you just seen a ghost," Maurice added.

"I think I just did," said Sally. She reached for her beer and noticed that her hands were trembling. "When I opened the door to the front bedroom, I saw a white shadow fall across one of the walls. A second later, it was gone." She struck a match against its flint strip again and again, until Booster took the matchbook from her and lighted one up. The tip of Sally's cigarette turned orange with fire.

"Jesus," Sally said. She blew a frantic fan of smoke from her mouth.

"It's the reflection of snow, combined with headlights," said Ronny. "A car probably went by just as you opened the door."

"It's too early for headlights," said Maurice.

"Not with a storm sky like I saw when I come in," Ronny argued.

"But it looked kinda like a woman," said Sally. "I swear. I ain't making this up. Grammie Fennelson always said this house was haunted."

"Go get us some beer, Maurice," said Booster. Maurice looked at him earnestly. No way in hell was Maurice Fennelson going up into that blasted room, in the dim afternoon light, no matter how many times Ronny called him *sweetheart* or *darling,* as Billy used to do.

"Tell you what," Maurice offered. "If someone goes and gets it, the case is on me." Damn them. They really knew how to hurt a man, right in the old pocketbook.

"Grammie Fennelson always claimed that the ghost of Jennie Monihan was in this house," said Sally. "She was the wife of the man who built it."

"Bullshit," said Booster. "Grammie Fennelson used to claim all kinds of crazy stuff. But she *could* stop blood, I'll admit that."

"There ain't no such thing as ghosts," said Ronny. His voice held the accent of authority. Ronny Plunkett had, after all, been around the goddamn world a couple of times.

"Jennie died in childbirth," Sally told them. "I wrote this all down for the historical society. Lots of folks claim they seen her ghost."

"Old-timers," said Booster. "Younger folks don't tell them kinds of foolish tales anymore. They got the television to entertain theirselves. That makes a big difference."

"Old Alfred Hart claimed he saw Bigfoot's footprint once," said Pike. He'd been listening to another playing of " 'Til I'm Too Old to Die Young," and speculating as to what Billy might've said about ghosts. "Come to find out, it was where three horses had all stepped in the same track. But Al still slept with a rifle leaning by his bed, right up to the night he died."

"Old-timers," Booster repeated.

"And old Sarah-Tom probably still believes there's alligators living in the sewers of Watertown," said Pike.

"Now, I'm not so sure *that* ain't true," Booster said. "They'd have plenty of Frogs to live off of."

"Old Sarah-Tom was so afraid of alligators hiding in the grass that she used to start up the lawn mower and push it in front of her every time she went to her garden for a cucumber or a tomato."

"Grammie said people used to see Jennie standing in that upstairs window," said Sally, ignoring them, "in the very room where her and that baby died. And she'd be rocking nothing at all in her arms, just rocking herself back and forth, humming a lullaby." Sally had, on the spur of the creative moment, added the lullaby part herself, enlarged the tapestry of Jennie Monihan's unfortunate life. Her voice had lowered itself to the sotto voce of ghost stories, captivating her listeners, especially the easily frightened Maurice. "Standing there in that white satin wedding gown of hers," Sally added. "Just rocking and humming."

"Boo!" Ronny shouted, and grabbed the nape of Maurice's neck with cold-beer-bottle fingers. Maurice flailed his arms lustily, knocking his Budweiser from the bar. It careened in spin-the-bottle fashion about the floor, leaving a foamy wake behind.

"Goddamn you, Ronny Plunkett!" Maurice said, his voice choked with fright. "That was my last bottle!" Now someone would *have* to go for a case, and Maurice would be damned if that case would be free.

"Maurice, hon," said Ronny. He had learned well in his apprenticeship to brother Billy. "You're gonna end up a Prissy Monihan before you die, if you keep this nervousness up."

"Don't you ever do that again," Maurice muttered.

"Laugh if you want to," said Sally. "But I swear I saw a shadow that looked a whole lot like a woman holding something."

"Maybe it was our case of beer," said Booster. "Somebody better go up there quick before she drinks it all." Laughter swirled again, the nimble bons mots of old Irish wakes, and new Irish wakes still to come—for hope, not religion, is the opium of the masses.

"What's so funny?" a voice asked from the door, and the partyers looked up in surprise to see Paulie Hart, the nouveau riche of northern Maine, standing there, a thin powdering of snow about his shoulders. "It's snowing like a bitch out there," said Paulie.

"Well, well, well," said Sally. "If it ain't the Howard Hughes of Mattagash. Where the hell you been?"

"Don't you ever try something like that again," Maurice whispered to Ronny.

"Money goes straight to some people's heads," said Booster, and winked. Paulie was still showing bewilderment, which the gatherers interpreted as *embarras de richesses*.

"It would go to my *crotch*," said Ronny. "Imagine all the female companionship you could buy for a thousand bucks." This was the thorn in the side of Ronny Plunkett's retirement: Mattagash had no professional whores.

"I'm surprised to see you hobnobbing with us poor folks," said Maurice, his nerves settling again. Where the hell had Paulie been with that thousand bucks when Maurice was open and going strong?

"What are you guys talking about?" asked Paulie. He kicked his toe lightly against the sign at the door, the two rivers shimmering blue beneath the light of the bar. "Did your sign fall down?"

"You know darn well what we're talking about," said Sally. She'd found another bottle of Budweiser, hiding beneath some Pepsi in the cooler, and uncapped it for Paulie. Now it sat next to Billy's on the bar, cold and waiting. George Strait had begun to sing again about the women he had married and divorced and moved away from.

"We're talking about the thousand dollars you won in the lottery," said Pike. "Of all the people who could've used that money and there you go and win it."

"He picked fifteen, seven, two, nine, and eleven," said Maurice, in a tone of confidentiality, as though the winning combination might be stolen and used again.

"I ain't won no lottery money," said Paulie. He'd already found the beer and tipped it up.

"What!" exclaimed Sally.

"It's been all over town for three weeks now," said Booster.

"You picked fifteen, seven, two, nine, and eleven," said Maurice.

"I didn't do no such thing," said Paulie. "I won a free ticket, but I wouldn't call that owning the goose that laid the goddamn egg."

"But you disappeared for all that time," said Sally. "We thought it was because you won the lottery."

"Or was it fifteen, seven, two, *eight*, and eleven?" Maurice asked, a look of concerned technicality on his face.

"It wasn't *any* of them numbers," said Paulie, exasperated, "because I'm telling you, I didn't win the goddamn lottery."

"Modest," said Sally.

"Where you been, in that case?" asked Booster.

"I ain't neither modest," said Paulie. "I'm tired, I'm thirsty, and I'm ready for a little party. Why the hell is this place so deserted anyway? I thought there'd be a nice crowd here. I drove nonstop all the way from New Milford, and in some pretty bad snow for the last thirty miles."

"So how come Beena didn't know you was in Connecticut?" asked Sally. "Beena didn't know where in hell you was."

"Holy shit," said Paulie. "Sounds like I'm gonna be in trouble back at the ranch."

"There ain't no ranch left," said Booster. "Charlie Hart's been camping out on Beena's couch lately."

"Your mother told Beena you just disappeared," said Sally.

"I swear," said Paulie. "She's my mother, but there's times I could strangle her. She was supposed to tell Beena that I had to drive my sister and her kids back to Connecticut pronto. You know how airheaded Sandy is. She decided in the middle of the night that she don't want to divorce that Wop she married. So I figured if I was already down there, I might as well spend some time with relatives. We got a bushel of them in New Milford."

"So why didn't your mother tell Beena that?" asked Sally.

"Mama don't like for me to be seeing Beena, her divorced and all. She says Beena don't wear enough clothes in the summers to pad a crutch," said Paulie. He killed the beer. Paulie had once finished off a cold Budweiser in three and a half seconds, a Crossroads record. Maurice had timed him. "You gotta get your throat to go straight up and down," Paulie had told his admirers, the losers. "You can't even *think* of your throat having a curve in it. You do, and you're a dead man."

"She's wearing enough clothes at this time of the year," said Booster. "You can be sure of that. But I bet she's hot to trot. She's got a temper as it is." He winked at Ronny.

"I wonder what else Mama told her," Paulie said, ruminating on where he was going to find another woman like Beena, what with the holidays coming on, not to mention the long cold winter ahead. "They already got Christmas lights up in Watertown," Paulie added sadly.

"She told her you hit the thousand-dollar lottery and then the road," said Booster.

"Shit," said Paulie. He had appreciated Beena's city experience when it came to *positions d'amour*. "Shit," he said again. He plunked the empty Bud bottle onto the bar.

"Well, here's to fortunes down the drain," said Ronny, and raised his own bottle.

"You don't believe in using the telephone?" Sally asked. "Why didn't you call Beena up yourself and tell her where you was? You're a big boy."

"Long distance?" asked Paulie. "All the way from Connecticut?" Sally shook her head. This from the man who spent a couple hundred a week on lottery tickets.

"Besides," Paulie added, "it's good for a woman to stew a little bit where a man's concerned."

"I wouldn't call what Beena's been doing with Charlie *stewing*," said Booster. "Although it rhymes."

"Oh well," said Paulie. "As far as women go, you win some, you lose some." It was the same philosophy he applied unsparingly to the lottery, but it seemed more the latter than the former in that case, too. "So anyway," he said. "What's been happening in this old town since I been gone? Any excitement? Where's Billy the Kid?" The others stared at him. With all the forms of communication available now in Mattagash, with telephones shaped like frogs in some of the better bathrooms, with machines that could rumble into the woods, limb a tree in eight seconds, and then cut it down where it stands, with all of that available, Paulie Hart still didn't know beans, even with the bag open. He was green as the grass that would eventually come back to Mattagash in the spring. It had been said of Paulie Hart before, and it was true. He had inherited more than the lion's share of the stupid gene.

"I tell you what," said Maurice. Where would he start? Probably with Mathilda Fennelson's death. The least surprising gem should always come first, and besides, she was Paulie's great-grandmother. "You go upstairs and bring us down another case of beer." Maurice was almost cavalier. "And we'll fill you in."

Sleeping the Dream:
Life in Anyone's Town

> anyone lived in a pretty how town
> (with up so floating many bells down) . . .
>
> someones married their everyones
> laughed their cryings and did their dance
> (sleep wake hope and then) they
> said their nevers they slept their dream
>
> stars rain sun moon
> and only the snow can begin to explain . . .
>
> —e. e. cummings, "anyone lived
> in a pretty how town"

*B*ecause of the thick snow, which was now circling Mattagash, Simon Craft was late delivering the mail. Amy Joy had been watching for the nose of his car to peek around the bend in the road. When it finally did, she had quickly bundled into her coat, waded through the snow piling up in her driveway, and was now waiting for him by the Lawler mailbox. She could feel the oppressive heft of the storm as it bore down, the wild power of it. In Mattagash, Maine, winter is like a weight that presses you down, holds you there until you think you can't breathe anymore. You just seem to black out and when you wake up, it's spring again. Amy Joy had learned, or so it seemed to her now, to bend with the weight of winter, to go with it, to survive beneath it. It's true that there were warmer places in the world, and some of them not all that far from Mattagash. Bobby Fennelson had found one of them. But there was that old rotting dream of *roots,* that notion of home, of heritage, of family scrapbooks that had been nagging at her for years. And now it seemed that, for some folks anyway, the roots run too deep to pull up and plant elsewhere. It has to do with something in the soil, maybe down there in the dark, quiet areas that the roots tap into, a little secret the roots have learned about survival.

And there was something else happening inside Amy Joy Lawler, something that middle age had done for her. She didn't seem to care so much now about raising her own family, about men she might marry, about the gray that was scattering itself in her hair, about what clothes were in style. Those were the things that nature taught you, when you knew how to look in the right places. The earth, the water, the sky, the stars, have been around a lot longer than McKinnons and Crafts and Fennelsons. Maybe that's why the answers lie there. It no longer frightened Amy Joy to admit that she might be in Mattagash forever, might die there, and take her own place in the Protestant graveyard overlooking the Mattagash River. Because the Mattagash River had been there a long time too. And it didn't bother her that maybe, if Sicily went first, Amy Joy might be compelled again to contemplate the wide places of the world. If that happened, then it happened, the way an earthquake happens, a storm, a flood. The way a star dies and suddenly disappears forever. You have no control over it, so you deal with it when it comes.

"Don't Mattagash look just like one of them paperweights that you pick up and shake and it snows all over everything all at once?" Simon Craft asked from his open window. His mail car had slid in on the waves of the storm, like a sleek gray fish, and up to Amy Joy's mailbox. She smiled. It did, indeed, look like the little towns in paperweights, the snowflakes so big and fat they could be artificial.

"What are you doing out on a day like today?" Amy Joy asked. "And so late? I thought you liked to sit out a storm." Simon nodded hardily, and then blew his perpetually running nose into a handkerchief. Amy Joy had always wondered, when a bad cold or a twenty-four-hour bug had passed around town over and over again, like something borrowed, if Simon was not the one responsible.

"I got caught in it," said Simon. "I never dreamed it would get so bad so fast. It's taking me forever to get this mail delivered. And you know darn well, judging by what's coming down now, that they won't even be able to find the gymnasium tomorrow. What a way to spend Thanksgiving! And my little grandkids has been practicing for that play since day one. They was gonna be two little Pilgrims. The cutest little outfits you ever saw. I tell you, they're brokenhearted over this."

"I need some stamps," said Amy Joy. She removed her mitten in order to get a better grip on the dollar bills in her coat pocket. Simon Craft was probably also late because, by now, everyone in town had been told how disappointed his little Pilgrim grandchildren were. Amy Joy knew that everyone in town received from Simon a sort of homogeneous gossip until he got down to the personal details of individuals.

"I just dropped a gas bill and two fliers off at The Crossroads," Simon announced. "Maurice is pretty long-faced over the vote they took yesterday."

"I don't blame him," said Amy Joy. "This should be a democracy, but with Prissy around, it really isn't." But Amy Joy should have realized that Prissy still had too much of the old loyalist blood pumping in her veins to give a hoot about such upstart notions as democracy.

Amy Joy was still waiting for her own mail, and finally Simon Craft stopped sorting through it and passed it on out the window.

"Booster's over there too," said Simon. "His skidder is broke down, and I suppose having a beer is better than twiddling his thumbs. You got a gas bill, too, and a couple of fliers," he added, pointing at the bundle. He blew his large nose again, a raucous bleat. "And it looks like your subscription to *Life* is running out. Oh, and you got one of them thank-you notes Lynn Gifford's been sending out to let folks know she appreciated the flowers and money and sympathy in her time of need, et cetera. Wasn't that the worse you ever heard of, though? I bet she sent out fifty of them notes just to folks here in town." Amy Joy was only half listening as she flipped through her mail. It was all there as Simon had reported it to be, but there was also a postcard, a lovely, colorful thing sporting large chunks of petrified trees, and eroded hills turning to yellowish rust in the sun.

"And you got a postcard," Simon said, "but it don't have a name on it. It's pretty, though. I suppose *you* know who it's from." He waited. Amy Joy nodded. *Missing You* was all the hand-scrawled message said.

"Yes," she said. "I do know." Simon was still waiting.

"Well, I don't push people to tell me where their mail is from," he said. "My job is to deliver it. And if I don't get going soon, I won't be able to do that. It's a darn shame that dinner is gonna have to be canceled, Amy Joy. There would have been plenty of eligible bachelors down there at the gymnasium for you to talk to." *Fifty-seven miles east of Winslow, Arizona, off historic Highway 66 is the Petrified Forest National Park featuring the Blue Mesa, Jasper, Crystal, and Rainbow Forests, where the best and most colorful specimens are seen.*

"You know what I been telling you about that bird of time," Simon was saying. "That bird of time is gonna end up like a Thanksgiving turkey if you ain't careful." She imagined him there with the children, careening about the trunks of polished wood, trees his ancestors never dreamed existed, trees they could never cut. She imagined Eileen, having a cigarette in the car, waiting it out, too hot for her suddenly, now that it was no longer too cold.

"That bird of time ain't gonna be able to lift itself off the ground pretty soon," Simon said. "I'd stop trifling with destiny, if I were you, Amy Joy." *Missing You,* the Y shaped like a delicate wineglass, the way he always made them, even in high school. In the center of the *o* he had drawn two eyes and a turned-down mouth. *Visit Agate Bridge, a single petrified tree spanning a 40-foot-deep arroyo.*

"You sure you know who that's from?" Simon asked again, and Amy Joy nodded, a sweet nod of remembrance. It was like a sad, lost bird, this card in her hand, arriving out of the blizzard, settling down beneath the storm, maybe like one of those Canada geese who lose their sense of direction and are forced to land in the strangest of places.

"The postmark is Phoenix, Arizona," Simon badgered. "I don't recall you knowing anyone from there. Course Eileen Fennelson is from Flagstaff. She already sent a few change-of-address cards to Mattagash. I suppose Bobby's settled in out there by now." Amy Joy looked at Simon's eyes, looked deep into those little cameras that had seen and photographed so many addresses, so many beautiful stamps, a million zip codes. Simon Craft, the town crier, the sexton, the keeper of the keys, the Pony Express in another place, another time. The harbinger of news both good and bad. Some jobs never end.

"Course that would have had to be mailed the very same day Bobby left," said Simon, "in order for it to get here." Amy Joy looked at the postmark. He was right. So Bobby hadn't visited the Petrified Forest yet. He must have mailed it from an airport, where racks of just such cards wait to be twirled by tourists who will never visit the sites. Of course, it would have been the airport in Phoenix. Eileen would have been waiting with the children for his arrival in Flagstaff. *There's something about having kids, Amy Joy, for some people, that you just gotta be there to see them kids grow up. Some of us even give up our roots to see it.* Amy Joy looked again at Simon Craft, the courier, dispatch, old Paul Revere, in another time, another place, rewarded for delivering good news, killed for the bad.

"So it couldn't have been from Bobby Fennelson, either," Simon kept on, a meaningful look in his eyes, a this-will-be-our-secret look. "You must have yourself one of them secret admirers."

"I guess so," said Amy Joy. There *were* some big secrets still kept in little towns. There were heroes everywhere, if you knew where in the storm to look for them.

"Well, I want to see you at the Christmas Arts and Crafts Bazaar, then," said Simon. "I hear tell some of the women have already started the planning of it. I'm hoping they'll go ahead and do the Thanksgiving play then. You oughta see the hats that go with them little outfits. Now I better get myself home. The missus will think I've gone all the way to the North Pole this time. I ain't seen another soul out on the road for the past two hours except, of course, for Dorrie and Lola. You'll remember they got that plow. Well, happy Thanksgiving to you and yours, and make sure Winnie fills out a change-of-address card." And then he was gone, in a spray of snow and gray exhaust—or was it a dappled gray horse instead of the mail car, already foaming at the mouth, somewhere on the speedy trail from St. Joe to Sacramento?

Inside the old McKinnon house, with evening coming on full speed, with the storm still intensifying, Amy Joy had just finished with her nightly bath. A towel around her dripping hair, she padded downstairs in search of Miranda.

Sicily and Winnie were in Sicily's old bedroom, already settled in. Amy Joy had brought the foldaway bed out of the hall closet until Winnie could purchase a comfortable twin-size. Then she and Miranda had packed up the meager belongings Winnie had scattered about her room at Pine Valley and, along with Sicily's things, had brought them home. Amy Joy had doubted almost immediately that it was a wise decision to bring Winnie along, but, at least so far, it was working out better than she ever could have imagined. Winnie was now the one to take up the slack in Sicily's life, to listen to the biblical quotes, even add to them. Winnie was the one to hear and appreciate any new gossip, and then share some in return. Winnie was the one to complain along with Sicily, while the two sat in front of cable TV, that there weren't enough families anymore like the Donna Reed family.

"I finally caught her home," Miranda said. She was just hanging up the telephone. "And I've told her where I am and blah, blah, blah, so now are you happy?"

Amy Joy smiled. "How *is* your mother?" she asked.

"Still the scourge of Portland, I'm sure," said Miranda. She bent over a sketch, at the little table Amy Joy had moved down from the upstairs hallway so that Miranda could spend her workday in the kitchen, overlooking the Mattagash River, where all the Mattagash light seemed to converge at once. "She says I'll be sick of Mattagash within a month and back in Portland, banging on her door."

"She may be right," said Amy Joy.

"I doubt it," said Miranda. "I was a stranger in that house, being raised by hostile Gypsies. I know, I just know, that they stole me from some nice normal Portland family. My real parents are out there somewhere, still mourning my loss, still putting fresh flowers on my bed when each birthday rolls around, burning candles in front of the only baby picture they have left of me."

"Did you tell her about our business plans?" asked Amy Joy. Earlier she had slid the precious postcard under a plate on the bottom shelf of the cupboard. Now, with the other household members busy with their own interests, she slipped it quickly into the pocket of her housecoat. She wanted to take it up to the privacy of her bedroom. She wanted to study each letter in the two words of the message. She wanted to read again the warm, touristy, sandy explanation from the Chamber of Commerce, or whatever, and then stare again at some of the colorful things that lay along U.S. Highway 66.

"I don't need to tell you what all she said," Miranda replied. She was studying a sketch, turning it at angles to catch the hundred-watt light.

"You might as well," said Amy Joy. "Although I can imagine."

"First she quoted statistics of how many new businesses go bankrupt within the first year," said Miranda.

"But we're only turning the toolshed into a shop for tourists," Amy Joy protested. "It's not like we're investing anything but my sweat and your talent."

"Then she asked how many tourists I thought I could sell to from a toolshed," said Miranda.

"Did you tell her that the owners of Mainly Maine in Watertown saw your snowflake sketches and agreed to take some on consignment? And Country Cottage, that new store, loves the Furbish lousewort prints you're doing?" Amy Joy asked. "Did you tell her The Tourist Trap in Caribou thinks that the pressed-leaf place mats I've been making all these years are quite the rage?"

"Of course I didn't tell her," said Miranda. "What difference would it make? The woman was born to rain on parades, especially mine."

"Did you tell her about the ad we're placing in *Yankee* magazine for mail orders?" Amy Joy continued. "Not to mention Furbish lousewort T-shirts and hats? I mean, dammit, they thought for years that plant was extinct and now here it is growing in Mattagash's backyard. The T-shirt will be a hoot with tourists. And did you tell her about the Christmas wreaths?" Amy Joy asked, remembering the thick, rich smell of balsam fir, imagining it filling apartments in cities where no such smell exists.

"No! Stop it already," said Miranda. "You're as bad as she is!"

"Sorry," said Amy Joy. The postcard again in her hand, she was struck by an image of an impersonal mail slot at the airport in Phoenix. Did he write the note while standing at one of those fast-food places she had seen so often in movies, where people eat hot dogs or a single slice of pizza while they wait for their next flight? "I'm done ranting. We'll just show her we mean business. I do agree, though, that you were stolen."

"By the way," said Miranda. "Winnie is much better now. I just took them in a bedtime cup of tea. She's stopped crying. She said that at least Mrs. Fennelson is now with her Maker." Amy Joy thought about this.

"These days, that could mean General Motors," she said.

"Whatever it means, she's done crying."

"Good," said Amy Joy. She glanced up at the clock. *The Golden Girls* had just started, possibly another reason Winnie's tears had dried. "She's been, as we've heard her say five hundred times already, expecting it any day now for almost thirty years."

"What do you think of this?" Miranda asked. It was a snowflake in shades of blue and white, shimmering, cold, wet, flaky.

"I like it."

"No two will ever be alike," said Miranda, "just like the real models. There are worse ways for a budding young artist to stay alive, don't you think?"

"Especially in Mattagash," said Amy Joy.

"I've got something I want to show you," Miranda said, and motioned upstairs with her long slender hand.

It was time for bed anyway, so after putting out all the kitchen lights and plugging in the timer coffee-maker, Amy Joy went in to say good night to Sicily and Winnie. Their TV show was just finishing up, and Sicily was looking for a pencil to begin her assault upon the crossword puzzle.

"Like I been telling your mother, dear . . ." said Winnie. She was already in her nightgown, her thin gray hair splayed about her shoulders like a messy cobweb. There was no doubt she had changed her mind about Amy Joy Lawler in the past few days. "I been expecting Mama's death for almost thirty years now. I might as well get on with my own dying. She's with her Maker now anyway, bless her soul." Sicily rolled her eyes up at the ceiling and found a pencil all at the same time.

"Ain't it nice that the Women's Auxiliary is gonna give that plaque to Daddy?" Sicily asked, and Amy Joy nodded. "They'll have to wait until the Christmas Arts and Crafts Bazaar to do it, but that's okay. Long as they do it. It's gonna say *In Memory of the Reverend Ralph McKinnon, Famed Missionary to China.* Ain't that pretty? He *was,* you know, probably the most religious man ever to come out of Mattagash." The truth, like plaques, is sometimes gilded.

"I wish they'd put someone else in charge of the Women's Auxiliary," said Winnie, "instead of that peaked-faced girl of Rose Monihan's."

"Good night," said Amy Joy.

"Good night, dear," said Sicily. "Don't let the bedbugs bite."

Switching off more lights as she went, Amy Joy followed Miranda, trailing her footsteps up the carpeted staircase, the reverend's staircase, then down the high-ceilinged hallway where Grace had trodden, where Marge, Pearl, and Sicily had trodden, and now younger women were coming, their footfalls still light and springy above the little red roses on the carpet. Miranda paused at her open door, at Pearl McKinnon's old door, and nodded her head into the room.

"What do you think?" she asked. Amy Joy stepped inside and looked about. There it was, the finished painting of Grace McKinnon, a young woman in the electric moments of her youth, one hand to her eye, shading it, staring out toward the river, and there, in the background, was the river itself, stretching past the house, snaking its way to the sea. Grace McKinnon in a pink dress, pink as the hollyhock blossoms she was the first to plant at the edges of the McKinnon house, her hair dark as Pearl's, dark and shiny as Miranda's own. Women and rivers. As far as the old McKinnon homestead was concerned, those were probably the two most important factors in its history: women and rivers, and the snow and the rain that had fallen on its roof and then gone into the making of rivers. And inside women there are other rivers that surface now and then to run, like winterbournes, rivers of love and hate and gossip and pain and hope and despair. Rivers of blood to bear children.

"She's absolutely beautiful," said Amy Joy, and outside she could hear the storm shift, like some old Edsel car grinding its gears, mustering its power. Downstairs Winnie's and Sicily's voices rose up, in their sweet old Irish brogue, some of the last old-timer's brogue in Mattagash. Nowadays, youngsters were talking like television sets. From the entrance to Pearl's old bedroom, Amy Joy could hear Sicily and Winnie doing their nightly cross-word puzzle, their door open, their words rising like steam, the house itself hissing warm air through its arteries.

"What's a five-letter word for 'opera house feature'?" Winnie was asking.

"*Porch*," Amy Joy heard Sicily answer. And suddenly the old McKinnon homestead became to her a kind of inn, one where there is always room for the Sicilys, and the Winnies, and the Mirandas, and even the Amy Joys. It was an inn full of women, women young, women in midlife, women old enough to die, women wise, women silly, women able to give birth, women past giving birth. And there would be new women come after them to take up the old roles, but the work would remain. Some jobs never end.

It was almost eleven o'clock when Amy Joy heard Miranda's voice outside her door. Minutes earlier, when Miranda had gotten up to use the bathroom, Amy Joy had listened to her footsteps tip-toeing past, and then to water being flushed through the veins of the house, then the tiptoeing back again.

"I saw your light beneath the door," Miranda's voice said. "Are you okay?"

"I'm fine," said Amy Joy, and it was true. The postcard from Arizona was beneath her pillow, where nice things belong, where dreams sometimes come true, where fairies are known to leave quarters.

"Good night, then," said Miranda.

"Good night," said Amy Joy. She heard the sounds of Miranda—footfalls, a hand scraping the dark wall, breathing, all the noises that were Miranda, inch along the hallway and then disappear. Amy Joy closed the book she'd been reading, *Favorite Poems of the American People*, and laid it on the night table. *O Western wind, when wilt thou blow, that the small rain down can rain? Christ, that my love were in my arms and I in my bed again!* She snapped out the light, fluffed her pillow up a bit, and then lay back hoping to sleep, maybe to dream. It was all right to dream. Maybe some-where, in the big cities of the world, there were folks dreaming of the country, of the orange and yellow hawkweed, the barred owl's doglike bark, the little crayfish that hide under rocks at the river's edge. And maybe those folks as well were too uncertain to make the big move. But sometimes, and Amy Joy truly believed this now, lives could be lived in that gauzy realm of wishing. Like postcards tourists send of places they haven't visited, maybe desire is the same as doing. Maybe desire is even better than doing. Maybe the Painted Desert would really be too hot, too lizardy, but on the card it abides forever lush. Grecian urns in the strangest of places. Maybe with desire as her friend, Amy Joy could live a lot of lives. Maybe she could even imagine all of Simon Craft's scraggly bachelors as potential husbands, what their children would look like, what cars they would drive, what house they might live in. All over America they could set up housekeeping, in ranch-styles, in Tudors, in three-cornered Capes, driving Toyotas, Chevys, Fords. Their children would be blond, dark, short, tall, gifted, burdened with dyslexia. Her mothers-in-law would all be wonderful and terrible. None of the pets would ever have ear mites. Amy Joy could sit on the back porch of the old McKinnon homestead, summer after winter after summer, and live, fully, a million different lives.

As Larry Monihan scooped by with the town plow, snow was beating against the windows of the McKinnon homestead and spiraling down beneath the yard light. He didn't hear the coyotes as they rattled off a few yowls from the back fields edging the woods. And he didn't hear the steady, calm breathing coming from the bedrooms of the old homestead. His mind was on other things as he listened to the scraping blade of the plow. It looked to him like he was going to have one hell of a busy winter. As he rounded the most treacherous bend in the Mattagash road, the lights of the plow swept across the yard of the McKinnon house—proud old house clinging for dear life to the banks of a proud old river. In the swirl of white snow, only the shutters stood out, black eyes open to the blustery night. Larry Monihan didn't know that, just moments before, a light had been burning in one of the upstairs windows, a little supernova, the heart of the house glowing. Then the old homestead disappeared into the raging blackness behind him.

Amy Joy didn't hear the scraping sound of Larry Monihan's plow inching along through the night as he did his job. She had already fallen asleep. And during the night, during that Thanksgiving eve turning into Thanksgiving day, *snow,* that old pristine slate, that old white blanket that sweeps away all the mistakes and gives everyone a fresh start once they're able to shovel themselves out again. *Snow,* more of it than the meteorologists down in faraway Bangor had even dreamed of. And with it came a whipping wind, a cold wild breath from the Canadian plains. It riled the white pines, scattering the most stolid cones and rippling through the needles. It shook the black spruce, the telephone wires, the old McKinnon house. It rattled the very stars. It moved toward

Mattagash like an ancient ghost, the smoky souls of all the old descendants come back for a second look. The wind played around the tombstones in the Protestant graveyard: *McKinnon, Lawler, Ivy, Mullins, Craft, Fennelson, Monihan,* some of the lettering too ancient to read, some still fresh from last year's harvest. At the Reverend Ralph C. McKinnon's empty grave, the wind circled listlessly, howling a coyote howl. At the Catholic graveyard the wind shifted, then came off the crest of McKinnon Hill with full force. It bent the tops of the goldenrod still decorating the back fence, scattered seed that would never find birth on the hard crust of winter. The crevices of the carved names caught the snow, the letters in GIFFORD turning white quickly, the K in PLUNKETT nestling flakes in its branch. When the weather warmed and the earth was moist enough, new names would sprout out of this landscape of the dead. People doing their jobs. But now, on this Thanksgiving eve, the wind tore at a plastic flower come loose from some veteran's grave bouquet. It rushed it along over the crust of the snow, blew it beyond the hill and down the slope of the Mattagash River bank. The flower was a pale pink, the red of the Veterans Day parade already bled out of it. It caught up within the roots of a dead birch, tangled with old growth, and huddled there, waiting, until the Mattagash River thaws itself in April and comes rushing along the banks, taking everything within reach along with it, beating its way out to the ocean, retracing the steps of the McKinnon ancestors. And one spring evening, while Amy Joy Lawler still lingers within the safety of her dream, the flower will go bobbing and dipping by, like a tiny boat, and she will come out of a fast sleep, snap her little bedside light on, certain she has heard something scraping past her in the night.